Redemption

SYN FRASER

SYN FRASER WORKS

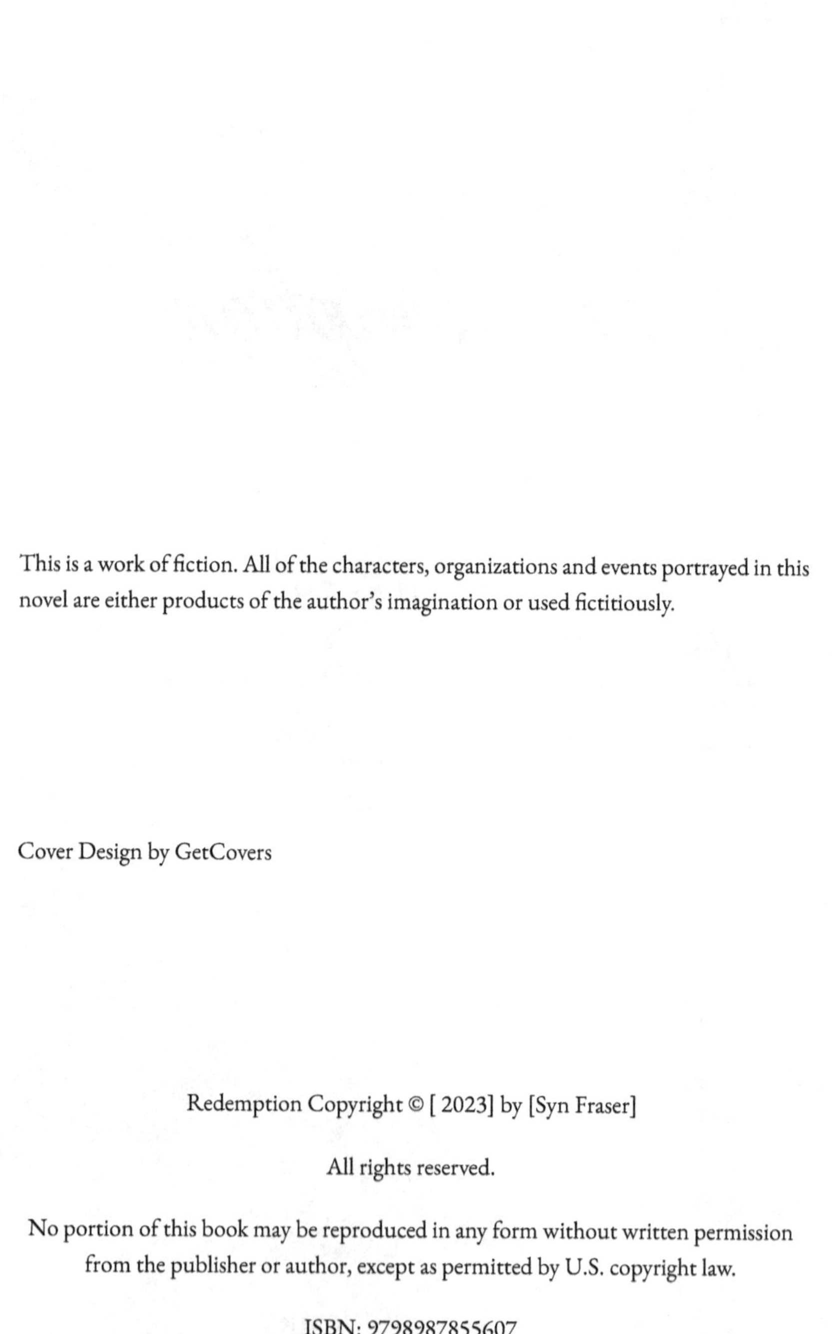

This is a work of fiction. All of the characters, organizations and events portrayed in this novel are either products of the author's imagination or used fictitiously.

Cover Design by GetCovers

Also By

Also By:
Reckoning

https://mybook.to/AUzhNyq

Solstier Chronicles:
Emerald Fire

https://www.amazon.com/gp/product/B0CV1VK8R1

Dedication

For Grandma Jack. The woman who taught me how to be kind, patient, and strong. Your memory is the compass of my life.

Chapter 1

Before joining the meeting, Nora pauses outside the mahogany door to take a breath. Soothing her nerves, she walks into the room to take a seat next to her sister. Ever since she'd arrived, an itch crawls over her skin until she's squirming enough to earn a scowl from Mallory.

"You're late."

A glance at her wristwatch reveals the opposite. When her lips twitch, she wipes it away with the back of one hand. "I'm actually ten minutes early."

"You were supposed to meet me at eight."

"Sorry. Everyone is getting ready for Oktoberfest. The roads are crazier than normal, even with the early hour."

"Which is why *I* left my place an hour early."

Of course, you did, Nora muses. It doesn't take too much digging for her to find the patience she needs to grant Mallory grace for her short disposition. Meetings like these suck and the two of them are banking up the experience.

When their grandmother passed, they'd both been too young to attend hers and Mallory was just into her teens when their mother's death shook the family's foundations. A simple summer night like so many before and after, except this one jumped Elaine Brennan's car over the Ninth Street Bridge. The result had been a devastating blow as they sat listening to a middle-aged man with receding hair drone on over her last wishes.

It had been eleven months and twenty-seven days since their mother had passed away when Nora discovered her father lifeless in his bed. She'd tried for months to ease her father's sorrow by cooking his favorite meals and playing card games on the porch. It all proved too challenging and bleak a life without the love of his life. The sisters lay asleep down the hall, blissfully unaware as Robert died in his sleep of unknown causes, the coroner unable to find an answer.

Fast forward a handful of years and they're back in a similar office to hear the reading of her grandfather's will.

"Why didn't you dress more appropriately?"

Nora's eyes flicker to her older sister, whose posture and expression betray her disapproval. Mallory's ivory business suit is a stark contrast to Nora's casual ensemble of new jeans and a silk blouse. The unspoken judgment between them is palpable, and Nora offers a soft shrug in response. She'd thought she dressed appropriately for the occasion, but clearly not. Mallory's eyes roll, conveying her frustration or displeasure at Nora's attire. *Oh well.*

Just out of sight, a clock ticks off every second spent in the room to increase the tension moving up her spine. As she sits and wonders over Brody's last request, fingernails pick at the leather stitching on her armchair. *Lord knows the man planned nothing beyond his next fishing trip, so what changed?* A long, audible sigh from her sister reminds Nora to settle her hands and focus her attention on something else.

The conference room is on the top floor of a skyscraper, deep within the heart of the city. A glass wall overlooks a mesmerizing view of the downtown core. Dark gray buildings shroud the streets and sidewalks in shadows as if they were trying to swallow up pedestrians brave enough to march between them. Their reflections roll across the glass pane as she enjoys the breathtaking view of bold fall colors.

A bookcase frames another wall with titles like Trial Techniques for Litigators and The Case For Standardized Discovery littering its shelves. She wonders if lawyers purposely sought these things just to show off their intelligence or need to be right.

The small touches of decor Nora spots are both extravagant and crisp. A painting of a little girl in a blue calico dress and white pinafore running after a butterfly hangs on the wall between two lovely curlicues of ironwork, which flow down from the ceiling to the floor. Two thick braids of golden hair trailed down the child's back. Behind her, tall grass shimmers in the sunlight. An ornate scrollwork of iron frames the painting with a floral design in black. Beneath the painting, a delicate wooden table holds a potted plant with tiny blue buds to match the dress.

"Did you remember to put money in the meter?"

The question jerks Nora out of exploring to stare blankly at Mallory while her words sink in. "Uh, yes. Two hours' worth. I think." A peek at her watch notes the time to ensure she's out of here before adding a parking ticket to her list of problems.

"You should be fine," Mallory assures her with a nod that never loosens her ramrod spine. Though her face is impassive, Nora takes comfort in watching her sister cross and uncross her long legs.

Across the mammoth wood table, a petite blonde with slender shoulders claims one of the dozen matching chairs. Her soft gray business suit produces tight press lines as if just picked up from the cleaners that very morning. Pale blonde hair cut in a neat bob at her chin smoothly frames her face, every strand perfect. While the picture of impressive posture, the incessant tapping of her pen off the notepad in front of her betrays her stoic appearance.

Another exchange of breath and Nora resumes distracting herself from the thoughts lingering in the shadows to travel over the stranger sitting on her left. Judging by the legs folded under his chair, once upright, he'll be tall. He pulls them in and stretches them out multiple times as if he has restless energy trapped inside his body. Clunky black boots make what could've been a graceful motion, clumsy. His dark head rests against the back of his chair, eyes closed to doze through the time it takes for this lawyer to arrive. The sun dazzling through the floor-to-ceiling windows casts shadows across him.

If Mallory thinks her attire is inappropriate, she probably had a stroke seeing him. His jeans fade from too many washes with holes in all the right places and a Metallica t-shirt with part of the logo missing stretching across wide shoulders. Casually comfortable doesn't really begin to describe it. Hell, he hadn't even bothered to shave the stubble that blankets a firm jaw.

From where she sits, Nora skims over the bold black lines of a tattoo inching up the side of his neck to disappear under his shirt collar. The contrast of ink against golden skin puts a tingle in her fingers to explore each intricate line thoroughly.

So far off the beaten path with her thoughts, Nora obliviously computes the flutter of thick lashes to reveal a pair of brown eyes watching her. As if on cue, his head cocks as he meets her curious perusal with an enigmatic half-smile before amusement flares to life in the depths of those eyes.

Caught, Nora inhales sharply and averts her eyes to the tall building in the distance. At least it wouldn't look back at her, she figures. On the off chance it did, Nora reasons the mishmash of attendants for this meeting would scramble to the nearest exit. She's contemplating the diamond-shaped dome of either steel or glass when the lawyer makes his debut.

"Good morning, I'm Daniel Brittain."

"Morning. I'm Mallory and this is my sister Nora."

"Good morning," she murmurs and accepts the handshake, head tilting. He looks far too young to be a lawyer of such caliber. *Maybe we've gone to the wrong meeting?* That her sister could make such a mistake is hard for Nora to swallow.

"Forgive my tardiness. Mornings are chaos around here." Mr. Brittain announces as he smooths a hand over his three-piece suit before taking a seat next to the blonde statue.

"For a firm this size, one should expect nothing less." Mallory offers, flashing her polite-without-warmth smile before smoothing the non-existent wrinkles from her knee-length skirt. Shiny black hair falls to her shoulders to frame a heart-shaped face and highlight silver eyes. While most men find themselves enthralled with her sisters' looks, the lawyer gives her a momentary perusal. *Hmm.*

"You're too kind." He takes a minute to pull a swallow or two from the glass of water in front of him, then withdraws a thick manila folder from his bag. "Shall we begin?"

"Actually, I'm rather curious how a criminal lawyer became the executor of my grandfather's will." A flare of irritation sparks within his steel-blue eyes before he blinks it away. While his smile is patient, Nora spots the tightening of his jaw. *Score one for catching him off guard.*

"You did your homework."

"I did." Nora offers a tiny smile before continuing. "You come highly recommended on Google. I know Grandad could be a handful, but I don't see him robbing banks or anything else that might associate him with the likes of such an attorney."

"Your grandfather didn't hire me personally. He hired the firm. And while I do have many areas of expertise, the criminal being my preference, I dabble in estates when it's needed."

Nora listens as the man ticks over his answers with a smile that never slips. She'd be lying if she said his professionalism doesn't impress a small part of her. The rest remains unconvinced. If one thought to ask, she'd confess her belief that they reserve his profession for cheats and liars, to begin with. Being so highly recommended only deepens her distrust.

"So, despite a firm of this size with countless lawyers, and your self-confessed dabbling, your superiors believe you are the best equipped to handle Grandad's will?"

"It appears so. Perhaps they thought I was sandbagging. Or that my caseload could use a boost. You'll need to ask them if you want exact answers."

"And your fee? I can't imagine you come cheap."

"You have no idea." His answer slips free before he can call it back, causing the stranger on her left to bristle. *Interesting.*

"You'll be happy to hear that the firm has waived my usual fee."

"Why would they do that?" Mallory chimes in.

"Something you'll have to take up with them. I'm afraid I'm not privy to all the details of running this firm. I have *several* meetings after this one, so if we could move this along, I'd be appreciative."

While not completely at ease with his answers, Nora stutters a curt nod, even though a buzzing sound fills her ears. As sweat beads on her upper lip, she sends up a prayer of thanks that she put on deodorant this morning! Pit stains in silk wouldn't go unnoticed long under Mallory's shrewd observations, not to mention Mr. Tall, Dark, and Broody sitting so close on the opposite side.

"As I mentioned over the phone, the sale of the property here in the city has closed, and the proceeds split. Brody asked that the two of you receive half. I will donate the other half to breast cancer research on his behalf."

Accepting the thin envelope, Nora drops it into her purse. If she ever needed confirmation that her grandfather was not of this world, his donation to the very thing that took his wife too soon shines a light on the wings he'd kept hidden.

"The meager life insurance he had covered the funeral and burial expenses, but there isn't much left beyond that, I'm afraid." Pages shuffle as Mr. Brittain thumbs his way through her grandfather's life. "The cabin up north and its surrounding property Brody left to, and I'm quoting here, *a steady and loyal friend, Kegan.*"

"Excuse me?" Mallory surges to her feet and slams her hands against the impeccable tabletop. With a slow breath, Mr. Brittain adjusts his wire-frame glasses and reads the passage again, his tone level and devoid of emotion.

"You can't be serious!"

"I'm always serious, Ms. Brennan."

"There's no way Grandad would leave that cabin to anyone but us knowing how much we cherished it." Whirling around to confront the man sitting next to Nora, Mallory jabs a finger in his direction. "How do we know he didn't con an old man who didn't know any better?"

"It would seem you're mistaken." Mr. Brittain assures her, spinning the folder around for Mallory to read the words herself. While the print is too small and the folder too far for Nora to make out herself, the sudden sag in Mallory's shoulders is all the confirmation she needs.

When the lawyer turns his attention to her, Nora could almost spot a twinge of compassion in his eyes before it's gone. "I can assure you, Brody was of sound mind and body when he asked this will to be drawn up and he was very clear on this."

"We won't continue to sit here and listen to-" Mallory hisses through her teeth until Nora lays a hand on her arm. Lips press tightly together on the rest of her sentence as she sinks into her chair with a loud plop to clutch tighter onto Nora's hand.

"As I was saying, the belongings at the cabin you ladies are free to go through as soon as you can. Keep anything you wish and donate the rest to a charity. Mr. Selkirk, you can retrieve the deed on your way out this morning."

"Uh, okay."

Nora shrugs away the goosebumps peppering her skin at the deep bass of Mr. Broody's voice. *Not now.*

"Mallory, Brody asked that I pass on his coin collection with the stipulation that you never sell it."

"Never!" Mallory seethes as if offended by the thought and accepts the wooden box. Fingers cling to its shape as if Grandad himself lay inside. Grief flickers across her face in soft ripples as lashes blink back unshed tears. On an exhale, her shoulders straighten and her spine snaps into place for the rest of the meeting.

"Nora, Brody asked me to pass on his favorite book. However, he has the same conditions. You cannot sell it and you must keep it safe."

Safe from who is the first thought that pierces the heavy fog of her mind. The second is why he would leave her a book she could probably order from Amazon. Once she realizes the lawyer is waiting for her agreement, Nora bobs her head and lifts her hands to accept the book wrapped in a piece of worn leather.

As if doubting her sincerity, the lawyer tightens his grip on the book, eyes locking on hers. For a breath of a second, Nora follows as his eyes shift from blue to violet and back again. The incoming chill from his expression sends a tremor through her limbs. Mr. Selkirk sits taller in his chair.

Once the moment passes, Mr. Brittain slides the book across the gleaming surface of the table towards her. Nora has just enough time to wrap her hands around it before he surges to his feet with a tight smile.

"I'm sorry we met under such sad circumstances, but should any of you have further questions, you're welcome to call me." On his way out the door, Mr. Brittain shakes each hand once more, his palm damp the second time around. As he rushes out with the blonde statue right behind him, the room hums with a strained silence.

Beside her, Mallory's temper rolls, waiting for a lit match that will bring the situation to an explosion. Before collateral damage can occur, Nora presses the book to her chest and stands.

"Let's get out of here."

Mallory's nod is more of a jerk, but she gets to her feet and leads the way from the room to a bank of elevators on their right. Fingers jab at the down button with more force than required as Nora withstands her glare.

"How could he leave the cabin to a total stranger?"

A shoulder jumps up and down while the metal doors slide open. With a step inside, Nora selects the ground floor so Mallory can press herself against the far wall. "Gramps said he'd been a loyal friend, Mallory. I don't think he *was* a total stranger. At least not to gramps."

"Kegan?" Spitting the name on a growl, Mallory fumes. "How good of a friend could he have been if neither of us have ever met him? At least I haven't, have you?"

"Trust me. I'm sure I'd remember if I had. Besides, you have a lot of friends I've never met." Nora reasons, pressing a thumb to her temple to ward off the looming headache.

"How are you not upset about this?" As the elevator begins its descent, Mallory presses a hand to her overly sensitive stomach.

"Do you see me dancing the jig, Mal? I'm not exactly thrilled, but it's what Grandad clearly wanted. I will not curse him for it."

As soon as the elevator settles and the doors open, Nora relaxes. Her long exhale serves to release the locking of joints as Mallory steps into the hall before she throws up her breakfast in the confined space.

"This guy could be a con artist, Nora, or a serial killer for all we know." With a shove of her shoulder, Mallory is through the glass doors and out under the warm sunshine. "I don't think I can just let this go, Nora. I'm sorry." The hug she wraps her in is long and fierce. "I'm going to make some calls and I'll see you and Eleni tomorrow for girls' night."

"I'll be there."

"That's good. It's your turn to host, Brat."

"Yeah, yeah. I remember," Nora mumbles while digging for her keys in the depths of her purse. With a warm smile, Mallory turns to glide into the driver's seat of her Equinox about the same time Nora locates the fob to disarm the alarm on her Jeep.

"What if I swear to be none of those things?"

The smooth sound of his voice freezes Nora in place as it glides over her skin to awaken a thousand nerve endings. A mixture of rough and clear, it brings to mind the image of expensive Scotch being poured over cubes of ice. Turning on the ball of her foot, she confronts their eavesdropper.

"Heard that part, huh?"

"Would've been harder not to, I think." Words fall from his tongue in a brogue thicker than Brody's had ever been.

"I'm sure." Lord, he is tall! Standing nearly a foot over her own five-foot-five frame, on legs the size of tree trunks, he makes an imposing figure.

In one hand, he carries a sleek, black motorcycle helmet, while the other buries itself into the front pocket of his jeans. Minutes race by before Nora acknowledges his lips are moving and his hand now hangs in the air, waiting for her to accept the friendly greeting. *What is the matter with me?*

"I'm sorry!" Taking his hand, Nora pumps it twice, thinking about the amount of heat it gives off. It hadn't been smooth either, like most men today, but worn through hard labor. *How long have I been shaking his hand? Let go for Pete's sake!*

"Nice to meet you. Brody spoke of you and your sister often."

"That would make one of us. I'm afraid he's never mentioned you."

"I suspected as much witnessing your sister's reaction. If it eases your mind, I'll sign the deed over right this moment."

"I admit I'm tempted to accept your offer, but I don't think I could see him again with that on my conscience." Talk about a stain on your soul! *Sorry Gramps, I know you wanted him to have it, but Mallory and I shamed him into signing it over.* Nora shakes her head to keep the darkness at bay and offers a genuine smile. "It's a pleasure to meet you, Mr. Selkirk."

"Kegan, please. I wish it had been under happier times."

"Me too."

Standing before her, Kegan shifts his weight from foot to foot as if he's eager to be some place else, yet he makes no move to leave. His free hand plows through short, dark hair before it scrubs down the scruff on his face. "Do you know when you'd like to go through your grandad's things?"

"Oh. Um, I should talk to Mallory first before I make any plans. Can I get back to you?"

"Certainly."

After he digs a small white card out of his wallet, Kegan pins the helmet between his legs long enough to scrawl his name and number across the back. Nora takes the time to scrub her own hand over her jeans before she accepts the card with a nod. "Thank you. And it was nice meeting you, despite the reason." With a wave of her hand, she twirls and closes the distance to her Jeep, eager to put an end to the morning.

Nothing Brody had ever told him could've prepared Kegan for Nora Brennan. She's fresh and quirky. At first look, nothing about her is extraordinary, aside from the sunset orange hair gathered in a low ponytail. Then he gets a glimpse of the personality hiding underneath, sparkling with an imp-like charm.

Hell, she doesn't even walk with flair. Each step serves the purpose of reaching her vehicle, completely unaware of the motion that's all hips and legs. The need Kegan experiences to cross himself unfurls within him until he's stomping the short walk to his bike.

"Get a damn grip," he scolds, earning a strange look from the elderly lady one space away. Nora is just another woman; he's met more than his share. One more won't be his undoing. Still, Kegan couldn't miss the voice in the back of his head, disagreeing vehemently.

Chapter 2

When Kegan first steers into the parking lot for Taps Bar, he battles with the temptation to ride off in the opposite direction. His phone reads ten-o-two, and already cars spill over the parking area, cluttering side streets within walking distance. It appears tonight they fill the small dive bar to capacity. *People.*

Sitting there, he focuses on the vibrations of the motor and the tremor of the machine beneath him. Anything but the sick feeling in his stomach.

"Buck up, Buttercup. Kill Colin later."

After another long moment in stillness, he leans over to pull the key. All that's left is a dozen steps to the garish blue door and the raucous sound that lies beyond. Even with the harsh glare of the neon lights, he struggles to see through dirty windows. *He better fucking be here.*

Deep breaths crisscross his head and chest. There's still time for him to turn around and leave. However, he can't shake the image of Colin's smug grin. Pocketing the key, Kegan climbs off his bike, his long legs devouring the short distance in seconds.

When he gives the door a tug, it opens unexpectedly, allowing a couple out into the night. Oblivious to him, they stumble towards a silver Honda two parking spots away. Shrill giggles, wet kisses, and awkward gropes impede the relatively brief journey.

Teeth set, he turns and forces himself to step over the threshold.

Coming in from what one can consider fresh air, the stench of sweat and stale cigarette smoke launch a merciless attack. Beside him, a big man with an impressive collection of tattoos offers Kegan a quick glance before perching on a small stool near the door. Muscled arms cross over a thick chest as he rests his back against the wall, watching the room with an intensity that is only gained by experience.

The number of people currently crammed into such a confined space would give the authorities nightmares. It isn't doing much to sway his desire to turn around and walk out, either.

Scanning the room, he notes the long bar on his right in sore need of a good polish and the two bartenders on the other side. On the wall directly to his left hangs a well-used dartboard. A collection of beer logos and gaudy neon signs overwhelm the one poster of drunk driving statistics. Several dozen round tables cover the worn wood floor from him to the karaoke setup in the back.

On the small, square stage, three college-aged girls belt off-key amongst slurs and mumbles. While the volume is deafening, the only obvious thing Kegan can pick up from their performance involves a wrecking ball. Searching from corner to corner, Kegan mutters a groan when a pretty brunette saunters his way. One manicured hand smooths over an exaggerated hairstyle while her lips curve into a salacious smile.

"You look like a man who knows how to curl a woman's toes."

"I do, huh?"

"Ooh," after a dramatic shiver and a flutter of clumpy eyelashes, she latches onto his arm. "I like a man with an accent. Where're you from, honey?"

While he resists the urge to shake her off, his lips twitch. For a quick second, he contemplates giving her an honest answer. *That'll clear the place out.* Instead, he replies with an automated response. "Scotland."

"A Scot," she croons. Heavy makeup mutes her soft blue eyes as they widen in surprise. "I've never met a Scot before. What's your name, honey?"

When her ample breasts press into his side, Kegan buries his hands deep into the pockets of his jeans. Oblivious to his plain disinterest, she prattles on about her recent ex-boyfriend while he scans the room for his target.

Hope unfurls in his chest when he spots Colin several tables away, entertaining two perky blondes. The sight of one sprawling across the table for better access to Colin inspires Kegan's eyes to roll inside his skull. "I see who I'm looking for. You have a good night, um?"

"Marcy."

Disentangling himself from her, Kegan tips a nod and flashes what he hopes passes as a friendly smile. "Nice to meet you, Marcy. Excuse me." Before she can put her crestfallen features to work, Kegan spins and surfs the sea of tables.

Twice he bumps into a chair in his path. The first guy simply grunts with the offense, then returns to his conversation. The second surges unsteadily to his feet. "What the hell, buddy!" One meaty fist slams on the table in front of him, mindless of the full glasses of beer teetering in response.

Taking a step back, Kegan plants his legs and withdraws his hands from his pockets. "Your chair is in the fucking way."

"I don't care if my chair is in the middle of the goddamn street." One thick finger jabs at the center of Kegan's chest. "Apologize."

His already dark mood festers in his stomach as a ghost of a smile appears on Kegan's lips. Tipping his chin towards his chest, he looks down into a pudgy face with bloodshot eyes. No doubt the man is accustomed to using his size for intimidation. Unfortunately, that's the last thing Kegan finds swirling around in his head.

A glance over the drunk's head shows Colin reclining in his chair with a shit-eating grin on his face. Behind him, Kegan's acutely aware of the big man at the door rising from his stool and the small squeak of relief the wood eeks out in the process.

Sitting at the table the drunk stood from, a smaller man gives his friend a quick jerk. "C'mon Joe. Let it go."

"Listen to your friend," Kegan warns. "Sit down and drink your beer."

"What if I don't?"

The second time a finger digs into his chest, Kegan's body tenses. A wave of acrid odors washes over him. Sweat, stale beer, and nicotine. Despite the rush of heat surging through him, he remains still. Locking eyes with his challenger, Kegan speaks slowly and methodically. "If you touch me one more time, I'm going to rip your fucking arm off and mount it over the bar there."

Even amidst a drunken haze, Joe's eyes clear for a fraction of a second. Reeling back on his heels, he folds his arms behind his back and stutters a nod. He spends another moment under Kegan's intense gaze before he stumbles back into his seat. A screech of metal on wood pierces the bar as he slides his chair closer to the table.

After pausing briefly, Kegan continues across the room, clenching and unclenching his fists with each step. Arriving at Colin's table, he takes a deep breath and releases it to regain a fraction of his composure. Dropping his weight into the remaining chair, Kegan shoots a dark glare in the face of Colin's obvious amusement, his voice tight. "Don't say a fucking word."

"Noted." Colin swigs the last of his beer and clears his throat. "Excuse us, ladies. I need to have a word with my friend here."

"Aw!" Blonde one moans, leaning far enough over the table to give Kegan a clear view down her shirt.

Blonde two simply shifts, her eyes lingering far longer than he'd like. When she stands from the table, she ensures her body brushes his side as she tucks a piece of paper inside his loosening fist. "Call me."

Colin's grin grows into one of barely contained-laughter. "You're such a stud."

"Fuck off, Colin."

"Alright. Calm down, for fuck's sake."

"Why do you insist on meeting here every damn time? There's got to be a better place in this city."

"I like it. It suits my mood."

Kegan smirks, dropping the piece of paper on the table in front of Colin. "That says more about you than you know."

"Eh. I don't care either way." Lifting his glass, Colin signals one of the two servers for a refill. "How'd it go this morning?"

"No fuck-ups, so there's that."

"Any problems with Melchom?"

Kegan pauses as the server approaches the table with a fresh bottle of beer. Pale blue eyes skip both him and Colin as she absently sets it on the table with a polite smile. Tucking a strand of near-black hair behind an ear, she mumbles something incoherent before turning to attend to another patron. "Did you know he's posing as a lawyer now?"

"I heard some idle gossip about it, but to be honest, I haven't given it much thought. So long as he's staying off my radar, I'm happy."

"Hm. I suppose."

"So? No problems then?"

"Nothing worth noting. There was a moment I thought for sure he was going to try something."

"He'd be stupid. His own bosses would skin him alive for just thinking of staging a coup."

"Any word about who the council is assigning to Nora?"

"*Heaven's Council*?" Colin sneers before a quick chuckle escapes him. "It was supposed to be Damien." One eyebrow arches as if reading the sudden tightening in Kegan's jaw. "Apparently, he's too big for such mundane things now. He's putting one of his handlers on it."

"Oh-kay. Which one?" When Colin refrains from answering him, Kegan presses his elbows into the table. "I need to know which one before I stumble over their fucking toes, Colin."

"Selena."

The steady sound of bass coming from several speakers around him smothers his groan. "When was the last time you spoke to her?"

"When I lost my command, and we fell."

"Christ. So not even in this century. This should be fun."

"Yeah, well, most of those winged assholes assume you've lost your mind for still taking my orders. So, there are no hard feelings if you want to back out. I'm sure I can get another watcher to serve as Nora's Guardian."

At any other time, if Colin had asked, Kegan might've jumped at the out he offers. Now, it's not just duty that propels Kegan forward, but loyalty as well. Keeping Nora alive through this transition is something he owes Brody. So, even while his fingers tap restlessly on the table, he gives his head a quick shake. "I'm good."

"Glad to hear it." Draining the new bottle, Colin takes a moment to dig a cigarette out of the pack on the table. There's a slight pause as he dips his head to light it and draws in a huge inhale. When he continues, Kegan fights to keep from waving at the puff of smoke that infects the air between them. "If you need any backup, Eleni and Jess are in the area. In fact, I think Eleni has already established contact with Nora."

"*That* should be interesting. Hopefully, I won't need to call them." If sending up a prayer at that moment would be any help, Kegan might've done just that. As it is, he doesn't waste the time. Heaven turned their backs on them a long ass time ago. Too many years for him to count.

No, he's better off relying on his own skills to ensure Nora reaches the end of this alive. *I've made worse decisions. Yeah, like accepting the transfer under Colin's command in the first place. Heaving a sigh, he stands. "I'll keep you posted.*

After Selena removes them from the human world, she notes an expression one could call amusement on her supervisor's face. Kegan's open hostility encourages a small smile to flutter across an otherwise somber face. However, the emotion is there and gone too quickly for Selena to be sure.

"I hope you're confident in this plan," Damien states in a quiet voice as Kegan storms from the bar.

"I am." She adds a quick bob of her head for good measure. "She's the Protector. We're bound to honor that."

"Every time I look, I see only disaster ahead."

"She'll learn. It always takes a little time for them to get their feet under them. Did you forget?"

Damien heaves a sigh. "Naming Nora his predecessor means he knew what he was doing. Or he was more senile than we originally thought."

"Considering the alternatives, I think she's perfect for the job."

"Perfection amongst humans is an illusion." The sharp snap of his voice draws her attention to the hardening of his ice-blue eyes. "What about Kegan?"

"He'll guard her, just as he did Brody." When his dark head quirks in obvious disagreement, Selena stumbles over the rest of her words. "He's honorable, Sir." The tip of her tongue darts out to wet her lips, her throat dry.

"If Kegan had an ounce of the honor you speak of, he wouldn't be in this situation. Would he?"

"I could make an argument for the opposite. It was his honor that put him where he is."

"You're saying he chose one loyalty over the other?" One dark brow climbs his forehead just before his lips thin.

Careful. *Selena shrugs her shoulder in what she hopes is a casual gesture. "Perhaps."*

"I fear your report relies too heavily on notions instead of the hard facts the council is looking for."

"You asked me to make an assessment. If you disagree, you could take your concern right to their chambers."

"Watch your tone, Selena. That sounded a lot like an ultimatum."

"My apologies. I didn't mean it as such."

"For now, I'll leave things as they are." Damien's cool glance in her direction inspires a rash of goosebumps to travel along her arms. "If things alter too far, I will intervene and it'll be you visiting their chamber."

"I understand."

"Let us hope you do."

While Damien fades from the human realm, Selena hangs back. His warning sits awkwardly around her shoulders as she tracks the path events should take in the not-so-distant future. Unfortunately, nothing with the humans is ever certain. Something like free will could alter the course with little trouble.

Shifting in the cool air, she places herself in Nora's bedroom. Moonlight gleans through thin blinds to whisper across the bed on the far wall, and two small tables on either side. Opting for the wooden rocking chair in the corner, Selena takes a seat, appointing herself as a guard until Kegan can take over.

With one big toe, she sets the rocker into a rhythmic motion that eases away some of the tension as minutes tick by at an alarming pace.

Chapter 3

"Hello Mr. Hadley, thanks for getting back to me." Nora braces the phone on her shoulder so she can better fight with the lock on her back door. Without a functioning porch light, the level of difficulty increases, inspiring her to make a mental note to replace the bulb this coming weekend

"I'm sorry about the late hour. My son just gave me your message." From her end, she can hear a brief scuffle over the phone and the offended *hey* that follows. "He should donate his brain to science so they can determine the long-term effects of video games."

"It's not a problem," she begins. "I was hoping you'd have that estimate for me." Once inside the kitchen, Nora turns on the lights to sound off the first of countless meows. "The board will want to review everything before I decide."

"Absolutely. I'll spend most of my tomorrow on a job up north, but I can drop it off on my way through town."

"That'll be perfect. Thanks again." Nora ends the call with a brush of her thumb and sets the bag on the table to scoop up the cat as it weaves its way between her legs.

"What did you do today, Handsome," she asks while scratching behind one ear. As he presses his enormous head deeper into her hand, the rumble of his purr sends vibrations along her arm. "Did you catch any mice?" One yellow-gold eye opens to regard her question as ridiculous in his usual quiet patience, drawing a chuckle from her. "So you napped. Again." His purr, now steady, responds to the scratch of her nails as he tilts his head left and right for the best angle. "When the kids named you, I looked it up. Ezio was a far more adventurous spirit."

Considering the late evening hour, her newly acquired cat is probably starving, but she is in no hurry to sacrifice his attention. "My day wasn't very adventurous either. Which is unusual for a center crammed with teenagers." As she suspected, Ezio delivers the first love bite to her fingers. "We need to work on your patience, Big Boy."

He answers with a slow blink before jumping to the floor with a thump. As Nora steals a moment to kick off her shoes by the door, Ezio resumes weaving himself around her legs until she retrieves the empty bowls from inside the laundry room. While she scoops dry cat food into a bowl and fills the other with fresh water, he howls over the lengthy process.

"I read somewhere that cats are supposed to be the quiet companion. You skipped that class, didn't you?" His long tail swishes across the tile floor as she approaches his favorite spot, eyes trained on the upcoming meal. "At least you keep my feet warm." Nora muses as she sets the bowls down to leave her cat to eat in peace while she forages in the fridge for her own dinner. The Darth Vader ringtone coming from her phone elicits a soft groan as she closes the fridge. On her way to the microwave, Nora answers in a voice she hopes disguises her lack of interest.

"Evening Carl."

"Nora. I hope I'm not calling too late."

And if you were? "Nope," she says. "I just walked in the door a few minutes ago." She smothers the yawn his voice inspires and programs the microwave for a single slice of pizza. "What's on your mind?"

"I'd like to call a meeting tomorrow morning. Hiller House is full, and we need to think about hiring more people. Or offload some of these kids to other homes."

"That's not an option."

"Nora."

"I'm not sending away kids that have already lost everything, Carl. If you think we need more people to share the workload, then let's do that."

"You hired me to track your bottom dollar, and right now, you're hemorrhaging money."

"We still have that grant coming in at the end of the month," she reminds him while filling a glass with the last of the soda to wash down the two-day-old pizza. *Tomorrow will have to be grocery day.*

"Just how long are you expecting it to hold back this flood?"

"According to my notes, it'll keep things afloat until we find a new benefactor."

"What about Mrs. Baft?"

His reply comes so quick that Nora suspects a little maneuvering on his part. "What makes you think she'd be interested?"

"She just pulled her funding from a charity over in Ankeny, so she'll be looking for a new tax break."

"I don't know." Maybe it's the way Carl answers, but Nora can't ignore the essence of crud gathering on her soul. "We may not have the same goals in mind."

"She's an old lady with a lot of money. What more do you need, Nora?"

Empathy? Kindness? "I'll think about it, Carl." *No. My answer is hell, no.* "In the meantime, I'll get with Rebecca and have her pencil in a meeting with you and the rest of the staff this coming week." The groan he answers with perks her interest. "What?"

"You're not including Zoe, are you?"

"She's part of the staff, Carl. What's your issue with Zoe?"

"She's young."

Nora smiles, "She's twenty-three."

"She acts like a fourteen-year-old," he spits back. "I don't see how anyone can think her dedicated."

"She was an unpaid volunteer for a year. Which means we didn't pay her for the work she did. Her personality makes her popular with kids, especially the young girls. So I put her on the payroll."

"Okay, Nora. You're the boss."

Despite the words, his voice sounds too sharp for her to believe he's on board, but she holds her tongue and settles for an eye roll. "You worry too much, Carl. Say hi to your wife for me."

"Yeah. Night."

After setting the phone to do not disturb, Nora tucks it into a back pocket before she tackles the now lukewarm pizza and room-temperature soda. "Carl isn't a bad guy," Nora explains as Ezio jumps up onto the chair next to her. "Gramps would call him a *Nervous Nelly*." The cat tips his head slightly, as if interested, before deciding otherwise and curls up for a nap. "You're right. I can worry about work tomorrow."

Tossing the paper plate in her recycle bin, Nora walks herself through a routine. After swapping out a load of laundry, she folds the towels and sets them on the table to carry upstairs with her when she goes.

A stop at the refrigerator allows her to add soda to the list on the door before she preps the coffeepot for the next morning. Armed with towels and her bag, Nora passes through the house to ensure doors and windows are secure, then climbs the stairs to the second floor.

Dropping the towels on the bathroom sink, she scrounges in the dresser and changes into a clean shirt, before disappearing inside the master bathroom. Brushing her teeth and washing her face, Nora eases the clip from her hair to let it fall around her waist and returns to the bedroom. Fingers rub over the tender spots left on her scalp as she places the phone on its charger and double-checks her alarms.

Ezio claims the bottom corner of the bed as she takes a seat to eye the book sticking out of her shoulder bag. More than once she felt a draw, a lure to satisfy her curiosity. If she unwraps the cover, she'll have an answer to her grandfather's last wishes. However, the chance he'd left her a farmer's almanac weighs heavily on the impulse.

"Oh, for Heaven's sake. Just do it." With a scooch of her hips, Nora retrieves the book and reclines against the half-dozen pillows. Stiff fingers complicate loosening the twine ties that hold a rough cloth in place. When she's able to brush it aside and get her first look at this special book, a small gasp seeps from her lips.

"Oh. My. Goodness." Each word is a whisper while her eyes register the cover. Definitely *not* a farmers' almanac. The first thing she notices is the brilliant blue stone in the center, anchored by strips of gold to form an intricate knot. While the mineral has lost shine, the stone glitters under the bedside lamp.

Cool air skips along bare arms and legs as Nora's head spins with an urgency that heats her blood. When she brushes her fingers against the stone, a tingle follows to release a soft fissure of energy. Her spine snaps to attention even as her vision narrows until all she can see is Brody's book. Pulling her hand back, she rubs it against the patchwork quilt to dispel the sensation as her imagination runs wild.

Straight ahead, through a gap in the small copse of trees, the sun sets on an impressive stone manor. Tall pines make up the surrounding forest to drip water after a recent rain, leaving the scent of wet earth inside her nose.

Once inside the keep, the scent of a fire burning and the crackle of dried herbs under her feet smother the rest of her senses. As if familiar with the path to take, Nora moves forward until her hand rests on a roughhewn banister leading to a second floor. Down a narrow passageway, she walks with the help of soft candlelight until she reaches a door. As soon as she shoves the cumbersome oak inward, the scene fades.

Quick as it appears, the image is gone, leaving Nora to question her sanity. A shake of her head eases any traces left behind as she lifts the cover. Uneven pages lay harsh under her fingers, its ink dulled to make most of the words indecipherable. Even if she knew the language.

"Why on earth would you give me a book I can't read?" A wave of emotion crests within her chest to kick up her heart rate. When did she get her hopes up exactly? Nora can't recall; but instead of finding answers, she finds more questions.

Clumsily, she re-wraps the book in what she now realizes is a rough hide with strange symbols branded all along the inner layer. After she snaps a couple of pictures with her phone, Nora secures the ties and lays the book on her nightstand. Climbing under the covers, she pulls the small chain for the bedside lamp.

In the darkness, Ezio lumbers lazily across her feet to settle into the bend of her knees. Across the room, neon green lights show the time to be well after eleven by the time her eyes close.

Kegan bolts upright, leaving the blankets to pool around his hips while he sharpens his focus. Traces of power fill his senses until they set off alarms with an ear-piercing frequency. While he scans every corner in search of the source, his teeth clench from the auditory assault. Goosebumps pucker his skin with the realization that hits him square in the chest. *Nora*.

Blankets sail as he scrambles over the side of the bed and into his discarded jeans. Every curse he's ever heard falls from his mouth as he snaps up his phone and scrolls through contacts. The second he can hear the other end ringing, Kegan takes a quick breath.

"Just die the way I taught you. With a smile."

Colin's greeting carries enough command with it to jerk Kegan to attention, his dark head reeling. "Excuse me?"

"You're dying, right? Calling to say goodbye? Why else would you call someone in the middle of the *fucking* night?"

"I'm not dying." Kegan's grin is slow to form. "You need to take this call." Across the line, he listens as Colin whispers something to whoever lies next to him. "Bad time?"

"And people say you aren't the smart one. Good for you." The reply comprises more snarl than actual words, increasing Kegan's grin.

"Nora's revealed the book's location." Saying the words aloud steals the air from his lungs all over again.

"You're positive?"

Kegan refuses to acknowledge the uptick in his heart rate when his friend suddenly appears in front of him. With a dirty look at his phone, Kegan ends the call before tossing it on the unmade bed. "You should warn someone before you do that. Hell, even genies require summoning."

"Do I look like a genie to you?"

If Colin is in fact a genie, he'd be a dark, irritable bastard, Kegan muses. Though the two stand at eye level, Colin is narrow in the shoulder. Still, the power that radiates off his old friend makes up for the leaner frame.

"Maybe more *Wishmaster* and less *I Dream of Jeannie*." Voicing the opinion has Colin giving him the finger.

"You're positive?"

"That you'd be an evil genie, or that Nora unwrapped the book?" The hard-line of Colin's jaw answers his question. "I'm positive."

"Well, fuck."

"Yeah."

"When?"

"Considering it was strong enough to wake me from a dead sleep, I'd say not more than a half hour ago. You didn't notice?"

"I had a lovely distraction."

A dark brow creeps up his forehead over the admission. "That's more than a distraction, Colin. No way it should've slipped by unnoticed."

"You mean the fucking alarms that never stop?"

"Never?"

"Nope. Twenty-four, fucking seven."

That revelation morphs his grin into a scowl. "Mine only go off with a flux of power, or when something needs a ticket back to hell." The sharp shrill of incessant ringing comes with a throbbing head and an aching jaw, and it's been less than an hour. He can't imagine hearing it *all* the time. "How do you keep your sanity?"

"Who says I have?" Tense shoulders bounce before he lights a cigarette and inhales deeply. "I've learned to tune them out. Kind of. But telling one, apart from the constant drone, isn't as easy as you'd think."

"This is a non-smoking room."

"Then you aren't getting your deposit back."

As Colin continues to smoke while pacing back and forth across the small hotel room, a thought springs to life. "How do you tune them out?"

"Whiskey and women work well."

"That's just replacing one distraction for another."

"Yes, but unlike you, my friend, I refuse to live the life of a monk." Colin's grin twists with the next plume of smoke. "I'm happy to drink, smoke, and fuck my way to eternity."

Scrubbing his hand across the back of his neck, Kegan steers the conversation into calmer waters. It's not that he believes himself above such indulgences. He'd spent more than a few centuries in little more than a stupor. *Now*, such behavior will only hinder his appeal.

"Have you come across anything useful?"

"You're seriously asking? No, asshole. Nothing."

"Someone has to know something."

"Yep," Colin replies while he crushes the cigarette out against the sole of his boot and lights another.

"Do you have to do that? You've been here less than ten minutes and the room reeks like a brothel. Housekeeping is going to have a cow."

"Fuck 'em." Though his answer comes swiftly, Colin cracks the patio door for some fresh air. "I've talked to anyone I can think of. Either they're all idiots or just exceptional liars."

"Just be careful. You go poking around too much and Selena is going to come down."

"She'd better bring fuzzy cuffs next time." A moment of sobriety follows his snarl to lift the shadows from amber eyes. When he next meets Kegan's gaze, the haze of couldn't give a fuck lessens. "They already banished us, Kegan. What more can they do?"

"I'd say not much, but they've surprised me a time or two."

"Yeah. Sounds like you're on the clock now, so stay on your toes."

"Will do."

As fast as he appeared, Colin leaves, but the acrid stench of nicotine and smoke lingers. Despite the cool fall breeze, Kegan opens the patio door as far as it'll go and makes preparations for tomorrow. Like it or not, he has a job to do, and he's not nearly close enough to accomplish it adequately.

The dark mood Colin shared rottens when he plows a hand through his hair to stumble across the raised brand. Immediately, every inch of his six-foot-four frame freezes. *Bastards*. With a curl of his lips, Kegan flips off whoever monitors their situation and steps into the small closet that serves as a bathroom.

Deep into a realm where innocence is a weakness and sins are welcome, an ancient evil stirs. After the final tendrils of power careen around the massive hall, breaths catch, and fingers flex. Upon a throne made of gold and gems, a tall figure lounges lazily. One by one, eyes look at Rome.

From his vantage point, a creature of the night would recognize the severity of the situation brewing. When he confirms their hopes with a nod of his head that drops black hair against his brow, it confirms Eli's reservation. However, the cheers that erupt from the crowd threaten to shake the foundations of Heaven itself.

"At last!" Rome surges to his feet, his breath catching. "Fate rewards our patience."

With eyes that shift from coal black to blood red, Rome searches the throng of faces until he spies Adriel near the back. Leaning against one of a dozen golden statues, his arms cross while his face remains impassive amongst the revelry. Sensing Rome's gaze, his head tips to meet it with steadfast blue-green eyes.

"Find that book. Bring it and whoever protects it, to me. Take my hounds. They'll answer to you."

From where he stands against the shadows, Eli observes Adriel snap to attention. The silent nod he offers swears a vow he'll return victorious as if his life depended on it.

In the silence, murmurs grow. A few wagers he'll fail while others remain optimistic. Whatever their opinion of his success; it's unanimous they don't envy him the task ahead.

When his master first assigned him to Rome, Eli was certain he'd die from sheer boredom. Armed with now valuable intel, however, perhaps he can persuade Shax to lift the ban. He no sooner completes the thought when his body hums over the prospect of walking among the humans once more.

Only after he ensures he can slip out, raising no alarms, Eli leaves the foul-smelling realm with a smile on his face. The promise of an upcoming visit to the world of mortal men and women heats his blood.

As Adriel traverses the winding halls, he attempts to settle himself. The heavy sound of his footfalls on the stone floor echo in his ears. He'd be lying if he said the deep cadence doesn't ramp up his body's temperature.

When he draws closer, sounds of laughter drift up the hall to meet him. Spine set, Adriel flexes his hands. Just outside the open doorway, he stops long enough to chase away what remains of his frazzled nerves.

Taking a breath, Adriel steps into the spacious chamber. The air is thick with the stench of sulfur and the sounds of chatter. Already revelers fill the large room. Some are dancing, and some drink. A few of the others engage in more intimate activities. This place serves as a den of debauchery and sin. The weight of its temptation presses on him like a physical force that takes a moment to subside.

He scans the room and notes the various groups of demons gathering around tables heavy with food and more drink. They look up when he enters, a few scowling over the intrusion. His silent gaze sweeps over each one until it lands on the familiar sight of Rayen's bent head near the back.

Though he obscures his face with the hood of his cloak, Rayen sits alone in the far corner. Adriel moves through the crowd with the ease of a predator, his eyes never straying from his intended destination. When he reaches the table, he selects the chair that places his back on the wall.

"They act as if Rome is already victorious," Rayen points out as his fingers circle along the rim of his cup.

Though his tone is soft, it commands Adriel's full attention with little effort. "They have faith in our fearless leader."

Rayen scoffs, his eyes never wavering from the cup set before him, and Adriel wonders which part is amusing. Fearless or leader? Whichever it is, Adriel refuses to put his friend on the spot by asking.

"I need a favor." Adriel begins and sighs when Rayen's gray eyes as delicate as smoke rises to meet his in silent speculation. "I need to know who Heaven is assigning to monitor the situation."

"I haven't left this place in years, Adriel. Why would you ask this of me?"

"Because you're the best Seeker I know."

"You're not taking this on alone, are you? You're good, my friend. But no one is that good, Adriel."

His soft chuckle dies when a succubus, scantily clad in sheer swaths of fabric, approaches the table. Ruby-red lips soften while her ivory skin sparkles under the light of a hundred candles that circle the room. Lifting a hand to halt her progress, Adriel keeps his tone casually polite.

"I'm not interested."

One graceful shoulder nudges with a lazy shrug. The movement shifts the gossamer material covering luscious curves, and he wonders just how intentional the action was. After a long glance in their direction, she moves onto friendlier territories.

Adriel leans back in his chair slightly. "Rome's instructed me to use the hounds."

"You're not serious."

Just then, a massive chortle cuts through the many conversations to pull his focus to the hulking figure near the center of everyone's celebrations. As the oldest of the triplets, Tobias has a reputation for vicious bloodlust and an unbridled fury to earn them the title of *The Hounds*. Similar in appearance to his younger brothers, eerie green eyes that burn with an incandescent heat set him apart.

"You can't control Tobias or his brothers, Adriel. Even Rome's hold over them is tenuous."

"I can with their leash." Once the words leave his mouth, it's too late to call them back.

"He'll hate you."

"Tobias can start plotting my assassination for all I care, so long as he follows orders in the meantime."

Chapter 4

Somewhere between consciousness and sleep, Nora finds herself in a small room. Straight ahead, they hang heavy material over the windows built into the stone manor to keep out most of the biting wind. Still, the chill is enough to push Nora closer to the fireplace and it's roaring fire.

The salty smell of seawater with each gust of wind is the first clue that she's dreaming since Iowa isn't known for its ocean access. Bare toes press down on the cold stones beneath her while she studies her surroundings.

The scent of wax hangs in the air from a dozen candles strategically placed to provide enough light to work under, and clings to her nose. The furnishings, though meager, appear stout enough to hold the large men that gather around the table. So absorbed in their task, they appear oblivious to her sudden arrival, lifting heads only to bicker quietly amongst themselves before returning to work.

Nora struggles to process everything around the thudding in her chest. In nearly every direction, a precarious stack of books limits room to maneuver. Long narrow tubes of paper scatter over open shelves and tabletops to fill any available space. She's in the middle of scanning every detail to remember later when her gaze lands on a man standing apart from the group.

Taller than most men, he boasts broad shoulders that leave little room for doubt regarding his strength. While the others dress in a simple fabric of coarse wool, he opts for a rich velvet. The material appears both thick and expensive, forming another thought. Royalty? If so, the lack of guards surrounding him leaves her to wonder if he's brave or just arrogant.

In the time it takes for her heart to complete a full beat, Nora notices his laid-back demeanor shift. Once relaxed shoulders, soon square up as a ripple of awareness crosses his back. His frame rigid, the man pivots off one leather boot in her general direction.

The shift in position catches the soft glow of candlelight to bathe pale hair with shimmering gold tones. Except for Kegan, he's the most handsome man she's ever laid eyes on. Breath stills in her lungs until they ache with a need to exhale while she trails eyes across a hard jaw and impossibly blue eyes.

Rather than being a pleasure to look at, his face rips the breath from her throat. Lips part on a mute scream as flawless features twist. Quick flashes of light snap within those eyes to scorch her with a look meant to frighten as his shock turns to fury. Moving to close the distance between them, an electric charge buzzes to stand the hair up along her arms.

"Who brought you here?"

Panic claws at her insides from the sheer ferocity of his words. Throwing a look left and right, Nora searches for an exit, her eyes landing on the heavy door not ten feet away. Can she make it before he reaches her?

"Better than this deer-in-the-headlights routine you have going", she mutters to herself. Balancing on the balls of her feet, muscles prime and bunch to propel her across the short distance when she jerks awake with a hard jolt.

Shoving herself upright, Nora fights to calm the demanding rhythm of her heart while every breath falls in a whoosh of air. She'd had bad dreams before. Hell, who hasn't? She struggles to recall one quite like that. *Wuh!* A glance at the clock shows her alarm, ready to go off, so she catches it early. "No way I'm sleeping after that."

She spends a few seconds working her legs free from the forgotten sheets and blankets tangled around her, then perches on the side of the bed to retrieve her phone. After swiping a finger to silence more impending alarms, Nora heads to the kitchen to start coffee instead of giving in to the cigarette her mind yearns for.

Freshly disturbed, Ezio pads along behind her, his meow starting off as a gentle nudge. Experience tells her that the longer it takes to fill his bowls, the louder his cries will become. Still, she makes a beeline for the coffeepot.

"When you first came here, you were quiet. Not a peep out of you." She observes as she starts the machine to brew coffee early. "Should I schedule something with Dr. Kerry?" Walking the short distance to his food bowls, Nora gives him fresh water, noting that the sound of cat food hitting his bowl quiets the howling sounds. "You've become a glutton."

While the BUNN finishes brewing the pot, Nora finds enough time to zap a breakfast burrito in the microwave. Then, armed with her favorite mug, she adds coffee, spoons in sugar and finishes it with flavored creamer before taking the first cautious sip. By the time she leaves for work an hour later, Nora is ready to tackle the day.

She should've called in. The two hours she's spent on paperwork tempts Nora to cry uncle. Instead, she moves the completed stack to a wire basket. Stretching side to side to work out the kinks taking up residence along her back, she then massages the tender spot the pen leaves on her index finger. With several more papers piled high, ready for her attention, Nora mutters a groan and pulls another stack closer for review.

"Got a minute?"

Spotting Rebecca just inside the door, Nora jumps at the quick reprieve from her morning's monotony. "You know, the paperwork is why people would rather sink than apply for grants."

"That bad?"

"At this rate, I could be done by next year." With a loud exhale, Nora caps her pen and waves in Rebecca, in like one would land a plane. "If you're here to rescue me, I may have to find room in the budget for your raise."

"I'm afraid I forgot my life raft at home." The brief smile Rebecca offers disappears under a pinched expression.

"What now?" As Nora's hopes settle around her feet, she can't help but wonder how she pissed Karma off.

"Mrs. Spinley from social services is here. She's wondering if we can provide a couple of beds."

"How many is a couple?"

"Two."

Nora stands, the news dropping her heart a few inches into her chest. "We'd be lucky to come up with one empty bed, let alone two."

"That's what I told her. Sister Francis said they could make room for the girl, but, as siblings, Mrs. Spinley would like to keep them together."

"I see. I'll go talk to her. Put in a call to Second Wind and see what they have available just in case. How old, do you think?"

"Maybe twelve and fourteen?"

"In that case, page Zoe to meet us upstairs."

"On it. Thanks, Nora."

The sound of her assistant's relief sets off a warning in her head. *Don't get your hopes up, Nora Brennan.* If she can't find space for both of them, she'll have to split them up. A prospect that leaves a cold spot on her soul. After her first experience with that scenario, Nora swore it'd also be her last. When she enters the common area where Mrs. Spinley waits, she settles herself to face the challenge head-on.

While the siblings stand together in the farthest corner possible, locked in a death grip, their caseworker sits at one of the short tables just inside the door. Not quite ready to tackle the children just yet, Nora takes a seat across from Mrs. Spinley. Experience taught her that a few extra minutes to adjust makes a world of difference with some kids. *Some.*

"Good morning, Margaret."

"Nora, good to see you." One hand slides a thick manila folder across the table while the other thumbs through something on her phone. "Sorry," she murmurs, tucking the phone into her open purse. "I just heard from Bramblewood. They can offer the brother a bed."

"Bramblewood is over by Cedar Rapids, not exactly visitation distance."

"I know." A heavy sigh lifts Margaret's shoulders, her free hand rubbing at a temple as if to ward off a growing headache. "The state has come a long way in terms of foster care, Nora, but I'm running out of options."

"May I?"

"Good luck. Neither one is much of a magpie."

With a nod, Nora stands and approaches the duo with a sense of calm she's far from feeling. Only after figuring she's close enough without invading their personal space does she take a seat on the table's surface.

"Good morning. My name is Nora Brennan. I run Hiller House with *a lot* of help. Who might you two be?"

"I'm Deacon. This is my sister Freya."

The boy, near fifteen, sets one of the first ground rules. *Speak to him.* Judging by the shadows haunting similar pairs of eyes, she can't imagine how much horrible the pair has seen in their brief lives. Their clothes, tattered and too small, are clean, however. "How old are you, Deacon?"

"I'll be fourteen this summer. Freya just turned eleven last week."

"You're tall for your age." His head lifts, the youthful jaw tightening under her compliment, though his eyes remain watchful. "Mrs. Spinley tells me you need a place to stay for a little while."

"Only until our Mom comes home, then we'll be leaving," he snaps.

"Okay. Well, while I try to see what we can do for you, are you hungry? I think they just finished serving breakfast a little while ago. If you hurry, you might catch it before they start their cleanup."

If the look Freya gives her brother means anything, Nora will wager they'd eaten little over the last few days. When the pair steps away to carry on a quiet debate, she forces herself to hang back and let Freya work. Taking on the job of protector, big brother soon relents with a begrudging nod in Nora's direction.

"Perfect. Follow me." Leading the two from the common room and into the hallway, Nora sighs aloud to see Zoe heading their way. At five-foot-one with bright purple hair and a sincere smile, she's the least intimidating person on staff. "This is Zoe. Zoe, this is Deacon and his sister, Freya. Would you mind taking them down for some breakfast while it's still hot?"

"Happily." If Deacon experiences any hesitation, his sister moves with purpose, dragging him along behind her.

Nora catches that while happy to follow Zoe to the promise of hot food, Freya's hand never strays from her brothers. After a deep breath, she returns to Margaret, who greets her with a quick nod, wraps up her phone call, and sets the ringer to silent.

"What can you tell me?"

"Deacon and Freya Webb," she begins, lifting the cover of her folder. "When Freya was two, their father died in a drug deal gone wrong. Their mother, Stella, was just picked up for selling meth to an undercover officer. Even with good behavior, I'm told she could get a few years."

"There's no chance of a family foster?"

"Deacon mentioned an uncle in Boston, but so far, we can't find any contact information on him."

"I asked Rebecca to put in a call to another facility near here, but they usually tailor to young men."

"You've seen how they are, Nora. Separating them would be beyond traumatic."

"I've called every place within fifty miles," Rebecca announces as she enters the room. The look of defeat on her gentle features prepares Nora for the words she grumbles next. "No one that takes both boys and girls has two beds."

"Okay, so maybe we get creative. Since Freya is eleven, we can bunk her in the pink section under Zoe. Deacon will need a bed with the teens. That's the snag."

Sinking into a chair beside her, Rebecca throws up her hands. "This is why most places have an age-out clause, Nora."

"I'm not opening that up for debate. Again." Either the set of her jaw or the look in her eye heads off whatever argument Rebecca came prepared to make. "It's not an option."

Margaret adjusts her thin frame. "What do you suggest?"

"We can move Tyr into the blue sector since he'll be eighteen in a few months. I'll have to ask Mark to be watchful of the other boys, however."

"Sounds like you have a solution, Nora, so I'll leave you to it." With a soft groan, Margaret shoves to her feet and buttons her green corduroy knee-length jacket. "In the meantime, I'll try to track down this uncle. I can be back to check on the kids in a few days."

Nora shakes Margaret's cool, thin hand, and accepts the folder on the Webb children. "I'll have Carl walk you down. He'll need to bring in their stuff, anyway."

"Won't take him long. There's only one bag between them." Margaret replies in a dry tone. "I'll drop off a few necessities for them."

"We'd appreciate the gesture. Every bit helps." Rebecca takes the folder from Nora and tucks it under her arm. "I'll get this filed in our system while you get them settled."

"If you need anything else for them, just let me know."

Nora nods. "Will do. Thanks again, Margaret."

The social worker chuckles, giving her head a gentle shake. "Pretty sure I should be the one thanking you."

After paging Carl, Nora leaves him to walk Margaret to her car while she goes in search of the Webb siblings. Since most of the resident kids moved on to study hall, school, or work, the lunchroom is near empty when she arrives.

Seated at a table in the back, Deacon and his sister carry on a quiet conversation, their guard going up the instant he spies her approach. Shadows fall into bright blue eyes as his shoulders square out for a fight. With a cant of his dark head, he whispers something to his sister that has Freya standing from the table and hiding behind his narrow frame.

"Take a breath, guys. We have the beds needed for you to remain together." Nora announces, seeing no reason to prolong their fear. "Still, Freya will need to bunk with the girls her age."

"She stays with me." Deacon's hand reaches out to grasp onto his sister's.

"I'm sorry, but I don't have the space to give you private quarters and in order to keep this place running for the kids in need of it, I have to abide by state guidelines."

Chin notches, Deacon unmoving in his determination. "Then we'll go someplace else."

Nora takes a breath and puts as much sincerity into her words as possible, lifting her palms in a gesture meant to calm his need for battle. "There isn't *someplace else*. I'm sorry Deacon. Outside of school, the two of you will have as much time together as you like, but, after lights out, she needs to be in her zone and you in yours. Can you make that work?"

Eyes burn in a youthful face until the hand Freya rests on his arm soothes his ire. "We won't be here long enough for it to matter," she whispers in a tiny voice.

Choosing not to argue about the length of their stay, Nora nods and moves on. "While you are here, there are rules. We'll go over them together so you both understand."

"We aren't babies, *Nora*. We know what rules are." Deacon's words clip free of clenched teeth.

The obvious disdain in which her name falls from his lips rises her temper a small notch, leaving Nora's voice soft but with a smidge of directness. "I'm sure you do, Deacon. We have a three-strike policy here," she continues, as if he made no objection at all. "Break the rules beyond that, and we'll have to place you somewhere else. Said place may or may not have room for Freya to follow. *If* that happens, you need to recognize that it's through your actions, not mine. Are we clear?"

"Crystal."

"Sir?"

How does one simple word set his teeth on edge? Lips thin as Adriel looks up from the reports in front of him to catch Cairn hovering inside the doorway. The weight of his gaze causes the empath to lower his. "What is it?"

As if the floor has become more interesting in the past few minutes, Cairn never lifts his gaze. Instead, he shuffles from foot to foot, his hands in a tight fold in front of him. When he answers, his words are so soft a mumble that Adriel can't make sense of them.

Leaving the report for later, Adriel lightens his tone. "Come closer." There's a shudder of movement before the empath complies with two meager steps forward. His eyes close while he pulls a slow breath. Once his heart rate evens out and his jaw loosens, he tries again. "Cairn? Look at me."

A long moment of silence stretches between the two men before apple-green eyes inch upwards from the floor.

"I apologize for my frustration," Adriel begins, "but I really wish you wouldn't call me by that title."

No doubt reading his now relaxed demeanor, Cairn stutters a nod. "How would you prefer I address you, Si-" knuckles whiten and Adriel chuckles over the slip.

"Can't you use my name?"

Surprise flutters over a serene face, his head tipping to one side. "With honor, Sir."

Adriel smiles at Cairn's willingness to comply with his request. Though an experienced warrior of hell, Adriel's always carried a soft spot for the Cairn.

Sitting behind his desk, Adriel finds himself taking a moment to observe the empath's features. Unique to his race, silver-blonde hair cascades down his back, and the gentle slope of his nose and the captivating shade of his eyes work together to create an entrancing effect. Shaking himself out of his thoughts, he straightens in his chair. "Now, what did you need?"

"You asked me to retrieve the leash, Sir. Adriel." With a tremulous smile, Cairn withdraws the medallion out of the pocket of his torn jeans and lays it atop the desk.

Adriel picks up the medallion for a closer examination. The etchings on the tarnished metal are ancient; the ruby in the center glows with magical energy. This leash is the key to controlling one of Rome's most powerful weapons. He'll not be happy to part with it. His next thought sends a shiver along his spine. "If anyone asks, I took the leash. Me. Alone. Do you understand?"

It isn't difficult to miss the way Cairn's shoulders immediately relax. "Yes. Thank you."

Tucking the medallion into his pocket, Adriel stands just as Rayen appears in the hall. "Thank you, Cairn." After another quick nod, the empath slips from the room.

"Did you even think this through?" Rayen leans against the wall, his concern coloring his voice.

"As much as anyone can. I don't trust Tobias. If I can bring him to heel, the other two will follow suit."

"And what happens when you give back the medallion? What's stopping him from coming after you later?"

Adriel's lips twist into a sly, confident grin. "He's welcome to try."

"Just be careful," Rayen warns. "I don't have many I consider to be friends."

"Have you uncovered anything yet?"

Rayen smoothes his jacket and takes a deep breath before responding. "Heaven appointed Selena to observe the situation and report back."

A flicker of hope ignites within Adriel's chest at the news. He hadn't prayed for it, but it arrives like an answer all the same.

As if sensing his relief, Rayen taps a fast rhythm with his boot on the floor. "Don't underestimate her, Adriel. She's just as powerful as you are."

"But unlike me, she spends most of her time up in the clouds. And observing means not interfering."

"And if she does, in fact, interfere?"

The two men exchange glances full of worry and determination.

Adriel's mind races with the possibility of Selena equaling his power. If that's true, she *could* pose a problem. "I'll bring a half-dozen Scavengers with me. If nothing else, they'll either be a valuable distraction or cannon fodder. Whichever it is works for me."

"Couldn't hurt."

"Do we know which Fallen took up the role of Guardian?"

"If it's who I think it is, you've got bigger problems than Selena, my friend."

After she steers her jeep into one of the remaining parking spots for *Maxine's Diner,* Nora checks the time. "Dammit." With a wrinkle in her pert nose, she grabs her purse and makes a mad dash through the rain.

Inside, *Maxine's* is more crowded than its parking lot. Far from one of the upscale places one can find in the city, this establishment runs with a *Mom and pop* atmosphere. One without a cute hostess to seat you. Where most consider a wine menu to be a mythical item seen only on television. Add the best chili-cheese fries on this side of Texas to the list and Nora immediately became a loyal patron.

With a shudder to shake off most of the rain, she searches the dining room for a particular face. *Did she leave? Tire of waiting, perhaps?* As fingers pick at the nicotine patch on her left arm, Nora cringes after another look at the time. She's in the middle of rehearsing an apology when the flailing of one arm draws her attention to a booth in the back. Arming herself with polite excuse me's, and hushed apologies, she weaves through the tables. When she's close enough to sink onto the vinyl bench, she signals one server.

"I was thinking you ditched me."

"Nonsense." Accepting the plastic cup of fountain soda, Nora waves off the menu to order her favorite. "Who would I possibly ditch *you* for?"

"Tom Hardy."

"Okay. Yes. For him, I'm sad to say you'd be on your own."

"Gerard Butler. Henry Cavill. I'm sensing a pattern here."

"Yes, and definitely yes." Nora laughs before pulling a swallow from the cup in front of her. "I guess I'm not as loyal to our friendship as I hoped."

Eleni laughs and pushes her food around on her plate. There was a time Nora would stare at her friend with unchecked envy. Wispy blue-black curls frame a slender jaw as her olive skin hints at a Greek heritage. Factor in the almond-shaped eyes of warm chocolate and the exotic lilt in her speech, and *presto!*

"At least you have good taste."

"Shamelessly," she answers with a grin.

"I keep saying it's a matter of time before some gorgeous hunk talks you into skipping town with him."

"Hm. Otherwise known as the apocalypse."

"You sell yourself short."

"No. I just prefer to keep my feet planted firmly in reality." *Unless you're counting last night's dream,* a tiny voice whispers. Unlike most dreams she'd had in her life, Nora awoke, recalling every single detail of that one. From the room to the scent, definitely, the enraged man coming after her. More than once today, she found herself lost in thought, trying to make sense of the whole thing. The sharp snap of Eleni's fingers inches from her face jerks her back to reality with a sheepish smile. "Huh?"

"I said, if you're the dowdy one, what does that make me?"

"The hot one." Nora smiles her thanks as the server returns with lunch. Armed with a fork, she makes quick work of diving into the plate of fries. Speaking around a mouthful, Nora sucks in a tiny whoosh of air to cool off the bite as she chews. "Everyone," inhale, "needs at least one." Inhale. "Lures in the unsuspecting."

"You shouldn't talk with your mouth full." Eleni lifts one finely sculpted brow. "How is that even healthy?"

"The fries or pouncing on the poor unfortunate souls left by the wayside in favor of your own preferences?"

"The fries, smartass."

"I'm sure they're not. But it's this or cigarettes." Spearing one fat fry slathered in chili and cheese, Nora tries to tempt her friend over to the dark side. "Try one?"

"I'll stick to my salad, thanks."

Although Eleni eyes her plate of cholesterol with open criticism, Nora notes she isn't making much of a dent in the pile of leaves she ordered. "Life is just too short."

"So, who's my hot friend?"

"What?"

"Everyone needs one, you said. Who's mine if it isn't you?"

"Jess."

"That was quick. Don't take time to think about it or anything."

Nora laughs. "No time required."

"You think Jess is attractive?"

"Duh! The man's a walking orgasm. With the playboy charm, in a let-me-talk-you-out-of-your-pantskind of way." For added emphasis, Nora rumbles a purr against the back of her throat and sits back to enjoy the look of pure horror on her friend's face.

"Ew."

"If he weren't such a player, I'd have acted on his purely physical attributes years ago."

"It's official. I declare you insane and admit you for a seventy-two-hour hold. For your own well-being, of course."

The friends laugh off the subject and move on to the next. Eleni is the let-off valve she needs in life. By the time the server clears their plates, she can feel the weight of her stress lessen.

Opting to cover the tab for her "tardy arrival", Nora digs around for the small red wallet swimming around in the shoulder bag she calls a purse. "Ah-ha!" She declares and drags it out into the light, unaware of the small white card stuck to the zipper. Her breath freezes inside her chest as the small card falls free to flutter onto the table, giving Eleni time to swipe it up with her cat-like reflexes.

"Kegan, huh? No last name?" Nora notes her friend turns the card over in her hands in search of further clues before she snatches it back to bury it deep within the abyss of her bag. "Interesting."

"It's Gaelic."

"How do you know that?" Eyes narrow, pinning Nora with a grin. "You looked it up, didn't you?"

"So?" The tips of her ears warm as Nora distracts herself by adding a tip to the bill and tucking her orange visa card inside the flap. "He's the one Mallory is having a stroke over."

"Oooh. You mean the guy with the cabin?"

"Yep."

"Why do you have his number? Is he hot? Are there possibilities there?"

"Stop. The only reason I have it is to arrange a time to go through the things Grandad left behind."

"So, he's not hot?"

"I don't recall." Nora grinds out, her insides flinching as the lie leaves her mouth. Of course, she recalls, any woman with hormones would remember. Eleni's smile widens as if picking up on the falsehood, but with obvious pity for her friend, changes the direction of her interrogation.

"Have you called him to arrange something?"

"No."

"Why not? Is he a perv?" Dark brows pinch in Eleni's forehead. "Should I tag along with you?"

"Of course not."

"Okay. Then what's the problem?"

"I'm not ready to box up his life."

"Honey," Eleni's voice softens, giving Nora's hand a squeeze across the table. "You're never going to be ready for that. You just have to do it."

"Yeah."

"Sadly, I have to get going." Eleni gathers up an armload of coat, umbrella, and purse, then plants a noisy kiss on Nora's forehead. "Unlike some people, I don't like to be late. See you tonight?"

"Count on it."

Chapter 5

By the time lunch is over, Nora's too distracted by current events, so she calls in to take the rest of the afternoon off. The slight drizzle she faced upon arrival turned into a full-on thunderstorm by the time she leaves the diner, drenching her light jacket before she reaches her Jeep. Setting the wipers to full, Nora cranks the heat and spends the rest of her day running from one dead end to another.

After braving the downpour half a dozen times, Nora's soaked to the skin, running back and forth from Jeep to store. The wipers' fight to keep up with the rain is near deafening as she crosses another name off the list. With only one remaining, any hope she clung to this morning dwindles to small embers. Still, she makes the short trek across town before calling it a day.

The lack of a sign on the front of the building has Nora passing it twice, only to backtrack again once she spies a meager logo down a narrow alley off Main Street. Parking as close to the door as the old buildings allow, she gathers up her shoulder bag and runs for the glass door. Above the door, a tiny bell rattles with a quaint jingle to signal her arrival.

From somewhere in the back, a young man in his twenties emerges, greeting Nora before she can reach the short counter. "Afternoon, I'm Andrew."

"Hi, Andrew. Quite a place you have here." Nora breathes while taking in the sight of hundreds of books lining every available shelf, leaving some to make haphazard piles here and there. The last time she can remember encountering so many books in one place was the trip to the library a month ago. "Hard to find, though. I think I passed you twice."

With a slow nod, the man adjusts thick frames; the lenses enlarging a pair of unremarkable brown eyes. "Yeah. My grandfather bought this place when there was less bustle. Can I help you?"

"I hope so since you're my last stop." Reaching into her bag, Nora pulls out the wrapped book and gingerly lays it on the counter. "I've inherited this book, but can't find any information on it."

"Hmm. You can't just ask a family member?"

"Afraid not. My sister is the only one left and seems just in the dark as I am."

"I'm sorry," Andrew murmurs while he pulls a pair of white cloth gloves over his slender hands.

"No worries," she assures him, her fingers struggling to untie the thick twine encasing the book. Swallowing a quick curse, Nora rubs her hands down the front of her jeans, only to find the wet denim problematic. Lips purse on the raspberry her exhale creates as she tries again. While in reality it probably took less than a few minutes, under the shopkeeper's scrutiny, those minutes feel more like an hour. Still, the loud gasp he makes when she lifts the cover eases some of her discomforts.

"Extraordinary!" Dull brown eyes flicker with small patches of light as his hands hover mere inches from the cover. "And you've no idea where it came from?"

"Sadly, no. My grandfather passed it to me, but I'd never seen it before this week. Let alone heard anything about it."

"Interesting."

"The lady I just left thought the symbols on the cloth appear to be ancient Egyptian."

"Hm. I don't think so." Andrew mutters, lips moving soundlessly as he spreads one side of the cloth over the surface. "Egyptian comprises more pictures than what we're seeing here, but I couldn't say for sure without a little time. I *can* tell you this, it's old."

"Okay?"

"The metal on the corners of the book here served the purpose of keeping the book's leather binding in place. Judging by the aging, that was some time ago."

"I noticed a lot of the ink faded from some pages as well."

Intrigued, Andrew lifts the cover meticulously to scan the first several pages. "What I can see reads like an old form of Gaelic. The pages confirm its age, though, so there's that."

"How do you mean?"

"Well, for one, they didn't make these from paper. This is animal hide."

"An-animal?" Nora swallows back the rise of her lunch as she recalls running her hand over said pages two nights earlier. "Any chance you can translate any of it?"

"Not without a bit of time, I'm afraid." The crash of her hopes must've been visible on her face as the young man rushes to soften the delivery. "Not that it can't be done, mind you, but the English language is difficult to translate into. Not to mention most of the words are indecipherable."

"I thought you might say that."

"It's quite a find, though. For sure. How much are you hoping to get for it?" Gone is his shy youthfulness, a calculating entrepreneur in its place.

"Oh, I apologize. I'm just trying to learn more about it, not sell." Closing the book, Nora replaces the wrap, knots the ties, and slides it back into her bag. Even if her grandfather hadn't made a stipulation to not sell, the idea of parting with it now leaves a knot in her stomach. With her right hand resting on its weight to assure herself it remains unmolested, Nora offers a friendly smile, wishes him a good afternoon, and heads for home.

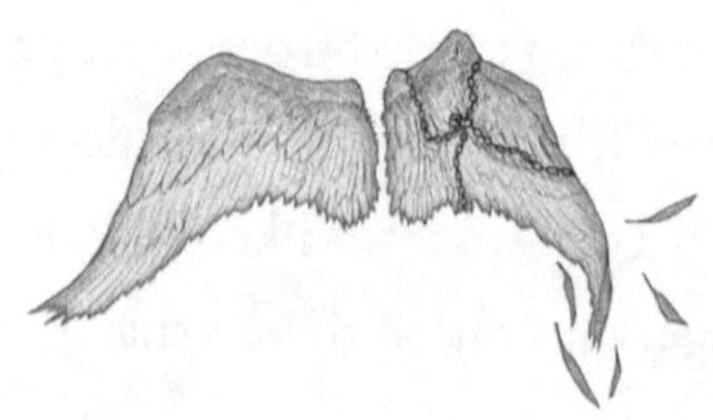

When another yawn creeps up on her, Nora covers it with a hand to steal a peek at the time. The movie is over and the popcorn gone;

the girls gather around the long coffee table to polish off the last of her tequila.

"So, the date was a total disaster?" Eleni asks before draining her shot glass without a wince.

Mallory answers with a giggle. "He seemed confused that I didn't jump at the opportunity to sleep with him."

Since her head is fuzzy from alcohol, Nora waves off the next shot. "Hell, I'm confused. On the phone, you said he was perfect."

"Omigod." Mallory flops backward to sprawl across the floor. "He was. Tall, good-looking with a smile that'll melt you at the knees."

"You don't know how many times I hear that exact thing," Jess offers as he enters the living room from the back door to take a seat next to Eleni on the couch.

"The tall part might be an exaggeration."

Eleni's barb inspires a frown on his rugged appearance before he wipes it away. Nora's surprise at his arrival earns her a good-natured smile. "Eleni texted, and said she might need someone to drive Mallory's car home."

Nora takes in her sister's very intoxicated mannerisms with a laugh. "I appreciate you lending a hand."

"Nah," he scoffs. "I've been itching to see what girls' night is for months."

"Mostly just playing catch up on our worst dates. Mallory's last guy holds the title so far." Eleni explains after consuming her eighth shot.

That was eight, right? How is she even still making sense? Nora wonders with a slight spark of jealousy. *You've had four and your brain is mush.*

Nora watches in fascination as Eleni pours herself another shot glass then sweeps her arm toward Mallory. "She was just telling us when he shifted from perfect to scumbag."

As she leans back on her hands, Nora's mind wanders as the conversation swirls around her. Reluctantly, she thinks back to her own disastrous date a few months ago and can't help but recognize a flare of regret.

She'd been looking forward to the blind date for weeks, building up an image of the man in her head that was nothing short of perfect. As soon as she saw him in person, she knew the fantasy was just that, a fantasy.

He hadn't been tall, or particularly good-looking. His smile certainly didn't have any effect whatsoever on her knees. Things Nora could overlook for the right fit. But what really killed it was the conversation or lack thereof. He'd barely said a word the entire dinner, leaving Nora to fill the silence with meaningless chatter. By the end of the night, she was relieved to be heading home, alone.

With a physical shake, she steers her attention back to the conversation in time to catch the tail end of Mallory's story.

"He kept trying to convince me that he was the best I could do. Like he was doing me a favor by wanting to hook up with me."

"Ugh." Eleni makes a face. "The worst."

Nora snorts in agreement. "I hate it when guys act like they're doing you a favor by showing interest in you. Like you should be grateful for their attention."

Jess nods, looking thoughtful. "I can see why that would be annoying. Personally, I think you girls are all amazing and any guy should consider themselves lucky to go out with you."

Despite her better judgment, Nora takes part in the next round of shots. "Most of the men I meet can't stutter out the words to ask me out, let alone get me into bed."

Eleni spares Jess a quick look. "Mallory has the inside track with the doctors and nurses."

No way." Filling her glass, Mallory drains it and pours herself another. "No dating in the workplace. It's bad luck."

Jess snorts. "Luck?"

Mallory shrugs. "You know those movies where people fall in love with each other while they are working together? Do you think they're thinking long-term? No way! Karma will come along and knock you on your ass down the line if you date in the workplace."

Accepting Mallory's shot, Nora drains it with a wince. Her face scrunches up as she fights through a wave of nausea. "It's a sad time when women have to turn to the movies for romance."

"Who said anything about romance?" Eleni asks on her way to the kitchen, returning with a glass of water she hands off to Nora. "Romance results in marriage. I just need a healthy sex life."

Jess laughs, shifting to the edge of his seat. "Hear, hear!"

"Well, since I won't be getting either in the near future, I'm calling it a night." Nora gathers up the dishes with Jess's help and carries them to the sink while Eleni searches for Mallory's coat.

"Learn to live Nora."

"Yeah, yeah. This coming from the most serious person I know." Considering her sister's alcohol consumption, Nora slips Jess her car keys and then does her best to assess Eleni's condition. "Good?"

"Don't worry." Eleni taps her finger to the end of her nose without a qualm. "I'll get her home safe."

"Thanks, El."

With a twist of the lock behind them, Nora cleans up the remnants of popcorn and then climbs the stairs to bed. Any other time, Gerard Butler is enough to swoon her troubles away. Tonight, he just brings to mind Mr. Kegan Selkirk, with a yummy accent of his own.

Already dozing, Ezio claims his usual spot when Nora reaches her bedroom. She takes less than five minutes to change her clothes, brush out her hair and rest her phone on its charger before she's turning out the lights. As she crawls under the blankets, she'd swear even her hair sighs. Already dozing, Ezio claims his usual spot when Nora reaches her bedroom. The lamp casts a warm, orange hue across the room as she changes into her night clothes and brushes out her hair. After dropping her clothes near the baize-covered wardrobe door, she places her phone on its charger and turns off the lights. As she crawls underneath the quilt, she'd swear even her hair sighs in contentment.

"I think it's time to bring in more staff for Hiller House," Nora mumbles, running a hand over Ezio's silky fur. His liquid gold eyes blink slowly, his soft whiskers twitching left and right with every stroke of Nora's fingers. "Maybe we can get Mallory to go over the accounts this weekend. What do you think?"

Nora yawns. "Hm. Good point. After she passes through the hangover phase." One hand continues to stroke his fur as Nora continues as if he's an active part of the conversation. "I saw Kegan over at Paddy's gas station today. Makes two sightings since Grandad died."

"Briarville isn't a big town, but it seems strange to see him around now and not before. Right?" She yawns heavily, too tired to worry or investigate further; instead choosing to accept that maybe she was just overthinking it all along. Not two long blinks later, Nora settles into a deep slumber.

Chapter 6

Unlike her last dream, Nora stares up at a massive castle with cliffs and the sound of a raging ocean serving as the backdrop. Relentless, the rain batters the surrounding ground, bringing a chill to the night air.

Conserving her body heat, Nora wraps her arms tightly around her waist and trudges towards the stone steps and the promise of refuge. Behind her, screams pierce the howling wind to fill her with dread.

Mud squishes between bare toes as she turns to see dozens of men, women, and children scramble to escape the soldiers walking out of the darkness, wielding swords. As they run for the same stone steps, the wet dirt runs dark with blood until it infects the surrounding puddles. Leg muscles prime as Nora latches onto the hand of the girl closest to her to propel them up the steps and into the castle.

Inside, the absence of fresh rain leaves the room stagnant with the reek of blood and sweat. Lifeless bodies litter the rough stone floor to tell Nora it's not any safer than outside but the many pleas for mercy on the other side of the heavy door push them further into the room to search for another escape route.

"We need to hide." Nora's voice cracks over the barely audible whisper and for a second she fears her companion either doesn't hear or, worse, understands.

After what seems like minutes, the girl answers with a frantic nod, sapphire blue eyes wide with fear. The young woman takes the lead to guide Nora through several rooms with even more bodies, accompanied by overturned furniture. Running the short distance beyond the kitchen, she stops at a small room built into the left wall near a crudely constructed table. After considering the rough shelves lined with food and other staples, Nora assumes the small room serves as a pantry of sorts.

Hushed whispers in an unfamiliar language slice through her thoughts until she stares helplessly at her companion. When she shakes her head in confusion, the woman gestures towards a door cut into the wood floor, partially covered by several sacks of potatoes. Understanding, Nora rushes forward to help drag enough sacks aside to gain access to the hidden door.

Stiff fingers wrap around a thick metal latch, though the cumbersome hinges hinder her first few attempts. Gritting her teeth, Nora gives it one last tug, her heart seizing as the bolt moves with a loud screech.

Frozen in place, the two listen for any sound of approaching danger before Nora lifts the door high enough to usher the woman into the dark pit. An afterthought has her taking an extra couple of seconds to shift one sack to fall carelessly across the door as Nora descends a stubby ladder into darkness.

The two women huddle as far within the blackness as the walls allow, their eyes watching the door above them. The screams that erupt randomly pierce the insulated room, gripping her heart with stiff fingers. "You're dreaming. Wake up." Lips tremble over the words as she rubs her hands up and down bare arms.

Overhead, footsteps stomp above them, drawing closer to their hiding spot. Time slows around her as loose boards sprinkle dirt in the wake of boots stamping too close for comfort. Behind her, Nora's nails dig into the soft earth as she wills herself again and again to wake up from this horrible dream.

When the attack comes, it happens so fast, she scarcely registers the blur of motion. One second, she's holding her breath, and the next, the door flies open. The bulk of his body smothers the light filtering in through the opening as his hand latches onto her companion's hair to drag her out. She experiences a flare of disbelief; her legs are heavy before fight-or-flight kicks in and she's up the ladder to launch her small body across their attacker's back.

Tiny, ineffectual fists pummel about his shoulders while hands yank clumps of dirty blonde hair from his head before she drags nails down the side of his face. The surprise of her attack lasts but a moment before a vicious roll of his shoulders flings her weight aside, slamming her into a makeshift shelf.

The pain that explodes across her back steals her breath, leaving her immobile to do anything but stare as he slits her companion's throat with zero hesitation. Blood sprays her attacker and the wall, staining the floorboards beneath before the metallic scent overpowers everything else.

"Wake up! Wake up!" No longer a muffled chant, Nora screams the words around the pantry-like room, drawing the attention of

their attacker. Shoulders bunch and roll as he spins his hulking frame in her direction, the blood-soaked dagger leaving a trail in his wake as he draws close. I'm dreaming! *Even as Nora assures herself, this is all in her imagination, she can't help but gape at the blood coating the very real-looking blade.*

The hand he fists into her hair slams shut her vocal chords against the scream rising in her throat. Hot flashes of pain explode along her scalp as he jerks her head back to expose the soft column of her neck.

Fingers scrabble over his, nails clawing and scratching before she abandons the struggle in search of a weapon. Hands skim across the dirty floor and stray potatoes in a desperate search that yields nothing promising. The tears that fall from her eyes cut a path over her cheeks, leaving a wet trail in the layers of filth as Nora prepares for the inevitable.

Her scream careens off the bedroom walls as Nora sits straight up in bed, blankets falling into her lap. Even after her breathing slows, her hands still shake when she shoves them through the heavy mass of hair clinging to her face and neck. Leaving Ezio to sleep, Nora climbs out of bed on uncertain legs and steps into the adjoining bathroom.

Twisting and twirling hair heavy with sweat, Nora gathers it into a loose ponytail. Her tank top soaked; fits like a second skin as she splashes cold water on her face. Drying off with a hand towel, she returns to her room long enough to swap out her sweat-soaked clothes for a clean t-shirt and a pair of Scooby-Doo boxer shorts, then pads silently to the kitchen.

Too early for coffee, and her rattled nerves preventing sleep, Nora decides on a cup of mint tea. Leaving the teapot to boil, she sets her sights on the snack cupboard, and its treasures of salty and sweet instead of the cigarette her brain suggests. When she looks back on it, Nora won't understand if the change comes suddenly, or if she simply doesn't notice.

Regardless of how; the air around her bites, shifting to become oppressive. Senses on high alert, something whirls around her to raise the hair on her arms and pepper exposed skin with goose-bumps. Fingers curl into fists, toes press against the tile as men appear inside her living room. Materializing out of thin air, more and more bodies fill the room until her whimper comes out strangled.

When the final three form a front line, Nora's fascination flees in favor of self-preservation. Arctic bands clamp across her lungs, migrating into her legs as the air around her spoils with an insidious purpose.

Clumsily, she inches toward the back door when a soft chiding sound halts her progress. Tracking the sound pulls her focus to the front three. Specifically; the one in the middle.

While the three of them appear similar in size and looks, the middle one far outweighs them in intimidation. His unnatural green eyes and feral smile pushes her to lift her chin a notch and locate the false bravado hiding somewhere within her.

"What do you want?"

"To feel the screams leave your body." Mr. Green Eyes answers, his words inciting the three to step forward in unison. Pace and cadence are identical amongst them, in his eyes Nora recognizes the promise of a savage death.

Kegan taps one Maison-Martin boot off the pavement to the beat of a Disturbed song while the minutes tick by. He's been sitting in the same spot for hours now without a good plan to get close enough to protect Nora. With the class of her neighborhood, however, his time is running out. Too much longer and someone is bound to call the cops. *Then what?* He couldn't imagine she'd believe any reason he'd be out here in the middle of the night, *not* born of perversion.

The combination of music and distracting thoughts have Kegan nearly tipping sideways when Selena appears inches from his face. As he struggles with the weight of the motorcycle, she jumps at the opportunity to yank the earbuds from his ears. The sharp pain that erupts behind his eyes promises to split his skull in two as he engages the kickstand and sprints up the front lawn, digging his phone out of one pocket.

Kegan clears the hedges and starts up the front porch when the other end clicks with a terse hello. "Nora's in trouble. I may need backup." Quick and precise, he ends the call and jams the phone into a back pocket.

At the door, heated blood primes his muscles for the upcoming battle as he tries the handle unsuccessfully. Before he can tear the door from the hinges, his head advises caution. Reluctantly, he reaches out to determine what he's facing.

He counts eight beings inside with Nora. The putrid stench tells him they're Scavenger Demons. Three of the eight are unfamiliar to him, therefore a variable in the equation, but the unique scent of Nora's fear forces Kegan to act.

With one well-placed boot, he kicks the door in, splintering the frame with a sharp crack. His unexpected arrival has several sets of eyes staring at him in shock just as Nora's soft green eyes lighten with recognition.

Roused from her bed, she hides in the kitchen on the far side of the house wearing only a t-shirt and a pair of men's boxers. Until now, Kegan never associated Scooby with arousal, but the tightness in his gut proves hard to ignore. Curls she kept contained during their initial meeting now fall in wild tangles over one shoulder. He allows himself another second to assess for any damage before addressing the intruders.

While the Scavengers pose a threat in great numbers, the other three hold the bulk of his concern. The shriek of alarms within his head remind Kegan to replace his earbuds and tap play on his phone to start a Shinedown track. Steady bass thumps against his eardrums as the lyrics to *Sound of Madness* disrupts the sirens. The smile he offers is slow to form.

"I don't have all night, boys." A crack of his neck follows a roll of his shoulders as Kegan withdraws two silver daggers from inside his leather jacket. With a finger crook at the demon closest to him, his small smile shifts to a grin. "Step up so I can send you back to your Maker." Their reply comes fast.

When several demons rush forward, he shifts from foot to foot, his daggers slashing left and right. Sending one back with a boot to the chest, he spins to confront the one on his right. Slowing his heart rate, Kegan blocks and dodges her attacks until he spots the opening to bury a dagger in her chest. The loud, painful screech that splits the air rattles the windows an instant before she disintegrates to burned ash.

"Friend of yours?" Sharing a look of shock amongst themselves, Kegan notes the change into a murderous fury. Since they hold the numbers, he changes his stance to one of defense.

Planting his feet, Kegan absorbs wave after wave of assault with relative ease. Switching from blocking their attacks, he counters with daggers or a well-placed fist. Sweat drips from his forehead, covering his back by the time Eleni runs in from the back door.

"Tell me," he demands while driving an elbow into an advancing demon, "you did *not* flash here!" The impish grin she offers is one he's seen many times throughout the centuries before she shrugs off his concern to enter the fray.

With her slight stature, she relies on speed and agility. Dodging the first, Eleni delivers a front thrust kick to another. There's a half a second between the sound of bones crunching and the scream of agony when one of the big ones drops like a rock, hands cradling his knee. The time Kegan spends assuring himself Eleni can still handle herself drops his guard long enough for a demon to jump on his back.

Driving a fist upward, Kegan fights to keep the stained fangs away from his neck while he attempts to shake him loose. Ineffective; he reaches over one shoulder to catapult him into one of his approaching comrades. Catching their friend sends a handful falling backwards.

Kegan stabs the next one, then finds himself toe to toe with the biggest of the three. Eyes that glow like hazardous waste conveys a fury. Fury he plans to vent on Kegan.

Shooting forward, Kegan strikes the first blow by dropping a shoulder and plowing into the demons mid-section. Unwilling to give up ground, he drives them forward until the two slam into an outside wall with such force, the house shudders. Searing pain blazes across his back before the vibration almost rattles his teeth. Jaw clenching, he growls hard as a blade collides with his shoulder blade directly beneath the flesh.

"Don't'cha just love the backstabbers?" Eleni asks with a laugh, wrapping a hand around the hilt. "Hold still."

While he's certain it'll take all her strength to pull the weapon free, he sags with relief the second she succeeds. With a twist of her hand, the handle twirls in her palm before she throws it into the crowd. The blade itself experiences several narrow misses before imbedding into another demon's chest.

Green Eyes momentarily forgotten, Kegan snags his backstabber by the front of his shirt. "You son of a-" he snarls through teeth. The headbutt he delivers drops the young demon into a heap on the floor, incapacitated. Pushing back the quick stun, he churns up a second wind to finish the fight.

Landing a hard right stumbles Green Eyes long enough for Kegan to toss his limping look alike through the remains of the front door. The next one to advance is reckless enough to drop her guard long enough for him to snap her neck with a quick jerk. He follows her limp frame to the floor to bury a dagger in her heart for good measure.

After a quick scan, Kegan spots Nora hiding just inside the curved archway. "We need to get her out of here!" Just as he catches Eleni's nod in agreement, something slams into his back, jarring the air from his lungs.

Falling forward, Kegan struggles for oxygen, leaving him open for a boot to the face. The force bounces his skull off the hardwood floor hard enough to dislodge an ear bud, allowing the sirens to reverberate between his temples.

When he blocks the next kick, Kegan smashes his fist into Green Eyes' knee, wrenching the bone out of socket. His scream is hardly worth noting before Kegan knocks him off balance. Exhaling, he pushes himself to his feet, takes a moment to reposition the loose earbud, and decides.

Running to the kitchen, he shrugs out of his leather jacket, only to pull it over Nora's bare arms before shoving a pair of boots in her hands. "Time to go. Grab her bag."

Chapter 7

While Nora muddles around the fog filling her head, she struggles to pull on her boots. More than once she has to hike up the long sleeves of the leather jacket for better access to her hands. Beside her, Kegan moves to turn the heat off the stove before returning to stand guard, his face impassive. The fading of the noise leaves Nora to wonder just how long her teapot has been whistling and how she failed to notice.

Along with the quiet, the fog lifts enough for her to snag one or two of the questions that pinball back and forth. *Who are these people? What are they doing in her house?* The complete lack of a logical answer trips her compulsive personality, adding a sour note to her words. "What in the *hell* is going on?"

Maybe it's her tone of voice, or that she spoke at all. Regardless, Kegan diverts his attention away from the living room. Eyes the color of chocolate rake down her entire five-feet-five height before meeting hers. Her question inspires him to plow a hand through his dark hair as lips press together in a grimace. The shadows in his eyes hover around the secrets he's keeping while the shaking of his head appears indecisive. Several seconds creep by as his brows pinch until he casts a look around her kitchen as if weighing what exactly to tell her. All her hope for clarity vanishes with the hardening of his jaw.

"I'll fill you in later. Right now, we need to go." In case the rigidness of his answer doesn't convince her, he clamps a hand on her forearm through the jacket to lead her toward the back door.

Are you sure you want to be leaving with this man? The tiny voice in her head pipes in as they near the back door, allowing her a fraction of a second to think things through.

While nothing about tonight lives in the same zip code as sane, he came to her aid. Had he not shown up when he did, she'd be dead. Nora harbors no doubts about that sad fact. Without question or hesitation, he'd put himself in harm's way. She can't help but feel grateful, even though that help will cost her a new front door.

"I have it," Eleni announces, joining them in the kitchen. The sight of her bag hooked on Eleni's shoulder raises more questions. *Why is she here? How did Eleni know she was in trouble? Who in the hell taught her to fight like that? Why didn't she mention she knew Kegan?* The last one lodges itself under Nora's skin to make her squirm. Kegan acknowledges her arrival with a grunt, his hand inches from completing their escape when all movement stops.

Unlike the frosty air from before, an unfamiliar sensation migrates through the house.

Wave after wave of oppressive energy surrounds them until she's sick to her stomach. As it builds in her head, she has to fight to keep from being sick all over Kegan's boots. Slowly, the pressure eases until its absence draws a heavy sigh from her. The exhale catches in her chest as a newcomer strides through the gap the broken door makes in the wall.

"I assume you're the Guardian?"

Guardian? Huh?

Kegan's close enough for her to catch the sharp inhale, his hand tightening on her arm. Back straight, he moves to stand in front of her, shielding her from whatever harm this new threat intends to inflict. A quick glance in her direction conveys a look of caution, even as Eleni latches onto her other arm.

"I am," Kegan deadpans.

"Figures. You're kinda the type. No offense." The newcomer walks with ease across the debris littering the floor, stepping over one man writhing in agony.

"The type that kicked the shit out of your guys? Yeah, none taken." With her field of view taken up by the wall of Kegan's back, Nora has to twist to peek around him.

About ten feet away, the newcomer bristles, annoyance thinning his lips. Without thinking, Nora lays her hand against Kegan's back, catching the twitch of muscles under his damp shirt. Her only thought is to suggest a bit of prudence, but the cords of muscles under her hand sidetrack that idea.

"The Hounds are sloppy, I'll give you that."

"Hounds, huh? Given their reputation, I expected," Kegan trails off, as if searching for the perfect word. The smile that lifts the corner of his lips has Nora swallowing a groan. "Better."

On his feet, with the help of one of the other two, Green Eyes teeters off balance, his glare murderous. "I'll show you *better.*"

"No. You won't." *Newcomer* cuts in, his tone quiet.

Nora observes Green Eyes quake with uncontained rage. "Rome'll want-"

From where she stands behind Kegan, Nora gapes when the newcomer's demeanor shifts. In an instant, the face that would rival any Spartan, wars with a black temper. Eyes the color of the Pacific Ocean narrow as another layer of steel hardens his jaw. "Do not think to tell me what Rome wants. Gather your brothers and wait in the car."

Brothers!

"But-"

As if deciding Kegan and Nora can wait, the newcomer moves closer to the brothers, his voice eerily quiet. "I brought you along to help me. Not go off all half-cocked, only to get busted up. Since none of you can be of actual help at the moment, you can wait in the car."

"*Wait?*" Green eyes blaze with the outrage that flares his nostrils and lifts his chin. "We don't take orders from," he pauses, baring his teeth as he spits out the words meant to insult, "*half-breeds.*" The warning the newcomer exudes gives Green Eyes a moment's pause before an arrogant grin overrides any sense of caution.

His movements smooth and nonchalant, as if he can't bother to put actual effort into his reaction, the newcomer shifts to stand toe to toe with Green Eyes. While the Hound stands a whole inch taller than the newcomer, he's on the losing end as far as perceived danger.

When the newcomer withdraws a gold medallion from his pocket, Green Eyes appears to second guess his ill-timed mutiny. Lips curl into a snarl at the same time he casts his eyes downward.

The instant he raises them again, Nora notes the hatred burning in his incandescent eyes, but with a wave of his hand, the newcomer brushes him off.

"Go to the car before I make you an only child." His words, while calmly spoken, vibrate audibly. As the triplets limp outside, the newcomer turns his full attention on her. "You'll have to forgive Tobias. While highly effective, he can also be a tad impulsive."

From where she hides behind Kegan's massive shoulders, Nora can't help but comprehend the deadly energy he sends in their direction. An ache lodges itself under her ribs for Kegan's well-being, her hand fisting within his shirt. Since Kegan's already bruised and bloody from the last go-around, Nora experiences some serious reservations about this new confrontation, fearing for his safety. The hand she places on his arm pulls his gaze long enough to voice her concern. "Let's just go. Please?"

Kegan gives his dark head a shake, his lips set in a hard line. "We can't outrun him, Nora. Not without a head start."

Newcomer releases a soft laugh, eyes alight. "I'm afraid he's right, child."

Nora bristles over the unsolicited agreement, putting a flare of bravado in her voice. "I am not a child, and I don't believe I asked for your *unbiased* opinion." Under her hands, she can feel every fiber of Kegan tense from her snarky response, yet remain steadfast in his position between her and the intruder. If she thought her words would put the stranger in his place, his bark of laughter leaves her gaping.

One hand clutches his side as *Newcomer* catches his breath. "I think I like you."

"Wish I could say the same," Nora clips.

Bowing gracefully at the waist, the stranger does nothing to hide his amusement. While wishing she didn't appreciate that smile on a purely female level, Nora moves closer to Kegan. "I am Adriel," the newcomer clarifies. "I've waited a long time to meet one like yourself."

"Having difficulty getting women to give you the time of day?" Nora asks with a saucy smirk, her confidence hinging on the proximity of her newfound Savior.

Another deep chuckle escapes him. An expression of pure delight adds a sparkle in Adriel's eyes and a twitch to his lips. "I *do* like you." Adjusting his attention to Kegan, his head shifts off to one side. "I don't suppose we can come to an agreement?"

"That isn't an option for me." While Adriel speaks softly, his strange accent coloring certain words, it's Kegan's that awakens Nora's inner fascination. She doesn't deny his thick Scottish accent teases her fancy, but the very sound of his deep bass brings her every nerve ending to attention.

"I thought you might say that." Adriel's heavy sigh snaps Nora out of her musings and plunks her back into the reality of her situation. Shrugging out of his coat, he makes a show of smoothing out the creases before laying it across the back of the couch. Without further warning, the two men lunge forward.

The series of punches and kicks they exchange makes Nora wince. Every blow that Adriel lands squeezes her heart. As they fall, Kegan's weight puts him on top to drive Adriel's head into the wood floor.

When Adriel attempts to right himself, Kegan's elbow prevents the movement. The loud crack of Adriel's skull bouncing off the floor sends tremors all the way to the safety of her kitchen. No doubt it's his own determination that fuels him to throw Kegan backwards with a boot, so he crashes through the long coffee table. The very piece of furniture she had spent weeks deciding on, shatters under his weight.

Moving too fast for her to comprehend, Adriel is on his feet and landing several kicks into Kegan's unprotected midsection. The final one lands hard, draining the blood from Kegan's face. As Adriel yanks him to his feet, Nora doesn't miss the wheeze of his inhale contracting what's sure to be broken ribs.

"Is that it?" A quick succession of blows accompanies the question, landing hard, intent on causing further trauma to the tissue surrounding broken bones. "I expected *better*."

Another toss lands Kegan near the doorway to the kitchen, his head connecting with a sick thud off the crown molding. Visibly shaken, he struggles to his feet with a toss of his head. About the time Adriel pulls a blade from his boot, Nora searches for some way to help Kegan.

Pulling and prying her arm from Eleni's grip, she snatches up the teapot. Judging by the heat the metal shell still emits, Nora prays it'll do the job an instant before she races forward. Fingers grip the handle, reaching the two of them just as Adriel sinks his blade into Kegan's left side, his shriek of pain loud amongst the quiet.

Drawing back, Nora swallows from the sound the metal makes connecting with Adriel's head. Tiny vibrations jar her arm, filling her with a moment of regret until she tamps it down in time for a second swing.

A splash of scalding water pulls a scream from Adriel as he retreats away from where Kegan still struggles to remain upright.

Trading the teapot for the discarded knife, Nora launches herself at his back, burying the blade just under his right shoulder.

Her intervention proves to be just long enough for Kegan to gain his bearings and tuck her behind him before Adriel's fist collides with her face. With a growl darker than anything she can imagine, Kegan lands a heavy left hook of his own. Kicking him backwards, he stops to ensure Nora's gently restrained by Eleni once again before advancing on his opponent.

"Didn't your mama teach you not to hit a lady?" Arming himself with a piece of the broken coffee table, Kegan wields it like a bat. The sharp crack it makes connecting with Adriel's skull rattles the windowpanes. It requires several more blows until Kegan appears satisfied Adriel won't be getting back up anytime soon. "Weren't expecting that, huh, Asshole." Spinning around, he grabs Nora by the arm and drags her out the back door with Eleni close on their heels.

"A-are you o-okay?" Nora wonders aloud, her boots slipping on the damp grass as she tries to keep up with Kegan's long-legged stride. When he comes to a stop near the parked motorcycle, he actively avoids her concern by busying himself with fitting the shiny black helmet to her head.

"Jess still isn't answering!" Eleni snaps, giving her phone a dark look Nora's only seen a few times over the years.

"We can't wait." Climbing onto the motorcycle, Kegan assists Nora with climbing on behind him, then turns the key. The initial shock from the cold leather seats sucks the air from her lungs as she instinctively shifts backwards away from it.

As if misinterpreting her action, Kegan throws a stern look at her over his shoulder, his words clipped. "You need to hold on."

In the time it takes Nora to override her body's response, the press of her thighs warms the seat a fraction. Teeth clamp across her lip as she leans forward and holds onto his sides. With a growl, Kegan takes her hands in his and wraps them around his waist tightly. The heat emanating off his back turns her gasp into a purr as she shifts closer.

"Take care of her," Eleni instructs in a voice tight with emotion.

"Just call me when you're safe. Get a hold of Jess and remind him of the importance of answering his fucking phone." Kegan offers Nora another once-over to satisfy himself of her readiness before skipping his gaze to Eleni. "If that doesn't work, I'll give him a refresher course myself."

Eleni opens her mouth to say something when Adriel stumbles out of the house to draw their attention. With a kick of his leg and a turn of the wrist, Kegan brings the motorcycle to life and races them down the street at the same time Adriel staggers into the waiting car.

"Here they come!"

Kegan mutters under his breath as Nora's voice sounds close to his ear, and gives the machine more throttle. Her squeak of alarm tells him she's unprepared for the lurch the machine makes, which tightens her hold around his waist. The action creates a flash of pain to explode along his left side. Stifling the groan, Kegan shoves back the wave of darkness teetering so close to his consciousness and distracts himself with their escape.

A series of lefts and rights takes them through the slumbering suburbs until he glimpses a sign on their right, and the freedom it hints at. Once again ill-prepared, Nora's scream rips through his head as he nearly lays the motorcycle on its side to catch the on-ramp for the freeway.

"Please stop doing that," he grumbles, with no hope of her actually hearing him.

Blasting their way onto the freeway, Kegan curses when the thick traffic forces him to weave out and around the vehicles between him and success. To keep the speeds he's pushing and the distance between them and their hunters, Kegan swerves them through tight spaces and near misses. *At least she's stopped the screaming*, he muses.

Quick reflexes steer them out of the way of a merging pickup truck, around the black Prius and into the fast lane. In his right mirror, Kegan catches Nora closing her eyes. Her head shakes weakly until she buries her face against his back, where each exhale soaks his shirt with liquid heat. The contrast to the frigid fall night sprinkles his skin with goosebumps. *Goosebumps. When was the last time he'd experienced those?*

Spotting Tobias on their right puts his musings on the back burner. With the slower traffic ahead clogging the lanes, Kegan gives Nora a heads up before he rolls the dice on a risky maneuver. "Hold on!"

Snapping his teeth together, Kegan releases the throttle with one hand and he squeezes the brake with the other. Speed combines with momentum to lift the back tire from the pavement. After a quick bounce, he steers them around the back end of a car and onto the waiting exit ramp. Pushing speeds well above the posted limit, he steers them around the spiral curve to the dark, two-lane highway below. *The lack of streetlights will cover your escape.* If any part of Kegan remains undecided about his *life's a bitch* status, the rub against the back tire is a solid argument.

"Son of a-" Another hard rub sends the motorcycle to fishtail across the road, forcing him to fight for control. The acrid scent of burning tires clogs his nose and ignites his temper. "Fucker!"

Front and back wheels continue to fight each other for purchase as he realizes the futility of his efforts. On a growl, he twists, despite the blinding pain, and wraps his enormous frame around Nora's. A full millisecond later, the motorcycle crashes into the street to skip them like rocks across a pond.

The first bounce almost rips Nora from his hands, forcing Kegan to tighten his grip in time for the second. Tiny rocks in the asphalt rip through his jeans and t-shirt, tearing at the flesh underneath to aggravate pre-existing wounds.

He's rewarded for his foresight to put the helmet on Nora when her head snaps sideways with a hard jerk to ricochet off the road. He catches the third and final bounce with his hip and shoulder. White-hot pain floods his body as they skid across their lane of traffic and into the ditch just beyond. The tall, wet grass serves as a temporary balm on his inflamed skin.

Stuttering an exhale, Kegan's hands roam to check Nora for injury. His relief at seeing her chest rise and fall fills him with a moment of peace that shatters under the sound of a car screeching to a stop on the road ahead. Car doors open and close.

In his weakened state, Kegan has no hope of fending off Adriel a second time. Seeing no alternative, he grips Nora tight to his wounded side and tries to flash them to safety. Opening his eyes, he curses aloud to see the dark, starless sky above them. For the first time in a long time, his heart races as a cold sweat breaks out over his skin.

"Can't you *fucking* help just one time?" Kegan vents at the night's sky, preparing to send out the distress signal to any Watchers in the area. The crack of lightning announces Selena's arrival just as she appears between them and the road. Her tone chiding, she reprimands the advancing demons with a wag of her finger, then places Kegan and his charge in the safety of his hotel room.

Chapter 8

Once Kegan and Nora are safe, Selena shifts her form within the air to place herself in the cold, damp city of Boston. Overhead, faint traces of dawn creep through the sky to curl and stretch out its long fingers.

Entering Colin's bedroom, her face heats, catching him in a moment of passion with a busty blonde. She has little doubt he's aware of her arrival, though unwilling to call a time out for her benefit, so she moves up to the rooftop to wait him out.

While shades of gold, rose and pumpkin color the once gray sky, Selena chews over the nails on her left hand. Damien is sure to find out about her actions tonight. The promise of his displeasure lodges a knot in her stomach. While she tells herself she can handle the heat, stand her ground with sure footing, a small voice in her head remains doubtful.

The situation wears her patience thin when she peeks tentatively inside Colin's bedroom once more. The soft sigh she makes seeing his female companion sleeping while he stands in front of the many windows is one of relief. *Right?*

As thousands of humans begin their morning commute with a flurry of activity on the street below, Colin looks on. Despite cracking the window open for fresh air, rich tobacco and acrid smoke fills the room, cloying around Selena's senses when she emerges completely. The ripple of awareness that cascades across his strong features tells Selena he's alerted to her presence.

"I didn't do it," he snaps. Bare from the waist up, the muscles in his back stiffen like corded bands under scarred golden skin. "Even if I did, you can *fuck off*."

"I'm aware Colin. You weren't even there." Selena whispers as she moves to stand at one side. From her position, she can see his stubborn jaw flex, and emotions flare in his whiskey-colored eyes. "I had to intervene, and we both know how my supervisor is going to react."

Colin shot her a sidelong glance and raises an eyebrow, the corners of his mouth turning upward in a wry smile. "It always comes down to how scared someone is of Damien, doesn't it?"

"You know how he is about bending the rules, Colin." Selena says, a hint of desperation creeping into her voice despite her attempt to remain composed. "He's ruthless in following protocol."

"Yeah, I have firsthand knowledge. Or have you forgotten?"

The atmosphere becomes charged with tension as Selena holds her breath, her jaw tensing at the thought of becoming another example. "Saving Kegan's ass puts mine on the line."

"What are you babbling on about now?"

"Adriel and the Hounds made an attempt on Nora. Kegan stumbled."

"Is he okay?" When Colin pins a look in her general direction, genuine concern outweighs his irritation.

"Banged up, but he'll heal."

"How did Adriel find her?"

"I'm not sure." Even before she finishes uttering the words, Selena meets a snarl of disbelief. "I don't know," she insists.

"Who would?"

"I imagine that's a very short list."

"How helpful."

"If you continue stumbling around asking the questions you're asking, you're going to get a lot of unwanted attention." She intends her words to be taken as a warning, but the hatred they encourage burns brightly in those expressive eyes.

"Good. Figure I'll either get answers or piss enough of you off to finish the fight you started."

"Me?"

"*Angels.*"

Selena exhales more out of habit than necessity. "Your temper is going to bite you one day."

His smile is quick, and full-blown to reveal even white teeth. Before her, Colin's expression shifts from bitter to a level of dead-sexy only he can pull off. Even with the history between them, she'd have to be dead to ignore the effect he inspires. "It's common knowledge that I bite back. Sometimes on request."

"Your base, juvenile barbs, won't work on me." His answer is in the casual shrug of one shoulder as he crushes out his cigarette and lights another. "If you want answers, you need to see Azrael. But you'll need to be quick about it. As soon as you ascend, so will *he*."

"Fuck him and fuck Azrael."

"I'm serious."

"Not. Going. To. Happen."

"Colin, you're acting like a child."

"Fuck you."

"He was your friend once."

"Pretty sure *was* and *once* are the keywords in that sentence."

"Either put on your big boy pants and talk to him, or stop poking around."

A billow of white smoke rides the air on his long exhale, his eyes trained on the small group of school kids boarding a big yellow bus on the street below. Several minutes tick by in silence, his face so unreadable that Selena nearly writes it off as a lost cause. Turning on one foot, she prepares herself to have a meeting with Damien when Colin's question gives her pause.

"Why are you helping me?"

It's her turn to distract herself with the flurry of activity that fills the city as she searches for the best answer to give him. She could be diplomatic or political, of course. Neither of which will defuse the bomb Colin lit the fuse on centuries ago. Teeth worry over her lip as she opts for honesty.

"I never wanted you to fail, Colin."

"Bullshit."

"We had our differences, yes, but you held my respect as well. On the day your regiment received sentencing and punishment, my heart was one of the heaviest."

"And I'm a monk."

"You can believe what you like. If you want answers, Azrael has them. We both know you're the only Watcher that can ascend that far, so do what you want."

"I always do.'"

As Nora comes to, she finds a soft bed beneath her and warm blankets tucked in around her. Inside her skull, the furious pounding warns her of the dangers of opening her eyes, but she doesn't listen. Colors of burned orange and a crimson red sunrise flood the small room, placing a grating pain in her head until she closes them again.

Next to her, the bed dips under added weight. Without warning, a warm, calloused hand rests on her forehead, her flinch of surprise releasing another painful moan.

This time, when she opens her eyes, she does so carefully, absorbing the blurry image in doses. Her brain registers a day's growth of stubble surrounding soft lips, close enough for her to notice the dried split in the bottom right corner. Further up, she registers his straight nose and the heavy bags under a pair of dark eyes. *He looks worse than I feel.*

"You're awake." While that declaration eases most of the lines around his mouth, faint traces remain.

"What happened?" She croaks around a tight throat, her hand lifting as if to ease the swallow sticking halfway.

"We crashed." Rising, Kegan disappears from her line of sight, only to return with a glass of water. "I absorbed our landing as much as I could, but you bumped your head." Large hands slide under her arms to lift her upright, situating her amongst a mound of pillows that he piles up behind her. His touch is electric through her t-shirt, and all too brief. "Sip slowly," he instructs as he places the glass in her hands.

The first wash of cool water entices a smile to flirt over her lips, encouraging another swallow. Only after every drink becomes easier than the first does Nora trust her voice. "Thank you."

"It's only water. How do you feel?"

"I have a firm grasp on an elephant love-tap, but nothing seems broken." Nora indulges in a few more sips of water before she sets the glass on the bedside table. "Where are we?"

"My hotel room."

"How? You said we crashed."

"Um." Eyes dart around the room as he answers, "a friend."

"O-kay." Too late, Nora recalls the injuries he'd sustained on her behalf. The sight of his right arm pinned to his side tells her he's nursing damaged ribs. On his left, visible under the white cotton of his t-shirt, Nora spies a large, square bandage. "Are you okay?"

Her impulsive question fills his face with surprise, lifting dark brows a second before his head cocks to one side as if confused. Judging by his reaction, Nora wonders about the last time some-one expressed concern for him. In the small hotel room, the two of them less than a foot apart, her heart breaks considering all the possible answers. As if sensing her runaway emotions, Kegan attempts a smile.

"I'm fine."

"You look drained. As if you could sleep an entire year away."

"You don't need to worry about me."

Sensing his vulnerabilities aren't open to debate, Nora changes the subject. "Where'd you learn to ride? The Grand Prix?"

"We'd have made it if they hadn't rubbed the back tire." His hand scrubs along the back of his neck as he glances out the patio door. "Contrary to popular belief, I don't have eyes in the back of my head."

"You're right. I'm sorry." Her soft admission whips his head around to stare at her, eyes full of bewilderment. Averting her gaze from his, Nora smoothes a hand across the thick comforter. "I don't understand what's happening. But you saved my life, Kegan. Thank you."

Time slows as Kegan rocks back and forth on the heels of his boots. One hand clenches and loosens at his side. Seemingly uncomfortable with her gratitude, he looks ready to bolt. Instead of running from the room, however, he manages a quick bob of acknowledgment.

"Thank the Heavens, you're awake!" Eleni declares as she whirls into the room in a flurry of activity. After dropping her armload by the door, she sets a cluster of styrofoam cups on the small table and approaches the bed. Chilly hands frame Nora's face to tilt her head left, then right for a closer inspection. "Are you okay?"

Nora shakes off the examination. "I believe so."

"More than we can say for your house," Jess muses as he sets the carrier containing her clearly distressed cat on the bed. Oblivious to the dark glares Eleni and Kegan aim in his direction he leans down to press a kiss to the top of her head. "Glad to see you're okay, kid."

Nora could laugh that someone just over the legal drinking age refers to her as a kid, but questions regarding her house take precedence. She already resigned herself to replacing the front door. Perhaps things look worse in the light of day? "How bad is it?"

Eleni is the first to answer. "It'll be fine," she murmurs and presses a warm cup into Nora's hands. "Figured you could use some coffee."

"What does that mean?" Nora's thumb scratches over the soft Styrofoam. "It'll be fine?"

"It means Kegan's hiring a crew to make sure everything is perfect before you get home." Eleni busies herself with passing out the remaining cups before folding up the cardboard carrier and setting it aside. "For now, I've thrown some things into a suitcase for you, and Kegan already has your bag."

"Suitcase?" The first two swallows of caffeine do nothing to clear up the situation, so Nora takes a few more. "Why do I need a suitcase?" While she'll give them points for being discreet, she catches a quick look between Eleni and Kegan, his hand scrubbing across his neck in a gesture that's becoming familiar. "What is it?"

Before Kegan can muddle his way through an explanation, Eleni speaks up. "We have plenty of time to go over all the details. Right now, we need to come up with a story for the police."

"Police?" Nora's stomach drops an inch at the same time her fingers tighten on the cup. When she awoke a short time ago, she couldn't help but assume her nightmare was over. She'd write it off as a bad acid trip, or too much tequila before bed and go back to her merry, oblivious existence. Talk of the police only chases her further into the proverbial rabbit hole.

"One of your neighbors called them this morning when she saw your house." She can tell that Eleni isn't enthused about the police involvement from her set jaw and the way she spits the words at her.

"The one with all the plastic gnomes in her yard," Jess supplies as he twirls a set of keys around one finger. "We barely got out before the cavalry arrived."

"Mrs. Muller," Nora grumbles. Since the coffee loses its appeal, she sets the cup next to the glass of water and lifts her chin. "We'll just tell them the truth. Some men broke in and you guys helped me escape."

Kegan's lips curve into a smile. "I don't think it's going to be that simple." From across the room, he stands with his arms crossed loosely, nursing his injured side. It's the first he's spoken since her friends arrived, and despite the little shivers running across her body, Nora would've preferred he remain silent. An air of arrogance rides high on his shoulders, his amusement clear in the twitch of his upper lip.

"Why not?" Nora presses.

"We can discuss that after you get a shower," Eleni interrupts.

Nora's eyes narrow. "You want me out of the room so you can talk about me?"

The smile Kegan answers with is anything but apologetic. "Yes."

Weighing her options, Nora settles on a shower. Not like she's getting any answers sitting here. Besides, the temptation of soap and hot water is too strong for her to resist. *You still may not get the answers you want*, the voice warns. *True, but at least I won't feel like a dirty hamper in front of fine male specimens.*

As soon as the bathroom door shuts behind Nora and Kegan catches the sound of running water, he moves off the wall with purpose. "I'm doing what now?"

"It's the least you could do after wrecking her house," Eleni clips.

"*I* didn't wreck shit," Kegan snaps.

Eleni gives him a pointed look. "It wasn't me, crashing into everything. Smashing furniture."

Tearing a lid off one of the to-go cups, Kegan levels a glare on Eleni. "My bad. I should've accounted for Big, Bad, Demon having a thing for racquetball."

"All I'm saying is it's been years since you've had a good fight. You're bound to be a little rusty." Eleni flicks a wrist in a flippant manner.

The urge to snap her neck cascades into his hands, but Kegan settles for pulling a squeak of submission from the thick styrofoam cup. "I'm not in the mood to deal with you today."

"How bad is it?" Jess asks, cutting Eleni off from further irritation.

Kegan shrugs. "I'll heal."

"You need sleep to heal, you know that." Bracing a hip against the patio door, Jess continues to spin the car keys around one finger.

"I couldn't close my eyes until I knew she was okay." Fingers curl as he recalls the hours he spent at her bedside, waiting for her to wake up. For the first time in centuries, Kegan sent up more than a few prayers on her behalf.

"Any idea who the big bad is?" Jess asks while the sound of jostling keys aggravates Kegan's headache.

"No. But if you run across him, do *not* underestimate him." When the keys continue to spin, Kegan's teeth set. "Stop it." Jess blinks with a look from him to the keys in his hand before settling the small weight within his palm. "Thank you."

"He said he brought the Hounds with him for help. Help with what?" Eleni asks, ripping open the seal on a package of flavored sunflower shells to pop one in her mouth.

"Hounds? As in Hell?" From his spot, Jess barely glances up as the truth seems to register.

"That'd be my guess. The one he called Tobias has a hard on for Nora." Kegan adds, his sense of possession infecting his blood at the thought of Tobias's grubby paws on her. At first, he'd mistaken the look of desire for bloodlust. Closer inspection revealed he wants Nora for way more than what her death will provide. Over his dead body. *Careful, it might just come to that.*

"You're just full of good news," Eleni gripes. "Care to tell us what's going on?"

When the shower cuts off in the next room, Kegan has a full image of Nora standing in the empty tub, naked from head to toe, her skin glistening. Would the same freckles that dust her nose sprinkle over the rest of her? Is her skin as soft as it appears? He could spend hours imagining the sight she'd make if not for the fingers Eleni snaps in front of his face.

"Hello?" Eleni presses.

"What?" Kegan snaps.

Eyes roll with Eleni's frown. "What's going on?"

"That'll take more time than we have." Kegan hedges, shooting a quick glance at the closed bathroom door.

"Fine." Eleni airs. "What does it have to do with the book you nagged me to grab last night?"

"Old women nag." Kegan grinds. "I simply remind."

Jess laughs as he checks his phone. "Uh-huh."

"There isn't much to tell you," Kegan stalls.

The sound of Eleni's teeth cracking sunflower shells raises the meter on Kegan's irritation. Pouring another handful into her palm, she lifts her eyes expectantly. "Why not?"

"Eleni." From his position, Jess braces a shoulder on the patio door, his tone chiding.

"What? Can you say you're not curious why demons would chase them down city streets, Jess? Awfully brazen if you ask me." She adds with a look Kegan can see a mother giving her child.

She's a dog with a goddam bone at this point. Maybe it's the countless years he'd spent in wonderful solitary, or maybe she's always been this annoying. At this point, Kegan leans toward the latter. "The book draws them when it's exposed. I don't know why they want it, but it's my job to make sure they don't get it."

Eleni badgers. "Who's they?"

Kegan takes a drink of his coffee. His eyes close with the hot flood of caffeine on his tongue. "No clue."

Unsatisfied, Eleni presses. "Where did this book come from?"

Kegan jumps a shoulder up and down, mindful of the pull in his ribs. "I don't know."

"Why do they want it?" Eleni asks.

"Don't know that either." His shoulder dances once more before he pours half the cup of coffee down his throat.

Eleni growls, pointing at him with a fist tight around shells. "If you don't stop with the shoulders, I'm going to box your ears."

Kegan struggles to keep his face blank as the pixie thinks to threaten him. Jess's deep chuckle makes his restraint pointless. "You can't even reach my ears."

"Kegan, I care about this girl." Eleni states. "She's my friend."

His coffee loses its appeal, forcing Kegan to set it on the table. "I get that, but you're asking the same questions I'm *still* asking."

"Okay." Eleni quiets for a moment. "How did this book find itself in Nora's possession?"

"Brody was the last Protector. When he died, he willed it to Nora," Kegan says.

"Why?" Jess chimes in.

Kegan offers the only answer he's certain of. "It has to remain within their bloodline."

"If you knew this book was going to bring demons to dinner, why not warn her?" One hand rests on Eleni's hip as she does her A level best to intimidate him.

"Sure. And spend the rest of eternity in a padded room. Why didn't I think of that?" Kegan snaps mid-whisper.

Before Eleni can respond to his sarcasm, Nora emerges from the bathroom. Dressed in a pair of jeans and a soft shirt the color of moss, she looks refreshed and capable. While she isn't skinny by today's standards, his gaze moves over the lush curves any man would appreciate. The sight of her hands combing through wet, tangled curls puts a hitch in his pulse. As she secures the mass to the back of her head with a lethal-looking clip, Kegan catches an itch to tear it free and bury his hands in the heavy mass.

"Alright." Nora's eyes flit across the faces in front of her, each one carrying it's own expression of guilt and secrets. "Time to talk."

Chapter 9

Kegan watches as the whirlwind that's Nora descends upon the Chinese takeout that Jess brought with him. As she eats her chicken and broccoli, her gaze shifts from Kegan to Eleni, a hard glint in her eyes. "Well?"

"What answers do you need?" Kegan leans against the nearest wall and shoves his hands deep into his pockets.

"Every last one." Nora replies simply. "But that pinch in your eyebrow tells me I won't get them."

A ghost of a smile flirts across Kegan's lips. She's quick. Maybe the odds are in her favor. His answer is just as quick. "Not yet, anyway."

"So, let's start with how you two know each other and why you didn't tell me." No one could mistake the barb in Nora's voice as she aims a long stare at Eleni.

"Kegan and I did some work together a long time ago," Eleni hedges. "I never put two and two together."

Jess snorts. "Because Kegan is a household name."

"Exactly." Nora's smooth brow furrows. "He works with you at the museum?"

"Er, yes," Eleni stammers. "Well, no."

As direct as she'd been with him earlier, Kegan recognizes the temptation to let her flounder. Since time isn't on their side, he decides to throw her a life raft. "Eleni, Jess and I fought in the same battalion."

Nora's head leans to one side. "As in the military?"

Kegan's dry chuckle earns him a dark glare from Eleni. His uninjured shoulder offers a shrug. "We may as well tell her. It'll make keeping her ass alive a lot easier."

"Agreed," Jess chimes in, raising his hand.

"Fine." The bravado Eleni used to interrogate him earlier is missing from her voice. In its place is a soft mumble Kegan finds slightly amusing. Crossing to the patio door, her hand rests on the flat handle, the other she uses to beckon Nora to follow. "Excuse us, boys."

"This should be interesting." Jess settles himself in an empty chair, rotating it to give him a clear view as the events unfold on the patio.

The moment Nora steps onto the patio, there's a heavy weight wrapping her in a tight embrace. Resting her elbows on the wrought iron banister, she looks out over the city while her friend gathers her thoughts. Nothing could've prepared her for what she's about to hear.

"I'm just going to say it plain," Eleni says, her eyes on the streets below as she speaks. Hands tug at each other like they're having an argument over where to settle. She can't help but notice there's a slight delay in the words Eleni says compared to the determined set of her delicate jaw. "We're angels."

Nora's initial shock washes over her body like a chill, raising the hairs on the back of her neck. She stands for a long moment in silence while her brain computes the information. Eleni and Nora stare at each other in silence, eyebrows raised. The meaning of what Eleni said sinks in. Yet, angels aren't supposed to look human. *Are they?*

Mentally, she dusts off the memory of Sunday school where she first learned of angels. Tall, golden-haired with massive wings and shiny halo's. They don't stand before you, inches away, dressed in jeans and a fuzzy pink pullover. No wings. No halo. Her question tumbles free before Nora can give it further thought. "Where's your halo?"

After a small smile, Eleni's hands settle while still forming a tight knot. "Technically, we're fallen angels. No halo, I'm afraid."

"Fallen, as in, Hell?"

Serene features twist as chocolate eyes darken. "Those are stories people made up. Based on no actual fact or research." As if aware of the bite in her tone, Eleni takes a breath. "We fell from Heaven.

But we have no association with Hell, Nora." Closing the distance, she moves to stand beside Nora. "Please don't be afraid of me."

The plea is so faint, Nora almost misses it. Her mind starts to race, spinning through her past experiences with Eleni in search of something that she'd missed before. Was there more hidden beneath the surface? After further reflection, Nora realizes there'd been nothing that could have alerted her. "I'm not afraid of you, El. That doesn't mean I'm not pissed."

Eleni's face softens and she nods. "I can understand being pissed."

Nora clenches the banister as she cautiously weighs her words. "You're all angels?"

"Fallen. Yes."

"Are there more?"

Eleni lips twitch. "Hundreds."

"And you just run around pretending to be human? Why?" Nora could think of a hundred things she'd do if she had the freedom Eleni does. Making a life in Podunk, Iowa, isn't one of them.

"There's a little more to it than that, I'm afraid."

"Why did you fall?"

When Eleni's smooth attributes fall, Nora experiences a rush of guilt for having voiced the question. A tiny spark of emotion bursts within her eyes. Her bow-shaped mouth quivers until Eleni regains her composure. "That's a long story. It's going to take a longer explanation."

The whoosh of the sliding door pierces their bubble a second before Jess pokes his head through the opening. "Colin needs us to check out a few things."

"To be continued." Eleni reaches over and gives Nora's hand a squeeze. "I'm sorry I didn't tell you. I hope you can understand why." A long exchange of air fills the space beside them. "Kegan's an ass. But he'll do whatever it takes to keep you safe. Okay?"

This can't be real! This cannot be my life! Teeth worry over her lower lip as Eleni hovers, waiting for some form of acceptance. Nora opens her mouth twice to give it to her. Nothing but gasps come forward. The desperation in her friend's eyes complicates her drawing a breath. A knot tightens in her stomach, twisting and pulling until her guts cringe in response. Reading the stuttered shake of her head, Eleni pulls her in for a hug.

"I got you."

The words brush Nora's ear in a warm rush of air. Her arms are stiff when they wrap around Eleni's smaller frame, borrowing the strength she needs to manage with a nod. "Okay, El."

By the time Nora steps in from outside, her face is pale, her hands shake, but her chin lifts all the same. *Score one for gumption,* Kegan muses. No sooner does the hotel door click shut behind Eleni than her shoulders square before she pins a speculative look at him. Alone with her, Kegan refuses to examine the nervous energy pooling in his stomach.

"What?" Kegan pulls a drink from his forgotten cup, his face twisting over the wash of cold coffee. With a grunt, he steps into the bathroom to pour it down the sink.

"I'm just trying to imagine you as an angel."

He laughs. "Think nicer." Rinsing the cup, he sets it aside to toss in the recycle bin later.

"Why were you nicer?"

"Because I had no reason to be otherwise?"

Nora's nose wrinkles in a similar fashion to her grandmother, and Kegan catches his smile before it has a chance to grow. "And now you do?"

"Let's just sum it up to say I'm bitter. I fell from Heaven. Lost most of my friends. And have spent centuries watching you guys stumble around like toddlers, fucking everything up."

"Fair enough." Picking up the container of Chinese food she'd left on the table, Nora picks through now soggy chunks of broccoli. "You are an ass."

"Probably. But I'll do what's needed to make sure you're alive at the end of this thing. If you can't put faith in me because of my winning personality, then put your faith in that one fact."

"I can do that."

"Good."

"Why were those things in my house?" Nora rests against the chair back and swaps between eating and enjoying her coffee. "They weren't human, were they?"

The question effectively throws cold water on whatever Kegan's feeling to whip his head around. "Demons. Most of the ones you encountered, we call Scavengers."

Nora's voice cracks. "Scavengers?"

"Mhmm. Most of your high-level demons use them for their numbers." Even as the color drains from her face, Kegan presses on. She wanted answers. He'd give them to her. "The triplets you met are the Hounds of Hell."

"As in dogs?" Nora frowns. "But, they were men."

"Things down under come with a bit more twists, I'm afraid."

"So, they're men? Why do the stories say they're dogs?"

"Because people wrote said stories?" Kegan grins. "They're warriors. Honed in battle, their bloodlust and sadism make them formidable opponents."

"And the other guy?"

"Him, I don't know."

Nora spends the next couple of minutes quietly eating her food, lost in thought. Thankful for the quiet, Kegan checks his phone for any messages from Colin. Still nothing.

"What were they doing in my house?"

"Um."

"Looking for you." The matter-of-fact way that Kegan answers inspires a sudden rash of rapid blinking on her part.

"Why me? It isn't like I sacrifice small animals or practice summoning the devil."

"That's complicated."

"As in, you don't know."

Tucking his phone into a back pocket he meets Nora's skeptical gaze. Even if she accepts their story of angels and demons, she's clueless about the danger surrounding her. In his book, that makes her a walking tragedy. His redemption hinges on pulling this off. "You have something they want."

"Please don't say my virginity. Because I gave that to Scotty Pinter years ago in a less than stellar performance."

Don't laugh. Do not laugh. Inhaling deep around the pain in his sides, Kegan counts to ten twice until he's sure he has the urge under control. "It's not your virginity." His ability to utter that sentence with a straight face amazes him. He makes a mental note of it just in case he needs it for a character witness later on.

"That's good. I'd hate to seal our fate over a pale memory."

"Nora, I know you need answers, but it's not safe for you here."

"Here, as in this hotel room?"

"We need to get you out of town."

The second he speaks those words aloud, her head shakes. In a matter of seconds, she resembles one of those bobble heads so many humans stick in their cars. "I can't just up and leave. What about Mallory? And Hiller House?"

"Mallory will be safest, far away from you."

"You don't know that."

"I'm sorry. But any contact with you puts her in danger. All we can do is hope she stays under the radar. If it'll make you feel better, I can have one of my mates check on her."

Nora's teeth chew on the corner of her lower lip as she digests her new reality. When she lifts her head to look at him, Kegan recognizes the spark of determination in her eyes. How many times had he seen it in Brody's?

"No. Sorry. I can't just up and leave my life."

"Nora, be reasonable."

"None of this is in the same ballpark as reason." Nora snaps, tugging on a pair of socks before shoving her feet into the boots from last night. "I have too much going on to just leave it all in the hands of someone else." As if to emphasize her decision, Nora jerks hard on the shoelaces to make a strangled bow.

"You'll sacrifice us? To keep your life uncomplicated, you'll sentence us to death?" Kegan's aware of the different levels of shock she experiences, but his breath remains even. Pushing to her feet, she moves to stand inches from him, her head tilted back so she can lock eyes with him. Hands rest on the gentle flare of her hips as her chin lifts a notch higher.

"That's not fair."

"Fair?" Kegan chuckles. "This isn't kindergarten, Nora. If you insist, we'll protect you here. And we will die. You need to understand, this isn't a game."

"I never said it was."

Indignation rolls off her in suffocating waves. Hands ball into small fists as she wrestles with the temper he intentionally lit. When her eyes snap with an unspoken fury, it takes Kegan's breath away. *Damn, she's beautiful*!

A gentle shake of his head dislodges the fanciful thought and steers him back into the logical frame of mind he's clung to for so long. "If we stay here. Everyone of us will die. And then, many, many more. So, what's it going to be?"

"Fine." While she concedes, Nora's voice is tight and brittle. Her mouth opens as if to say something before she thinks better of it and snaps it shut once more.

"Great. I'll take you to meet with the police and then we get the hell out of Dodge."

The color drains from her face and he wonders how long it'll be before Nora loses the food she just inhaled. With a series of swallows, she rests a hand on the carrier housing a howling cat and frowns. He can't be sure, but the word she grounds out sounds an awful lot like, "Apocalypse."

Chapter 10

Tires screech as her Jeep comes to a halt outside the local police station. As Nora pries her nails from the armrest, she monitors the hood for a white flag to emerge from the engine.

Like he seems to do everything, Kegan drives with an intense desire to get from point A to point B. She unclenches her jaw before her teeth can shatter and escapes to solid ground. After spending several minutes inhaling fresh air, Nora starts across the parking lot. The heavy footfalls behind her drawing her up short.

"You don't have to come in with me," she offers. A dark eyebrow arches up his forehead in silent speculation, and Nora fights the desire to squirm.

"I think I should be there to sell the story we came up with."

"I just didn't want you to have to wait, is all."

"Waiting with you or in the car is still waiting, Nora. And until we're out of this city, I'm not taking my eyes off you." Kegan points out, jamming her car keys in his front pocket.

"Fair enough." Despite the tension between them, she spies a faint smile before he wipes it away. What would a genuine smile look like? Nora would stake her life on toe-curling and crosses the lot of police cruisers.

The sight of Mallory stomping out of the building just ahead puts a stumble into her step, her supply of oxygen running light as her sister spots her. Forcing a touch of lightness into her words, Nora attempts to avoid an unpleasant confrontation. "What are you doing here?"

"I got a call saying someone vandalized your house. Thought I better come down and make sure you were alright." The moment Mallory registers Kegan behind her, her concern slips, chilling her expression. "Why is *he* here?"

"He brought me." Her words leave her mouth like one would drop an anchor. Nora doesn't have to wonder if the innuendo takes hold, since Mallory jerks her head back as if physically struck.

Silver eyes narrow as her sister takes a step back. "He's why you weren't home when whoever broke in last night? Right?"

"Yes, but it's not what-" Nora's words stumble as she absorbs the sight of Mallory's clenching hands.

"Save it, Nora." Mallory's eyes change to a gunmetal steel, her tone flat as she moves to brush past them.

"Mal, wait-"

"I can't. I'm late for work." Not more than a second passes before Mallory whirls to confront her. "You know how I feel about him. That you'd spend the night with him in any way is a kick to the teeth." With a hiss, she jerks her arm free and puts some distance between them. "Whatever. You do you."

"I'm sorry." Kegan offers in a quiet tone less than two feet behind her.

Though spoken simply, Nora couldn't miss the regret in his voice. "Not your fault." She could chase after her sister and spill all the horrible details needed to mend the rift, but at what cost?

"Why did you let her think that we-"

"Slept together?"

"Yes."

"Better than pulling her into the mess I'm in. She'll understand." Shoulders roll as Nora climbs the steps. Shoving through the glass door and approaches the front desk with her best smile. Behind the tall counter, a young man lifts his blonde head to regard her through a pair of wire-frame glasses.

"Can I help you?"

"My name is Nora Brennan. I'm here to see Detective Evans."

"Is she expecting you?"

"She is." Kegan confirms, stepping forward to lay a hand across the small of her back in an ancient propriety gesture that flushes her face with heat.

A quick scan of his clipboard has the young officer offering a stiff nod. "Elevators are on your right. You're going up to the third floor."

"Thank you." Nora murmurs before moving promptly to the bank of elevators and away from the heat of Kegan's touch. It'd taken a while for the two of them to agree on a believable story to tell the cops. Now that she's here, Nora doubts her ability to pull it off. Especially if he continues to touch her.

On the third floor, Nora's heart seizes at the dozens of desks arranged strategically around the large open room. Sweat dampens her palms as she wills her feet to move, only to have her brain override the signal. Now what? As if sensing her panic, Kegan slips her hand between his, diverting her attention to his body standing close enough for her to inhale the scent of his soap.

"You okay?"

"This won't work. I'm a horrible liar, Kegan."

"Brody told me a few stories." His head dips until his face is but a breath from her ear. With his face hidden, Nora's forced to imagine the smile he wears as he continues. "Something about abandoned ferrets getting loose in your mother's laundry room."

Nora chuckles with the memory that plays in her head. Her mother had been livid after finding the wild pack of rodents running amok through the strictly organized room, making quite a mess of things. In a few short unsupervised minutes, laundry soap dusted almost every inch, clumping within the spilled fabric softener. Her only saving grace had been her grandfather. If not for him, her mother may have followed through on her threat to tar and feather the five-year-old.

"That was a long time ago." Nora sobers and shakes her head.

"True. You're older now." With a quick tug, Kegan guides her across shark-infested waters, of ringing phones, boisterous conservations and disgruntled civilians until they come to a stop at a desk in the far left corner.

"Detective Evans?"

Peeking up from her paperwork, she glances from Kegan to Nora with ice-blue eyes; her smile all business but pleasant as she sits a little straighter. "Yes?"

"I'm Nora Brennan." Practicing her statement for the third time leaves her stomach in turmoil. "I was told to come see you."

"Of course." Pushing to her feet, the detective clears away what she was working on and digs out a yellow legal pad from beneath an impressive stack of files. "Please have a seat." After gesturing to a pair of metal-frame chairs in front of her desk, she continues her search. "I just had your file a minute ago. Ah! Here it is."

"No rush." Nora assures her after taking a seat next to Kegan. She refuses to dwell on his proximity, fastening her attention to the detective flipping the file open.

Pen in hand, the detective begins, her tone short and polite. "Why don't we start with yesterday?"

Sweat gathers on her skin until Nora's clothes begin to stick. "H-how do you mean?"

"Just walk me through your day." Clicking the button on her pen, Detective Evan's hand hovers an inch from the notepad, ready to write whatever falls out of Nora's mouth.

"O-okay." With a swallow, she trudges ahead. "Um. I left for work about eight. Everything appeared normal. I t-took a late lunch to meet a friend and spent the rest of the afternoon running some errands."

"The friend's name?" Detective Evan's eyes peek up from the paper in front of her.

"Oh, Eleni P-pappas."

"Great." The detective makes quick work jotting the name down in tall, plain print. "What sort of errands did you run?"

"A bit of shopping." Nora's fingernails pick at the nicotine patch on her arm until Kegan plucks her hand away and settles it firmly within his. "I'm sorry. What?"

"I need a list of the stores you went to." The detective clarifies, snagging a small notepad from the corner of the desk to pass it over for her use.

Kegan sits forward. "Why is that important?"

"Anyone could've made Ms. Brennan as a target and followed her home," Detective Evans explains. "Your name is?"

"Kegan Selkirk."

Another quick scribble of her pen and Detective Evans adds another name to her list. "And what do you do, Mr. Selkirk?"

"This and that mostly." Kegan replies, his smile full of warmth and charm. "A lot of side jobs."

Blue eyes blink as the detective glances up to better study Nora's companion. The click, click, click of a pen increases the uneasiness in Nora's stomach, but the slight squeeze of a hard, calloused hand on hers reminds her to relax. *As if that's possible.* With a swallow, she uses her free hand to write the names of the shops she stopped at before passing the notepad back across the desk.

"I can't imagine that pays very well." Detective Evans sits back in her chair while shrewd eyes narrow.

"I inherited some money when my parents passed, so they're more to keep me busy than paying the bills." Kegan's the first to break eye contact, as if embarrassed by the admission.

"I see." The damn pen scribbles even more before the detective lifts her head to smile at Nora. "Please, continue."

"After that, I went home." Nora shrugs and prays the action appears as nonchalant as it's meant to. "Did some laundry, took a shower, fed my cat and watched a movie with Eleni and my sister Mallory."

"But you didn't stay?" Detective Evans brings the pen to her mouth. The sharp snap of teeth chewing on the hard plastic increases the pressure building in Nora's stomach.

With a smile that oozes more charm than Nora could've expected, Kegan pulls her against his side. A thumb drags mindlessly along her bare arm to frazzle the nerves underneath as he answers for her. "We met at my hotel room."

His response causes one of Detective Evans' eyebrows to inch up her forehead. "Why pay for a hotel when you can stay at her place for free?"

"Privacy." The way Kegan purrs his reply brings a flush to Nora's cheeks. "Her sister is notorious for popping in unannounced. I live out of town and don't get back here near as often as I'd like. So when I do, I prefer not to share."

Dear Lord. Nora groans and waits for the ground to open up and swallow her whole as she recites the Alphabet in her head. The hand she scrubs across her face draws the detective's scrutiny, putting a quick squirm in her seat.

Kegan's chuckle is deliberate and full of adoration. "She's shy."

The nod the detective responds with is brief as she makes more notes before moving on. "Any idea who would want to break into your home?"

"Honestly?" Nora squeaks, "no."

Pen scribbles out notes before the detective resumes her chewing on the one end. "Is there a chance it's connected to a kid or two at Hiller House?"

Icy dread fills Nora's bones. "How so?"

Once again Detective Evans sits back in her chair. "I'm sure you know that a few of them have colored pasts, complete with terrible childhoods and absent parents."

"A few, yes." The racing of her heart slows with the implications the detective makes regarding her children. No way are the police going to pin this on one of them. "We have a strict curfew. If one of them broke it, I'd be the first one contacted." Her tone chills as the smile she offers wavers just a tad.

"I have to ask these questions, Ms. Brennan," the detective murmurs in what comes across as a chiding manner. "Nothing about this case is making much sense."

"Like what?" Once again, Kegan's hand tightens on hers as he chimes in to give her a moment to collect herself.

"For one? We found rather expensive items still in the home. For two, most robbers don't resort to busting down doors, too noisy." Detective Evans offers a skeptical smile before continuing. "Attracts unwanted attention. So there's a personal element here that we're not seeing."

"I can't see any of my kids doing something like this." Nora vows in a thin tone. "They're good kids, mostly."

"The sad fact of reality is that most of them are, in fact, *not* good kids. At least not yet. They each come with a history, behavior, or attitude." Detective Evans sets her pen on the desk and folds her hands across the top. "The way the intruders ransacked your house leads me to believe whoever did it was looking for something. Any idea what that could be?"

When she first sat down, the switch on her nerves kicked into hyper-drive. Now, Nora experiences a flush of heat start in her core and surge through her limbs. As the detective spoke about the children at Hiller House, her nerves stabilize, her body switching into protective mode. When she answers, her voice is steady. "No."

"I see." Heart-shaped lips purse as Detective Evans re-reads her notes. When she lifts her head, the suspicion clouding her slight smile is unmistakable. "This is enough to give me a starting point. If I have any further questions, I'll call."

"We were planning on a few days up north." Kegan begins while helping Nora to her feet. "That won't be a problem?"

"I don't see that it should be." Detective Evans murmurs while sliding her notepad into a drawer of her desk.

Kegan shakes her hand, then drops an arm around Nora's waist once more. "Thank you, Detective Evans."

Nora has just enough time to flash a genuine smile before Kegan leads her toward the bank of elevators they came from. A casual peek over his shoulder produces the makings of a scowl, inspiring Nora to do the same.

From her desk, Detective Evans stands watching their exit with an expression of either curiosity or suspicion. Instinctively, Nora's fingers curl within Kegan's a second longer than necessary. Her next thought leaves her feeling restless.

"I need to call Rebecca." Nora clips. "Make sure she can verify no one broke curfew last night."

"You think she'll go after the kids there?" Kegan raises an eyebrow.

"It'd make sense." Teeth chew on the inside of Nora's cheek. "I'm not sure she bought any of what we said in there."

"Don't panic." Kegan assures her in the deep voice that awakens every nerve ending hiding under her skin. "She has nothing to prove otherwise."

"Maybe." His air of confidence grates on Nora. *Easy for him to say. It's not his life that's imploding.* The itch at the base of her skull grows until she's near trembling. For the last twelve hours, her life has dipped into the twilight zone. With each hour that passes, Nora loses more of the hope she has of it all returning to normal once this is over. Twice, she tries to pry her hand from his, both times he tightens his hold.

As the doors glide open, Kegan pulls her into his arms, lifting her off the floor to settle within his arms. Nora's gasp of surprise does nothing to cover his wince of pain, yet it doesn't stop him from sampling her mouth. Long strides carry her into the confines of the elevator as two more pin her to the metal wall. Her confusion takes a back seat to the taste of coffee on his tongue, the press of his lips knocking the dust off her hormones.

Nora sinks into the wall of his chest, lost in the feel of his fingers delving into her hair to angle her head back with soft shards of pain along her scalp. When he scrapes his teeth over her swollen lower lip, she's unable to hold back the moan rising inside her. As his free hand skims along the flare of one hip, her hand clenches into his shirt for purchase. A second after she swallows the groan he offers, he steps back.

With a cough, Kegan jabs at the button for the ground floor. "Let's get on the road."

Straightening her clothes with a trembling hand, Nora inhales beyond a tight throat. *What the hell was that? And what are the chances they can do it again?* Peeking up at him under lidded lashes, Nora watches as he smooths his shirt, his face a mask for whatever emotions bubbling under it.

His almost imperceptible nod at the security camera on their right lends some clarity to Nora's jumbled thoughts, biting back the heavy sigh on her lips as his arm winds around her waist to hold her close. *It'd been for show. You're an idiot!* As surely as if he'd thrown cold water in her face, Nora reigns in her racing heart and levels her eyes on the doors in front of her. *It's going to be a long damn day.*

When Rome strides into the main hall, his arms cross at the site of Shax lounging sideways across his chair. Legions of Rome's demons hover nearby, sharing tense looks between them. Once his temper reaches them, one by one, they scatter from the chamber in a flurry of quick flashes. With a growl, his glare locks on the poor excuse for a demon left behind.

"You can either remove yourself from my seat, or I can remove you. Choose."

"Temper, temper Brother." Shax mumbles while inching off the far side of the seat, out of Rome's reach. "No wonder you have so little visitors. Your hosting needs work."

"A host has *guests*. Since you don't fall into the category, I see no reason for an exception."

"Ouch, Brother. Having a bad day?"

"I'm not your fucking brother, so cut the shit. Why are you infecting my home with your foul stench?" Rome's sneer blooms across his face while his hands fist at his sides.

"I hear you've sent some men after the book?"

"What do you know of it?" After a quick blink, Rome's eyes narrow into tiny slits.

"More than you. A lot of myths and few facts."

Air puffs out of Rome's lungs while Shax draws out his little game. A jerk of his head summons Cairn for service. Rome just hasn't decided what service he'll ask of him yet. Either keeping his unwanted visitor honest, or disposing of his rotting corpse. With a quiet nod of acknowledgement, the empath moves to stand rigid in a far corner of the room. The more Shax drones on about what myths he's heard over the centuries, Rome leans toward having his corpse removed. "Just get to the fucking point. What do you want?"

"A small piece of the pie."

"No."

It takes a half a second for Rome's answer to produce a flame in Shax's eyes. Wiping his nose with the back of his hand, he stands to his full five-foot-eight height, eager to make himself irreplaceable. His nervous smile pulls Rome's attention to stained, jagged teeth. "I'm told your men encountered one of the Fallen. Sent them running like whipped puppies, he did."

"You think you can help with that?" Rome laughs then. A deep rumble that doubles him over as he fights for breath. "You? When was the last time you were in any kind of fight you didn't need to rig?"

"I may not be strong like the rest of the brothers, but I have something most don't."

Wiping a tear from the corner of one eye, Rome coughs back his next round of laughter and braces a shoulder against one of the alabaster columns. True, Shax never seemed to master the physical aspects of being a demon, but he'd read everything he could get his grubby hands on. A trait that makes him valuable to Melchom. If he can play this right, there's a chance he comes out on top and rids himself of the little parasite as well.

"Speak plainly, Shax. I'm losing what patience I have."

"In order to tap into the power the book holds, you need a descendent of the bloodline."

"The Angel is protecting her."

"How have you survived this long?"

Taking a step forward, Rome's voice takes on a hard edge. "By getting my hands dirty. A concept you have no experience with."

"Okay. Okay." Shax's hands lift as he searches for an escape route from confrontation. "There is another one of a different bloodline. One that has the spell we require."

"We?"

"Partners. You and I."

"If I decide I don't need a partner?"

"Then I suppose you go it alone. But we both know why you want the book. Does your master?"

Violence ignites within him, its heat flowing amongst his blood, while fingers flex with an urge he recognizes. From the corner of his eye, he notes Cairn stepping forward, no doubt sensing the tidal wave churning within him. The effort it requires shaking the emotion loose leaves his muscles twitching.

With work, he could retrieve the book with no help from Shax. Should he try, he wouldn't live long enough to start the ritual, let alone complete it. There's a saying that comes to mind about keeping your enemies close. Rome prefers to keep them in another part of hell altogether. Yet, in this, it seems he has very few options.

Chapter 11

Colin ends his phone call on a curse. His confidence in Kegan's abilities is absolute, but the situation is growing more complicated. Between the book, Nora, Adriel and now human involvement, he can see no other option but to pay Azrael a visit. Even though he resigns himself to the decision, he spends the next ten minutes stomping a path around his living room.

"I know I'm going to regret this," he mutters, crushing out what remains of his cigarette before ascending.

Almost instantly, his body jerks against the stimulation. With every electrical surge, muscles twitch as sweat beads out from his pores. Part of him toys with the idea of turning back, but he sets his jaw and pushes forward. It isn't long before he regrets that choice.

Pressure builds inside his skull, his joints throbbing from the force as he draws closer to his destination. Between Heaven and Hell, Azrael's realm is off limits to the Fallen, but not unreachable.

When bolts of lightning split the air with a consistent ear-splitting crack and blinding intensity, he has no choice but to shut his eyes as the hair on his arms stands on end.

The impact his feet make with the compacted ground crumples his legs, pitching him forward onto his hands and knees. White heat sears across his skin once he forms completely. Teeth clench as he draws one slow breath after another to seal off the trauma into a small compartment so he can see clearly. Unfortunately, it does nothing for the throbbing behind his eyes.

"Where'd you come from?"

The voice is small, pulling his gaze to a child about seven years old. The sunlight behind her makes her blonde hair translucent as it falls around a heart-shaped face. Her simple blueprint dress falls just shy of a skinned knee and dirty feet. In her arms, she clutches a worn teddy bear with one eye and a crooked ear.

"Hell," he croaks.

She accepts his answer with a solemn nod, her expression wary as he climbs to his feet. Brushing off the thick layer of dirt from his clothes, Colin catches the stiffening in her spine as her eyes dart around for her best chance of escape.

"Before you go running off, maybe you can help me." While she says nothing, the tilt in her head offers a slight flare of hope. "Do you know Azrael?" With a mute nod, she studies him for any sudden movement. "Can you take me to him? I don't know how long it'll take me to figure out this maze on my own." She spends a full minute considering his request before she coaxes him to follow with a crook of her dainty hand.

A chuckle rumbles deep within his chest as his tanned hand palms a full breast, causing a chirp of delight. The purr that his thumb elicits cranks up the dial on his hunger. As damp lips inch up the side of his neck, Melchom's growl slips from his throat. With a groan, he relaxes into the softness of the body behind him while his hands romance the curves of another.

When he left this morning, he hadn't intended to return with playmates. After a brief work meeting and calls to clients, he stopped off at the coffee shop one corner over from his condo.

Two cups of coffee and a blueberry bagel later, he's ready to be on his way when his senses zero in on Lillian and Rachel at a corner table. Even if he couldn't overhear their conversation, the long looks in his direction followed by soft laughter whispers a clue to the topic of their conversation.

Still, getting them to return with him to his condo took finesse and a great deal of charm. When Lillian's nails score a path over his chest, Melchom deems the effort worthwhile. There are worse ways to spend an afternoon. He'd experienced them, in fact. This was far better.

Turning his head, Melchom nuzzles the breast closest to him as Rachel's lips skim along his stomach. The scrape of her teeth across a hipbone causes his lips to falter over the dusky red nipple and his body tense. So intent on the paradise he'll find in Rachel's mouth, Melchom is unprepared for the agony that assaults him. Glittering violet eyes snap open the instant he realizes he's ascending.

Fury erupts within his blood just before he hits the ground, hard. With a grumble, Melchom flops onto his back, his lip curling as hot dirt covers him like a second skin. "Sonofabitch!" His roar ricochets off nearby buildings, shaking the windows in their frames. *He couldn't have waited twenty fucking minutes?* "The fucking angel is going to die."

Manifesting clothes, Melchom dresses himself in his customary jeans, black button-down shirt and Jimmy Choo boots. Dragging a hand through ruffled hair, smoothes it away from his face to reveal dark violet eyes and two red studs under his lower lip.

A quick view of the area tells Melchom where is he, but not the why. Lillian and Rachel forgotten, he plows through the crowded streets with one purpose. Find Colin and remove his lungs. The thought produces an image that encourages a hint of a smile. Adjusting to the pain in his crotch, he begins the hunt.

He's pacing! Another look at his phone does nothing to slow his steps across the wide porch while he waits for Nora and Eleni to arrive. The small voice in his head reminds him it'd been a bad idea to let her make her own way to the cabin. "I needed space." *I'll bet*, the voice replies in a way that inspires his lips to curl.

From the moment he'd met her, Nora plucks at his nerves as if he's a fine-tuned guitar. While he won't lose any sleep over the physical effects of stress, the psychological ones are another story. Of all the ways he envisioned his eternity, locked in a padded cell isn't one of them. The sight of her black Jeep bouncing up the winding drive postpones the funny farm. For now.

Stepping off the porch, Kegan lumbers across the gravel drive-way to meet her. When she jumps out of the driver's seat with a bright smile aimed in his direction, it puts a hitch in his step. Her white cotton shirt clings to full breasts, hinting at the delicate lace hiding underneath. In the V of the neck, a silver angel's wing pendant hangs from a silver chain precariously close to the swell of her breasts to taunt him with a luxury it possesses. He groans inwardly when even white teeth nibble her lower lip as if suddenly unsure of herself.

"Where's Eleni?"

"Right after you left, she got a call about some emergency at the museum. Said she'd get a ride up with Jess."

"She was supposed to stay with you. What kind of emergency does a museum have?"

Eyes the color of fresh meadows, narrow under his tone. Her chin hitches slightly before she turns to offer her back so she can unload the car. "I don't know. I didn't ask. And I'm not a child, Kegan."

"Then stop acting like one," he snaps. Reaching into her vehicle to sort through what she needs pulls the denim tight around her ass, enhancing the full curves. His mouth suddenly dry, he backs up a step to spend the next minute counting the needles on a nearby pine tree until his body temperature regulates and he can better focus on the situation.

"Do you need help with anything?" Yes, a heavy blanket of dust covers his manners, but he asks, anyway. However, he won't deny the shake of her head, leaves him relieved. Unsure of what he should do, Kegan shoves his hands into his pockets and rocks back and forth on his heels.

He'd never put much effort into an awkward silence. Experience taught him it's better to leave such things alone. More often than not, breaking the ice ends with one person drowning. "I'll, uh, go get a room ready for you." Her complete lack of reply tells Kegan she's touchy over his behavior. *Too damn bad.*

Charging his way into the cabin, Kegan makes a beeline for a bedroom door. He needs to find some footing, a semblance of control, or the long term is going to kill him for sure. The years he'd spent with Brody had been quiet, the two men living together with mutual respect that formed a solid friendship. Any hope he has for a peaceful existence with Nora quickly escapes as he opens a window for a bit of fresh air.

Retrieving a quilt from the bench in the corner, Kegan makes quick work, changing the bedding. Swapping out a pillowcase, Kegan gives it a sound whacking before moving onto the other. Hopefully, she doesn't complain about his room choice. There aren't many to choose from and he didn't see her comfortably sleeping in Brody's. That it also places her furthest away from his room has no bearing. *Right?*

"Are you okay?"

Spinning in surprise over her silent approach, loosens his grip on the pillow to send it flying into her face. After a muffled *oomph*, a smirk dances in the corner of her mouth as she picks up her attacker and smoothes out the wrinkles. *Kill me now.*

"Just when I think something is harmless, it attacks. There's no chance of the bed swallowing me in my sleep, is there? I could always go to the motel at the edge of town."

Kegan brushes off the grace of her banter as the flush of heat creeps across his neck. "You startled me, is all."

Boy, won't the other Watchers have fun with that one? Big, nasty Kegan startled by a mere slip of a woman. Accepting the pillow, he sets it next to the other and moves to make a retreat from the shrinking bedroom. The sight of her cat carrier in the hall wrinkles his nose.

"What is *that*?"

"Ezio. Eleni didn't think you'd mind, and I couldn't very well leave him home."

"Why the bloody hell not?"

Nora pauses, picking at her thumb as she shifts from side to side. "Because demons know where I live. Not that I think they'd bother themselves with one cat, but I don't see them ensuring he doesn't get out either. I didn't want to risk losing him, too."

Damn it all to hell! How's he supposed to say no now? Kegan opens his mouth to tell her to take the fleabag outside, but nothing comes out. "Just as long as he's litter trained." *What?* Despite the reward of her bright smile, Kegan slips into the hall, kicking himself all the way back towards the living room.

Free from his prison, Ezio careens through the house, weaving between Kegan's boots so tight it nearly trips him. With his sights set on the long couch dominating the room, the cat settles in to begin a very intense grooming routine while Kegan fishes the phone out of his back pocket.

"This is Jess. Your dime is my time."

"Just thought I'd check in. Nora and her cat finally made it," Kegan states casually. No need to advertise his restlessness over the phone. One great mystery is how Jess hasn't lost his tongue by now.

"Wait. She brought the cat?"

"Yep. As we speak, he's enjoying my couch."

"You hate cats."

"Thank you. I wasn't aware."

"Well, if the girls' safe, the rest is all gravy. Am I right?"

"What the hell does that even mean?" Kegan growls into the phone, trying to ignore the sounds of grooming that border on obnoxious. When that doesn't work, he picks up an oven mitt and chucks it with satisfactory aim. With a hiss, Ezio jumps back. His long back arches as he puffs up twice his normal size, ready to strike.

"Try it furball. I'll end up with a new pair of slippers."

"Slippers, huh? I never would've guessed." Unable to contain his laughter, Jess gives in with a hoot. Irritated warnings from Kegan only fueling the noise.

"One day, Squirt, you're going to laugh yourself right into an ass stomping."

"This *Squirt* will give you a run for your money, Old Man. I'd be more concerned if I didn't already know you're too brittle to stomp more than spiders."

"You aren't much bigger."

"Bite me."

It's Kegan's turn to chuckle with a shake of his head. "Thanks for the offer, but no. You don't have the necessary attributes for me to get anywhere near you with my teeth."

"Be thankful for that; I'd never leave my bedroom." Laughter dies off in exchange for a more serious topic. "Colin wants us to monitor the police involvement. Once we're satisfied it's contained, we'll be on our way."

"Sounds good. Be careful." Hanging up, Kegan once again finds himself alone with house guests. A hand scrubs across the back of his neck as he looks out the patio door at the tree-lined backyard. Strange, being purged in the pits of hell doesn't sound so bad at the moment.

Chapter 12

Just after dinner, Nora makes herself at home with several of Brody's books. Tucked into the arm of the couch, she folds her legs beside her while she thumbs over the first book. With a slow stretch, her cat nestles against her feet, paws kneading the soft blanket covering her lap.

"That is the laziest cat I've ever seen."

Nora offers a soft laugh as she scratches the top of his striped head. "He *is* pretty lazy. He's earned it, though."

"How so?"

"He was a stray. Old enough for the vet to think someone just dropped him off one day."

Kegan struggles to focus on what she's saying instead of her hands scritching her cat's head. His stomach knots with an unexpected desire to have her hands on his skin. Smothering a groan, he rejoins the conversation once he chases the temptation free from his brain. *For now.*

"Half-starved, flea infested and drenched by the spring rain, I found him using my porch for shelter. Took me two weeks to earn his trust to come close enough for me to grab."

"Why bother? You could've just left food out and been done with it."

"My father had just died. The silence in the house was maddening. I didn't even notice how far I was falling into depression until he arrived." As she talks, her hand strokes over the round head near her lap, nails scratching across a cheek until Ezio answers with a purr and Kegan suppresses another groan.

Knowing all too well the feeling she describes, he jerks out a nod. One surrounded by family and chaos tends to flounder in solitude. Having spent so much time on his own, it's the company he finds challenging. Still, the respect he finds for her recognizing her mental state and working to change it surprises him. How many had he lost to their own despair? *Too many.*

"Can I ask a question?"

Drawn from his quiet contemplation, he posts himself against the archway between living room and kitchen, his answer automatic. "Better than most."

"I'm serious." Full lips twitch with a ghost of a smile.

"So am I."

"How well did you know, Grandad?"

"Hm, very well." It wasn't the question he'd expected, so Kegan releases the tension gathering in his shoulders. "We met shortly before Elsie died."

"That was over ten years ago. You've been a part of his life that long?"

"Mostly."

Nora closes the book on a finger to mark her place. "You were friends?"

"Not at first, no. But we found some common ground to build a friendship."

"What kind of common ground?"

When Kegan searches her face, he finds no manipulation or calculating coyness, only curiosity. "We were both lonely."

"Oh."

Silence stretches around them, so Kegan busies himself with tidying an already immaculate house. He's straightening her shoes by the door when her next questions stills all movement.

"How did you meet?"

Internally, he answers with, *when he became the books protector.* Outloud, he hedges. "That's a hard story to tell." After he readjusts the shoes once more, he glances in her direction to note a look of amusement.

"I'm sure the word difficult doesn't appear in your vocabulary too often. I'm confident you'll muddle your way through the telling."

"We should probably wait for Eleni and Jess."

"Why?"

So you don't go running screaming into the night and get us both killed. Grasping for the first viable excuse, he shrugs. "I hate repeating myself." From the way her head cocks to the side and the pucker of her lips, he'd guess she's unsatisfied with his answer. The action of her closing the book with a soft clap only to sit straighter against the couch confirms his suspicion.

"I doubt they care. On the slim chance they do, I'll give them the cliff notes."

He stands as the voice in his head warns him about dropping her into the pit of her new reality. "It's getting late. We should turn in."

"It's seven thirty. What aren't you telling me, Kegan?"

"There's a lot I haven't told you. Most of it, none of your business." Unclenching his jaw, Kegan paces back and forth between the couch and the patio door.

"It's a simple question. Why won't you answer it?" Her eyes narrow as she latches onto an earlier theory. "Does it have to do with why you fell from Heaven?"

"Of course not!"

"Then what?"

"And you'll believe whatever answer I give you, huh? I doubt it."

"Well, I certainly seem to have accepted the bizarre fact that you're an angel. Even if you're far from the stereotype. That has to count for something." Her brows knit. "I don't think you've lied to me yet, so I'm more inclined to believe you than you think."

His feet stop long enough for him to pin her with a look that leaves her squirming. "I'll never lie to you, Nora. Even if it makes you wish I had."

"Ditto."

"What?"

"Ditto. It means, um, me too." Her head bobs for emphasis, the action dropping a curtain of hair across one cheek. The temptation to brush it away shoots into his hands so rapidly, he's forced to jam them into the pockets of his jeans.

"So how did you meet Grandad?"

On an exhale, Kegan allows the words to spill forward. "We met when Brody inherited the book from his uncle."

"The book?"

"Uh-huh. The one he left you."

"So, this is all because of some damn book I can't even read?"

"You tried to *read* it?" Kegan meant his question as more of an inquiry, but he buries his intention under the thundering of his voice.

"It's impossible. Most of the words have long since faded, and the language is all but dead, as far as I can tell."

"*Bloody hell, Nora.*" Plowing a hand through his hair, he tries to find any measure of patience this one female requires. The small meager measure he locates carries a warning of its impending absence. "It's not a simple book. You must've felt its pull when you first looked at it. A need to possess it that boils within your blood, yes?"

"I only felt curiosity."

Judging by the lift of her chin and the hard glint in her eyes, he's willing to bet his eternity that she'd just lied to him, after professing so charmingly that she wouldn't. *Well, that lasted all of five fucking minutes. Humans!* The revelation sours his mood and flattens his tone.

"The same curiosity that overruled whatever common sense the good Lord gave you? Exposing it repeatedly to the world they meant you to hide it from? Broadcasting not only its existence, but its location over and over again for them to track."

"Who's them?"

"For fuck's sake, Nora. Demons. They're going to come for it."

She collapses against the couch with a huff of breath, her voice small. "It's a book." Fingers bury in the blanket covering her legs as she trudges through the information she'd prodded so hard for.

Taking several steps forward, he puts something similar to compassion into his warning. "It's more than that. More important than even I know." Ducking his head, Kegan meets her eyes before continuing. "They will come for it. And they'll stop at nothing to get their hands on it. Unless I can keep that from happening. Do you understand?"

When his words chase her from the room as if the Hounds are already on her heels, Kegan admits he could use a refresher in empathy. The sound of her strangled sob pitches his stomach as he straightens.

"Should've waited for Eleni," he grumbles softly, and retrieves the book that dropped from her lap on her exit. He's unprepared for the force of raw power slamming into his senses before she's running into the room, book in hand.

"Take it!"

Kegan's chest seizes as he jumps backwards, edging himself along the opposite side of the room with her in quick pursuit. The pain he prepares himself for never comes. Only untapped power. Tiny tendrils scrape against his mind at the same time it seeps into his blood to assault him on every front. Closing his eyes, Kegan dashes around the end of the couch as she tries to close the distance once more. "I can't." His usual clear tone cracks from the strain of keeping a lid on the growing desire to take her up on her offer.

"You can keep it safe, Kegan. I can't." Shoving the book in his direction once more, Nora appears oblivious to the war she's creating within him.

"It's my job to keep *you* safe. And I swear to you, I will."

"Please, Kegan. I want my life back." One long study exposes the desperation within her eyes, a tremble in her chin. He hates that he's the one who put them there, but better sooner rather than later, he reasons. "One without demons, and threats of death, motorcycle accidents, and concussions," she continues.

"Stop." With Nora pressing the book against his chest, he can feel its influence clouding his judgement. Fighting for some space, Kegan slips beyond the counter and into the kitchen as the nerves just under his skin vibrate. *It'd be easy*, he tells himself. *Hell, she's offering it to me!*

Soon, Heaven and Hell and everything in between would bend to his will. He used to think himself above the pettiness of revenge, but with this book, he could right the wrongs against him and the garrison. Eye for an eye. Sweat coats every inch of him as his fingers curl with the tingle to take what she's offering. On a growl, he turns to grip the counter. "Put that fucking thing away!"

Something about his voice pierces the fog of her female hysterics to put a stop in her pursuit of him. When she speaks, he can relate to the sorrow that stains her words. "Please."

"I cannot take it." Unwilling to even glance in her direction, Kegan counts the specks of granite within his countertop until the throbbing between his ears fades.

"I don't understand."

"Just put it away. Please." With the sound of her footsteps receding, he takes the time to find what remains of his control. Shudders skid along his back to send tremors into his legs. The idea of how close he'd come to throwing everything away douses his senses in ice-water. The shuffle of bare feet on his wood floors alert him to her return long before she speaks.

"Are you okay?"

"No." His response to the unexpected question is automatic. Righting himself, he turns to see Nora hovering just inside the kitchen, fingers curling together in front of her. The picture she makes with her face flushed, wide eyes and a tangle of loose hair touches something dormant inside him. For the first time in a long time, Kegan puts in the effort to keep the bite out of his voice. "I will not throw away everything I've worked so hard for, only to condemn myself to horrors worse than Hell."

"How am I supposed to live with this thing for the rest of my life, Kegan?"

"It'll get easier. You can do this, Nora. If you couldn't, Brody would've never left it to you."

"So, wait, you're going to be with me forever?" Already wide eyes grow until they threaten to swallow her face.

"Until you die, yes. That's my job."

"How am I supposed to have a life with you around as a spectator? My dating life is already non-existent. You're going to make every guy that asks me out feel uncomfortable!"

"I'll take that as a compliment."

"What's the alternative," she demands. "There's a glitch in the matrix somewhere. What is it?"

"Judging by how your last round of questions turned out, I think you've interrogated me enough. Especially since you didn't even buy me dinner first." He brushes past her slight frame with an inward flinch. "Let's save the rest of your questions for our second date, huh? Leave a little mystery." He drags a hand through sweat-soaked hair, his words heavy. "Goodnight Nora." Turning on his heel, Kegan retreats to his bedroom before she can mutter anything in return.

With the aid of a small desk lamp, Andrew hunches over a desk near the back of the otherwise dark store and pours through one book after another. He has no way of knowing how long the young man had been at it, but judging by the pile of discarded books, it'd been quite some time. Without a clue where to start, Adriel harbors little worry over the so-called research.

Inching his way around a narrow passageway clogged with shelves and boxes, he stays hidden amongst the shadows. Gradually, the air warms, pulling a reluctant glance from the young man to search the shadows near where he stops.

His movements too quick for the human to compute, Adriel rushes forward to loom over the young man, his hands splaying across the desk's surface. Shock filters over unremarkable features, eyes wide as he shrinks back into his chair.

"Lord, have mercy," he declares, pressing a hand to his chest.

"If I'm here, I'm afraid it's too late for that."

"W-who are y-you?"

"My name isn't important, Andrew. I'm here for some information."

"This appears to be old. Where did you get it?"

Adriel pulls back to follow Andrew's eyes to the leather bracelet encircling Adriel's right wrist. Made up of several leather pieces, the braid lays flat after countless years in the same position. Despite his mood, he does nothing to hide the smile tickling his lips.

Humans are such elaborate creatures, ones to avoid. Aside from the righteous and evil paths one can take, there are hundreds of avenues just under the surface. It left an unpredictable lot that Adriel prefers to steer clear of.

"Yes. It's old. Andrew, tell me about the visitor you had."

"How do you know my name?"

"Why do you insist on asking insipid questions?" Fingers snap sharply when Andrew's attention strays to the bracelet once more. "You had a visitor. Did she come in alone?"

"Such a strange accent you have. I don't think I've ever heard it before."

"Andrew. Focus!"

With a physical jerk, the young man snaps to attention. Adjusting the thick lenses on his face, he squints to see Adriel above the glow of the desk lamp. "Yes. She came in alone."

"She had no one with her? A large man, perhaps? Maybe waiting for her outside?"

It didn't take long for the curiosity that propels Andrew through life to give way to something else. Considering the tremble in his lips, the sweat on his brow, and the occasional furtive glance, Adriel would say he's more than a little anxious. It takes no effort on his part to delve beyond the educated demeanor the man portrays to locate the rather dull child underneath. As he probes, he finds no recollection in the man's memory of anyone resembling the Angel.

"She came alone. I s-swear it. I-is this about the b-book?"

"What do you know of it?"

"Only what I've found. I didn't get a good enough look to remember everything, and the text was challenging to translate. Still, I found a few things of interest."

Adriel reads over pages of scribbled notes, granting Andrew an extra sixty seconds of life. Before summoning Tobias and his brothers, he tucks the pages inside his jacket for later. Knowing he won't get any further information from the shopkeeper, he conveys a look at the Hounds and steps back.

"Compensate him." The green glow of Tobias's eyes isn't nearly as unsettling as the sneer that creeps over an otherwise handsome face. While the Hounds go to work cleaning up yet another mess, Adriel summons Rome's Drau. "Cairn!"

A cool rift answers his bellow to reveal the lanky man. Upon seeing Adriel as his summoner, he bows regally at the waist, his eyes hooded. "Yes, Sir?"

"Don't call me that," Adriel snaps, tuning out the screams flooding the small store. From where he stands, he has an unobstructed view of the Hounds, tearing at the small man, pulling his frail body in different directions. "Inform Rome that I've located the trail. It might take another day, but I can track it now."

A lack of response brings Adriel to full attention. All too late, he catches how Cairn reacts to Tobias's playtime. While the screams are enough to give him a serious headache, he's no Empath. Cursing himself for his reckless behavior, Adriel palms a blade to sail it across the room, sinking to the hilt in Andrew's chest. Among the silence, he faces the anger flashing in Tobias's eyes. The hound steps around the mangled body in confrontation, but the step Adriel takes in answer forces him to reconsider his actions.

"My apologies, Cairn, I wasn't thinking. Do you recall the message to take to Rome?" Only after Cairn jerks his head does he invite the Drau closer, careful not to touch him. "Give these to Rayen. And only Rayen," he instructs, easing the folded papers into icy hands. Once Cairn swears to it, Adriel releases him to return to Rome. With any luck, he'll have located the book by this time tomorrow. Now there's just the matter of the damn angel.

Chapter 13

When bright sunlight streams through the windows to greet her, Nora answers with a groan. When did the nights become so short? After a night of dreams that alternated between Kegan and the book, she wakes more exhausted than when she first climbed in bed. Where the books dreams are chaotic and confusing, dreams of Kegan are the opposite. Images of him naked, in a giant bed so she can trace the inked lines of his tattoo flash within her mind to bring a tightness to her belly. While the temptation to remain in bed whispers seductively in her ear, there's a to-do list that just won't wait.

Nora grunts in a soft protest as she forces herself to sit upright. With a swing of her legs over the edge of the bed, she stretches left, then right to work the kinks from her back. Sweeping the wild tangle of hair from her face, she secures it with an elastic band at the nape of her neck. Once she recovers her discarded white cotton shorts from the floor, she tugs them on and darts across the hall to the bathroom.

A splash of hot water chases away what remains of the cobwebs, followed by a scrub of cleanser for good measure. After applying a thin layer of moisturizer, Nora completes her routine by brushing the fuzz off her teeth then heads to the kitchen in search of coffee.

At the counter that just out from the wall, Kegan dwarfs a stool with a cup of coffee and a newspaper in front of him. Dressed in jeans and a gray pullover, he completes his attire with familiar black boots. Hair still damp from a shower, falls over serious brow while his clean-shaven jaw adds a finishing touch on the sight he generates first thing in the morning. Adjusting to it is going to require effort on her part.

"Coffee cups are in the third cupboard on your right," he directs without lifting his eyes from the paper in front of him.

Nora grumbles a quick reply and retrieves a thick white cup covered in pink and red roses. Without her usual creamer, she settles on a splash of milk and extra sugar before claiming a chair at the table.

"Not a morning person?"

Her eyes close as she relishe's in the first few swallows of coffee. With a crook of her lips, she offers a quick shake of her head. "No, but you are."

"Hm, is that a question or a statement?"

"A bit of both, I suppose," Nora admits while keeping her eyes on the cup in front of her instead of the lazy smile flirting across his lips.

"I'm not really a morning person either. I just get up early enough to balance it out." Kegan stands and starts re-folding his newspaper. "What do you have planned for today?"

"I thought I'd check in with Rebecca and Mallory. I should probably start going through some of Grandad's things as well. Is there still a church in town that accepts charity?"

"There is." Kegan's gaze skips over her briefly on his way to the sink. Once he dumps the remnants of his cup, he takes the time to rinse it out before turning to towards her. "You don't have to accomplish it all on day one, you know?"

"I know, but I'm hoping to find some clues about the book of destiny."

"Destiny, huh?"

Nora grins. "It sounds better than the book the fubar'd my life."

Despite his cool demeanor, Kegan allows a chuckle to escape. As if realizing his slip, he moves toward the front door. "I have some errands to run in town. Stay inside while I'm gone."

Left at the table, Nora mulls over the almost brute-like behavior. *He could've asked nicely.* The habitual withdrawal he succumbs to leads her to believe he can't be in the same room with her for too long. The optimist in her chalks it up to a solitary nature. The realist reminds her he'd live with her grandfather for who knows how long. "So it's a *me* thing," she concedes. As she sits with her coffee, Nora distracts herself with how much the cabin hasn't changed since she spent her summers here as a kid.

Never a fan of wallpaper. The first thing her grandmother did was peel it off the walls and paint them a pale sunflower yellow. As the sun rises, it streams through wide bay windows to light up the room quickly.

Complimenting the walls, Grandad painted the cupboards a washboard white, replacing the wooden nobs with yellow-gold handles. In between the straight rows, Nora spots a framed needlepoint that reads, *Grandma's kitchen, kids eat free*. The memory of her grandmother rocking away the hours with her needlepoint brings a serene smile to Nora's mouth.

More than once she'd tried her hand at the craft, but lacked the patience to keep her thread from tangling into knots. Where Mallory's had been flat and relatively recognizable, Nora had been distraught when her finished product lay in a lumpy mess of knots and repeated mistakes.

Wiping her tears, her grandmother simply offered her loving smile before proudly displaying both pieces directly under her own. The sight of it still there thirty years later puts a lump in Nora's throat that the coffee can't wash down.

Rescuing her from memory lane with the first of several meows, Ezio hovers just inside the kitchen until she slides away from the table to rinse her empty cup. With a to-do list weighing heavy on her mind, Nora fills his bowls with food and water, then returns to her room to dress for the day.

The struggle to keep his gait even instead of breaking into a run toward Brody's old Chevy surprises him. Kegan spent centuries preparing for the worst situations. Doomsday. The apocalypse. Even Jess's ridiculous zombie invasion. None of it prepared him for Nora.

As he sat reading the morning paper, Kegan told himself he was immune. Co-existing with humans isn't as foreign to him as it might be for other Watchers. Then, she emerged in shorts and a tank top, her hair mussed from sleep. More than once his eyes stuck on the creamy expanse of skin and smooth legs. Hell, the sight of her toenails sporting a bright shade of purple brought a smile to his lips. The scent of her shampoo, when she shuffled past him, awakens the beast he recognized during the fiasco in the elevator. The memory brings the texture of her lips and the way they moved under his to the forefront of his brain.

"Are you ready to admit you're in trouble," he grumbles to himself while fishing for the keys. Coming up empty, he experiences a rush of panic at the prospect of having to go back for them. Just as he resigns himself to hotwiring the engine to avoid further contact with Nora, his fingers brush the lone key and plastic keychain deep in his right pocket.

"I just need actual sleep," he reasons. "I haven't fully healed from the other night. One good night's sleep and I'll be fine."

Of course, to do that, he'll need to physically sleep. Last night, he lay there as the twilight hours crept by at an agonizing pace, sleep the furthest thing from his mind. Instead, he entertained thoughts of the kiss he shared with Nora and how soon they could start on a sequel. That alone chased away any hope he had for serenity.

"Not going there." Kegan's teeth set as he raises a shaky hand to start the truck. *Getting involved with a human now only serves as a complication.* "I'm fine," he declares to the empty cab of the truck. *Even as you continue to talk to yourself?*

Putting the truck in reverse, he drives the distance to the sole convenience store in town. By the time he kills the engine, Kegan's nerves settle. He refuses to consider his distance from Nora as a factor as he stomps across the gravel parking lot.

"Good morning Kegan," Mrs. Fie croons.

The glass door glides shut behind him as he returns her greeting with a wave and makes his way along narrow aisles lined with basic staples meant to save one a trip into the nearby city. He takes ten steps when her daughter Celeste darts in from the backroom, smoothing her hair and straightening her shirt.

"I've got the register Mom, why don't you rest for a spell?"

From his position two aisles away, Kegan notes the slight bristling in the stance of Sandra Fie. After making a display of checking the time, one pencil-enhanced eyebrow arches. "It's not even nine-o'clock in the morning." One hand brushes over her dark orange silk shirt decorated with brightly colored butterflies, fingers adjusting the individual buttons.

"I know Mom. But you didn't sleep well last night. A quick break isn't asking too much. Is it?" When Sandra relents with a toss of her head, it takes all his willpower not to return his items to the nearest shelf and leave. From the corner of his eye, he notices Celeste take up a position in front of the register, her eyes studying his every move.

Oh, she's pretty enough, he readily admits. Maybe one of the most sincere people he's met since moving to the area. Celeste busies herself with an ailing mother, a barely-breaking-even general store, and raising a young boy alone since his father ran off. She's relationship material. Messing around with her will only lead to her heartbreak since he has no desire to pursue a relationship with *anyone*. His arms are full of creamer, sugar, and an overpriced can of coffee when he approaches the counter.

"Can I get anything else for you?"

"No. Wait. A pack of Marlboro Lights might be a good idea." He's not sure what brand Nora used to smoke, but the way she picks at those little patches, he'd bet she'll be killing someone soon. He hadn't spent the last several centuries toeing the line just to have his appeal railroaded by a nicotine-depraved fiend.

Fingers freeze over ancient keys as Celeste processes his request. "You don't smoke."

He can't miss how her voice cracks on the observation or how clear blue eyes darken with unspoken emotions. "Probably the one habit that never stuck with me. But I have a guest up for a while and I'd rather not give her a reason to be cranky."

"*Her*?"

"Mm-hmm. One of Brody's granddaughters is up to sort through his belongings." Taking the paper bag, he looks at the green neon numbers on the register and counts out the correct bills to hand her. "Thanks, Celeste. Don't work yourself too hard."

In less than a minute, Kegan's out the door and halfway to his truck when he senses her terse smile falter. While he tells himself the brush-off is for the best, he can't help but hate himself a little more. His sour mood continues throughout his errands.

By the time he returns to the cabin, the site of his new motor-cycle has his heart skipping a beat. Sitting not ten feet from the garage, the machine glitters under the morning sun.

Shiny black paint sparkles in contrast to polished chrome. At any other time, Kegan might mull over such an expense for two or three weeks before deciding on a cheaper option. With Jess's encouragement, he'd acted on impulse. Instead of the guilt he'd prepared himself for, he registers a rush of adrenaline at the thought of opening her up for the first time.

"You've more than earned it," he reminds himself. Sacrificing the last one to keep Nora alive was a small price to pay, one he'd make again. As he kills the engine on the truck, Kegan snags the brown paper sack and heads towards the cabin, his steps lighter, his sour mood abated. Until he registers the sound coming from within.

His cringe absolute, Kegan climbs the porch, shutting his ears down against the country music blaring loud enough to shake the foundation. Stomping beyond the front door, he takes a moment to absorb the scene that greets him.

Amidst a mess of open boxes taking up space in the living room, Nora bounces and dances from one to another. One bare foot taps along with the smooth bass as she stops to drop an armload of coats into one open box. As the singer croons on about someone being as sweet as strawberry wine, Nora resumes dancing long enough to put a gentle sway in her full hips, an act that leaves his throat suddenly thick.

The heat spreading within his blood encourages a detour on the way to the kitchen to stab a thumb against the power button of his stereo. He completes a half-turn until he can address the look of shock on her delicate features. Hands fit against her hips in a gesture he's becoming familiar with as her mouth opens.

Bracing the bag in one arm, Kegan holds up two fingers with his free hand, stalling whatever tirade she's about to start. "Two rules. One, do not play country music in this house. Two, don't make me listen to that *stuff*," he spits through a tight jaw, "in this house."

She'd showered in his absence, a fact he tries not to dwell on. Dressed in a pair of jeans and a black Avengers t-shirt, she shifts side to side on painted toes. At the back of her head, wet curls form a pile, twisted within itself, mindless of the loose strands gracing the soft slope where shoulder meets neck. Still wet, the strands rest against flushed skin, leaving it damp in a few places.

In his mind's eye, Kegan can see her standing under the spray of his shower. Follow the path the water takes over lush curves, flat plains and the deep valleys that make up her small five-foot six frame. The image his mind creates burns itself into his brain so flawless, he resorts to shaking himself to dislodge it.

"I may be wrong, but those rules mean the same thing."

"So long as you understand, we'll get along fine." Dodging to her left, Kegan stomps into the kitchen to set the bag on a counter.

"Are there any more rules you'd like to mention? You know, so we can continue this getting along thing?"

When she closes the distance between them, Kegan gets a whiff of her shampoo. Grapefruit and some sort of mint. As he breathes deep, his stomach tightens in a way he refuses to acknowledge. The quiet anticipation settling around her graceful brow tells him she's waiting for an answer while he busies himself with unpacking the small paper bag. "I had one about no cats and no distractions, but you've already broken those." After he pulls out the pack of cigarettes, he tosses a nod in her direction as they hit the countertop. "You're welcome."

"I quit."

"Right. The way you're always picking at those little patches says otherwise. Besides, your mood affects everyone here."

"You're the only other person here."

His smile is quick. "Precisely."

Her pert nose wrinkles in response while the glitter in her eyes draws his attention to the temper ticking up a few degrees. "So you're the only one allowed to be an-" Kegan lifts a brow in silent speculation, waiting to see if she'll finish her train of thought. A soft shake of her head follows a loud exhale as she attempts to change the subject. "This is some of the stuff I thought could go to charity. If you don't want it, that is."

"Why would I want your charity?"

"Why are you being so prickly?" Hands plant on her hips once more while her eyes search his face for an answer.

"I didn't think I was." Prickly isn't the word he'd choose to describe his current mood, and it's all her fault. Picking Ezio up off the floor, Kegan scratches behind one ear. Better than reacting to the sight she makes, all ruffled and flustered. Stroking the cat's silky fur instead of all that creamy skin will have far less disastrous consequences for him.

"Whatever you say." Tossing her hands in the air, she offers him a view of her back as she retreats toward the living room.

"Look, Princess, I'm here to keep you alive. Not to walk on eggshells or cater to your every whim."

The obvious disdain in his voice brings Nora around full circle at the same time air pushes from her lungs in a hiss of surprise. He thought only to establish a better perimeter around himself, but the flash of hurt in her eyes drops an ache in his chest. Before he can fumble his way around with an apology, her cat responds to her shock with a sharp hiss of his own. Back arching, he puffs his tail. The only thing on his feline mind is escape. Claws slice into Kegan's arm as he frees himself to land on the floor so paws can scrabble at the smooth wood for traction until he's able to bolt to the safety of her room.

"Bloody hell!" A hand clamps over the gouges that run the length of his forearm as Nora retrieves a towel she runs under cold water before offering it as a compress. "Might be a great idea to have that thing declawed."

"I'm learning to expect such ugliness from you." Pressing the towel against his arm, her head cants to better assess the damage. "Do you know how cruel that procedure is? What it does to them long term?" He didn't have to see the fire in her eyes to know she's angry. The raw emotion trembles inside her voice as her shoulders shake.

"My bad. Better to let the little buggers peel the flesh from your bones."

"Oh, puh-lease. It's a scratch. You're acting as if he cleaved you in two."

"Wasn't for lack of trying."

Snapping her gaze to his, heat floods her face, enhancing the sprinkle of freckles across the top of her cheeks. The blaze in her eyes shifts from anger to something else while her soft lips curl, adding a level of mockery to her sarcasm. "What is it with men, huh? Beaten in a bar fight, impaled on a battlefield, these are injuries you all wear as a badge of honor. Dying on your deathbed without so much as a whimper of pain. But a paper cut or cat scratch and you act as if you're on the way to meet your *fucking* Maker!"

Kegan can't pinpoint exactly when the air changes from confrontation to attraction, but before he can steel himself, his lungs seize. A fraction of his size, Nora stands toe to toe in defense of her cat. Breasts rise and fall heavily while her hands ball into fists at her side. *Does she mean to hit him? Would she dare?*

Anger explodes across her face, hurling shards of light into her eyes shortly before the dark clouds emerge. The sight she makes snaps what remains of his restraint. Gripping her shoulders, Kegan pulls her flush against his chest.

The kiss starts out demanding, taking without hesitation. As he explores every hot inch, his tongue curls against hers before dragging it across the edge of her teeth silences any protests. With a moan, she melts against him, her hands twisting into his shirt for leverage. The sound of her pleasure heats his skin with a spicy tingle, rousing each nerve ending.

Sweetened coffee clings to her tongue, her hands climbing to his shoulders as he softens the kiss to taste rather than take. When she catches his lower lip between her teeth, Kegan emits a low growl and lifts her off the floor to settle them on his couch.

Stradling her across his lap, he nibbles the corner of her mouth as his hands travel up the slope of her back. The brush of her fingers before the scrape of nails along the back of his neck clenches the muscles in his stomach.

You're drowning, he warns himself as one hand knots in the back of her shirt while the other rips the fat bun loose to bury his hand in the depths of her hair. Its cool weight cascades over his forearm to bring a rise of goosebumps in contrast to the inner fire Nora stokes with every moan.

Her soft growl when he suckles at her bottom lip nudges him closer to the tipping point. So consumed, he realizes too late the feel of her fingers in his hair. The sensation of them grazing over the raised brand on the back of his skull effectively douses him with ice water.

Releasing her mouth, Kegan plucks her off his lap to take several steps in the opposite direction. As he paces left and right, he refuses to examine the erratic thumping in his chest, or just how snug his jeans have become.

Questions spring to life in her eyes to smother his desire under the shame. His mouth opens to offer some lame excuse until he thinks better of it, and stomps out the front door to take out his mood on a couple of training dummies waiting for him in the remodeled garage.

Chapter 14

It's early evening when Jess and Eleni arrive at the cabin. With a mumbled hello in Jess's general direction, Nora drags her friend away for some much needed girl talk. Minutes later, while Eleni reclines against the pillows and Nora wears out a path in the carpet, she catches her up on the current events

"So, he kissed you?"

"Mm-hmm. Twice. Well, the first one shouldn't count." Nora adds as she walks back and forth from the bedroom door to the window.

"Why not?"

"I'm pretty sure it was just for show. To sell the story, we told the cops." Nora stops at the window. Not ten feet away, she stares at a family of raccoons and the knocked over trash can beside them. As if sensing danger, one by one they scamper off into the trees to disappear into their dens. *Serves him right.*

"Gotcha. What about the second one?"

"Yeah. I don't know how that one happened. One minute we were fighting about battle wounds and the next I'm sprawled across his lap."

"Wait, battle wounds?"

"Long story. It doesn't matter now. Anyway, we were both mad and having a disagreement?" She wonders aloud while pressing a thumb against the growing headache. "Then we weren't."

"Did you enjoy kissing him?"

Heat spreads across her cheeks as she recalls her enthusiastic response to his touch. "That's so not the point."

"So, yes?"

"The man is a walking, talking poster for Sexual Education Eleni. I'm fairly certain he'd have tempted Mother Teresa."

"Duly noted. I'm not seeing the problem, honey."

"The problem is when he's not kissing me... he can barely stand to be in the same room. He's so rude and dismissive."

Nora resumes pacing as she notices Eleni stifling a laugh. "Kegan has being an asshole down to a science," she says.

"What am I supposed to do? I've been nice, and it doesn't work!" Nora blows out a frustrated breath and pulls her hair back in a tight ponytail.

Eleni shrugs. "Don't be nice then. Fight fire with fire."

"El."

"I'm serious. If he wants to be an ass, treat him like one."

After taking the next several minutes to contemplate her friends' suggestion, it leaves Nora feeling uncertain. She can't deny a piece of her agrees with the theory, but she's not oblivious to the squeeze it places on her heart. Is he gruff? Certainly. Serious? Most definitely, although there were moments of something else. Something that softens his strong exterior and melts the hard glint in his dark eyes.

"Penny for your thoughts?"

Nora looks up to meet Eleni's sharp eye, then resumes her trek across the floor. "I don't know. Sometimes, he's different."

"Different how?"

"Vulnerable. Almost."

"We are talking about the same man, right?"

"I can't think of another word for it. This morning, as things were becoming heated between us, I experienced his desire. And I saw the regret in his eyes after he switched gears."

"What made him switch gears, then?"

Nora mentally wanders back to the moment she found herself on his lap. The wall of his chest against her, his solid thighs beneath her, coaxes her to give in willingly to the hunger of his mouth. The subtle scent of his soap invades her senses as he explores every inch of her mouth with an eagerness she hadn't prepared for. As he responds to her sounds of pleasure with his own, she came undone. The vibration of his deep growl crumbles her restraint like the walls of Jericho.

Needing to be closer, her hands drift over his arms, coming to rest on his shoulders. Fingers flex on the corded bands of muscles before moving to encircle his neck. When his mouth breaks contact to nuzzle the crook of her neck, Nora recalls the tightness in her belly.

Nails graze the exposed skin at his neck to pull a shiver from him an instant before she registers the scrape of his teeth along the column of her throat. Enthralled, Nora slides her hands up to his hair, holding him to her as its soft texture wraps around her long fingers. The shudder that escapes him pulls a sigh from her lips, a breath before he went rigid beneath her.

Her voice is hardly audible to her own ears as realization hits her. "I think it was his scar." Fingers float along the air as she recalls the texture. "A raised one on the back of his head. As soon as I touched it, he went cold." When Eleni fails to respond, Nora's eyes rest on her, the silence heavy between them. The image her friend portrays leaves a knot in her stomach where seconds before heat had pooled.

Now sitting cross-legged on the bed, Eleni's graceful jaw locks, her hold on the blankets resembling more of a death grip. Amber eyes, usually warm and inviting, lay flat and cold, completing a deadly expression.

"El? Eleni? What is it?"

Eleni pulls in a slow breath while the murderous glint in her eyes fades to memory. Her words thrum inside the closed room with an emotion Nora can't quite pinpoint. "Something for him to tell you."

"But-"

"For now, we have ourselves a girls' night." Scrambling off the bed, Eleni offers an exaggerated wink as she latches onto her hand. "I'm sure Mr. Uptight and Grumpy must have alcohol around here somewhere." As Nora allows herself to be led along, she stores the image her friend made talking about Kegan's scar away to be analyzed further at a later date.

"So how is it they know more about the book than we do?" Jess asks as he selects a card from his hand to discard on the growing pile.

"Probably because they learn that sharing is caring as little demon children." Shortly after his backup arrived, the girls had gone one way, the boys the other. The girls eventually emerge from Nora's bedroom to raid his liquor cabinet.

From where he sits at the table, he gathers bits and pieces from the chick flick they are determined to enjoy. Opting out of the movie, deciding the DVD player would need to be burned, the boys start a card game.

"Well, I don't know about you, but I will feel better with a little more knowledge on my side."

Not touching that one. Kegan draws a card off the deck. Staring at it for a moment, he wonders if it's the one he needs. He's off his game tonight, a fact he blames on Nora. Should've never kissed her again; it's reckless. No matter how sweet those lips had been, Kegan *is* going to learn from his mistakes. *Any time now.* "Any thoughts on those book dealers?"

"Hell, no!" Jess picks up Kegan's discarded card and slides it into his hand. "The police were crawling all over the scenes by the time we got there. Someone in the department leaked a theory to the papers about animal attacks. *Morons*."

"Doesn't inspire much confidence in today's law enforcement. I don't think animal attacks inside city limits are frequent, especially behind locked doors. "

"I don't know; some might say it's not a far leap from stealing picnic baskets to picking locks."

Kegan's eyes roll. "You're an idiot."

"Whatever the theory, the police aren't going away, and if Detective Something connects the dots, we could have some explaining to do."

"Detective Evans," Kegan offers. "And they can't pin anything to Nora, yet."

"Hope you're right." Scooping up another discard, Jess presents a winning hand. "What is that, three in a row now, Sparky? Losing your touch?"

"Or you're cheating."

"Sure! It's finally my turn to kick your ass, and I have to be cheating."

Kegan grins as he tosses his losing hand into the discard pile. "It's the only way you *can* kick my ass, Squirt."

The clock shows midnight when the girls are halfway through their second movie and several bottles of alcohol. After the fourth card game, he stands. Nora is giggling over everything, and Eleni slurs more than her speech. *Time to call it a night*. Experience tells him they will need all the rest that time allows for the next couple of days. Calling a halt to the marathon, Kegan switches off the television, amongst protests and some vicious name-calling.

Backing him up, Jess lifts Nora off the floor to set her on her own two feet. Eleni, insisting she doesn't need help, takes a minute to steady herself upright. "How about we call it a night?"

"Can't do that," Nora slurs.

Eleni gives her head a shake, her arms shooting out to keep her balance. "Nope.

Scowling, Kegan tries to put this image of Eleni to the Guardian he's come to know and trust with his life. "How are you drunk?"

"Beats the hell outta me, but I'm quite enjoying it." Eleni jabs at his shoulder and stumbles sideways. "You should try it."

"What did you get into?" Kegan scans the room, noting the several now empty bottles on the coffee table. The bottom drops out of his stomach when he spies a familiar red label bottle, laying on its side, drier than the Sahara. "You drank all of it?"

Eleni hiccups, rocking side to side just to stay upright. "Hm, guess so."

"What was it?" Jess steps forward just in time to keep Nora from falling over the rocking chair. Once settled, he releases his hold and takes a cautious step backwards.

"No fucking clue." Kegan gives the bottle a tentative sniff, but finds nothing worth mentioning. "Colin gave it to me last Christmas."

"Wait," Jess frowns. "You got something from Colin, for Christmas? I didn't even get a damn card."

Kegan shrugs. "He likes me better than you." Setting the bottle down on the table, he attempts to reign in a very intoxicated human, and one shitfaced angel. "Time for bed, girls."

"Nope." Eleni's rapid blinking gives him a headache, but she stands her ground.

Lips thin as Kegan searches for patience. "Why the hell not?"

"Because I'm not tired," Eleni snorts.

"Me either." Nora raises her hand to be included while leaving the other on the rocker for balance. "We need to do something."

The boys share a perplexing look over their heads. The last time he checked, entertainment is not in Kegan's job description and there's no way he's willing to start a new trend.

"What you need to do is sleep off the booze." Jess flashes his best smile, a smile that has won him more hearts than Kegan will count. Thankfully, the only reaction it seems to inspire is him slamming a considerable fist into his friend's face.

"That doesn't work on me, Buddy." Nora murmurs with a wobbly shake of her head. "I'm immune to a stunning smile."

Eleni snorts loud enough to make them all jump. "I think that depends on the smile, *asteri mou*. Besides, I'll tell you what you should be doing." She continues, perching precariously on the back of the couch, thoroughly missing the fierce expression Nora aims at her. "You need to get laid."

The roaring laughter Jess explodes into, covers Nora's offended squeak. "I get laid. I just don't kiss and tell like some people."

"Honey, I love you, but solo sex doesn't count." Eleni uses an elbow to lean against Jess's side. "I'm talking good ol' fashioned, sweaty, body aching, toe-curling sex."

Jess grins. "Can I volunteer for that?"

By seconds the situation grows uncomfortable, as if the thermostat had gone haywire, warming the room by several degrees. The quick acceleration of Kegan's heartbeat and the breath catching in his throat, he chalks up to unfamiliar chaos invading his life. After he railroads the subject and gets the girls put to bed, all will be well again.

It seems simple enough until Nora hits Eleni with one of the couch pillows. Falling backward off the couch and onto the floor, Eleni bounds up awkwardly and retaliates. Between shrieks of outrage and hysterical laughter, the girls beat each other with every stuffed item they can get their hands on.

"Your turn." Kegan shoots a pointed look at Jess.

Eyebrows arch as Jess begins to frown. "Huh?"

Kegan clarifies, "It's your turn to break it up."

"Nuh-uh, Bub." Hands raised, Jess backs up to the safety of the kitchen. "I only have a few rules, and not getting involved in catfights is one of them. I say we wait them out; I give it ten minutes until they pass out."

It's almost an hour later when Kegan nearly nudges Jess right off his barstool. Every pillow has exploded for one reason or another and his living room lies in shambles.

"They're asleep." Passed out on the hardwood floor, using each other as pillows, the girls snore gently. The cat, who retreated when all the commotion started, now lays tucked along Nora's side.

"Thank all that's holy; I've never seen El so-"

"Unhinged?" Stepping carefully through the debris littering the floor, Kegan swallows a growl with the sound of chips and popcorn crunching under his heels.

"I didn't know angels could get drunk."

"Me either. I don't know what was in this bottle, but she'll feel it tomorrow." Reaching down, Kegan gathers Nora from the floor to cradle against his chest. Shifting in her sleep, she nestles closer with a soft, breathy sigh. Emotions and desire slam into him unbridled. If she wasn't passed out drunk, he would've taken her to his room right then. Instead, he lays her down on her bed and takes a moment to tuck the covers in around her.

Brushing the hair away from her face, Kegan grants himself a moment to watch her sleep, her tiny hands twining up under her chin. Somehow, she's working her way past his defenses. Steadily Nora chips at a wall he put up as much for her protection as his own. Strange how he can't locate the ambition he needs to repair the damage.

"Where were you before all this? Why come into my life now?" Kegan spends the next minute searching for an answer before tiptoeing out the way he'd come. Pausing with the door cracked, he waits for Ezio to jump up on the bed before shutting it with a quiet click of the latch.

"Feel like we got the short end of the stick yet?" Jess asks, grabbing the box of trash bags from under the kitchen sink and tossing Kegan the broom.

In the world's most significant understatement, his living room is a mess.

Piles of pillow stuffing lay in clumps; overturned, one small table lies against a far wall, and the rocker sits crooked on one leg. Movie munchies litter the floor along with the DVD's Eleni had swiped off the shelf with a stray pillow. His plant lay on its side, spilling black dirt on the floor, and his couch rests on its back from the girls crashing into it. The whole thing resembles something one might see after a barroom brawl, not a pillow fight.

Kegan has indeed gone rusty, though he refuses to put his combat skills in that category. He's seen drunk women in his time, and while those experiences varied, his living room never became the target. Making a mental note to lock up any remaining alcohol, he sweeps while Jess sets the furniture upright.

The two work quietly until the cleanup is nearly finished. Kegan freezes when a whisper of trepidation skips down his spine. Meeting Jess's eyes, the two of them register the disturbance in the Symphony a second later. Something is outside, moving around, feeling, and testing the perimeters Kegan had put up yesterday.

"Did you put up a barrier?"

"Of course. As soon as I got back. But it's not impregnable." Trading the broom and dustpan for his weapons, Kegan runs out to the backyard with Jess close on his heels.

Whether from them or the demons spilling in from the tree line, the motion lights kick on, illuminating the entire wooded area. Leaping over the railing, the boys take up a line of defense. With a bit of skill and a lot of luck, they might keep them away from Nora long enough to get an additional barrier set up. Off on Kegan's left, Jess prepares himself for the attack, his blonde head already bobbing to the music blaring from his headphones, reminding Kegan to put in his own.

Tapping play on his phone, the bass of a *Disturbed* song fills his head, drowning out the Symphony just in time to meet a voracious demon. Blocking the wild swings, he knocks his opponent to the ground, sinking a blade into his heart.

Since the Scavengers couldn't cross the barrier on their own, someone stronger must be hanging back, waiting. With Eleni out of commission; sleeping off the losing battle with alcohol, Nora would be defenseless inside. They are going to have to keep the fight outside.

Reaching out with his senses, Kegan attempts to pinpoint the swell of power to get Adriel's location. The distraction nearly costs him as a pair of blades sweep an inch from his throat.

Chastising himself for the lack of focus, Kegan meets her next attack with the broadside of his blade, each movement smooth in its parry with her. The clash of metal sends small vibrations up his arms, forcing his fingers to flex tighter on the hilt. Seeing the opening, Kegan sweeps her legs out and punches downward into her chest, ensuring she lands on the ground with a solid thud. However, the twirling blades of her ally prevent Kegan from finishing her.

Dodging his advance, Kegan moves with practiced ease, jumping back to avoid the wide arc aimed for his midsection. Using his sword to deflect what he can't dodge, he draws on patience. There will be a flaw, a hiccup in the attack; he only needs to see it.

Heaven must be on his side, for the first time in a long time, because he doesn't have to wait long. Instead of swinging outward when given a chance, the demon draws back, allowing Kegan the opportunity to press his attack. Swinging out to force a block, he slides a hidden dagger through the webbing connecting the ribs and pierces his heart.

Two more demons press their luck, pushing Kegan to use skills he thought long lost. Only after their ashes clump into the damp grass does he draw in a breath. From the corner of an eye, he catches a demon sneaking around for Jess's blind spot, weapon drawn.

With a football tackle, Kegan takes him out; his fist connecting with a very stunned adversary. Spinning a lethal dagger between fingers, he slams it home, watching the demon erupt. "Fuck you too."

Seeing Kegan without a proper weapon, several demon's attack, causing him to retreat, rolling back to his blade. Meeting the arc of their furious attacks, he keeps his movements quick and concise, conserving energy. Sweat coats his skin, resulting in his clothes becoming sticky and cumbersome.

Dodging and countering, he holds his own with fast reflexes and a long reach. Two more replace where the last one falls, and then he worries. *There are too many.* A quick look shows Jess on the verge of being overrun by their numbers as well.

If this had been a battle of honor, Kegan would've fought with honor. However, this isn't some ancient battlefield, and losing isn't something he can afford.

Drawing off the residue of his energy, Kegan peppers the yard with lightning. Bolts of electricity stab the moist ground, burn the grass, and skewers a couple of demons. Pulling on that much power forces agony to slice through his body, stealing the air from him with a straightforward pass.

Pressing the heel of his hand to his left temple to ease the pressure, he drops to one knee. Despite the mounting pain, he gives the yard another pass of lightning, ensuring the remaining demon's give their battle plan a second thought.

Behind him, Jess swears so loudly, Kegan can hear him over the music, screaming into his ears. Taking up a position over him, Jess allows him a moment to recover. Under the assault, the demon's shimmer out from the yard, putting much-needed distance between them and the house.

"That was the most stupid thing I have ever seen and trust me. I've seen a lot." Jess gripes, helping Kegan to his feet.

"Worked, didn't it?" The queasy feeling in his stomach multiplies as soon as he's vertical. Kegan swallows, breathing in gulps of air to keep from throwing up on Jess's boots.

"Not the point, Asshole. If you'd been on your own, they would've torn you apart." Grabbing his dropped weapons, Jess helps him back to the cabin. "Not to mention if that didn't work, I would've been on my own."

Jess is right. It had been careless to draw on powers he knew would drain him. Much like anything else, the skills granted to them come with consequences now.

"Honestly, I didn't think it would even work."

"If Eleni wasn't sleeping off her binge, you wouldn't have to resort to such tactics. I'm half tempted to drag her drunk ass out of bed myself."

"Don't." Kegan massages the severe ache under his temples. "She's in no shape to fight off anything but her pillow. And talking to her right now isn't going to help the situation."

"Fine," Jess seethes. It's unusual for the laid-back Watcher to be this upset about anything, so the sight of his face flushed red, and his eyes snapping fire takes Kegan by surprise. "Well, it works, and now you remember how much it hurts, don't you?"

It'd been so long, the reality of its effects had waned. *The memory is fresh now, though*! Had Jess been anywhere else, Kegan wouldn't have lived to see the end of this battle. Pressing the heel of his hand on the pain splitting his skull, Kegan struggles to keep the strain from his words. "I'm going to need you to put up a second barrier."

Chapter 15

While Colin follows his tiny guide along the winding streets and alleys, his already sour mood blackens. Under the relentless sun and humidity, his fitted black tee becomes damp with sweat, his jeans sticky and uncomfortable

Another handful of lefts and rights leads them past what serves as a neighborhood bar full of enough music and laughter to rattle its foundation. When the next left brings them to an alley full of people as dirty as what remains of their clothes, Colin's ready to call a halt to the whole adventure. Gesturing to the end of a dirt driveway, the girl offers a small smile before running off in the opposite direction.

Fastening a tenuous grip on his temper, Colin starts up the packed earth, his eyebrow lifts at the flowerbed he passes along the way. Crimson Begonia's compliment full Goldenrods and Impatiens, the color of a summer sky as they grow among a myriad of flowers in diverse shapes and colors. As if in agreement, several bees fly from one bright petal to another, their gentle buzz resonating in his ears.

Nice to see while he and his soldiers spent centuries stewing, Azrael has been working on his green thumb. The thought tightens his chest and strangles his breath.

"Put it away," he grumbles. "You need answers." Answers Azrael supposedly has in spades. "Just get it over with so you can go home." As much as that idea chafes at his being, he marches up the porch steps.

Just ahead, an ornately decorated door swings open before even one boot reaches the threshold. On the other side, Azrael steps into view, apprehension visible on sharp features. Shadows in pale blue eyes tell Colin he isn't happy over the unannounced visit. *Good.*

"How are you here?"

Briefly, Colin recalls a time when the two of them had been close friends. Nothing one wouldn't do for the other; a fact time had tested more than once. Now, at best they're acerbic acquaintances.

"I took up selling Avon. You were the first one that came to mind." Since it's pointless to keep the animosity out of his voice, Colin doesn't waste time on the effort. Brushing past Azrael's lean frame, he stomps through the large foyer, keenly aware of the dirt each step leaves on pristine marble floors.

"You shouldn't be here." With a look over his city, Azrael heaves a groan and shuts the door behind Colin.

"Tell me about it. Hurt like a bitch if we're being honest." Colin's boots thud into the room Azrael obviously uses as a study, judging by all the paperwork. Dropping his bulk into the leather chair behind his desk, Colin props his boots up on one corner, ignoring the crinkling of papers. "So this is it, huh? This is where you've been hiding all these years?" He casts a look around the generous room with a skeptical eye, as Azrael does his best to ignore his presence.

Unlike the indifferent marble of the foyer, Azrael covered this floor in several area rugs, each color and pattern clashing with the last. He lines three of the four walls with intricate metal shelves, each shelf full to the brim with various books and red leather-bound ledgers. Tall bay windows allow the afternoon sun to lighten every corner, expelling whatever might linger in the shadows. Colin can't help but notice the lack of any personal touches in the room. This is where Azrael spends most of his time, yet no one would ever find a trace of him after he's gone.

"Why are you here, Colin?"

The sound of unrestrained patience pulls him from his musings. Never one to dance around the bull, he squares his shoulders and meets Azrael's look, head on. "I'm told you have answers I need."

"And who told you this?"

"Selena."

The scoff that bursts from Azrael's mouth is unfitting for his impeccable appearance and regal stance. Still, Colin spies something of intrigue in his once trustworthy eyes.

"What?"

"I don't know that I'd listen to anything that spills from her mouth. Word is, she's one step away from being hauled before the Council."

Azrael's revelation set his teeth on edge as fingers ball into fists within his lap. He takes a couple of breaths before he curbs his reaction and avoids the baited trap. When he speaks, he adds a level of calm into his words, despite the furious pace his heart pounds out.

"It's that well-informed gossip that brings me to your door."

Azrael moves deeper into the room, ignoring one of the empty chairs to brace a shoulder against a row of shelves. "They could brand me just for you being here without me saying a word."

"That seems extreme." He resists the urge to touch the one hiding under his hair and asks, "Figured they'd give that up for something more humane, maybe nail pulling."

"I don't find you funny."

"I wouldn't worry your sorry ass over something like that. Word is you have friends in high places. Not everyone can say the same."

"You had friends Colin. We, uh, *I*, was one of many to speak on your behalf."

"Is that before or after you reported my company to the council?"

"You know, that wasn't a simple decision for me."

"Do I? Shit, I'm smarter than I give myself credit for." Colin's fingers ache from clenching them too tight for too long. The knot in his stomach grows with every passing minute he spends dredging up the past.

"Colin-"

"Save it. That's not why I'm here." Releasing the breath burning within his lungs, Colin fills the nearby tumbler with the bottle of whiskey on his left and pours the contents down his throat. After two more, Colin meets the flutter of annoyance on Azrael's immaculate features. "You know the answers I'm looking for."

"They attached you and Melchom at the hip. The dark to your light. When one of you shifts realms, the other goes too. And knowing all this, you expect me to babble like some teenage girl."

"Oh, I'm sure he's here. Which makes the time you have to spill what you know very limited." Colin's head tilts. "Isn't that what you do best? Gossip? I'd have brought a nice scotch if I thought it would help." With a derisive chuckle, he shakes his head. "Actually no, I wouldn't."

"There's nothing I can tell you."

"So I was right, and you're just like the rest of them. Setting us up to fail. Should've made it a ten-dollar bet."

With a groan, Azrael scrubs a hand over his baby smooth face. "What do you need to know? Not want Colin. *Need.*"

"Where did it come from?" A deep chuckle that sounds more like sarcasm than amusement explodes from Azrael's chest to surprise him.

"From you and your fallen comrades."

"What does that mean?"

"Everything one of your soldiers taught, each secret they murmur during a lover's embrace; recorded."

"Recorded? How?"

"Thanks to Emma, the McKinnon line recorded the information on pages in a language she shared with their bloodline. Once the Brennan clan could locate all the pages, they sealed them away in a tome. With a little help, of course."

"Of course," he seethes. "Why don't I remember any of this?"

"Considering the Fallen created the mess, it seemed taking the knowledge away from you, *all* of you, was the best course of action. No way could we risk a repeat."

"Why wasn't the book destroyed?"

"That's above my paygrade."

"What happened to the McKinnon clan?"

"The Council dealt with them."

"Figures."

"Colin, the knowledge they had attained was dangerous."

"And the Brennan bloodline became a Protector of our secrets," he utters to himself. He'd be a fool not to recognize the pain in the back of his throat, the queasiness in his stomach. If he'd been more vigilant in monitoring his troops, this never would have occurred. The weight of his inaction settles across his shoulders. Systemically, they add to the burdens he already carries, leaving a mark on his heart and a stain on his essence.

As the vapor of sleep lessens, Nora shifts with a sound somewhere between a groan and a croak. The action makes her aware of the ache hammering her brain and the howl every muscle releases in protest. With a hand to her head as if to ward off the cumbersome hangover, she sits up.

Considering the amount of sunlight that filters through sheer curtains, it's already late morning. *Too blessed early.* However, the drum solo carrying on between her ears makes more sleep impossible. It doesn't take her long mentally to scratch off her to-do list and replace it with tylenol and a nap.

Throwing off her blankets, Nora scoots out of bed slowly to give her awkward legs as much warning as possible. Peeking through lidded lashes, she shuffles across the room, stubbing her toe on the wooden footboard.

"Sonofabiscuit," she seethes through teeth as she hops backward to the bed to better inspect her foot. Agony throbs within the tip of her pinky toe as it fattens to twice its usual size. A large part of her begs her to call off the search for painkiller in favor of crawling back under the blankets, what's left reasons the search of tylenol more essential than ever.

Gingerly, she stands, putting the bulk of her weight on her good foot as she shuffles across the natural oak floors into the hall and towards the kitchen. That she's upright encourages Ezio to remind her of his missed breakfast as he winds around her hobbling legs, his yowls multiplying in frequency and volume. Despite her gentle nature, Nora struggles with the temptation to nudge him along until they reach the livingroom and she's able to sidestep him.

Even in her sleepy state, she registers the state of the large room. After the cage fight Eleni started the night before, she expected to find the room in shambles. The haze of her recollection brings a memory of her swinging wildly and knocking Kegan's African Jew plant sideways, dumping thick black dirt across the floor. Instead, everything stands in its rightful place. Debris from their drunken feud cleared away. A knot lodges itself under her ribs as she considers her upcoming apology.

Playing it out in her head, Nora can see herself offering her most sincere *I'm sorry*. Kegan's face is full of barely contained patience as he looks down at her. She knows disappointment will taint his goosebump inducing voice as if he expects better from her. Just when she'd assume his lecture had reached its climax, that one eyebrow will creep up his forehead for good measure. Watching the reel leaves Nora with an urge to rip that strip of hair from his face entirely.

Inside the kitchen, Jess stands over the stove, challenging himself with how much racket he can create. Twice, he lifts the pan on the burner only to adjust the way it sits with a clang. Apparently satisfied, he cracks eggs into the skillet while whistling a fast-paced tune. The urge to smother him with a towel cascades down into her arms with such ferocity, Nora balls her hands into small fists to resist the impulse.

"Hey," she croaks, mindful of the hangover, her voice never reaches beyond a whisper. "What could you possibly be doing to make so much noise?"

"Making breakfast," he answers hesitantly before turning. As if unfazed by her irritable demeanor, a grin twitches across his lips. "Kegan said it was my turn to cook."

Just the mention of his name puts a snag in her breathing that she covers with a groan as she approaches the sink. "Maybe try to cook with less enthusiasm," she grumbles while filling a glass with water from the tap. From the corner of her eye, she catches his lazy nod while she begins her search for anything resembling aspirin. Because of her average height, Nora starts with the cupboards she can reach. As she moves along, having zero luck, she's vaguely aware she's closing the doors with more force than it requires.

"What're you looking for?"

"Tylenol. Aspirin. Ibuprofen. Anything that will help with this damn hangover."

"Drank too much last night?"

Nora scowls, shooting him a quick look before turning her attention to the last cupboard within reach. "Well, it's that or brownies have taken up residence inside my skull and are currently rearranging the furniture." His loud chuckle earns him one more glare as she resorts to climbing up on the counter to reach the taller cupboards. Nora resigns to her fate until she catches sight of the little white bottle nestled among the wineglasses. *Go figure.*

"What in the bloody hell are you doing *now*?"

Dropping the bottle with a yelp of surprise, Nora covers her ears against the ungodly roar coming from the back of the house. As the sound of Kegan's boots thump across the distance, she retrieves the bottle from the empty sink and holds it close, unprepared for the feel of his warm hands on her skin as he pulls her down from the counter. "I just needed the Tylenol," she reasons quietly, unwillingly absorbing the full impact of Kegan.

Considering the damp curls clinging to the back of his neck and falling across his brow, he'd already showered this morning. Shaved too, she reasons as her fingers twitch to brush along his smooth jaw. The subtle scent of his soap reaches her nose, toying with her senses until her stomach is tight, her breath shallow.

When he leans toward her, Nora's breath stops, her heart pressing pause on further beats as she falls into his dark eyes, burning with something she can't quite name. For a brief second, she readies herself for the taste of his lips, and the arms that'll snake around her waist only to pull her close. So the scratchy texture of the blanket he wraps around her bare shoulders, snaps her eyes open. He'd never intended on kissing her again. Idiot! Heat infuses her. A bright red wash that paints her skin from hairline to toe.

"Don't touch me," she spits, shaking off the world's most harsh blanket. "You've been avoiding me as if I'm Typhoid Mary, so don't go grabbing me now."

"Now, Nora, if you'll only-"

"Stuff it Grumpus. And while you're at it, you can stuff that stupid charm of yours as well." Gripping the tylenol tightly with one hand, she retrieves her glass of water on her way back to her bedroom. She will better assess the full weight of how complicated her life has become once she's had more sleep.

Kegan counts to ten, twice, as Nora limps back to her bedroom. The voice in his head rages for him to scoop her up and carry her off to his room that he's left physically restraining himself. Fingers clamp onto the granite counter so hard, for a moment he worries, which will give first. The stone or his fingers?

Funny, when he stepped out of the shower less than five minutes ago, he couldn't deny he was feeling more than a little refreshed. The sight of Nora perched up on his kitchen counter wearing nothing but bra and panties definitely knackers any feelings of optimism he might've embraced. He'd seen her to bed fully dressed the night before, so when she emerged with her clothing missing, his body longs to uncover the secret.

The image of her skin against the lilac underwear sears into his brain, lodging itself with his strongest memories. Flawless feet of creamy skin gleams under the sunlight streaming into the kitchen, highlighting every stray freckle from the top of her head to her painted toes. The contrast her pale skin makes with the loose hair falling beyond her shoulders steals his breath and any coherent thought.

She's almost to her doorway when Nora spins around, confronting him from a half a house away. Although her voice never journeys beyond a tight whisper, Kegan hears every word as if she'd been right in front of him.

"I may not be the nicest person in the morning, I can admit that. But I don't go around shouting at people. You don't want me climbing on your precious counters? Then put shit where others less fortunate in the height department can *fucking* reach it." Whirling about, Kegan catches the quick snap of her door latching behind her.

Heat unfurls within his chest, snuffing out his oxygen. His ears register the muffled crack as his fingers bite down into the granite. *Too late.* Pulling his hands back, Kegan plows one through his hair, all too aware of the tremble his restraint puts in his legs. Jess's whoop of laughter directs him to the only witness of their exchange.

"Grumpus," Jess asks with a rueful shake of his blonde head, his wide grin provoking Kegan's temper. "I rather like it. I may have to use it. Think she'll mind?"

"You saw nothing, got it? If you don't wipe it from memory, I'm happy to do it for you."

Holding his hands up, a rubber spatula in one, Jess shakes his head. "Nothing to worry about, Chief. I saw nothing. Saw what? What was I supposed to see?"

"Just cook your damn eggs."

"Got it. Loud and clear. But between you and me, I'm still saying my prayers of thanks before bed tonight." Jess calls after his retreating figure.

You and me both, Bub. Kegan's heart slams with a furious tempo as he storms out to the garage for a grueling workout.

Wrapping his hands, he counts to ten again. Never has he met a woman like Nora, and if he's being honest with himself, he's losing his grip.

"You're in control of your emotions. Your emotions aren't in control of you," Kegan mumbles over the old mantra. He can't recall the last time he felt the need to recite it back to himself.

Squaring off with the heavy bag, the *wop* of his first punch brings a fraction of calm with it. When Brody asked him for his word to keep her safe, he'd readily offered it. *Wop, smack.* Unfortunately, the only watching he wants to do has very little to do with her protection. *Thud.* How gallant of him, huh? Punch after punch peppered with a random knee or elbow strike makes the bag dance in the ceiling's anchor.

When was the last time he'd been so affected by one woman? Kegan can't recall a face, let alone her name. Sure, he'd get looks of uninhibited interest over the years, but he stopped acting on them a long time ago.

In the beginning, everything was new and intensified with so many unfiltered emotions flooding their systems. Over time, those emotions became easier to contend with, making his solitary existence easily attainable. Until now.

Kegan was expecting the same lack of emotion when he first met Nora. Instead, every passing minute multiplies her intrigue and his infatuation. *Christ*, the memory of her mouth haunts his waking moment, the promise of more flooding his nights, stealing away into his dreams. "Face it. You're screwed," he snarls before breaking into another round of abuse on the heavy bag.

Chapter 16

Melchom storms along the manmade streets, his mood unsalvageable. Opting for a nearby alley where the traces of Colin are strongest, he's assaulted with a smell that makes him gag. Lined on either side with dirty degenerates, their foul smell curls within his nose, rolling his stomach.

"I know why you've come."

Pinned under his hostile glare, the young woman shrinks inside the one-room house, her heart hammering audibly as he moves to follow. Just inside, Melchom takes a moment to allow his eyes time to adjust to the lack of light that illuminates a bleak interior.

Thin planks frame the small house, once fresh, now dull and dingy from a lack of care. Along the back wall, a simple kitchen sits with a stove and a refrigerator straight out of the eighties. On his left, stands a meager twin sized bed, topped with a lumpy mattress, a flat pillow and a threadbare blanket. Straight ahead, she stops near a wooden table with three chairs tucked in around it. One rests at an awkward angle because of a missing leg, the other lacks a back piece, leaving only one of any use.

"You have my attention," Melchom says slowly, the fragile hold on his patience weakening with each second she withholds vital information.

"I know what he's here for."

"I don't know who you're used to dealing with, girl, but stalling is only going to piss me off."

Suddenly unsure, the woman scrambles closer to the door at the back of the kitchen before attempting her best smile. He imagines at one time stunning; the expression falls flat, absent of any shine, the time spent here dulling her feminine attributes. "I want something in return."

"Of course you do." With a roll of his eyes, Melchom leans against an exposed wooden beam, hoping it'll bear his weight for the duration of this conversation. With a nod of his dark head, he only half listens as she whines petulantly about the time she's spent here.

"Why so eager to leave and give up your chance at Heaven?"

"I'm not going to Heaven. Most of us here already know that."

"Nothing is ever certain until the big guy decides. Besides, it might be better than where I'd put you."

"Nothing is worse than sitting here while others move on."

"This place serves a purpose. Few would risk messing with Azrael's plan." She fails to pick up on his warning, preoccupied with a scraggly strand of what may have been luxurious, golden hair. In life she was probably a beautiful creature, a human with looks often unchallenged. Whatever choices she'd made, earned her a ticket to the benchwarmers realm, the time spent here leeching away her essence.

"Are you saying you can't get me out of here?"

"*Can't*, no. I'd say by the look of you, you're still paying for every foul deed you've dealt out. Each one siphons off your beauty, draining the vibrancy of that human soul so many cherish above all else."

"Foul deeds? If that's the case, why are there children here?"

"The beings you see as children are *virtues*. They work with Azrael to determine who moves on for judgement. Once you pay your debt, you may move on, the direction you'll go, I cannot say."

"I can. And I'm done waiting around for the ax to fall. So, are you going to get me out of here or not?"

Nora swings back and forth on the porch swing as the sun drops into the horizon, painting the soft blue sky with shades of orange and a rose petal pink. Soon, the leaves would change with the season as the weather turns cool and damp. She can't help but remember this being her favorite time of year to spend at the cabin. In the past, her visits came with a sense of quietness and serenity the real world couldn't tarnish. "After your performance this morning, you could use a little quiet," she notes, blowing a cooling breath on the cup of tea that warms her hands.

She's always been clumsy around boys. A fact she accepted in her early teens after developing a crush on the high school quarterback. Realizing she's unprepared for the feelings Kegan invokes is a vast understatement since the man makes her act like a blubbering idiot twenty-three hours of the day. Perhaps if he'd been more homely, with horrible hygiene, she'd find it easier to be herself.

"Not like the angels are going to come down and strike him ugly now."

It isn't as if he's a nice person, either. Most of the time, he regards her as a nuisance to tuck away in a corner far away from him. On the rare occasions his defenses slipped, and he warmed her with the hungered embers sparking to life in his eyes. They didn't last long, nor changed his brutish demeanor.

"You okay?" Sidetracked by her scattered thoughts, Nora never heard Kegan approach until he stands over the swing, blocking out the vibrant sky before her.

Plastering a smile on her face, she jerks out a nod. "Just thinking."

As if taking her response as invitation, the swing sways off-kilter as he takes a seat next to her. Using a boot, he gives the swing a heave to resume the rocking motion. "About anything particular?"

"Besides the scene I made this morning?"

"I wouldn't call it a scene, exactly."

"Even if I'm able to chalk up my mood to the alcohol, you saw me in my underwear, for Pete's sake!"

Heat creeps up the back of Kegan's neck over her not-so-subtle reminder. With a cough, he scrubs a hand down his face and pins his eyes to something on the horizon. The rhythm of her heart keeps track of the seconds before he actually voices a reply. "If it makes you feel any better, you're not the first I've seen in their knickers."

"Yeah, that doesn't help," she replies with a soft mumble, then pulls a drink of her tea. The sound of his light chuckle puts a tilt in her head, his profile giving hint to a small smile. When he looks back at her, Nora registers a look of pity in his eyes instead of the interest she'd been hoping for. Inwardly, she flinches and gives the swaying trees on her right her full attention.

"Best to forget it ever happened," he offers in a smooth tone. "I have."

"Right." *Just kill me now.* The two of them sit for a while as the sun sinks just beyond the tree-line, illuminating the fall colors with a golden glow. Turning away from thoughts branding her pathetic, Nora focuses on some questions, certain to put a damper on the fire that settles at her core. "In the spirit of forgetting, how about telling me some secrets you guys are keeping from me?" If asked, she'll admit it was mildly rewarding to see shock ripple across his forehead.

"Um, er, what makes you think we're keeping secrets?"

Swallowing the snort rising in her throat, Nora presses. "For one, you seem relatively at ease with deadly weapons. Eleni, who by the way has been my best friend for years, turns out to be an ass kicking combat specialist, angel, *and* a friend of yours."

"I wouldn't say, *friend.*"

"Whatever. You three ooze secrets. Somehow I've ended up in the middle. I think you can spare a few answers."

He's quiet and still for so long Nora fears she's pushed too hard and he's fixing to run in the opposite direction. His uncertainty trembles around his words when he answers, giving her a tiny peek at his vulnerability.

"I don't know how to do that."

"Okay, I'll go first with a tiny secret of my own." Nora drops a shoulder just enough to close the distance long enough to whisper in a conspiring manner. "There are these things called conversations. Words put together can form sentences. You say a few, then I say some and so on. For an excellent conversation, we have to take turns."

His faint chuckle tightens her skin. "I've met no one like you," he declares with a smile, relaxing into the swing's back. It's the first time Nora can recall ever seeing him truly at ease since their meeting just a few short days ago. *Days ago? Has it really been so brief?*

"I see so much of Brody in you, but Elise too, yet there's enough of you in there to still make you unique. It's unnerving, annoying, and endearing all at the same time."

"I'm going to take that as a compliment since you ended it on a positive note."

As if taken by surprise, his laugh explodes from his chest, warming the evening air with his rich baritone. In the heat of the unexpected emotion, tiny lines crinkle around his eyes and his lips flutter into a crooked smirk. Unlike his previous smiles, this one reaches his eyes to highlight gold particles buried in their depths until they glitter sharply to soften their warm brown depths.

"Three questions," he states, his lips still twitching as he holds up three fingers. "Make them good and I'll explain the best I can, so long as you promise not to go running off screaming into the night. It's getting dark and you won't be able to see as well as I do. It won't take me long to run you down. Okay?"

She's aware most of what he said was important, but Nora can't help her mind from wandering off to the idea of him chasing her down in the ever darkening evening sky. The idea has her pulse leaping in her neck, her breath coming out in audible pants. Dazed, she spies Kegan's eyebrow lift, dragging her back into reality, kicking and screaming.

"Uh, yes. We have a deal."

"Good." Settling his shoulders, Kegan rests his head against the back of the swing while using his foot to continue the rocking sway. "Ready when you are."

"Have you always been an angel?"

Kegan's gaze is so intense that it shatters any attempt of ease he hopes to portray in an instant. Pleased by his reaction, Nora hides her smile behind her cup of tea and wonders just how honest he'll answer.

"Yes. Though we're not actually considered angels any longer."

"Does it count as a question if I ask for some clarification?"

Kegan chuckles, shaking his head. "I suppose not. We've held many titles over the ages. Guardians, Grigori, Watchers, the Fallen."

"So, where are your wings? Every depiction of an angel has wings."

"Most do in their angelic forms. As punishment and part of our shame, we became unworthy of such things."

"Punishment for what?"

Kegan studies his boots for a long time, inhales and exhales, unmoving beside her. So much time passes, Nora figures he's done answering her questions and relaxes beside him, tucking one foot underneath her to enjoy the gentle motion of the swing. Whether it's the effect of the chamomile, the rhythm of the swing, or the warmth he gives off, it isn't long before her eyes feel heavy. When he speaks, the soft lullaby of his cadence only adds to the tranquility surrounding her.

"They sent us to Earth to monitor humanity. Something complicated mankind from the start. Unlike anything previously created. When God made you, choosing you as the object of his love, he put you on a pedestal of sorts. All but one followed his lead. But there was so much we didn't understand, so we were to observe and learn."

"What didn't you understand?"

"Why two men would fight to the death over a patch of dirt that matters little in the grand scheme of things, bathing in the death of thousands? How one of you loses a loved one and becomes inconsolable in their grief. So much so that the one left behind will sometimes follow."

"Can I ask what the scar is on the back of your head?"

Heat floods Kegan's face. Whether irritation or shame, Nora can't pinpoint. Beside him, the sound of his teeth grinding is obvious. "It's a brand," he spits, without ever releasing the pressure of his jaw.

"Why would they brand you?"

"Because we were no longer angels. We are now considered, Fallen."

Awake now, Nora inches closer, her chest expanding. "I'm sorry." Eager to settle his ruffled feathers, she latches onto a relatively simple question. "Why does your brogue sound different from Grandad's?" Unprepared for the next question, confusion skitters across his features. She's aware he was expecting her questions to resemble the Spanish Inquisition, but if she's learning anything about Kegan, it's keeping things simple.

"Brody grew up closer to the Lowlands, I favored lands further in the North. I spent most of my time in a small village near Kintyre, so much so that it colored my speech." Raising his gaze, he studies her for a long moment, so intently Nora struggles not to squirm. "Is it rank?"

"Rank?"

"Mm, horrible. Disgusting, displeasing."

The small voice in her head warns Nora to keep her cards close to her chest and to leave their interaction light. "No," she begins, "not in the least." Did her voice sound as breathless to him as it did to her?

However, her response sounded to him; Jess stuck his head out through the patio door, saving Nora from another brush off. "Hey, you two, Eleni wants to order pizza. If you don't want to be drowning in anchovies, I suggest you get in here."

"Yeah, that's not happening," Kegan declares. "Over my dead body."

"Sounds fair to me." Eleni replies from inside the house, the bickering fading as Kegan pulls the glass door shut behind him. Opting to remain outside, Nora studies the night sky and contemplates everything Kegan had said.

She can't imagine what it must be like to watch humanity from afar, to observe their every moment and emotion, all while being unable to fully comprehend the complexity of their actions. It's no wonder Kegan acts the way he does sometimes. She imagines being constantly bombarded with the intricacies of human behavior is overwhelming.

She'll admit, it all sounds like something out of a fairy tale. "In that case, let's hope Disney is writing my story and not the Grimm brothers."

Fingertips squeeze against the cup in her hand. When Kegan spoke, his words carried weight. They came off authentic and sincere. It's true her perception could read wonky with the strange connection she feels to him, but Nora can't shake the idea he was being honest.

As she sits in silence, her mind wanders to the kiss they shared. She remembers the way his hand felt on her skin and the heat that spread through her body the instant their lips met. *Does he think about it too or has he "put it away"?*

As Rome's legions drink and celebrate the predicted outcome, he lounges on his self-proclaimed throne. Now and then his eyes drift to the pair of Succubi dancing for his pleasure, scraps of sheer fabric scantly concealing voluptuous curves. Every so often their brazen display levels a familiar ache in his groin, but mostly, he battles a yawn. At least until he senses another's presence.

"Out!" Rome commands to bring the celebrations to a halt. As his voice ricochets around the marble columns, his soldiers screech to a stop, bowing out in quick reply. The only demon left stands in the back with an arrogance Rome itches to rip out of him. "This is the second time you come uninvited. What's stopping me from ripping your spine out, leaving you to bleed on my floor?"

Instead of the hesitance Shax should've felt at that threat, he merely smiles an unconcerned smile. "I've come to discuss our deal."

"We never struck a deal." Rome sneers, pushing himself to his feet. He'd be damned if Shax gets the better of him. Slight wisps of smoke rise off him, speaking volumes about his current mood.

"Have you considered my offer?"

"I have, though I still don't see how you can be of any use to me. At. All."

"Well, I can point you in the right direction regarding the ancient bloodline."

"My men have already located the bloodline."

"The other one."

"How did you know there were two? Where are you getting your information?"

"They're called books, Brother." Shax heaves a dramatic sigh. "The point is, I know who you need for the translation. Do you want her name or not?"

Shifting his attention to the demon huddling amongst the shadows, Rome waves him forward. "Bring Rayen to me." When he looks back, Shax is picking over food left out on one of the banquet tables. "Anything else you bring to this partnership?"

"It's rather straightforward." Shax laces his tone with boredom, reckless as far as Rome is concerned. "I have a tool at my disposal that will put the book in those big meaty paws you call hands. However, I lack the soldiers to put it into play. That's where you come in."

"Obviously."

"Your men get word to the Brennan girl about our little bargaining chip, and she's guaranteed to deliver the book herself."

"Any tool you have can be mine. You destroyed. The book mine. Alone."

"I had a feeling you'd go there, which is why it's currently under the guard of Chayante warriors."

Rome didn't hide the incredulous shock tainting sharp features. The Chayante people are long respected warriors made up solely of women. "How did you manage that? No way you have the coin required to buy their services."

Shax shrugs, his face already showing the victory he'd just won. "You have two options left. You can accept my proposal, or I can inform your Melchom of the upcoming rebellion. I'm sure he'd like to know you plan to unseat him from his throne."

Fire explodes in tidal waves, spreading quickly to heat every drop of Rome's blood. He could smell Shax's fear from here. The demon reeks of it. His sudden hitch in breathing only confirms Rome's suspicion. If there's anything worse than arrogance, it's fake arrogance.

It's quick. So fast, Shax barely registers the threat before Rome's hand clamps around his throat. Squeezing until he can feel the blood pounding against his fingers, he pulls him forward to balance precariously on the tips of his toes. "Never threaten me again."

Chapter 17

The second her dream changes, Nora's on alert. The lure of the mist muddies her mind until the bed Kegan had been waiting in shifts to a clearing. Tall trees provide the meadow with shelter from the drizzling rain often experienced in the fall season.

Like every time before, Nora walks forward on bare feet, the wet grass squishy compared to the rough stone of the manor's floor. Inside, fires roar in monstrous fireplaces to ward off the bite of the damp weather outside.

As if set to purpose, she creeps up the winding stairs, her hand hovering over the roughhewn banister as she reaches the second floor. Spying the door ahead with a light of recognition, her breath stills as she pushes it open.

As before, men circle a round table, bent tirelessly over their work. This time the wind and rain falls lazily, its chill hindered by the heavy material covering the windows. The only recent addition to her dream stands near the back, watchful of the work being done.

Dressed more commonly than the furious male model beside him, his stature screams importance. Long, thick legs plant themselves firmly, his leather boots stopping at mid-calf. Several inches shy of his neatly pleated kilt. Each fold lays precise, the bright colors reflect flawlessly amongst the rich candlelight.

A plain white shirt tucks into the waist of his kilt, sleeves rolled over the massive forearms crisscrossing his chest. At his throat, the collar remains open, strings left to hang as the simple cloth embraces a wide set of shoulders. Over his left, he drapes a piece of his kilt, securing it with a round silver pin. Through her study, Nora assumes he intends to appear relaxed. Missing the mark entirely.

Even as she gets her first real clue where her dreams are taking her, the epiphany soon fades.

In the harsh lines of his face, warm chestnut hair and vivid green eyes, she discovers a man closely resembling her father. While his prominent nose and full mouth are identical, a deep scar runs from brow to jaw, separating him from the face she cherished.

Where her father's face carried classic, beautiful charm, this mans' is unyielding. Trials of a severe life carve and shape his appearance and personality. The deep-seated blaze in his eyes and the set of his mouth tell Nora he'll kneel for no man.

"You!"

Blurted so sharply, the urgency pierces her fog of a dream and pulls her attention to the golden-haired model. Eyes so clear a blue it hurt to look at, radiate his accusation, forcing her back a step. This time he moves too quick for her to anticipate, clamping a hand around her wrist.

"You're wasting time," he snaps, pulling her off balance. Fighting to free herself, Nora claws at his vise-like grip while her heart tries to make room in her throat.

The intense desperation twisting his handsome features sends a shiver along her spine. When her scream tears from her body, it splits the room's heaviness. Undeterred, blue eyes scorch with desperation as he searches her face. "You must listen to me. We have little time." Breaking free from his hold, Nora tumbles backward, prepared for the collision with the floor. She wakes and bolts upright in her bed.

Wrestling for air, Nora's mouth opens and closes like a fish out of water as she scans each corner of her room. Blankets coil around her hips and legs to constrict movement, her t-shirt wet with sweat clings to her upper body, impeding her ability to draw a full breath.

"It's just a dream. Just a dream." Nora rambles over and over, waiting for the dizziness to pass. Peeling away the blankets from her legs, she pushes an unsteady hand through her heavy hair and climbs out of bed. Content that all is right with the world, Ezio continues to slumber.

Bridging the hall to the bathroom, Nora changes into fresh clothes and braids her damp hair. After brushing her teeth and splashing cold water across her face, her heart slows and her body relaxes. Lately, her dreams are taking on a horror movie quality she's unequipped to rationalize.

It's while drying her hands on a towel that she exposes the blemishes marring her arm. Spanning the width of her wrist, several red splotches darken her fair skin in the shape of long fingers.

No way is she crawling back in that bed now. Returning to her room, she exchanges her clean pajamas for jeans and an oversized hoodie before tiptoeing out to the kitchen for coffee. Outside, the sky is still dark with the early hour, morning not yet ready to break the stillness of the house.

Approximately five minutes later, Nora tucks herself in Kegan's rocking chair with a fresh cup of coffee, staring out the patio door into the backyard. Busying her mind from anything remotely disturbing, she wonders about Hiller House and Rebecca.

Not that her friend is incompetent, but Nora is eager to get back and lose herself in the familiar. By the time her cup is empty, she makes a note to call after breakfast and check in with everything there when she senses movement to her left.

His approach is a shuffle without the aid of his lumbering boots. Her lip quirks at the sight of his bare feet under folds of denim jeans. Sitting there with the empty cup in hand, she realizes it's the first time she's seen him without his boots or a *shirt*. Fingers squeeze the ceramic mug while eyes greedily feast on what she now declares breakfast.

Tanned and muscled, his golden skin glimmers smooth aside from the patch of hair spanning from chest to stomach. Nothing about Kegan boasts of Hollywood beauty, or finely sculpted muscles. No, he holds the look of a warrior, his physique honed in battle instead of a gym. He almost reaches her when her attention snags on the tattoo from the lawyer's office.

Scaling the column of his neck, it splays over one shoulder to descend across his corded back, only to disappear under the waist of his jeans. Nora breathes around the sudden desire to trace each line with great care, paying homage to the artist. As her body responds with an eagerness she'd never felt before, she has to choke down the purr rising from her chest. The sound jolts Kegan to a stop not six feet away.

"You're up early."

His usually smooth voice is rough from sleep, lending a thickness to his words that Nora finds sexy as hell. Sometime over the last few days, a switch appeared on her hormones, one he instinctively knew how to flick with minimal effort.

"I didn't sleep well, but I put coffee on."

Extending her the courtesy of nodding his thanks, Kegan sets his sights on the kitchen. After a moment of muffled activity, he returns with a cup in hand, perching himself on the arm of the couch a safe distance away.

"What's keeping you from sleeping?"

"Bad dreams." Any other time, Nora might've felt silly over her answer. This morning, the traces of her dream hang heavily around her shoulders to keep silliness at bay.

"Feel like talking about it," he asks, eyes on his coffee.

Nora mulls the offer over for less than a minute before she's rambling off every detail she can recall. When she finishes her tale, Kegan carries a distinct look of concern in his eyes until he blinks it away, forcing a smile that never reaches his eyes.

"Disturbing, I'll grant you that. Still a dream, though."

"Was it though?" Setting her cup on the table in front of the couch, Nora scrunches up her sleeve to reveal the distinct bruises on her arm.

She remembers the night she and her friends snuck out of the house to catch the premiere of *Nightmare on Elm Street*, and the fear she had of sleeping. This is worse. Her fear must've been obvious because instead of blowing it off, Kegan sets down his cup and pulls her into the safety of his arms.

While the warm scent of his skin swarms her, strands of hair snag on the stubble of his jaw as he brushes his face over the top of her head. The weight of the arms he wraps around her offers more stability than she thought possible, consoling her frazzled nerves. Eager to absorb the comfort he offers, Nora twines her arms around his waist, her heart leaping at the soft sigh he breathes in response.

Heedless to one of his arms falling away, Nora's lungs seize up when his thumb brushes the curve of her cheek. Unable to stop herself from leaning into his touch, she smiles when he doesn't pull away, draining the tension of her stiff muscles. As his thumb continues its path along the side of her face, it dips below her chin, giving a spark to the hope within her chest. At the nudge of his hand, Nora allows him to tilt her face upward to meet his waiting mouth.

Because of their difference in height, Nora must extend on tip toes to taste his coffee-flavored lips. Framing her face with his hands, Kegan kisses her with a gentleness that leaves an ache in her belly. A shudder cascades across his back and under her hands to contradict the restraint he shows. His moan in response to her nipping teeth adds dry timber to the fire, threatening to consume them both.

Stepping in between his knees, Nora presses her body closer, accepting his growl of appreciation as a reward. While he busies himself with learning the curve of her lips and the taste of her tongue, her hands glide up the wide expanse of his back. Now and then, her fingers will graze the raised edge of a scar, but instead of breaking the moment like last time, she pushes the information aside for a later conversation. When her nails faintly score his skin in retreat, Kegan offers a deep groan, arching into her touch.

In the dark halls of her mind, she admits his larger size thrills her. Her reaction to him is primal when it awakens a need within her and stokes it to fruition. Angling her head, she delivers an unspoken invitation to take the kiss deeper, stumbling over a moan when he's happy to comply. Less cautious and more claiming.

When he breaks the kiss, Nora lets out a soft whimper, embarrassed and excited all at once. A shiver runs through her when he moves to her throat. One hand latches onto the curve of her hip to anchor her in place, while the other uses her long braid to tug her head further back. The hunger he keeps contained is now awake and impatient. All she can do is hold on for the ride, lost in the tide at the scrape of his teeth.

"Who's turn is it?"

Her face hot, Nora jumps back, a hand to her mouth. The disappointment crashing over Kegan's strong features makes her heart flutter. Avoiding Jess's amused grin, she backs away with a nervous stammer and flees to her room, leaving Kegan to fend for himself.

"Sorry Chief."

"Don't worry about it." Dumping his cold coffee in the sink, Kegan pours himself a fresh cup while Jess digs around in a drawer for one of his skillets.

"Why didn't you say anything? I never would've interrupted if I'd known."

Bracing his hip against the counter, Kegan attempts to wash away the taste of Nora's lips with his coffee. "It's for the best."

"What is?" Looking fresh and rested, Eleni joins them in the kitchen, glancing back and forth from him to Jess.

"Nothing." Kegan clips.

Jess grins. "I walked in on Kegan and Nora, enjoying a little one on one time."

Kegan's lip curls. "Snitch."

"What does he mean, one-on-one time?" Eleni asks, lips pressing together when Kegan answers with a shrug of one shoulder.

"It's nothing." Kegan says.

"Didn't look like nothing. Looked like a lot of," Jess pauses, embracing his flair for the dramatic, "*something*."

Kegan growls. "Hey, Squirt, how about you worry about your damn eggs and shut the hell up?"

"She's my best friend, Kegan." Eleni explains. "I don't appreciate you playing games with her."

"Who says I'm playing games?" Kegan sets the cup on the counter before he crushes it in his hand. "It was a lapse in judgement. And after you left Jess and I to fend off another attack, you're in no position to tell me what I should or shouldn't be doing."

Heat floods Eleni's face a second before she glances at the floor. "I apologized for that. It won't happen again."

"Doesn't change the fact that I almost died, Eleni."

"This isn't about me. This is about you and my best friend." Eleni crosses her arms across her chest as her eyes narrow. "You're standing there saying it was a mistake, and I'm sure she's not even in that ballpark. It's not right."

Kegan stares at the ceiling, wondering if Eleni is right. He wouldn't be tied up in knots where Nora is concerned if he was simply playing games. A lapse in judgement, definitely. But can he say it was a mistake? Did he regret kissing her again? *Not one bit.*

As Eleni continues her lecture on poor impulse control, breakfast loses its appeal. Dumping the still hot contents from his cup, Kegan tries to put some of his friend's fears to rest. "It won't happen again."

"Uh-huh." Eleni snorts. "And if it goes further than it did this morning? What then?"

"It won't." Kegan gives his head a shake.

Eleni pauses. "How can you say that and mean it?"

"Because *that* is a dead-end street." Kegan answers in a flat tone.

Ears perked, Jess spins from the stove. "What do you mean?"

"I've already put in for my release. I won't jeopardize it." His admission hangs in the surrounding air, adding to the shock on Jess and Eleni's faces. The bafflement that follows splinters his heart.

"You're not serious." Jess's usual boisterous voice comes out strained.

Kegan nods. "As the Pope on his deathbed."

"How?" Eleni demands. "Why?"

"Christ, Eleni, it's been *centuries*." Kegan reasons, "Centuries with no end in sight. I'm surprised more haven't asked before me."

"So, what?" Crossing the kitchen, Eleni stops at the round table. "You're going to roll over and play dead?"

"I don't expect you to understand, Eleni." Kegan sighs, his chest heavy. "You've always been able to mingle in their world, but I can't. Hundreds of years with the same droll is enough."

"Boo-hoo. We all feel like that now and then." Eleni pokes her bottom lip out in a mock pout. "Right, Jess? It's a rough patch. But you can't just throw the towel in over a mid-life crisis."

"Mid-life crisis," Kegan laughs. "I'm pretty sure I hit that five hundred years ago."

With a shake of her dark head, Eleni softens her tone. "You can't give up now."

"Why not?" Kegan challenges. "Tell me why, Eleni. Honestly. I'll fight the same fights, probably the same demons, from here until the end of time. Forever."

"If you say uncle now, it will have meant nothing." Eleni struggles to find something in his eyes, her shoulders drooping with whatever she finds there.

"Newsflash El, it meant nothing!" Kegan's roar rattles the kitchen windows. "I did nothing! I followed the commands of my superior and out of loyalty or friendship, hell maybe weakness, I looked the other way while you and others did whatever you damn well pleased. Did you even think about the rest of us? The ones you condemned when you chose your love for Caelan over duty?"

Amber eyes snap with a controlled fury, Eleni's fist thumping the table. "Don't you dare put this on me."

With a shake of his head, Kegan brushes past her, tugging on a pair of boots left by the door. Sliding his arms into a hoodie, his hand rests on the door handle as he chooses his words carefully.

"I'm not blaming you, El. But spending forever paying for someone else's mistakes is a long time."

"Uh, that's my shirt." Jess says simply.

"I'm going for a ride." The door frame shakes with the force of the slam, Kegan's boots thump on each step as he picks up the tail end of the conversation.

"I fell in love too, El." Jess begins, his voice taking on a more serious note. "I think we need to admit what some of them pay for isn't entirely fair. Maybe that's why so many have gone rogue over the years. Cut him some slack." Kegan's laugh is humorless as the weight of Jess's hidden logic sinks in. *Who knew?*

"I hope you know what you're doing. Sending Colin on that field trip was reckless."

Selena lifts her eyes from the events below to meet Damien's grim expression. Squaring her shoulders, she bobs her dark head. "They need answers."

"The Council forbade the Fallen to have any contact with us."

"I'm aware. I'm also aware they can't do their job properly without all the facts." Once again, she looks down to see Kegan stride to his motorcycle a short distance away. She'll never admit it out loud, but there is a hole in her being where the Guardians used to be.

"You miss them."

It's not a question. Damien doesn't ask, he states. "Yes," sensing his rising annoyance, Selena continues. "They weren't like the others. I remember them being funny and carefree. Even Colin had a different demeanor back then. Calm with a leisure smile, ready with sound advice or a strong shoulder."

"Their difference became their downfall," Damien warns, his voice less steady than before, "be careful."

"He was already poking around. I offered a clue in direction before he could step on too many, um, toes."

"You aren't supposed to offer him anything."

"You seem especially concerned. Is there something you're not telling me?" The chances of her winding up before the council members grow with every decision she makes. Should the worse happen, nothing Damien could say would save her. She's not entirely certain he'd say anything. As her superior, her actions reflect on him as well. Selena's been careful to leave their laws intact, but even she's aware she's becoming an expert at bending them to her will.

"Don't tell me you don't have a soft spot for them."

"I won't. I remember how the Fallen used to be. Do you? If memory serves, you once thought of Kegan as your closest friend. Regarded with respect, and he was a bigger charmer than Jess ever thought of being."

"I remember, better than even you."

"Now look at him. This punishment has broken his spirit and beliefs, eroded the foundation he built for himself. All he can do is pray for it to be over."

"That was his choice to make."

"*The mischief that the two of you could get into was truly beyond belief before they transferred him to Colin's order. Can you tell me you don't have a soft spot for him under all your duty?*"

The doubt Selena plants alongside Damien's convictions doesn't last long. When she looks again, his dark eyes snap with renewed vigor, his jaw tight. "Enough." Around them the air snaps, clouds responding to the turmoil she can sense within him. "I am not here to debate with you. I only wanted to warn you. The Council is watching. If you aren't careful, they'll reel you in."

He disappears before Selena can reassure him of her intent. Sending up a silent prayer soothes over the sharp edges of her nerves enough to continue her plan. With their combined strength, the Guardians should emerge victorious. If not, it will leave her alone to answer for it all. After another prayer for guidance, she perches atop the refrigerator to watch the events unfold.

Chapter 18

With an exhale that ruffles her hair, Nora swaps out her book for a new one. Hours ago, she'd disappeared in her grandfather's room, determined to find some clue about this mysterious book. If she's honest, hiding out from the others after yesterday hadn't sounded too bad either. What initially seemed like a good way to distract herself became tedious under his vast collection of books.

Altogether disorganized, he crammed books, notes, and his mementos wherever they would fit. On a shelf with scattered biographies, she'd found the bass trophy he'd won several years back, followed by a collection of children's fiction.

During her hunt, Nora found one book she'd written in the third grade for a class project in between a book about Abraham Lincoln and the Revolutionary War. She refuses to think about the time she wasted as she sat there staring at the embossed pages riddled with typos and childlike drawings.

Her gaze lands on a leather-bound journal squeezed between two fairly generic book spines when her phone rings. As Mallory's name lights up the display, Nora's teeth nibble over her lip.

"Mal," she breathes into the phone.

"Good morning, Juju."

"I'm pretty sure I'm officially too old for nicknames." Nora mutters with a wince and rests against the wall behind her. She can't be sure how long she's been digging through books, but the pressure behind her eyes eases when she takes a break.

"*No one* outgrows the nicknames their parents give them."

"How are things?"

"Work's been busy, I meant to call sooner but I've been pulling a lot of doubles lately. Figured I'd check in and see if you're still alive."

"Oh-kay. I've been going through Grandad's things little by little. Anything I think you'd like to keep, I'm putting in a separate box for you to go through."

"Thanks, Nora. I'm not ready to see that place."

"I know. Do you know how much of a packrat he became? The man kept everything."

"Anything good?"

"Well, he framed the poem you wrote in the Ninth grade. It's hanging over his dresser as we speak."

"I'm shocked Kegan hasn't cleared all that out by now to get the place on the market."

"Mal," she sighs, "he's not like that. Him and Grandad *really* were close."

"Uh-huh." She could hear Mallory take a deep breath, exhaling slowly. "I didn't call to fight with you, Juju. I worry about you."

"I know." Nora's ears perk at the weight of exhaustion coloring Mallory's voice. "Are you okay?"

"For the most part. Influenza A is going around at work. Pretty sure I gave it an internal couch to stay on for a few days."

"Drink lots of water. Get plenty of rest, too."

"Wow. Maybe you should be the nurse and I'll be the kid wrangler."

"You'd be lucky to make it through the first day without the police hauling you away."

"True. Young kids are a snap. It's the asshole teenagers that'd get me."

"None of them are assholes, Mallory."

"Bullshit. Do you remember how bad I was as a teenager? The girls are all attitude, drama and independence with some tears and snot thrown in. Boys are suddenly ten-feet tall and bulletproof, with the sex drive of a wild stallion in a herd of willing mares."

Nora laughs until Mallory's yawn reaches her end of the phone. A glance at the phone shows the conversation has only been a few minutes. Yet, her sister sounds like it's been hours. "Did you call Dr. Lewis?"

"I'll call him tomorrow if I'm not feeling any better."

"Okay, get some sleep."

"I'm on it. And Nora?"

"Yeah?"

"Take care of you, huh? You're all I have left."

"You too Mal. Love you."

"Love you more."

Nora reminds herself how capable Mallory is to calm her worry brewing under the surface. As she tucks her phone into a pocket, a sharp rap on the door draws her attention in time to see Eleni poke her head through the meager opening.

"Hey Lovie, you've been in here for hours."

"I thought maybe I could find some answers in here."

Slipping into the room, Eleni closes the door behind her and takes a seat next to her on the floor. "Honey, I love you, and you know I adored your grandfather, but the chances he wrote any insights into life are slim."

"Life? What? I was talking about the book."

"Oh!"

"What did you think I meant?"

Eleni smiles sheepishly. "Kegan."

Nora scoffs and busies herself with stacking the books she'd went through into piles. "If I want answers about him, I won't go digging through old books. I'd ask you."

"Me? Why me?"

"Eleni, I'm not an idiot."

"I never said you are." A thin line creases Eleni's forehead.

"From the outburst I overheard this morning, I assume there's a bit more to it, though."

"A little, yes."

Her friend casts a longing glance at the door as if judging the time it would take to escape before offering a simple shrug of slender shoulders.

"Are you sure you want to know? 'Cause I'll tell you if that's what you want." Nora's jerky nod adds a shadow of resistance in Eleni's eyes, but true to her word, she stumbles forward. "Okay, here goes."

"When they sent our battalion to observe human life on earth, it became clear that many of us found them to be without logic. Raw and emotional creatures with strange habits."

"Kegan said, the array of emotions we expressed overwhelmed your kind."

Eleni pauses for a moment and cast another longing glance at the door before continuing. "That's true, but it was also your varied nature. One man or woman would sacrifice their family for their own happiness, despite their upbringing. While another would rather sacrifice themselves for family. No two humans are the same."

"Are angels?"

"In most cases they are if they exist in the same choir. Archangels differ in traits and personalities, but the rest are fairly the same. If you put a choir of angels in one room, you'll get one opinion. And you can bet your booty it'll be the logical one."

"Your regiment was different?"

"Not at first. In the beginning, we were a lot like the others. Honorable, dutiful. Over a span of countless years spent amongst your kind, your proximity changed our structure. Gradually, we experienced emotions, and many of us became mired in the quicksand associated with such things."

"So, because you felt happy or sad, they punished you?"

"Not exactly," Eleni answers with a wistful smile. "Because of emotions, we began to see the world through their eyes. Celebrated when a crop grew or when the hunters were successful. We cried with the death of a friend. Soon, we loved. I doubt any of us were quite ready for what followed."

"You mean falling?"

"I mean marriage, children, families to surround us until the warmth of Heaven became a distant memory."

"All of you?" Nora does her best to ask as nonchalantly as she can manage, but mentally, she's preparing herself to hear about Kegan's past love.

"A few clung to their soldier's duty. Refusing to allow humans' impulsive and unpredictable nature to sway their purpose. Kegan was one of them."

"But they fell anyway?"

"Our council said they were negligent in their orders. That they should've reported our transgressions, so they could mete out a just punishment. In the end, they punished Kegan and the others with the rest of us."

"Did you love someone?"

As the two friends sit, the tick of her watch thunders between them. When a wave of complex emotions stain Eleni's graceful features, it makes Nora squirm. Did she cross a line? If she delved too far into an abyss that didn't concern her, would Eleni forgive her? Squeezing Eleni's hand with hers, she's about to brush her question under the carpet when her friend answers.

"Caelan. He was a warrior in our village." Her words are so light when she speaks, Nora strains to hear them. "Arrogant and impetuous, he also wore an amiable smile. It wasn't long before my thoughts centered on him, his image plaguing my dreams. When I finally allowed myself to love him, it was the happiest I ever remember being."

"What happened to him?"

"They killed him, along with our children."

Nora gasps, her free hand flying to her mouth. "That's horrible! Was it another village?"

"I think Kegan has finished dinner by now." Her eyes full of shadows, Eleni attempts a light-hearted smile and fails before climbing to her feet.

The boys are already sitting at the table by the time Nora and Eleni arrive. Jess offers a smile that would drive most women wild. The toe-curling sensation shooting through her over Kegan's half-hearted attempt in comparison is more than a little annoying.

Eyes devour him as Nora draws closer. Damp, his chocolate brown hair appears darker than usual, his skin still slick from whatever workout he'd been doing in the garage. When he meets her eyes for one moment, the heat she finds there is scorching.

Long, skinny tendrils of his desire slip beyond her defenses, spark her nerves like flint to wood until her body thrums with its effect. Nails bite into the tender pads of her palms as she maneuvers to the one empty chair, fighting to ignore how close he is even as his unique scent floods her sense of smell. Wincing with the unexpected sharp pain exploding in her shin, Nora shoots an accusing eye to Eleni, only to be meant with a lazy grin. The look in her eyes all but screams, *you're welcome* before she casts them toward Nora's plate.

Dinner, right? Picking up a knife and fork, she digs into the contents on her plate, methodically dancing between steak, potatoes and grilled asparagus. While she's refusing to dwell on the exact level of yummy Kegan carries around with him, she feels no such qualms over the food he'd thrown together. When she lifts her head to say just that, she notices him scrolling through the music on his phone, updating his playlist.

"Why do you guys always seem to have those within arm's reach?"

"You'll have to be more specific," Kegan replies curtly, without ever looking up from his phone laying flat on the table.

Nora's voice tightens. "The earbuds."

"That would be because of the Symphony." Jess answers, gesturing to Kegan with his fork. "Some hear it more than others."

Nora's head notches to the right, as if she'll better understand Jess's reply after a different viewpoint. "The Symphony?"

"It's a constant loop of Heavenly music in our ears." Jess answers. "Some call it a gift, some a curse."

"Gift my ass," Kegan snarls, closing his playlist with a solid swipe of his thumb.

"It plays constantly, no matter what?" Nora gapes for a moment then catches herself. "Like, twenty-four, seven? What about when you sleep?"

"Every second of every day." Eleni speaks around a mouthful of steak. As if aware of how it might look to the others, she blushes and takes a moment to chew her food before continuing. "The only time it lets up is when an evil presence is within the vicinity, yet we never seem to know what that presence will be until it's trying to kill us."

"Yeah, instead of the music, we get blaring DEFCON 5 alarms that'll split your eardrums." Jess adds, holding up a wireless earbud in one mammoth hand. "Playing our own music drowns out most of the distraction."

Nora nods as she pushes asparagus around on her plate. "So, all Watchers carry them?"

Kegan is quick with a lazy grin. "Unless they want to roll the dice on early execut-"

As deafening bursts of energy snaps against the air to ricochet around the kitchen, it cuts Kegan short and separates him from his chair. The light bulb overhead brightens until she's certain it'll shatter in its socket as Kegan drags her from her seat and places her behind the wall of his back.

Jess and Eleni choke off entry to the kitchen when the overwhelming sense of oppression increases within the walls that battle to contain it all. Nora's ears strain with the need to pop as a man falls inside the living room, narrowly missing the stout coffee table.

Extending on the tips of her toes, Nora peeks around Kegan's arm to see a man sprawled across the floor. Abandoning his best impression of a broken pinata, the stranger shoves himself to his feet with a grumble, the scent of burnt hair heavy enough to pollute the kitchen with its stench.

"Shit man, you have a helluva way of announcing yourself," Kegan declares, rushing forward. "Are you okay?"

"Yeah, looks like that hurt." Jess remarks as he loosens his defensive stance and slides one of his daggers back inside his tall boot. Nora isn't sure how he armed himself before the fight.

Brushing off the dense dust covering his clothes, the stranger takes a moment to flip Jess off for his obvious observation before his whiskey-colored eyes land on her. A slow minute drags on as Nora tells herself not to flinch from his attention. "You must be Nora. I'm Colin."

"Sorry, Nora Brennan, Colin Arundel." Kegan's hand gestures to her and back.

"Arrendelle? As in Frozen?"

Colin snarls with a shudder. "Do I look like a fucking Disney character to you?"

Nora's head stutters from side to side as she takes in the newcomer.

His towering frame is closely similar to her protector. But his carries the majority of his lean muscle tightly. Handsome features carry a deadly awareness, almost as if he's prepared for anything to jump from the shadows. Dark stubble adds a level of sexy to full lips she's only ever associated with Kegan. In fact, standing next to the object of her sex-deprived obsession, the stranger's subtle flaws may as well be on full display.

"Your hair is smoking." Nora isn't sure if the dirty look he shoots in her direction is for noticing or pointing it out, but he drags a hand through its dark curls, regardless.

"So, children," Colin rubs his hands together, "what have I missed?"

Nora hangs back as the Watchers settle in the living room to bicker about which details are most important to clear away Kegan's now cold supper. As she scrapes remains into the trash, she listens to Eleni and Jess argue over the effects certain alcohol has on a Watcher before Eleni shoves Kegan under the proverbial bus regarding his control or lack thereof on his hormones. Peeking over her shoulder, she catches the promise of retribution glittering in Kegan's dark eyes.

"Wait, what alcohol did you get into that made you drunk?" Colin fishes around a pocket for a moment, scowling when the pack of cigarettes he produces is a charred mess.

"I don't know," Eleni squawks. "Ask him." With a glare, she stabs a thumb in Kegan's direction.

"It was the bottle you gave me for Christmas."

"Oh." Colin laughs. Despite the hard exterior, Nora blinks over the melodic tune his laugh carries. "I got that from Jericho."

"That figures." With a mutter, Eleni slumps back in her chair. "The shit he makes isn't any more refined than moonshine. He could've put puppy tails in it for all we know."

"Yet, you drank all of it." Kegan reminds her with a shit-eating-grin on his face.

"I want to know why Kegan gets kick ass liquor for Christmas and I don't even get a card." Arms cross Jess's chest, his pointed look aimed at the newcomer.

Colin shrugs one shoulder before tossing the charred cigarettes on the pristine coffee table. "I like him more than you."

"Told you." Kegan grins.

Jess scoffs loudly and moves on to mention a second attack that earns him a dark scowl from Kegan and a gasp from Nora. No one had even *mentioned* another attack. "Bastards," she mumbles under her breath and stacks the plates inside the sink.

"Sounds like we're in more trouble than I thought." Colin muses aloud.

"Of course we are," Nora breathes, clearing away the last of the dinner dishes, her patience beyond thin.

"What was that?"

Whirling around, Nora meets Colin's look of amusement, her hands resting on her hips. Ignoring the warmth in her cheeks, she repeats herself with a clear voice to avoid any confusion. "I said, of course we are. None of you ever come bearing good news. I should be used to it by now."

While his head rocks from the venom in her voice, Colin's full lips twitch. "You realize it's rude to eavesdrop."

"It's also rude to drop in on people uninvited." Nora snips. "And I mean *drop* in every literal sense of the word."

"Nora is having dreams," Eleni pipes in.

"I'm not a shrink, Eleni." Colin replies with a laugh.

Eleni nods in Nora's direction. "Show him, Lovie."

Tossing her eyes, Nora blows a raspberry and walks forward to show the bruise spanning the width of her forearm. His eyes sharp, Colin leans closer, his hand resting just over her skin, measuring the marks the same way Kegan had done earlier. As he draws back, she can't help but get the impression of wheels turning inside his head.

"You thinking what I am?" Colin asks.

Kegan's reply squeaks between ground teeth. "Hell yes."

Eyes like amber darken an instant before Colin's jaw hardens. "I wonder what they want with her."

"Who?" Nora asks.

"Heaven only knows, I'd wager it's nothing good. Never is with them," Kegan flings in reply, ignoring Nora's interruption.

"Them?" Nora prods. "Who's them?"

Ignoring her, Colin shakes his head. "I don't know where I'd even start asking questions here."

"Hello!" Nora waves an arm to ensure they still see her. "I'm standing right here. I don't see why you two must talk around me."

Irritation flares in Colin's eyes while Kegan's carry only concern. When he answers in a tender voice, the sound not only warms her skin, it raises her level of worry. *The only time he speaks with any sort of care is when your life is in danger.* The tiny voice in her head whispers loud enough for Nora to latch teeth to her lip.

"There aren't many choirs of angels that can enter someone's dream state. Guardian angels, Raphael and Archangels are the only ones I know of," Kegan begins. "I doubt a Guardian angel would wait so long to reveal itself, and I don't see you needing deliverance from Raphael, so that leaves one of the big seven."

"What are you dreaming about when he appears?" Eleni moves to sit on the edge of her seat.

With a gasp, Nora automatically turns her attention to her dreams that end with Kegan naked and agreeable. The memory of his six-feet-plus inches sprawling across a monstrous bed brings a flush to her cheeks and a hiccup in her breathing. The knowing smile curling across Colin's full lips brings those thoughts to a screeching halt as she attempts to recall the question. When she finds her voice, her usual light tone sounds rough and shaky to her own ears. "The book, usually."

"How very interesting," Colin replies smoothly, with a light of intrigue in his eyes that sets Nora on edge.

Chapter 19

After Colin leaves the same way he arrived, with less crash, the Watchers sit discussing everything they'd learned. Excusing herself from the conversation, Nora ducks out to the back porch to enjoy the cigarette she tells herself she isn't craving. Still, when nicotine floods her system with the first long drag, her shoulders relax while her mind races.

A week ago, her life was simple. Maybe a touch boring in some areas, but overall, she was content with it. Now, its shredded remains lay squarely at the Fallen's feet. Because of their inability to keep state secrets, this real-life horror show squashed the hell out of everything else. Admitting it, even to herself, sets her teeth on edge.

Exhaling, she sulks as every well-laid plan escapes along coils of white smoke. The night sky allows each one to hang for a moment before dissipating with no show of remorse.

As minutes tick by, the tension in her body lessens with each drag. On the horizon, darkness cloaks the large copse of trees surrounding the property under a dense blanket. Without the warmth of the sun, the growing breeze chills from the approaching storm, brooding within the air. Overhead, hundreds of stars glimmer with a white glow to bring a touch of magic one rarely views in the city.

Bracing her elbows on the railing, Nora allows her thoughts to drift from her current situation to the conversations she'd had with Kegan and Eleni. When he'd told her why his kind fell from Heaven, Nora hadn't detected an ounce of bitterness in his voice. However, his outburst with Eleni made it clear he's harboring some resentment for his punishment.

Try as she might, she's unable to comprehend the level of betrayal he must've felt. Stripped of his wings, forced to live among the very species that had enamored so many of them, branded as a renegade for eternity. *Branded*!

Her sob claws at her throat at the same time a tear threatens to slip free. If she's honest with herself, she can't help but excuse some of his ogre-like behavior.

"He's still an ass," she grumbles, crushing out her cigarette before tucking it into a pocket to dispose of later. *Part of you enjoy's it*. Her inside voice snickers. "A small part. Microscopic."

When the wind kicks up, to pull at her crocheted sweater, Nora clutches the sides together to huddle deeper into its paltry shelter. Goosebumps pepper her arms after a series of shivers trickle across her back. Winter will be here soon, then Christmas. Her heart twists with the hope she'll be able to celebrate with Mallory like she does every year. "Don't even go there," she warns, slipping inside the cabin as the storms shrieks its fury.

Kegan notes the precise moment Nora returns from the porch. In that instant, his skin tightens and breathing becomes difficult. The regular rhythm of his heart turns into a mariachi band and she hasn't even drawn close.

Clenching his teeth together, he tries to concentrate on the laptop's small screen and whatever Eleni is pointing to. Squeezing his eyes shut, he opens them to read the information for a third time, cursing when he still can't retain it. Shoving the computer across the table towards her, he pulls in a tight breath.

While Nora had been outside, Jess had the idea of tracking the bloodlines tied to the book. The spark of hope he felt after locating the Brennan line soon fades under the wallop of reality when every other search turns up nothing. Now that she's within a stride's reach once again, he finds his focus non-existent. *That's not true.* No, he's laser-focused, just not on the things he should be.

Instead of narrowing down potential lines, one mortal woman hijacks his thoughts. From where he sits, he can smell the nicotine and kicks himself for not only noticing but for the uptick his pulse gives in response. She wants to put herself in an early grave. That's her business. *It's your job to make sure she doesn't. No. It's my job to keep the demons from killing her and taking the book for themselves,* he argues. His principles are far from convinced.

"Hey Lovie," Eleni calls, lifting her eyes from the computer screen. "Jess has an idea for tracking the second bloodline."

"It would be easier if we knew what name we were looking for," Jess admits with a rueful grin.

"Great." Nora's lighthearted tone, full of charm and mischief, is gone. In its place, Kegan picks up a roughness of churning emotions broiling just under her tough exterior.

If he'd been a better man, he'd put himself in her shoes and note the devastating effect all this is having on her life. *Pity that man died a long time ago.* What remains of the man he used to be is enough to get him from one day to the next until someone reviews his petition. After that, maybe he'll find a small semblance of peace.

"Feel like helping me go through some ancestry records?" No sooner are the words out of Eleni's mouth and Kegan is suppressing the urge to kick at her from under the table.

"No. I think I'll take a bath and head to bed." The faint sound of Nora's feet shuffling across the bare wood floors leaves him fighting for air.

True, he wanted her far away from him, but now it's all he can do to keep himself in his chair and not stalk after her. His jaw tightens so hard against the demand of his body, he prepares himself for the sound of cracking bone. *W*

hat's the matter with you? I don't know, his mind screams. Even with the daunting task in front of him, all he can think about is Nora, naked, in his bathtub.

Would she fully submerge herself? Let the heat from the water soothe the chaos she's battling within herself? Her short frame will extend until her painted toes reach the other side of the deep basin and he can almost hear the sigh she'll release. Is her hair up? Free from the water? Or does it fall to float around her ivory skin in a sharp contrast? Painfully, Kegan shifts the image to explore the hidden valley her body carries until it reaches the soft curve where ribs meet breast. Pinching the bridge of his nose with thumb and forefinger, he shakes loose the image and adjusts the fit of his jeans.

"I seriously hope you know what you're doing," Eleni grumbles.

"If we narrow down the surname we need, we'll be able to build the family tree within a few years. More or less." When Kegan looks up from Jess's chicken scratch penmanship to meet Eleni's glare, one eyebrow lifts as he sits back in his chair. "What's wrong with you now?"

Jess chuckles while his fingers tap over the flat keyboard. "I'm just taking a wild stab at it, but I think she's referring to Nora."

With a deep frown, Kegan lifts a hand. "What about her?"

Faint traces of amusement flicker in Jess's eyes as his lips twitch until he turns his attention to Eleni. "And people say I'm the dense one." Jabbing a thumb in Kegan's direction, he continues. "Are you sure Colin said he knew what he was doing?" Eleni nods, her expression darkening with each passing second. When he finally turns his gaze back at him, Kegan notes a slight shadow emerging in his pear-green eyes. "You, my friend, are in some serious trouble."

"What are you talking about? I swear most days, you don't even know," Kegan growls. "You just babble along until something sounds good."

"Nora!" Eleni and Jess shout in unison.

Kegan blinks. His dark head rocks backward for a heartbeat before he glances over a shoulder to see if she'll come running from the bathroom. He refuses to examine the large part of him that hopes she will. Clad only in a towel, to ward off the arctic air on wet skin.

When she doesn't, he wrestles with the pinch around his heart. Tearing his eyes from the hall, his words fall from his lips on the grumble he can't swallow. "You don't need to shout. My hearing is perfect."

"I swear, you're so fucking clueless." Eleni drops her pen with a snap.

"I am keeping my distance from her, El. None of us can afford the distraction," Kegan reasons. "And I will *not* risk the disaster sure to follow."

Eleni snorts. "Has it occurred to you that Nora may not like to hear the word disaster associated with getting too close to her?"

"You know what I mean." Heat creeps under Kegan's shirt to the back of his neck. Shifting in his chair, he searches for a comfortable position when all his body wants to do is respond to the need that carves a hole in his stomach at the mere mention of her name.

"Dude, you have woman troubles. And unless time has struck you stupid, those are much worse than anything further north." Jess jabs a finger toward the ceiling for good measure, bringing a scowl to Kegan's mouth.

Pushing to his feet, Kegan beings to pace. "I've never had woman troubles and Nora is just fine."

"Never? Really?" His blonde head shifts from Kegan to Eleni, eyes wide with confusion. "What am I doing wrong?"

"We don't have enough time left to explain all the things you do wrong," Eleni deadpans.

"Whatever. Look Buddy, it's simple." Jess begins, "If they say *fine*, or *nothing*, in an argument, worry. If she says something like *forget it*, or *I got it*, duck and cover. If she tells you it *doesn't matter*, then you better pray hard, because you can bet your baby-makers it matters."

"You're an idiot." His tone indifferent, Kegan gives his head a shake, retakes his seat and narrows his attention to the list in front of him. Even as he blows off their concern, he can't help but wonder if they're right to be worried. It's been a long time since he'd gotten close to anyone other than Brody.

Just because he believes things are fine, doesn't mean she does. But if either of his friends expect him to inquire on her feelings, they don't know him as well as they think. Every part of him would opt for being pig-roasted in Hell for eternity before he opens that can of worms.

Tossing from one position to another, Nora peeks at the bedside clock with a whimper. For hours now, sleep eludes her, her head full of too many things to allow any sort of calm. More than once she'd contemplated how all this will play out, and what sort of life she'll have after. The nausea that follows such thoughts leaves her battling with a wave of dizziness. Fisting the chunky comforter, Nora pulls in a slow breath and directs her thoughts away from the promise of a bleak future.

Nearly two hours ago, the house fell quiet, Ezio's soft snores as he slumbers beside her unrealistically loud to her ears. Her bedsheets are scratchy and uncomfortable underneath her as her feet brush side to side. Each wrinkle they encounter adding to a level of awareness until Nora's ready to scream her frustration. *What is wrong with me?*

Throwing her back to the clock, Nora adjusts her pillow. A hand rubs over her blanket, as searches for sleep. Each minute that passes draws her body tight. *Is he already fast asleep? Thankful for a lull in the chaos that's taken over his existence?* With the thought, an image of him assaults her senses as she wonders how he sleeps.

Does he wear pajamas? Or nothing? Maybe he settles on something in between? The idea of all those glorious inches open for exploration leaves her fingers clenching into tight fists, her chest tight.

Giving up any pretense of sleep, she eases the blankets away from her and perches on the edge of the bed. On the floor, her toes sink into the plush carpet and her hands grip the side of the mattress. Standing, Nora brushes aside the bundle of nerves that stretches and contracts inside her, latching onto the decision she's made.

Crossing to the three-drawer dresser, she studies her reflection in the mirror that rests across its polished surface. "You can do this," she mumbles, waving a hand across the cold sweat covering her bare skin.

Her movements are slight, and with great care as she undresses, folding her t-shirt and shorts before laying them on the foot of her bed. Pulling the band from her hair, Nora's fingers gently tug her hair free from its braid to drag a brush through its length. Once it shines under the silken moonlight filtering into the room, she arranges it strategically in front of her. There are too many thoughts pin-balling for her to nail down a specific one, so she shoves them aside and steps out into the narrow hall.

It's only a handful of steps to his door, but she takes them at a snail's pace, her feet silent on the floor. For a heartbeat, she pauses outside his door, her palms damp over the probable outcome.

Nora had never considered herself forward, or frisky. Delving into the deep end of the pool, she struggles with the itch in her limbs to run back to the safety of her room and lock herself in. Instead, she turns the handle, half-expecting it to be locked and dead-bolted.

When it inches inward noiselessly, she drags in a lungful of air before crossing the threshold. On another side of the cabin, the moonlight that streams through his windows gleams across a tall dresser on one wall, a monster-sized bed on another. Teeth sink against her lower lip and fingers curl as she shuts the door behind her.

Chapter 20

"What are you doing?" Kegan sputters in a hushed voice, causing her to jump. Whatever confidence she'd been feeling to get herself this far must've fled, leaving her to resemble a deer in the headlights. Not that he studies her reaction long, he's too busy burning the image of her into a memory so stout, it'll carry him through however many years he has left.

A dull buzz fills his ears as he takes in every dip, valley and plateau of her body. She's gorgeous, standing there, shadows drawn to her glow. Lush hair to rival the richest sunset falls in wavy curls around her. While she pushed the majority behind her, she lay enough in front to cover her breasts, lighting a fire under his intrigue.

Light, the waning moon spills into the room, casts shadows on the creamy skin of her stomach. Delicate, it dances over the flare of her hips and curves of her calves, caressing their roundness. Laying there frozen, lust grips him so tightly it unfurls within his chest. With a hiss, Kegan grips the light sheet covering him to keep himself from crossing the yawning distance between them and hitches one of his knees up to hide his reaction.

What is it about this woman that encourages his body to respond like some horny teenager? Unlike every other woman he's met, he's unable to locate any form of control. Even now, as his mind catalogues every reason he should send her away, his body screams for the pleasure he'll find among her lush curves.

"What are you doing here?" He demands once more, his voice thick and rough with the thirst coursing through his veins. Hunger ignites his skin, settling into the pit of his stomach to burn slow and hot. Her words are light and breathless when she finds her voice, forcing him to strain to hear them.

"I'm tired of waiting around for you to decide if you want me."

His heart pounds, deafening his mind. He holds his breath to calm the adrenaline and oxygen flooding his body. The rush of euphoria and fear is potent enough to leave him dizzy. *Is he ready to confess his attraction? Can he live with himself when their time is over and he becomes the primary source of her pain? Would her memories of him serve as a balm or a bard?* His decision to not risk it is fast and secure. "Go back to bed."

His dismissal notches her chin in that stubborn tilt he's learning all too well. Instead of moving towards the door, she simply shakes her head. The movement draws the curtain of hair shielding her breasts to shift insignificantly.

"Go back to bed, Nora." His voice sharpens, his mouth dry. Again she refuses, watching him, her vibrant eyes smoldering with her own desire. "I could always cry rape. Bring the others running in here."

"Yes, you could," she concedes, her lips twitching with a ghost of a smile.

With a foul curse on his tongue, Kegan throws off the covers and stomps across the gap. Fingers bite harder than he intends on the soft flesh of her upper arm, her muffled gasp reaching his ears as he spins her toward the door. If his grip hurts her, she doesn't show it. A blush creeps over her skin with his blatant rejection, her teeth nibbling worrisome across her mouth. When he looks into her face, the emotions churning in her eyes, shatters his resolve. "Aw hell."

On a sigh, he lowers his mouth to hers. The brush of his lips, soft and light. Too much pressure will ignite him like a match doused in gasoline. Heat blooms inside him, burning into his limbs until it reaches his core. There, it quickly pools into a raging inferno within his chest. Framing her face in his hands, he samples her honeyed lips again. The contact rips control from his grasp, awakening a blaze of lust and wanton desire.

As he breaks contact, Nora draws in a breath of air. When he nibbles across the curve of her jaw, marveling at the softness of her skin, a moan escapes her. Her nails score slightly along thick forearms, to latch onto his broad shoulders as he buries hands in her hair. Delving deeper, he drags one hand down her back toward the base of her spine. Her moan joins his groan as she arches against him.

Just as her eyes grow heavy, he pulls back to meet her gaze, hunger nipping at his heels. Releasing his hold on her, he plants his hands on the wall on either side of her and shivers when he catches the growl slipping from her throat. Counting to ten, Kegan struggles to find coherent thought hiding amidst the primal need. His voice uneven, he forces the words from his lips. "You need to be sure. I won't stop this time."

"Promise?"

Nerves fire simultaneously as she drags a hand to the back of his neck, holding onto him as she stretches on the tips of her toes. With a heavy sigh, she claims his mouth before he can utter the words that will break the spell between them. Slow and lazy, her lips probe at his. Their sweetened taste falls to the wayside by how supple they are under his. His breath sucks in sharply as he engages the lock on the bedroom door.

Setting his jaw, he doesn't hide the intensity in his dark eyes as they consume all five-feet and change of her full figure. The sight of her lips swollen and wet from his attention lodges a lump in his throat. Breath stalls as Kegan calls on every strand of control he has left to lift her gently from the floor and lay her across his bed. The tremble in his legs plays on a loop as he lowers himself beside her.

"I'm going to take my time," he promises, his voice heavy with a desire that steels his breath as he brushes his lips across the slope of her collarbone.

True to his word, he takes his sweet time exploring every inch of her, first with eyes, then hands, followed by lips, tongue and teeth until she's squirming, her soft sounds of pleasure filling his ears. "You're so fucking beautiful," he rasps.

Wedging a cotton-clad thigh between hers, she whimpers as Kegan applies pressure against her core, the sound nearly his undoing. Small hands roam across his back, her nails biting at his shoulders as he pays homage to one breast, then the other. The gentle brush of his tongue over sensitive nipples brings Nora's back off the bed, desperate for more.

Kegan's deep chuckle rumbles inside his chest before he draws back to torture her further with his fingers. Moaning desperately, Nora twists and turns her body deeper into his touch. Her responsiveness making him second-guess his ability to keep his promise. Teeth set as he drags in as much oxygen as he can.

With a hiss, he replaces his thigh with his fingers. Leaning over her, Kegan devours her mouth while his fingers strum the chords at her core until she's panting beneath him. He swallows every plea squeaking beyond her lips until her teeth catch his lips to jerk his body taunt.

Continuing the slow torture, he stokes her hunger until her body trembles, nipping at her ear when her nails bite at his shoulders. Her body tightens, her back arching against the bed as she lifts her hips deeper into his hand a second before she's erupting with her release. As she rides the waves of pleasure coursing inside her, Kegan buries his face against her neck, inhaling the minty scent of her hair.

Before he can locate his composure, the feel of her hand cupping him through his sleep pants locks his jaw, his arms quivering from supporting his own weight. "Greedy little minx. Patience is a virtue." Was that his voice? He can't seem to recognize it, heavy with lust.

"I wasn't aware this was a lesson," a growl accompanies her rough voice. "Maybe you've gotten rusty."

The laugh that escapes him rumbles through his chest, easing the quaking in his limbs, temporarily. "I'll show you rusty."

Easing off her long enough to strip out of his pants, Kegan resettles with a steel grip on his restraint. Fingers glide over her satin smooth skin as he dips to tease another kiss from her lips, her moan of response quick. The soft whimpers of her hunger prod at him as he wraps an arm around her hips to drag her closer.

Bracing his weight on an elbow, he buries himself into her welcoming heat. With a tiny groan, Nora lifts her hips to bring him deeper inside her, building the pressure beyond his control. As he moves in long, languid strokes, Kegan drinks in everything, engraving this moment to a memory that eternity can't tarnish.

She fits within him perfectly; her smaller frame tucked neatly into his. Every rock of his hips sends Nora spiraling closer to a precipice, her face tucked against his neck. Clamping his teeth tightly, he struggles to contain the liquid fire spreading through his body to consume every thought.

When her body explodes around him, he gasps for air. Burying his face in her hair, he counts to ten in a sad attempt at restraint. With the gnawing urge settling across him, Kegan realizes this is as close to Heaven as he can hope to be. Too late, he understands that it's close enough.

Fingers bite into her hips as he lifts her for one last thrust. Pleasure tears free, similar to the cry ripping from his throat. With a soft whimper, Nora pulls him close, her body welcoming his ecstasy with a shudder. A full minute passes before Kegan hauls in a shaky breath and rolls over, taking her with him. Nestled into his side, her chest rises and falls unsteadily. He tells himself he can stomach the look of regret on her soft features, prepares himself for the blow.

Lifting lashes carefully, he looks into her upturned face, amazed. Those same eyes that have haunted his dreams now sparkle with satisfaction. The corner of her lips upturned. Searching her face, he finds no regret or uncertainty for the moment they just shared.

The observation renews an ache in his groin for round two. Skimming a hand along her soft curves, he grins when she trembles with renewed awareness. In an instant, he's lifting her up to straddle his hips. One hand sinks into the curtain of hair that whispers across the tops of his thighs, and he palms her neck to bring her mouth closer.

Without a word, she rocks her hips just enough to bury him to the hilt within her lush folds. His moan of pleasure disappears in her mouth as his body tenses and strains with the hunger she feeds so effortlessly. Her soft chuckle vibrates against him a second before she's nipping at his bottom lip, her hips tilting in such a way it sends a tremor all the way through his legs.

The weight of her hair falls around him when she leans forward to caress the tattoo on his neck with her tongue. Her smile cheeky, she peeks up at him from under the veil of thick lashes. "I plan on tracing every inch of this before the night is over."

Lord, have mercy!

Safely inside the tree-line, Adriel observes the cabin. Careful not to solidify completely to set off the wards the Angel put up, he gathers information on the human. The interesting turn the situation takes gives him a little leverage. Set on a new plan, he slips away, only to reappear in the small town a few miles away.

Celeste uses a thumb to rub at the headache forming as she locks the front door behind her. With dawn an hour out and sleep eluding her, she tackles her day earlier than usual. Though slight, the cool breeze runs its icy fingers along her face, slipping up under the light jacket she grabbed on her way out.

Fall is over, soon winter will be upon them. She makes a mental note to have the plumbing checked in the trailer before it turns too cold and starts down the worn path leading to the back of her small store. She isn't six feet from the back door when something grabs her attention.

Scanning the darkness, she searches for the thing that causes an uptick in her heart and the wave of apprehension settling around her shoulders. Eyes strain and ears tune while she taps her thumb and forefinger together. On more than one occasion she meant to replace the store's back light and its outdated meager glow, but like most things, it falls low on her list of priorities. After scrubbing her clammy hands down the front of her jeans, she forces one foot in front of the other.

"Now I know how gazelles feel," she mutters. With the house further away than the store, it makes more sense for her to push forward, but she second guesses her decision with each step. The sound of a twig snapping from somewhere behind her vibrates her spine. A half turn on the balls of her feet brings her in line with the sound, but searching the layers of shadows turns up nothing.

"Good morning, Celeste."

Whirling around, she takes a step back to see a figure sitting rather nonchalantly on the few steps leading to the store. Polite and articulate, his voice rings with sophistication. Yet, he appears nowhere near the part. Despite the cool temperatures, he lounges on the rough cement wearing black jeans and a dark shirt he leaves open at the collar. His scuffed leather jacket drapes over one knee as he studies her with peculiar sea-blue eyes.

"H-how do you know my name?"

"Does it matter? I am Adriel," he says effortlessly, standing to his full height several inches above her. "I know many things about you." His first step towards her sets off alarm bells, leaving Celeste to search for a quick exit. "I have no intention of hurting you."

"Intention, huh?" One step backwards, and another inches her that much closer to her trailer. "That's a loophole word. You use it to reassure me while leaving your options open."

"I suppose that's true." Never once does his voice raise above the slow cadence he uses to dull her senses, encouraging a false sense of security. "I won't hurt you. How's that?"

"What do you want?" Any other time the walk from store to home and home to store seems so quick, Celeste barely starts the journey before it's over. Now, it might as well be another country for the progress she's making.

"To help."

"Help what?"

"You, of course."

"Oh, of *course*." Celeste smirks. "You don't strike me as the charitable type."

"I don't do charity," he says, his tone flat. "A favor for a favor."

The ease with which he speaks strangely quiets her nerves, lulling her fear into skepticism. When he circles her, his steps create a harmony in time with her heart. It takes a great deal of effort to focus on what he's asking and not what he's doing. "What kind of favor?"

"I can give your mother her health back."

"That isn't possible."

"For me," he pauses, "it is."

"For you? What are you then? Some sort of faith healer?" She lifts her chin at his sudden bark of laughter, her eyes rolling when it continues for more than a few seconds. "Or not."

"Nothing I do is based on faith. I can help her. It's that simple."

"In exchange for what, my soul?"

"Your soul doesn't interest me."

Is she really considering this? It all sounds insane and impossible, based on some B rated SciFi movie. Still, her mother's oncologist gave her mother three months, nearly seven weeks ago. Time is running out.

As if plucking her thought straight from her head, Adriel steps in front of her, sincerity lining his Spartan-like features. "The question isn't, why would you, but why wouldn't you?"

"What will I have to do?"

"Oh, it's rather simple, I promise." He draws a few lines over his chest, full lips hinting at a ghost of a smile. "Cross my heart."

Chapter 21

It's well after dawn by the time Nora drifts off to the steady sound of Kegan breathing. It isn't long before his room changes into one she's never seen before.

Beyond the covered openings that serve as windows, hard rain falls as if Heaven itself weeps.

Somehow, she knows something bad happened here. She can't locate where the memory comes from, but Nora is as sure of it as her own name.

While the moonless sky drenches the land in shadows, wrath washes over the stone manor and its surrounding village. Wave after wave of violence rips sleeping figures from their beds, spilling their blood across rough floors of packed earth and hard stone. The whole thing is over in minutes in an event that leaves countless dead and only two alive.

One lays forgotten, nestled inside a stout cradle near the foot of an extra wide bed.

Bundled in a coarse wool blanket to ward off the chill from the rain, one small fist slips free to shake with its growing cries. Tears fall over chubby cheeks red with distress. A pair of brown eyes study her desperately, begging for human contact.

On the floor next to the cradle, a set of parents lay dead. Their spilled blood stains the stones, rendering them helpless to offer comfort to the small child. Assuming his age to be less than a year, the child couldn't possibly comprehend the events leaving him an orphan. "It's the cruelty in the air it's reacting to," she murmurs, more for herself than anyone else.

"Hush, hush now, M'Lord," an elderly maid croons as she scoops up the bundle of blankets, pressing the babe to her bosom. "Frannie's got ye." Only once the child quiets with the occasional hiccup does she turn. The motion shifts Nora's attention to the beautiful man who's been haunting her dreams.

Unaware of her presence, he whispers something for only the maid to hear. As the two talk, Nora instinctively rubs at the fading bruises spanning her left forearm. After a bob of her head that drops several strands of gray hair across her brow, the maid accepts the leather pouch and heavy medallion with an awkward curtsy. Ensuring the blanket bundles the babe tightly, she runs from the keep.

Unfazed by the rain drenching her frail form, the woman puts some distance between them and the dead left behind. More than once Nora wraps her arms around herself to ward off the chill that never quite reaches her bones.

Keeping pace with the retreating figure proves difficult as they wind through a grove of tall trees only to climb a fat hill and dart across the meadow to a small thicket of bramble bushes. Several times,

Nora loses her footing on the slick grass, opening the distance between them as she rights herself.

Never once does the maid look back, not even when she reaches the wide steps of a neighboring keep. Deep lines wrinkle her weathered face as she explains the child is now an orphan, pleading with the Laird to offer his home.

Persuading the stoic man seems like a daunting task, but the small woman beside him accepts the babe with a kind smile. Relief cascades across the maid's ancient features as she presses the leather pouch into the Laird's hands.

With a look that takes years off her face, she hangs the medallion around the babe's neck. The long chain drapes over slight shoulders until the scrolling metalwork rests on his stomach. None of them are ready for the dagger she pulls out of her cloak and without a moment of hesitation, plunges it into her own heart.

The sharp ring of an alarm shatters Nora's dream, throwing her back into reality. Blinking against the remnants of sleep, she rubs a finger over her eyes to dispel the image of the maid committing suicide. Even from under the warmth of the blankets, she shivers from the icy rain on her skin. The scent the fallen leaves and the harsh coppery scent of blood clings to her skin.

With a shudder, Nora reaches across the empty bed and silences the alarm, her ears picking up the sound of the shower turning off in the adjoining bathroom. Just like that, her dreams fade with the image of Kegan under the hot spray and all those golden inches of bare skin.

Rolling, she flops onto the pillow that carries the scent of his soap. "What is wrong with me?" Sex has never ruled her life before meeting this man. Now she thinks of nothing but. "Get a grip," she whispers, giving her head a shake as if clearing an etch-a-sketch.

"Sorry. I forgot to turn those off."

Tilting her head, Nora cranes her neck to get an eyeful of Kegan wearing nothing but a towel.

To her, it appears as if every inch of his six-foot-five frame is molded from hot metal. His wide shoulders sent a thrill through her the night before, dwarfed by this man. His narrow waist and hips barely keep the towel in place, encouraging him to clasp the terry cloth in one hand. Choking down a groan, she finds her voice.

"I needed to get up, anyway."

"Is that so?" Crossing over to the bed, Kegan presses a kiss to one bare shoulder, the scruff of stubble shaved smooth this morning. Twisting, she sinks her hands into his wet hair and guides his mouth to hers.

This time, her shiver has nothing to do with imaginary rain as his hands roam under the blankets to cup one breast. Not even her moan of pleasure can drown out her sparked curiosity when her fingertips graze the raised brand on his scalp. Like before, he freezes against her, breath still as he draws back a fraction of an inch.

Nora chooses her next words with great care, her voice tender as she searches his face. "Will you tell me about this?" In his dark eyes, a storm brews.

"I already did."

"Not entirely."

"The Council ordered us all branded before we completed the fall."

"Council?"

Kegan frowns and takes a seat on the edge of the bed. "Think of it as an *unbiased government*." The way his lips curl at the end of his explanation leads Nora to believe it's anything but unbiased.

"Why would they order you branded?"

"So that others would see it and know of our shame."

"Shame for what?" Fixing the blankets across her chest, Nora leans back against his many pillows, smiling when he shifts with her to tuck her body against his heavy frame.

"We spent so many years around humanity that many forgot or made the choice to forget, our rules. Many became derelict in their duties. Brought before the Council, they meant us to answer for our crimes. Judged as rogues, they carried out our punishments swiftly, sentencing us to eternity amongst the creatures we envied."

"You envied *us*?"

His chuckle is soft and humorless as he brushes a thumb up and down the curve of her shoulder. "I can't speak for everyone, but for me, it was the emotions your kind are privy to. The vibrancy in which you live. Even your horrible experiences run so deep that for a long time, I couldn't imagine it. As many of us began experiencing emotions in ourselves, we became addicts."

"And that's bad?"

"Maybe not in theory, but definitely in practice. What you need to understand is they made us to be impartial, a silent spectator for all things human. Before we knew what was happening, many had formed friendships, teaching things we shouldn't have."

"Eleni says she fell in love."

"Caelan," he answers with a nod. "She wasn't the only Watcher to fall prey to such powerful emotions. Many of us took husbands or wives. Had children."

"If you all fell as a unit, then what happened to the children?"

When he finally answers, the despair she hears in his voice brings a rash of goosebumps to her skin. "One by one, Heaven erased them."

"Erased them? What does that even mean?"

"The Council ordered their Seraph's to hunt them down and dispose of them. Husbands, wives, entire families slaughtered in one swoop of *justice*."

"Justice?!"

"They weren't natural, Nora. Yes, children and therefore innocent. But they had no hope of co-existing without ruling over man."

"Everything in my being argues against slaughtering children."

"I understand. It's part of who you are. But what if just one Nephilim brought pain and suffering to your people? Drunk on power and entitlement, it destroys everything in its path. Could you condemn a natural-born child to live under that kind of tyranny?"

"I suppose not." Minutes tick by as Nora wrestles with the question riding on the tip of her tongue. She tells herself it was a long time ago, and it doesn't matter. One breath, then two as she studies the hard slope of his jaw. Before she can turn tail and run from it, the words rush from her lips. "Did you have a family?"

"No." Dragging a thumb along her cheek, Kegan meets her look with an intensity that leaves a throb in her stomach. "There were humans I cared for. Many, I considered friends. But none before you invoked such emotions in me." Her chest tightens with his admission, but before Nora can push any further, the rumbling of her stomach fills the quiet. "I think I've kept you in bed long enough. How 'bout some breakfast?"

The question is barely out of his mouth when he's out of bed, eliminating any hope of temptation. On his way to the dresser, his towel drops for a clean pair of jeans. Her groan of appreciation strangles in her throat at the sight of him. From where she sits, she studies the tattoo that starts at his neck, wraps across the expanse of his back, and over roped muscles to settle against the opposite hipbone. A warm flush heats her skin as she recalls following each graceful line with her tongue. And the sounds of pleasure he made. All too soon, a clean t-shirt sufficiently covers all but the trails along his neck.

Scowling her displeasure, Nora chides him for the quick striptease before climbing out of his bed as naked as she arrived. Instantly, her light complexion carries a pink hue as she looks anywhere but at him and scrambles for his discarded shirt. Shrugging the thin material across her shoulders, Nora lets the tails graze at mid-thigh as she buttons each button.

Rolling one sleeve, then the other, she looks up to meet Kegan's voracious expression. All he has to do is look at her with heat pooling in his eyes and she knows, without a doubt, he wants her. The monster inside her rears its head, awake and hungry. No sooner does she note the lazy grin twitching across his lips before she launches herself into his arms.

Kegan catches Nora with ease as her legs wrap around his waist. One hand clasps her to his chest as he turns to brace her against the wall. Using his body weight to pin her there, he focuses on the buttons of her shirt. He grins as her mouth nips its way across his jaw, squirming under his roaming hands.

One hand dips down to squeeze her ass while the other works one nipple into a hard nub. A moan leaks through her lips, its sound shooting straight to his gut. Now that they've crossed the invisible line, his hunger grows quickly into an insatiable ache. "We're going to hell, *mo chridhe*."

She rocks her hips forward; her chuckle vibrating against his chest. With a whimper of need, she peels the shirt from him in one smooth pull. Her purr kicks his lust into overdrive as she runs her hands across his skin, leaving a trail of heat in her wake. "But what a way to go."

Murmuring his agreement into the crook of her neck, Kegan tastes the salt on her skin. Palming her other breast, a hiss sneaks through his teeth when she tugs on the zipper of his jeans. Her growl of desire stutters the beat of his heart, ceasing all thought aside from losing himself within her depths. As he spills into her waiting hand, Kegan's legs give a shudder before he claims her mouth in a kiss that leaves them both breathless.

Wasting no time, Nora guides him to the center of her body. Rough fingers grip the curve of her ass to lift her higher against the wall. Breath stalls in time for him to sink into her heat, his groan of pleasure ripping beyond his throat. While their combined sounds of pleasure dull the sound of someone trying the handle, the frantic banging pierces through.

"Go away," he roars, teeth set on edge, with Nora writhing in place. The intentional tilt of her hips brings him deeper within her until his eyes roll back.

"Nora's bed is empty. I can't find her." The thick door muffles some of the panic in Eleni's voice, but not all.

"She's with me." Grinding the words through his teeth, Kegan moves his hips in long strokes. In one breath she whimpers, in another, she growls with frustration. Fingers scrabble across his back for purchase, one hand snaking up to give his hair a tug.

He faintly registers the small *oh*, Eleni responds with before he wraps a hand in Nora's long curls, jerking her head back an instant before he plunges into her core. The wail of pleasure he drives from her steals his breath and draws his balls tight. Just like that, his focus shifts to prioritize her orgasm before he finds his. *God willing*.

"Good morning, Sir. Rome is waiting for you in your office."

Melchom's mood blackens with the mention of his next meeting. After the last couple of days, his hands itch to throttle someone. He's not even picky about who that someone is. With a mumble of thanks to George, he searches for an inner calm as he opens the door to his office.

Standing near the bookcase, Rome feigns interest in the several tomes lining the shelves. Melchom registers the demon's steady heartbeat from the doorway as his eyes narrow in on the aloof stature. Either the demon has been spending lots of time in Hollywood, or like the others, he's clueless about recent events. If his suspicions are correct, Rome will slip up at some point. Melchom can only hope that day is today.

"Have a seat." Slipping behind the sizeable desk, Melchom lowers himself into the leather chair with a small sigh. When Rome remains rooted in place, he gestures to a chair directly across from him before shuffling loose papers into a workable pile.

"I'd rather stand."

"What makes you think I give two shits what you'd rather do? Sit your ass down. I talk up to no one, least of all you," he snarls. As Rome trudges his way to the designated chair, Melchom mentally makes a mark as strike one. Two more and he can use the demon for the punching bag he always should've been.

"Why have you summoned me?"

"Something has caught my attention. I'm wondering if you know anything."

"Something?" Lava-like eyes widen as Rome sits back in his chair. "Like what?"

"Surely you've felt the disturbances all over our realm." Melchom arches a brow. *How had the demon not noticed the fluctuation?* One finger taps on the now empty surface of his desk, his curiosity piqued. "The scale is tipping back and forth, and I'd like to know the cause."

"Why ask me?"

"You're the first asshole that came to mind." He wasn't, but he'll choke before Melchom utters anything to the contrary.

"I have done nothing to your precious balance." As if to emphasize his innocence, Rome shifts his attention to neatly manicured nails.

"It isn't my balance you should concern yourself with. Tip the scales too far in one direction and I'll be the least of your worries." Melchom's tone takes on a hard edge as he forces Rome to meet his stern gaze. "That is a promise." Strike two, he ticks off while reclining in his chair.

"I'm not the one messing with them, so why should I worry?"

"If you insist." Melchom stands from his chair and edges the desk, muscles compressed with the need for a good fight. "I've given you a chance to get ahead of this. If it is you, there are no laws forbidding any reprisal, I deem justified. You think your existence sucks now? Wait until I nail your ass to my wall."

"Is that all?"

With a wide grin, Melchom uses the toe of his boot to tip Romes' chair, forcing the demon to look up at him. "Is that all? What?"

"*Master.*"

Chapter 22

"As long as we keep Nora and the translator out of reach, the book is worthless to them," Colin confirms for the second time since Kegan put the call on speaker.

"That won't be easy," Jess chimes in from his stance at the patio door. "It's not like protecting honey from Pooh, you know."

"From who?"

"Jeez, Colin! Watch a fucking cartoon once in a while."

Nora grins, hearing Colin's scornful snicker as she sets a cup of fresh coffee in front of Kegan. The look he rakes over her in return steals her breath and knots her stomach. "Do we know how to locate this translator yet?"

"Azrael sent me an image of their family crest. I've asked him to look into a few of the names Jess emailed me." Kegan swipes at the incoming text message as Colin continues. "Your family bound the pages Nora. With the help of Michael, they placed the enchantment. Which is why it must remain within your bloodline."

"And the other bloodline?"

"Azrael couldn't find much on them. There's a rumor some survived long enough to change their name and flee to Europe. But so far, nothing concrete."

As the phone displays the image Colin sent over, a chill drags along her spine. The only other time she's seen this precise metalwork was in a dream. Shaking her head, she retreats a step, drawing Kegan's furrowed brow in her direction. "What's wrong?"

"I-I've seen that b-before." Nora squeaks as she continues in her retreat.

Something in her face spurs him into action. Shooting to his feet, Kegan rushes forward to tilt her chin upward. The concern brewing in his chocolate eyes centers on her, chasing away the cold tendrils of fear. "Where have you seen this, Nora?"

"In a d-dream. Everyone was d-dead. Bleeding on the floor. Except for a small child and an old m-maid. She spoke to someone briefly, then bundled the baby and took it to another family to raise. Once they swore to raise the child, she killed herself."

"Demons?" Jess muses aloud, his eyes drifting from Kegan to Eleni.

"No." Colin's voice bites through the speaker. "*Angels.*"

Eleni blinks and sits up straight for the first time since the call began. "Why would they wipe out an entire bloodline?"

Kegan remains quiet for a moment as he pulls Nora into his arms, running a hand over her cool skin. "With the information the book supposedly contains, they'd be a genuine threat."

"To whom?" Jess demands, his tone incredulous.

"To everyone." Colin's short answer snaps against the phone speaker in a flat voice.

"Damn," Eleni breathes. "That's harsh."

Colin's snort fills the air. "Are any of you surprised?"

"So, if my family enchanted it, the demons don't just want the book. Do they?" Nora's eyes flit to Eleni, Jess, and then up to Kegan. The hard clench in his jaw confirms her fears even while he couldn't voice them.

"I'm afraid not." Any other time, she might appreciate Colin's direct approach. Today it leaves a pit in her stomach.

The severity of her reality threatens to be her undoing, her mind struggling to contain all the information they fed her since this whole thing began. Sweat drips down her back, coating the palms of her hands as the danger she's in finally comes down full bore. When faced with the choice of mental breakdown or irrational humor, Nora opts for humor.

"You couldn't have been crazy, could you?" She stabs a glare at Kegan from under her lashes. "Not even for me? I'd have found a nice *old* lady to take care of you."

"An old lady, huh?" Lips twitch as Kegan wraps an arm around her waist.

"Hell, yes! You think I'm going to let some woman in her prime take advantage of you in your fragile state?"

With a bark of laughter, Kegan kisses the top of her head. Inhaling the scent of man and soap, her hands tremble. Though he muffles her words with his shirt, Nora is confident he hears them just fine. "My life goes up in smoke and you find your funny bone. That's a little twisted of you, Mr. Selkirk."

His grin borders on naughty while the look Kegan drags over her stokes heat within her core. "I never said I wasn't just a little twisted, *mo chridhe*."

"So what do we do?" Eleni questions, bringing them all back to the task at hand.

"We keep doing what we're doing," Colin replies. "Keep Nora safe, find the translator, and Rome's plan will fall through."

"Question." Jess raises his hand. "Assuming you aren't talking about a city in Italy, who's Rome?"

"Kegan, you said the man who attacked you is called Adriel?"

"Yep. Bastard cheats."

Colin sighs. "He works for a low-level demon by the name of Rome. Nothing extreme, but we shouldn't underestimate him."

"Let's hope they don't come armed with cats," Nora muses.

"Huh?" Eleni asks.

"What?" Colin clips.

"Why cats?" Jess's head cocks quizzically.

"Men are funny like that," Nora explains.

Kegan chuckles and tugs on a loose strand of her hair. "Brat."

"I think I'm out of the loop." Eleni snaps.

"I think that makes three of us." Jess grins.

"Well, I'm going to rattle Azrael's cage and see if he came up with anything. In the meantime, Nora, see what you can learn about this book." The faint sound of a lighter flicking a flame comes across Colin's end of the phone. "If we can render it useless without the translator, it will increase our chances."

"I might need to install an app to translate it for me." Nora muses. "But I'll do my best."

"Sounds good." Jess offers a nod as he rotates his shoulders.

Nora sets her phone down before it ends up out a window and shares a defeated look with her watch. After Kegan double-checked the barriers surrounding the cabin, the Watchers continued to argue strategy. How much work they're getting done with earbuds blaring to drown out the hum from the exposed book, she can't be sure. "Probably making more headway than I am," she grumbles and shoots the book a frosty glare.

How does Colin expect her to learn anything? Even the writing that isn't faded beyond recognition is so old, Google translation is floundering. Her latest inquiry came back with someone named Hamish wanting to be castrated.

"Highly unlikely." Digging a thumb against her right eye, Nora calls for a break and scrolls through her contacts until she lands on Mallory. The call almost goes to voicemail before her sister's weary voice cracks over the line.

"H-hello?"

"Mal? Are you okay? I've been calling you."

"Sorry, sweets. I've been sleeping off this flu."

"Did you call Dr. Lewis?"

"I did. He said to get plenty of rest and drink lots of water."

"Shouldn't you be over this by now?"

"I think I'm through the worst of it," Mallory says around a tired yawn. "Blew through a lot of my energy reserves, though."

"Okay. Well, get some sleep. I'll call you tomorrow. If you're not feeling better, then I'm coming home."

"Don't cut your vacation short over this. I'll be fine."

Nora's nose wrinkles as her stomach flips. She hates lying to her sister, but the others felt certain the truth will only endanger her. *You can apologize later, when this is over*, the nagging voice assures her. It doesn't make her feel any better. She forces a lighthearted tone into her words, intending to stay below Mallory's big sister's radar. "No worries. There's always another vacation. Talk to you tomorrow."

"Yeah." Yawn, this one is longer than the last. "Tomorrow. Love you."

"Love you back." Her thumb hovers over the red telephone icon for a bit before swiping it to end the call. Her instincts kick into hyper-drive, unconvinced Mallory's illness has anything to do with the flu. She makes a note to mention it to Eleni and dives back into the task in front of her.

Time passes in a blink as she digs from one journal to the next until the sharp rap on the door catches her attention. "One second," she calls, wrapping the book securely in the leather cloth before climbing to her feet and opening the door.

On the other side, Kegan looks up when the door opens, plucking one earbud free. His expression is identical to the one Mallory wore after eating sour patch kids for the first time. She's spent enough time around the man that she's come to read his subtle cues, steeling herself when she catches the hard set of his jaw.

"What's wrong?"

"There's been a development. Thought you'd like to join the conversation."

"No one can make *development* sound as foreboding as you do," she teases lightly, following him out to the living room. Jess and Eleni gather around the phone he'd left on the coffee table to retrieve her, their expressions roughly the same as the one he wears.

"What's up?"

"Hello, Nora." Colin's polished Irish lilt pours through the phone, bringing a shaky smile to Nora's face. "How are you coming with the book?"

"I've made some progress. Nothing with the translation, of course, but I thought if Grandad had the book as long as I think he did, he would've kept notes on it somewhere. It's just a matter of finding the right journal."

"I see. Let's hope luck is on your side."

"Luck, huh?" Nora's lips quirk at the notion of angels relying on luck.

"Right now, luck seems to be our best shot," Colin replies flatly.

"So, what's this development that has everyone looking like my cat just died?" As she asks, her eyes dart to where Ezio snores at one end of the couch, very much alive.

Colin chuckles. "Azrael went through the list of names we gave him to find our best bet."

"And?"

"She's a language professor at Iowa State," Kegan deadpans.

"Iowa State is just over an hour from here. Isn't this good news?" When no one volunteers an answer, she looks from Eleni to Kegan, waiting for the proverbial shoe to drop.

"She's under the influence of a Mercurian." Colin explains between the sound of him lighting yet another cigarette. *Jeepers, the man is a chimney.*

"Oh! Okay. A Mercurian. Of course!" Nora's hands rest on her hips as she flashes the same death glare she uses on her kids at Hiller House. "What the *hell* is a Mercurian?"

"They're another choir of angels." Colin supplies in a vague tone that's hard for her to read.

"Oh." As if picking up on her relief, Kegan shakes his head, effectively deflating the ray of hope flickering in her chest. "Not oh?"

Kegan's smile is tight. "We're forbidden to have contact with them."

Her eyes close with a heavy sigh. When she opens them, Nora notes not a single expression has changed. "So, they won't help us?"

"Probably not. Getting a bunch of pencil-pushing pansies to break a rule is like taking a nun to your senior prom." Jess's dry directness cuts the tension in the air.

"Does anyone have a plan?" Nora asks as she physically shakes the image Jess created free from her brain.

"Jess and Eleni are going to make the drive to Iowa State and see if they can get a moment alone with this professor," Colin says. "Take your charm."

"If anyone can talk a strange woman into coming home with him, it's Jess." Kegan's remark earns a chuckle from Colin and a flip of the finger from Jess.

"I guess I better make some progress in those journals." Nora attempts a confident smile.

Jess keeps to the shadows under a large oak tree as he studies the campus. Every sense is alive with the close presence of the Mercurian. Between his ears, the symphony skips like a scratched record, setting his teeth on edge. The vast amount of students milling from one building to another makes a fight reckless. They can't risk waiting too long and miss the professor altogether, either. Pinning Eleni with a look, he offers a crooked grin.

"You have a plan, right?"

"Working on one."

Shrugging away the sound of reluctance in her reply, Jess looks on as a kid a short distance away executes tricks on his skateboard. With every giggle from the group of girls, the young kid becomes a little more courageous. As the board teeters, drawing attention to his upcoming demise, the crowd of onlookers multiplies. Reaching out, Jess steadies both board and rider to clear the metal railing and land smoothly at the bottom of the steps.

The dull ache that comes with tapping into his powers requires a thumb massage, but is well worth it, in his opinion. Wiping out in front of a gaggle of females is mortifying for a kid his age. *Hell, who are you kidding? Wiping out at any age is detrimental to a man's ego.*

"We need to tread lightly, Jess."

"I am."

"I'm serious," Eleni snaps, jerking him around to face her. "This Mercurian won't offer a warm welcome and we can't afford to scare this girl off."

Jess casts a look at his steel-toe biker boots, then passes Eleni a dramatic wink. "Guess I should've changed first." After a roll of her chocolate eyes, she starts off towards the prominent building on their right. Following a quick shrug of his shoulders, he lumbers off after her.

His calloused hand touches the glass door a beat before demons swarm them. Too late, he realizes the stutter of the Symphony he attributed to the Mercurian instead belongs to the large group of Scavengers.

The presence of human witnesses prevents Jess and Eleni from doing little else, but fight them hand to hand. While it puts the two of them at a serious disadvantage, he plans on making the scum work for their conquest.

Chapter 23

When Nora stumbles on a quick passage about the magic surrounding the book, her heart leaps into her throat. While deciphering his sloping scrawl takes as much effort as the book itself; it's more than she had five minutes ago. She reads the four lines twice more before Kegan pokes his head inside the room.

"You plan on eating today?"

"Hmm. Maybe," she mumbles, gasping when he snatches the journal from her hands.

"Nora. You need to eat."

"I'll get something for lunch. I promise." When a brow hitches up his forehead, she has to curl her fingers in to keep from ripping it off his face. "I promise," she repeats, steadfast.

"*Mo chridhe*, it's past suppertime."

"What?" With a twist of her head, Nora looks to the window over her shoulder. The waning daylight would explain the eyestrain she's been battling for some time now. "I didn't realize."

"I know," he concedes, picking his way through the littered floor to take a seat next to her. When he passes the journal back, Nora earmarks the page for later and abandons it to her lap.

"You've become obsessed with this."

"I can't just sit here while you guys do all the heavy lifting. I may not know how to fight like one of you, but research is *my* domain."

"Brody was the same way. He spent countless hours in here after Elsie passed."

"You were with him for a long time?" Taking one of her hands in between his, he traces a finger across the knuckles, an absent nod his only response. "How is it we never met?"

"When Brody took on the responsibility, his only stipulation was that we keep you and your sister safe and unaware."

"And then he dies and drags me into this nightmare, anyway."

"Hm, I suppose. I don't think I've been that bad. Have I?"

"You didn't top the list of my most favorite people. That's for sure." Nora's chest tightens when Kegan snakes an arm around her waist to pull her across his lap. A hand rests over his chest, the other slipping behind his neck.

"And now?"

"Now, I'd say you make the top ten."

"Ten?" Full lips quirk into a playful smile as he inches a hand under her t-shirt to splay along the small of her back. The small contact ignites the nerve endings under her skin until her core clenches. "Do the other nine make you see stars?"

"Mm, no. I can't say they do," she stutters, teeth scraping against her lip as she fights the urge to squirm. When his fingers dance around to the slope of her ribs, a coherent thought becomes improbable.

"Good. I make you see stars, *yes?*"

"Oh!" Her breath rushes out when he eases the fabric of her bra aside to torture the hard nub hiding underneath. "Entire galaxies," she purrs, giving up the fight on squirming. When her hip brushes against his obvious arousal, his heavy growl is its own reward.

"You make me crazy," he croaks before peeling her shirt from her to drop it across a tall stack of books. In a flash, the fire smoldering in his eyes sends heat to the tip of her toes.

When he leans forward to trail kisses across her shoulder towards her neck, Nora's grip on him tightens. Lungs burn with the need to exchange air, but she won't risk any movement that will break contact with the scrape of his stubble surrounding velvet-like lips.

The bookworm in her shudders when Kegan clears a path with one swing. She shudders for a different reason when he lays her back, following her to the floor. Eyes close as she drowns under the press of his mouth on her skin and the playful torture of his fingers going from one breast to the other.

With a moan, she wraps her legs around his hips to draw him closer to her center. His growl of satisfaction instills a quiver in her arms as she buries her hands in his hair. There are plenty of moments when she wishes she could rewind the clock to a time before the book came into her life. Kegan isn't one of those moments.

A finger drums a brisk beat into the arm of his chair as Rome awaits Rayen's arrival. The second he received his report, an empty sensation invaded his stomach. Patience will never be a trait he studies in, but the longer he sits here, the worse it becomes.

His army gathers inside the great hall, some drinking and celebrating. Several men cleared out an area for a round of friendly sparring until it morphs into something a little more severe. A handful of the women take to dancing under the pale candlelight, a good number of them without the restriction of clothing. None of it holds his attention for longer than a few seconds. At most. So when Shax strides through the middle with a dozen Chayante warriors at his side, Rome has to reign in his initial reaction.

Lifting a hand to calm the immediate tension his legions suffer at the sight of an age-old enemy within their borders, he stabs a glare at the little toad, openly gloating. Bravado shines inside his dark beady eyes, his head lifting in a vain attempt to look down at his troops.

"What's the purpose of *this* visit?"

"I come with a gift, Brother."

Teeth grind as Rome fights to remain seated, his hands shaking to disembowel the malady that continues to reek up his halls. "And that requires you to arrive under their protection?" His head jerks at the warrior on Shax's left. That she's the tallest is a coincidence.

"Well, when one considers your open hostility towards me, one can never be too careful."

"How can someone as offensive as you purchase their services?"

"We struck a deal. A fair deal, I might add. One you shouldn't concern yourself with."

Any hope of restraint threatens to deteriorate over Shax's false arrogance. Rome catches the race of his heart as fire sears his skin from head to toe. His drumming finger increases the tempo while he wrestles his normal temperament. "What is this *gift*?"

The tall warrior with platinum hair and brilliant blue eyes gives the others a slow nod before the numbers part for the two marching forward. Between them, they haul a human, listless.

As they approach, Rome stands and meets them halfway, still a good distance away from Shax in case his temper does indeed snap. A close inspection of the human rewards him for the precaution.

What he can only assume was once a rich tan fades under a sickly complexion. Eyes like liquid silver stare back at him, dull and unfocused. Tangled hair as dark as a moonless night hangs limply around a heart-shaped face. Unable to stand under her own power, each warrior braces her weight, the tips of her toes barely scuffing his marble floor. Her satin nightgown hangs shapeless around what might've been an attractive figure.

"What's this supposed to be?" He speaks low, each word carefully enunciated.

"Leverage."

The other Brennan, he assumes as he schools his features. "She looks near death!" His first thought was they'd found some poor soul addicted to the drugs of humanity and hauled her down here to please him. One whiff of the scent she gives off, and he picks up the essence of the creature that haunts her, draining her life like a leech on her soul. "You allowed an incubus to feed on her?"

"Humans are our food. Why should this one be any different?"

"Just how stupid are you? Round down." One boney shoulder hitches up then down as if he couldn't care enough to entertain Rome's question. "How am I supposed to make use of her like this?"

"If not for Eli, you would have *no* leverage. I'm sure you'll figure something out."

If Rome were to study his reflection, he'd see steam rolling from his ears. Rayen's arrival serves as a moment of collection as his small party parades their trophies to the front. Wild cheers shake the foundations as every demon catches sight of his prize.

Two of Rayen's best wrestle the difficult prisoner across the floor, his hands bound in front of him. Beneath torn clothing, Rome spots more than a few fresh wounds, some grave. Dried blood gathers under his nose and across his right cheek. One green eye sports a nasty bruise while the other eyes them with blatant disgust.

"Is this the Mercurian?"

Shoving the man forward, Rayen drives him to his knees with a vicious elbow to expose the brand hidden by yellow-gold curls. "This is one of the Fallen," he replies with candid measure. "He and his little partner took out seven of my best before we subdued him."

"Why would a Mercurian involve itself with his kind?" Shax's repulsive features contort.

"Does anything about my face say that I care to find out?" When the stench of the angel becomes too much for him to stomach, Rome ushers several demons forward. "Place him in one of the empty cells. Leave his hands bound."

No sooner does he deal with the first hiccup before Rayen orders the remaining two prisoners brought up for closer examination.

The first is a curvaceous brunette with a regal bearing. The gentle characteristics of her face are beautifully subtle. Long, slender fingers fold on top of each other, her binds tight enough to leave welts on her unblemished coloring.

The woman beside her is a blubbering mess of sweat, tears, and snot. Her blonde hair carries a heavy tint of red as it falls just below her jaw. A pair of brown eyes, red and puffy, casts furtive looks around, debating the level of her safety. The number she came up with must've been rather low as she wails once more.

"The one making the horrible commotion is your translator, Master." Rayen nudges the silent woman from behind just enough to force her to take an additional step. "This is the Mercurian Shax warned us about."

Cries pierce the room as the Chayante warriors descend on the brunette like a pack of wild dogs. The group wrestles to draw first blood, pulling the angel in several directions. The moment she loses her balance and crashes to the floor, fists and boots rain down in a frenzy of activity. Blood and clumps of hair trash the immaculate marble as she struggles to deflect the worst of the blows. Once his ears catch the sound of a blade unsheathing, Rome calls a halt to the ruckus.

"Enough!" The thunder of his command results in his own soldiers taking a step back, eyes lowering. As the only one not affected, Rayen steps into the crowd of Chayante's, and drags the brunette within the safety of his own men.

"What is the meaning of this?" Eyes burn with a blue flame as the tall warrior squares her shoulders. "We had a deal."

"Not with me." Rome smirks as the blood drains from Shax's sallow complexion. As much as he'd prefer to relish the moment, better sense prevails. "However, considering our partnership, I will honor the terms of your arrangement. The Mercurian is yours." From where he stands, it's hard to miss her sigh of relief. "After I have the book," he adds, allowing his temper just enough latitude to change his onyx eyes to a blood red.

At the counter, Nora spreads every journal that mentions the book in front of her. Two passages comprise one sentence. Another contains an entire paragraph. As she reads them again and again, the sharp sizzle of meat hitting the pan on the stove snags her focus. She smiles lazily while Kegan obsesses over just the right amount of sear on the steak.

"You know, I could've just nuked a burrito."

With a long glare over his shoulder, Kegan arches a brow at her. "I do not *have* frozen burritos."

"Jess brought some."

"That figures." Lips press at the same time he completes an eye roll that rivals any teenage girl. Fighting off the giggle bubbling in her chest, Nora chews on her thumbnail until he turns his attention back to the stove.

With a shake of her head and a silent laugh, she returns to her journals. Grandad had done some extensive research on the book while he'd had it, narrowing down several possibilities. The stone makes the most sense to her. The first time she'd laid eyes on it, the pull was strong. She recalls the fizzle of magic against her fingertips that night. What she brushed off as an overactive imagination now makes complete sense.

"I think I found something."

"Yeah?" Moving the pan off the stove, Kegan leaves the steak to rest on a plate while he crosses the kitchen to lean across the counter. "Not another secret fishing hole, I hope."

Despite the uncomfortable tingle in her hands, Nora laughs. Grandad *loved* his fishing. More than any of them could've fathomed. "No. This one mentions the stone as the source of magic."

"Makes sense. Harder to enchant a bunch of makeshift pages." Twisting on his heel, he grabs the plate and sets it in front of her, pushing the journals aside. "Eat." When he returns with a knife and fork, he offers a smile to curl her toes. "Please."

"I will. After you put your earbuds in."

A dark scowl wipes away the smile, his arms folding across his chest. "That doesn't really work, you know. I can still feel the power calling my name."

"Would you rather go without?" A series of emotions play on his face. He'd been unprepared the first time she unwrapped the book. The events are still clear in her memory. Judging by the immediate locking of his jaw, he remembers as well. Fishing the small black earbuds from a pocket, Kegan cleans up the kitchen.

Fetching the wrapped bulk from her shoulder bag, Nora removes the rough leather to inspect the stone with a sharper eye.

It doesn't appear any different from before. So clear a blue, Nora can see the anchor points below, holding it to the cover. Like the first time, the smooth surface catches the overhead light to twinkle prettily. It *looks* like any other beautiful rock. Harmless.

The moment she brings her fingers close, however, the magic gives off a dull buzz. With a brush of her middle finger, a tingle settles in the tip, shooting into her hand.

Pulling her hand away, Nora rubs her fingers against her palm as she reads the journal's paragraph one more time. The epiphany comes quick, and without giving herself a chance to second guess it, she picks up the steak knife and pricks a finger. Teeth pin her lower lip between them as she positions her finger above the stone to let two little beads drop. The effect is instantaneous.

The glow builds quickly, emanating from within the stone until it radiates a bright light. As if caught by a gust of wind, the book opens and pages flip with a soft whoosh. She loses count of how many pass her eye when they stop just shy of the middle. A blank page upon an earlier inspection now sports random letters and symbols as dark as drawn blood.

Once the change reaches Kegan's dulled senses, the pan he's washing clatters into the stainless steel sink. "Mother fucker," he growls out amidst grinding teeth, propelling his large body beyond the gap to slam the book tight. "What the hell are you doing?"

Nora's head jerks from the half-roar, half-mutter so close to where she sits. Narrowing her eyes, she lifts her chin and meets his fury boldly. "Testing a theory."

"Christ, Nora. Forget the splitting headache you just gave me. You just lit a beacon for all sorts of terrible things that'll keep you awake at night."

Resting a hand over his, she observes the soft tremble working its way up into his arm. Her temper diffused, she meets his pained expression with one of tenderness. "I'm sorry. I didn't think about the fallout."

"Just tell me it was worth it."

With a frantic bob of her head, Nora sorts through jumbled thoughts to give the best explanation when the front door crashes open.

A blast of frosty air sweeps through the living room to barrel into the kitchen. Inhaling past her teeth, she rubs hands over bare arms to ward off the chill. Her tiny squeak of surprise gets lost in the wind's cry when Kegan plucks her off the stool and plants her behind him.

Every muscle in his back primes for battle. On either side, his fists open and close while he stretches his neck, first left, then right. Suddenly, as if someone flips a switch, his rigid stance relaxes. Craning her neck around him, Nora covers her gasp with a hand as Eleni collapses to the floor.

"Omigod!" Rushing to her side, Nora kneels next to her friend, searching for the source of the blood that soaks her shirt. When she reveals a deep gash just under her ribs, she uses her hands to staunch the flow.

"Eleni?"

Nora figures the fact that her skin is cool and sweaty to the touch can't be a good thing. Once she brushes away a few loose curls, she discovers several scratches and bruises staining exquisite skin. When she gets her friends' attention, it takes longer than it should for Eleni's eyes to focus on her.

"El," she croaks and forces a swallow beyond a tight throat.

When she speaks, her voice sounds rough and uneven. "Jess."

"What happened?" Kegan demands after doing his best to rese-cure the front door. "Where's Jess?"

"She doesn't need this right now."

"Let me get her to the couch." With a tip of her head, Nora blinks to see Kegan standing just off to her side. When did he move? Not trusting her voice, she nods once and scoots back on her heels so he can sweep Eleni into his arms. The moment she settles, Nora is by her side again.

"I need to know what happened, Eleni." Kegan insists, his voice hard.

"*We* need to stop this bleeding." Nora snaps. "*Then* you can interrogate her."

Without a word, Kegan disappears into the kitchen long enough to re-appear with a clean hand towel and a glass of water. "I do not interrogate."

"Your offense is incredibly cute," Nora informs him as she folds the towel in a tight pattern and presses it to Eleni's side. Her quick flinch and sharp hiss of air compels her to apologize.

Kegan's soft grumble is just loud enough for Nora to hear. "*Cute* isn't the word I'd choose."

"Oh?" With a tilt of her head, she studies him as she applies pressure to Eleni's side. "Do you have a better one in mind?"

"Handsome. Deadly." Lips flash a crooked grin at her, her stomach tightening in response. "Sexy as hell," Kegan adds with a wink.

"While I do agree with those descriptions, my point is you do, in fact, interrogate." Peeking under the towel, sours her banter with Kegan. "This isn't working. She needs a hospital."

"No hospitals." The tense shake of his head kills the argument Nora is ready to launch in her friends' best interests as he digs his phone out of a pocket. From her spot on the floor, she can hear the other line ring several times until a gruff voice replaces it.

"We need you. Now." Kegan bites short, cutting off the irritated greeting.

Maybe it's a sixth sense, or maybe he picks up on the same level of stress in Kegan's voice that she does. Whatever the case, Nora blinks once and then Colin is standing in their living room.

Instead of asking for details, he takes in Eleni's current condition. "Fuckers," Colin snarls, his vintage brown combat boots devouring the space between them. After a deep inhale, he places a hand across Eleni's forehead, his strong jaw tensing as whiskey-colored eyes burn bright with an incandescent fire. Less than a minute later, Eleni's wounds begin to close and fade.

Thirty-seconds after that, Colin staggers back, blood soaking through his blue t-shirt across his right side. The scrapes and bruises he took from her rest over his face long enough to raise a few questions before they fade just as Eleni's had done. His eyes normal once more, Colin hovers. "Tell me."

Eleni draws a full breath tentatively and holds it a moment before exhaling. "They were waiting for us at the college."

Kegan steps forward to stand beside Nora. "They?"

"A dozen Scavengers." Muttering a groan, Eleni pushes herself upright until she can swing her legs onto the floor. "There were too many humans for us to fight with weapons. Didn't stop them, though."

"Yeah. That's the bitch with following the rules."

"Not that Kegan doesn't have a point, but I'm glad you didn't expose yourselves. Where's Jess?" Colin asks, his tone gentle for the first time since Nora's met him a few short days ago.

Eleni's face pinches. "A tall demon took him," she whispers, her hands fisting at her sides.

"Now what?" Kegan turns to Colin, his expression grave.

"Are you okay?" As Kegan and Colin argue over their plan of action, Nora continues to scan Eleni' for any trace of her injuries.

"The only injury remaining is to my pride, *asteri mou.*" Squeezing Nora's hand, Eleni attempts a smile. "You have my word."

"Well, we can't just storm in after him. They're bound to expect us to do something just that crazy." Kegan grumbles behind her, snagging Nora's attention.

The deep rasp of Colin's sigh hovers for a moment. "How did they know we'd come for her?"

"Do I look like a demon whisperer to you?" Kegan challenges, pacing within the confines of the living room. He scrubs a hand across the back of his neck and levels a pointed look at Eleni. "You should've had Jess's back."

"Not much I could've done." Eleni's face hardens, her eyes narrowing. "They outnumbered us."

"Yet you escaped, and he didn't." Kegan points out ignoring the elbow Nora jabs in his ribs.

"Don't get all grumpy on me, asshole," Eleni hisses. "Next time, I'll play house with Nora and you can run the gauntlet."

"What'd you just say?" His question is strictly rhetorical since Nora's certain he heard Eleni's low blow just fine. His voice shakes, shoulders lifting from the insult.

"This isn't helping," Nora intercedes, caught between friend and lover.

"Nora's right." After a quick look from Colin, Kegan marches away, putting distance between him and Eleni. It isn't hard for her to miss the rigid set of his body.

"Where'd this come from?"

The three of them look. Colin and Eleni sporting similar expressions of confusion until Kegan bends down to retrieve a knife from the floor.

Approximately 10 inches long, the hilt sports a worn black handle with a makeshift crown on the end. Its silver metal gleams under the ceiling lights, highlighting several etches along the lethal blade itself. Even without knowing the significance of its presence, Nora studies the razor shape point and suppresses a shudder.

Eleni sits up for a better look. "One demon dropped it. I grabbed it on my way out."

"Colin." The worry Nora registers in Kegan's voice multiplies the tension in her bones.

"I'll ask around." While he projects the image of aloofness, the small tic in Colin's left cheek says otherwise.

Kegan nods settling the weight of the weapon in Colin's hand. "What can we do for Jess?"

"We can't leave him with those sadists." Eleni pipes in.

"I'm all for stabbing Rome right in the throat," Colin growls, "but any rescue attempt will leave Nora unprotected. *Which is what they want*, by the way."

Eleni gapes, her gaze moving from Nora to Colin. "So we do nothing?"

Several minutes go by with Kegan resuming his pacing. Eleni shoves herself off the couch to stare out the patio door, hands clenching. When Colin speaks, the sudden break of silence causes Nora to jump. "Have you learned anything about the book?"

Ignoring the warmth on her cheeks, Nora jerks a nod. "I think so. Let me show you."

Kegan hisses before taking a step back. "Do *not* even think of doing what you did earlier."

"I won't have to." Entering the kitchen, Nora opens the book. She takes about ten seconds to flip to the page she needs, then holds the book up for them to see clearly. "I spilled some of my blood on the stone, and this text appeared."

His head cants, taking a step closer. Thinking better of it, Colin retreats several paces back and buries his hands into the pockets of his jeans. "It's old writing. I can only guess at some of the translations. But I'd stake my wings, it's what they're looking for."

"We don't have wings."

"How do you suppose you travel as you do Eleni, without wings? You have them, you just can no longer feel 'em."

"So remove the spell on the stone and they'll lose access to the text."

"Removing any spell isn't nearly as fun as it sounds, Kegan," the tense set of Colin's jaw draws her attention. "It can even be quite dangerous."

"We don't have the time to go digging around Iowa for some homegrown hobby witch," Eleni snaps, her head turning back to the floor-length window.

"What if we remove the stone?" Nora pins each of them with a look. "If the spell is inside the stone, couldn't we just pry it off and lock it away?"

"In theory," Colin pauses as if thinking to himself. "I don't dare get anywhere near it."

"I'll do it." Nora decides, already digging in the drawers of the kitchen to find a screwdriver small enough to wedge in against the anchors.

"I'm not sure that's a good idea, *mo chridhe*." Kegan murmurs, his hand settling over hers for an instant.

"We have no choice but to try," Nora's teeth capture her bottom lip as her fingers tighten on the hard handle of the screwdriver. *Right?*

Chapter 24

The moment her shoe touches the bottom step, Celeste's nerves flee. Over the years, she's struggled to find the courage to walk this very path. Funny, she always imagined different circumstances.

The wooden steps creak under her weight as she tells herself she's doing this for her mother. It's possible Adriel lied about Kegan's relationship with Brody's granddaughter for extra incentive. So it couldn't be jealousy, she tells herself. Once. Twice. Then again, for good measure.

The warm amber flare of the porch light illuminates the distance between her and the door. Sweat gathers under her coat despite the crisp air. A few seconds pass by in the time she takes to settle on a decision.

A tug on the screen door has the hinges whining loudly, shattering the tranquil evening. Each breath is a war as she thumps her knuckles on the door. One more knock and she can return, saying she tried at least. Before she can even form the prayer, the door swings open. Standing in the open space, a tall man with golden eyes stares down at her.

"Can I help you?"

"I'm l-looking for Nora." Celeste stammers with a cringe, pulling in another stiff breath before Nora comes to the door.

"Hi, Nora, I don't know if you'll remember me."

"Holly's little sister, Celeste? Right?"

"Wow, yeah." Celeste blinks. "I wasn't sure you'd remember."

"Your sister and I would hunt frogs together. You came along once or twice."

"Yeah. Guess I haven't changed much over the years."

"Well, you're taller, and you finally had the braces taken off."

Regardless of her dry mouth and her rolling stomach, Celeste laughs. "Yeah."

"So," Nora flashes a friendly smile, "what brings you by?"

"I kind of need someone to talk to. One that isn't sporting gigantic handbags stuffed with Kleenex and chapstick."

"Gotcha." She takes the time to slip on a pair of neon green tennis shoes and a long sleeve sweater. "Let Kegan know I'm stepping out for a minute."

"I'm not so sure that's a good idea, Nora."

"You're on edge. I get it. It'll be fine Colin, you can see me from the porch. Okay?"

The tall man studies Celeste for a long minute and the urge to squirm rocks her nerves. Offering a shaky smile, she strives for the picture of innocence. Despite the tic in his jaw, he nods his dark head before stepping aside.

Nora grabs a sweater before joining Celeste on the porch and it takes all of her willpower not to run.

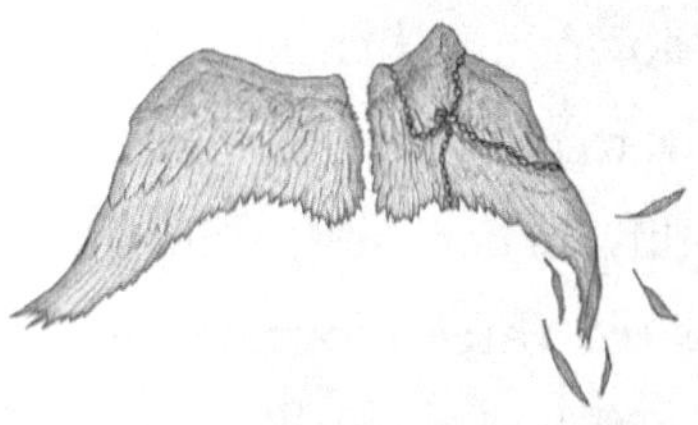

One hand holds the sweater closed while the other pulls her hair free from underneath. Her inner voice warns her to tread carefully now that she's beyond the safety of the house, but Nora brushes it aside. While she hasn't seen Celeste since they were in their teens, she's lived in the area for as long as Nora can recall.

"I must confess, I'm a little surprised you came to me," Nora says with a smile. "I haven't seen you or your sister since the eighth grade. How is Holly?"

"She's good. Trying to make it in Hollywood. Landed a couple of minor roles, nothing big yet."

"Oh! She's always had a flare for the dramatics. Good for her. Are you two still close?"

"No, she left town the second she turned eighteen. I'm hoping to get her home now that our mom is sick, but she's stalling."

"Your mom is sick?"

"Lung cancer." Celeste wanders down the short drive, kicking at loose pebbles. Her quiet response draws Nora closer to hear above the rustling trees. "Doctors say it's inoperable."

"I'm so sorry. I remember when cancer took my grandmother, most of us just felt helpless." Backing up blindly, Nora moves for the large rock near the edge of the property where they'd sit and watch the cars drive by as kids. Before her feet can find it, however, strong fingers bite down onto her shoulders from behind.

"You're a hard girl to get a meeting with."

With a sharp tingling in her chest, Nora tries to convey to Celeste the need to run as the three Hounds step out of the shadows behind her. Green eyes hover a little too close for Nora's liking as he brings a piece of Celeste's hair to his nose.

"You can let her go." Tears she attributes to fear streak across Celeste's cheeks, her shoulders racking with the occasional jerk. "She has nothing to do with this."

The one behind her tightens his grip as he gives Tobias a short nod. "Time for little girls to run home. Our deal is complete." The weight of his words causes her stomach to roll, her body heaving as if from a physical blow.

"I'm sorry," Celeste whispers, taking a series of steps backward.

"See that she makes it home. Alive, Tobias." Celeste's tiny squeak of fear comes close to sparking Nora's sympathy before falling short.

Once they are alone, she whirls around. She'd recognize that classic, beautiful face with strange blue eyes anywhere. "Adriel," she breathes.

Lips quirk into a wide grin as he offers a deep bow. When he rights himself, his eyes twinkle with mischief. "It's nice to speak with you one on one."

"I'm sure," she answers dryly, arms folding across her chest. "What do you want?"

"You should know the answer. Maybe you're not as smart as I took you for."

"Or maybe I expect you to have the balls to say it out loud. Guess we're both disappointed."

The sharp bark of laughter that escapes him leaves her skin crawling. Fingers scratch at the new growth of stubble covering a rugged jaw while he studies her.

"I *do* like you."

"Shame I can't say the same."

"The book, Nora. You're going to bring it to me."

"Is that right? You take arrogance to a whole new level."

"I make it a point to exceed expectations."

"You know, if this whole demon thing doesn't pan out, and trust me when Kegan finishes with you, it won't. You'd have a nice career in politics."

"Fuck that. I'm way too honest."

"What makes you think I'll just hand the book off to you?"

"Insurance."

His smooth reply just reaches her ears when he paints a small chamber against the inky black sky. The whole image flickers as if searching for a stronger connection, then settles within arm's reach of her.

The lack of windows makes the many candles in tall, golden candlesticks necessary. Deeper into the room, she can make out dark red coverings against white marble walls. Their weight gathers in large pools once they reach the smooth floor. On the left stands a thick door, the wood stained by time and god knows what else. In position at either side, is a guard Nora initially looks over until she registers the color of their skin.

The taller of the two flaunts jade green skin that shimmers under the soft lighting. Sleek, black hair falls over one shoulder, decorated with thick silver beads at various lengths. A long wooden staff stands erect in one hand, her clear lilac eyes alert. The second woman is a head shorter, her white hair cut in a bob style to frame an oval face. Brisk emerald eyes compliments her yellow-gold skin.

When the picture shifts like the zoom on a camera, Nora fights the compulsion to throw up all over Adriel's expensive-looking boots. The urge grows as she fixes her eyes on the large bed, one tanned foot kicked free from the covers.

Encircling the fragile ankle bones, she processes the sight of the dainty anklet Mallory has worn since her sixteenth birthday. She studies the tiny charms hanging lazily against her skin until the pit in her stomach threatens to swallow her whole. Once the image disappears, she spins around to confront Adriel.

"What have you done to her?"

"You have my word. I've done nothing to harm your sister."

"And I'm just supposed to believe you?"

"You can believe what you wish. All I require is your understanding."

Even as she gives a nod, her mind screams for an alternative. Once she hands over the book, there'll be no reason to keep her or her sister alive. *What choice do you have?* None, she reckons, the cold realization sinking into her bones.

"Excellent. Be here at dawn." For the space of a breath, Nora imagines a conflict of emotion in his eyes. "If you do not come alone, your sister won't survive. Are we clear?"

"Crystal."

Instead of leaving, he lingers for a moment, as if to say something else. The door to the cabin opening draws him short, his silent stare pained as Kegan calls for her. After a dismissive wave of his hand,

Nora heads back, doing her best to school her features before she reaches the porch.

Laying in bed, Nora listens to the steady sound of Kegan's breaths as the night continues its descent. With one arm across her hip, he fell asleep holding her close. Any other time, the familiar weight would lull her to her own dreams. Tonight it puts a twinge in her chest.

When Ezio shifts between their legs, Kegan draws her closer with a mumble too soft for her to make out. Using a finger to clear the hair from his face, she takes great care to memorize every detail. He would've made beautiful babies. The thought racks her with a silent sob as she drags a finger across his lower lip. Smooth to the touch, hot and hungry in a kiss. He's a walking contradiction. Severe with everyone else, gentle, greedy, and fun the instant they're alone.

Her heart twists as she wonders what memories he's carried for so long. Would the ones she adds be good or bad? Would he look back on their time with a smile or his usual scowl? She tells herself repetitively that he'll understand. So far, she remains skeptical. The longing his thumb creates brushing over a nipple drops her into the present. Her instant reaction flares with a groan, her back arching further into his touch.

"You're looking way too serious."

"You're supposed to be sleeping."

"Plenty of time for that." Rolling onto his back, Kegan pulls her with him. The sight of his playful grin strikes deep into her core as she straddles his hips. Her thighs clench when she notices the desire burning in his dark eyes.

Hands immediately move up his chest, marveling at the strength he hides under his skin. Hips squirm when one strong hand dips beneath the oversized t-shirt to skip along the curve of her spine. When he pulls her close, she takes his mouth in a kiss meant to leave them both breathless.

She has enough time to swallow his moan of approval before he tears his mouth away, trailing lips across her jaw. With a gasp, she holds onto his shoulders when he lifts her away, only to roll her over onto her back.

The shudder that courses through her when he situates between her legs is enough to curl her toes. Nora's eyes snap open when, instead of feeling the hard swell of his girth, she senses fingers. Dipping within wet folds, her hips lift in response, her moan stammering. Liquid fire spills into her limbs as she concentrates on the turmoil he's creating inside her body. Legs lock when he slips a finger, then two inside her. The harsh sound of his rumbling groan adds a quiver to already straining muscles.

"Kegan," she pleads, fingers grasping at thick forearms. The need to have him closer becomes a gnawing ache she can't ignore. Rather than giving in to the demands of her body, Kegan continues to play her like an instrument until she's exploding beneath him.

"Beautiful," he breathes, leaning in to claim her lips. Intense and greedy, Kegan devours her mouth like a dying man needing air.

Her whimpers and moans rush from her lungs in quick succession as she rides out her release. Hips buck wildly against his hand as nails nip and scrape over his arms. Panting, she collapses against the bed with a hard tremor, her legs trembling.

Determined to keep her recovery short, she purrs heavily when she feels his weight settling at her core. Air hisses through his teeth as he guides himself against her, pulling back just enough to rest his forehead against hers. Bodies freeze when he sinks deep in one smooth motion.

Hooking a leg with his arm, he pins her to the bed with a good share of his weight. When her body clenches tight around him, she cries out. Holding him tightly to her, she rides every dip of his hips, encouraging him with soft thrusts of her own. Sinking a hand into his hair, Nora gathers a soft fistful of his curls the instant she pitches with another orgasm.

"Christ," his teeth grind out, the rhythm of his thrusts increasing until she can feel his arms shake. Roping muscles knot along his back as he falls into his own release. Hard groans fan the side of her neck as he buries his face into her hair. When they collapse together in a panting, boneless heap of bodies, Nora catalogs the memory to last all the way to the end.

As she lay there with her head on his chest, Nora's heart thumps a vicious beat. Teeth work over her bottom lip as she draws a lazy finger over the lines of his tattoo. It seems like years since she first laid eyes on Kegan and this intricate design. In reality, it couldn't have been more than a month.

So intense on the pattern her finger follows, she jumps when the pad of his thumb brushes the side of her face. Lifting her eyes to his, her lips curve into a sleepy smile. "Do you believe in soulmates?" The question sends shadows falling into his eyes to smother the sparkle. She doesn't need the lights to know his jaw clenches over the question at the same time his chest hitches under her cheek.

"I don't have a soul, Nora."

"How do you know that?"

"They did not give us one. Souls are for humans. Not angels."

"Maybe that's the way it was supposed to be." Pushing up to her elbow, Nora stares into his face, his raw emotion clear. "I don't think you can experience emotions without a soul, Kegan. Hell, there are humans I doubt even know what the word means. If we're the only ones meant to have one, why do we have so many scary, *human* people on Earth? Where's their soul?"

"I see your point, but that still doesn't mean I have one." The brush of his hand across her nape inspires a rash of goosebumps to pepper her skin. When he cups the back of her head gently, her heart threatens to stop altogether. "If I did. I know without a doubt, you'd be my soulmate, *mo chridhe.*"

"That's good enough for me."

When she finally dreams, Nora grinds out a sigh, finding herself in the stone keep once more. Like every other time, men huddle with their work, hundreds of loose pages sprawling over the round table. Again, the handsome one looks on.

As if tuned to her presence, she's only there the space of a few minutes when he turns to confront her. This time, when he advances, she plants her feet on the floor. Chin lifts as the distance shrinks, his eyes burning with fury. Wait. Not anger, she muses. Urgency. Waiting for him to draw closer, she flinches backward, eyes narrowing.

"I'd like to skip the bruises this time. If that's okay with you."

His blonde head rocks back, then shifts in a makeshift nod of understanding. Sweeping his arm to the side, he gestures toward a set of chairs near the roaring fire.

"I am Michael."

Wuh. *She plops harder into the chair than she intends. Forget the smooth cadence of a sultry voice. His introduction has her mind racing to catch up. "Michael? As in God's army? Protector of Evil?"*

"You seem shocked."

"Oh no! Not at all. Why would it shock me to meet a frickin' archangel in my dreams? That's just the way my luck is going lately."

Even to her own ears, her voice raises more than a pitch or two. "Why are you trying to scare me?"

Identical golden brows arch high amidst his forehead, clear blue eyes cloud. "Scare you? In truth, you scared me."

"Me? Why?"

"I have watched your ancestors have these dreams over countless centuries. You're the first in your line to ever venture inside them. I was desperate to find out how."

"That's why you're Freddy Krugering my dreams? You're curious?"

"I'm what?"

"Nevermind. These dreams are about the book?"

"In part. Mostly, they mean to serve as a warning."

"A warning against what?"

"The very thing you're contemplating."

His eyes stab her so steadily, Nora resists the urge to squirm. He can't possibly know, she reasons. Untangling her fingers, she lays her hands in her lap even as sweat leaks through her pores.

"You'll give up your life?" Wrinkles mark his forehead as he searches her face for an answer he doesn't have. With a nod, she gives it to him.

"For my sister. Yes."

"What guarantee do you have he won't kill her, anyway?"

"He needs my blood to unleash the spell. And if Grandad's notes are correct, I'm the only one who can reveal the writing. If Rome wants it bad enough, he'll have to make a few concessions."

With a smile that reaches his eyes, Michael gives her a nod. "It seems you've learned a thing or two."

"Yeah, well, running for your life can inspire dogged determination." As they sit, Nora extends her legs to warm her toes by the fire.

"You've decided, then?"

"I have."

"Have you considered how your sister will feel when she learns what you did for her?"

Two men at the table break into a heated discussion over a particular page. Unable to catch the entire conversation, she can't help but watch as one lanky man gestures wildly at the page in question. When the rounder gentleman beside him shakes his large head, the two break into a tirade of unrecognizable words. The argument lasts no longer than a minute or two before a third man swaps the controversial item with his own. Round gentleman heaves a sigh that settles his frame deeper into his seat then begins work on a new page.

"Nora?"

"Hmm?"

With a patient smile, Michael repeats his question and Nora wonders if she just misplaced it the first time, or intentionally wiped it from memory.

"I don't have the luxury of worrying about what will happen. This is now, and now Mallory is vulnerable and needs my help."

"I see." Reclining against the back of his chair, Michael stares into the fire, his jaw locking and unlocking. However, he doesn't leave her to wonder long about his train of thought. "Where does he fit into all this?"

"Who?"

"Kegan." If she isn't mistaken, his voice carries a trace of impatience.

"He'll understand." Yeah. Right!

"You love him."

His flat tone compels her attention. She expects to find judgment and prepares herself for it. When she catches him pinching the bridge of his nose, it feels like something else. Fingers tighten in her lap for a millisecond as she pulls her legs back in and tucks one beneath her. "Last time I checked, I'm not a Disney princess ready to promise forever to a man I've just met." When he raises his head, he pins her with a hard stare.

"You're saying you don't love him?"

"I'm saying it doesn't factor into the equation. I won't be the reason your kind deals him any more damage." After everything Kegan and Eleni had told her the last few weeks, and learning the man he is despite it all, she'll be hell-bent if he suffers any more humiliation over a decision that is hers to make.

"You may not wish it to be Nora, but your heart belongs to him. As does his to you. Your death will ruin him and forever like that is a long time to endure."

She blocks out the image her mind conjures when Kegan will hear of her death and suppresses the frigid numbness creeping over her body. Straightening her back, Nora lifts her chin and fists her hands. "If you care so much, maybe you should make sure I don't die."

When Azrael looks up from his desk, his pen snaps in half, spraying the ledger he's working on with ink. "Dammit, Colin."

"Hey, don't blame me. I know my own strength."

With a look that could wither an entire forest, Azrael erases the ink on his hands and builds stacks out of the remaining ledgers. "What do you want now?"

"Not buying the whole Avon gig, huh?"

"No."

"You're smarter than you look." After dropping the dagger on the desk with a loud clang, Colin folds his arms. "What can you tell me about this?"

"Where'd you come across one of these?"

"During a scuffle with Rome's minions, one of them dropped it."

"Rome had this?"

Eyes roll as Colin counts to three. "That's literally what I *just* said."

"How did he find one?"

"Amazon? eBay? No fucking clue. What is it?"

"It's a Thronen blade. Before he fell, Azazel had several made. Melchom lost his first son to one."

"Shit." How in the hell did Rome get his hands on one? *Why would be a better question*, the tiny voice in his head points out. "If they're so dangerous, why not destroy them?"

"Not even we can destroy everything, Colin."

"True. Just pride, friendships, honor."

"Colin,"

"Whatever." With a swipe of his hand, Colin steers the conversation back on track. "If you can't destroy them, where'd they go?"

"It took Melchom decades to hide them all."

"Not well enough."

"If Rome found one, he's found more. Be careful."

"Yeah, yeah. Don't pretend you fucking care."

"I'm serious Colin. A blade like this will send any one of you into the ether. There's no coming back from such a fate."

Nora thrashing in her sleep, stirs him awake. Brushing a hand across her cheek, she relaxes a bit and settles with a sigh. No doubt the book again. It certainly has taken control of her life. Her breath even, she burrows closer to his warmth, drawing a smile along his lips.

During the last few days, he's decided. He's going to withdraw his plea for clemency. Living the rest of her life beside her means more to him than not having any time at all. There'll be plenty of time to re-appeal after she's gone. Right now, the idea of sacrificing even the tiniest moment with her lodges an ache in his chest.

Careful not to jostle her, Kegan eases out of bed and dresses in jeans and a white button-up shirt. Lost in dreams, Nora slumbers peacefully, her hair splayed up and over the top of her pillow. Leaning in, he places a kiss on her forehead, grabs his boots, and tiptoes from the room.

The store in town will open soon, and they used the last of the coffee yesterday. While he's thoroughly enamored with every personality she exhibits, the one before coffee he makes a point to avoid.

Chapter 25

Nora can't be sure how long she lay there, her breath measured, until the motorcycle roars to life outside. Coming clean to him now would be a mistake. Either he'd insist on coming along or he'd prevent her from going. "No. This is the only way to get Mallory out alive," she mumbles, stroking a hand over Ezio's thick fur.

The effort it takes to toss her legs over the side of the bed ends in a groan. A quick twinge of discomfort here and there after last night's lovemaking only provokes her queasy stomach. "You're doing the right thing." Although the nod of her head stutters, the words bolster her nerves.

To keep from disturbing Eleni's sleep, Nora steps lightly to her room. A scoop of dry cat food in the bowl beside the dresser brings Ezio running with a mere squawk. She dresses quickly in jeans and a t-shirt, her frenzied fingers tying and then re-tying her shoes. Since dawn already lightens the sky to a measurable degree, she pulls a brush through her tangles and secures the mass with a clip near the crown of her head. With her time running short, Nora locates a pen and sheet of paper.

With an extra pep in his step, Kegan arrives at the corner store just as Mrs. Fie turns the lock on the door. Flashing a crooked grin, he calls out a greeting and makes quick work of scanning the aisles.

"You're in a fine mood this morning."

On cue, Celeste steps out from the back room, her usual bright smile dim. "I'll ring him up Mom. Can you go over the cigarette order? It needs to go out today to get them in time for the weekend."

"Sure. Nice seeing you Kegan."

"You too, Mrs. Fie."

His arms full of a can of coffee, and a bag of doughnuts, Kegan approaches the register. "Your mom is looking well today. She feeling better?"

A loud sniffle precedes her uneven wobble of a nod. "She's having a good morning. Makes me think the worst is behind us."

He frowns, fingers dig his wallet from a back pocket. "Did the doctors ever say what was making her so sick?"

"They're best guess was pneumonia." Without looking at his face, Celeste rings up the few items.

"I think you're pushing yourself too hard. You look tired."

"A polite way of saying shit."

His frown deepens as a shiver of awareness trickles across his neck. "You know me well enough to know I'd say shit if I thought so."

"I'd like to think I do." As she reads off the total, he's aware of her eyes searching his face. "This is a new look on you. Almost chipper."

"I have a lady at home that doesn't do mornings. I'm hoping I can change her outlook." As the words leave his mouth, he refuses to believe the heat on his face is anything remotely similar to a blush.

Celeste drops her face into her hands and heaves a great sob to put a pause in his silent examination. Words blubber together amidst wailing cries loud enough to bring her mother in from the back room. Kind features twist as she runs to her daughter.

"What in Heaven's name?"

Still new to the whole compassion thing, Kegan pats her arm awkwardly. "Take a breath."

"I'm a h-horrible p-person," she snivels.

"No, you're not. C'mon. Whatever it is, can't be that bad."

"I am." When her body heaves with a great lungful of air, Kegan fears her cries are going to start up all over again, and fights the itch to make a mad dash for his bike. "I t-tricked her."

"Tricked who, honey?" Wrapping a frail arm around Celeste's shoulders, her mother does her best to provide comfort. The sliver of awareness around his neck falls into his chest. Sweat beads along the length of his spine as he finds the patience needed to get more information from Celeste.

"She was so n-nice to me. And I s-set her up."

When the pieces fall into place, his heart squeezes. Fingers grip the counter so hard the sound of tiny shards of wood splintering seems loud. "You don't mean Nora." The restraint it requires to not scream the accusation gives him an instant headache. "Right?"

"I'm s-sorry. I didn't have a ch-choice."

Confirming his fear does nothing to dilute the wave crashing into him. White-heat floods his limbs, shivering with the frigid numbness that follows. More than once he squeezes his eyes closed, willing the world to right itself.

Unfortunately, when he opens them again, everything remains distorted. The pain unfurling inside his chest threatens to bring him to his knees in this very spot as he runs through the events over the last two days.

He can't recall a moment when Nora was away from his protection. Most of her time spent with him or in the makeshift study. When had they approached her? How did they manage to do it without setting off the alarms he'd set? The thought lands like a punch to the gut, whooshing the air from his lungs, his vision swimming.

Celeste had come by to *talk*. That was the one and only time Nora was ever away from him long enough to be vulnerable. "Who?" He croaks, a twinge of pain in his jaw from clenching his teeth. Her whispered reply jerks his head back.

"Adriel."

"Motherfucker."

"I'm truly sorry, Kegan. I swear I'll make it up to you."

Leaving the coffee and doughnuts on the counter, he marches toward the door. When he forms the words in his throat, his voice is calm and devoid of the emotions rolling in his chest. "Start praying Celeste."

You're too late. The words ring in his ears before he even brings his motorcycle to a stop. He'd spent the last few decades inside the small cabin, and in the few weeks Nora was here, it changed. The windows attract more light; the walls feel less constraining as if the breath of life that follows her transformed the small house. In her absence, he can sense it drain away from the very foundation.

Taking the steps two at a time, Kegan explodes into the house and charges the short distance to his bedroom. Certain what he's going to see, he can't help but hold his breath as the door crashes open. The empty bed just ahead shatters his resolve. Crossing the room on stiff legs, he takes a seat on the now-cold mattress.

Thoughts whirl, chasing each other through the depths of his mind. It's one glaring question that sticks to his tongue. *Why?*

From the corner of his eye, he spies a piece of paper propped up on her pillow, his name penciled across the fold in large loops of cursive. He tells himself he already knows what it will say, but reads it anyway.

Her handwriting is obscenely perfect. A mixture of print and cursive flows across the faded blue lines as she explains how they took Mallory before asking him to look after Ezio. The realization she plans to offer herself up for her sister's survival creates a crack in the dam. His first instinct; to crumple the letter, demolish the words until they no longer exist.

You've failed her. Jumping to his feet, Kegan walks the path from wall to wall. When he took up the role, he had one task. Protect.

He's failed. Her being in a danger she can't fully comprehend is something he should've seen coming. Taking steps to prevent. It made sense for them to target her sister. What better way to bring her to heel? The emptiness spreading up from his gut consumes him. *Finish this.*

An arm swipes blindly, catching the objects on top of the dresser and tossing them across the room. Another swing sends the dresser sideways into the mirror, the sound of broken glass eerily similar to the ones echoing within his heart. His cry rips free as he strikes out, his fist blasting through the nearest wall. A hiss sneaks past teeth as he relishes in the pain that explodes in his hand before it too fades.

"What's happened?"

Without a glance, Kegan can sense Eleni just out of view. The panic he catches in her voice is a knife to the chest. Unable to find the words to explain the situation, he allows his legs to buckle. Dropping to his knees, he buries his face in his hands while fighting for one good gasp of air. The sight of his empty bed couples with his visceral reaction to bring Eleni close enough to rest a hand on his shoulder.

"Where's Nora?"

The moment Adriel escorts her to Rome's halls, onlookers swarm. Several hiss and spit profanities while others congratulate him on a job well done. Two demons attempt to lay hands on her, their dark intent gleaming in cobalt eyes. Reading their purpose, Adriel deflects both of them before sandwiching her between Tobias's back and his front. When they finally come to a halt, the noise increases with cheers and whoops of victory.

In awe of the sheer number of demons at Rome's disposal, Nora refuses to gawk. Her eyes straight ahead, she traces the small golden streaks in the white marble columns. With the book clutched to her chest, sweat gathers under her shirt.

On her left, someone strides into the cavernous room and all sound ceases. Dressed in black leather pants and a dark t-shirt, he continues a proud walk until he stops merely ten feet from her. Ebony hair falls around his face to soften sharp features. Crimson eyes take measure of her silent stature before a dark smile tips one corner of his mouth.

"This is the girl?"

Well, duh. Dipshit.

His melodic tone is careful and calculating within the silence. Numerous pairs of eyes burn into her skin, the hair on the back of her neck rising. When he takes another four steps to bring himself within arm's reach of her, he moves with grace. Every muscle bunches, then releases only to repeat the process. *What is it about these creatures? Even the evil ones are yummy. Someone needs to adjust their so-called balance.*

"Does she speak?"

"She does. Sometimes rather sharply." Adriel responds, placing a hand at her back when she feels the need to retreat.

"Maybe fear compels her silence." Casting a wide grin to his many minions, Rome creates a wave of snickers.

"Do not mistake my disgust for fear."

"Told you," Adriel says. She's certain if she could look, there'd be a smile on his face.

"Don't mistake my cordial nature for weakness."

Nora scoffs dramatically. "Cordial brings to mind tea parties with light conversation. The very air around you reeks with violence and hate. There's *nothing* cordial about you."

After cutting off the chuckle that slips from him, Rome offers a quick nod. "True."

"I want to see my sister."

"I want the book."

"Then it seems we're at a crossroads. Make me a deal and you can have the book." Even under the false bravado, Nora's nerves stretch. Only bracing her feet quells much of the tremble in her muscles.

"I don't make deals, human."

"This time, you do."

While he school's his features, a rush of light shoots through haunting eyes. When he speaks, his words thunder across the marble walls to draw a whimper from most of his soldiers. "I take the things I want."

"Careful."

Adriel breathes the word so softly at her back, Nora wonders if she's imaging things. Ignoring her damp armpits, she swallows and ventures head-on. "The book is useless without me. You can call my bluff and attempt to summon the spell you need by yourself. But you don't wear failure well. Am I right?" The second the words are out of her mouth, Nora cringes. She's just bartered for her sister's life. When he doesn't need her anymore, Rome won't dispose of her, painfully.

She can see the gears turning in his head, weighing the validity of her words before his gaze shifts to a slender man huddling in a far corner. Long, silver blonde hair falls across either shoulder, falling just short of his hips. When he meets Nora's curiosity, the vibrancy of his green eyes envelopes her in a strange level of calm. Whatever the question, the man gives Rome a slow nod in response.

"Whether you're telling the truth matters little. I have time to consider my options. Let's hope your sister can stay alive that long." A dismissive wave of his hand has Adriel gripping one shoulder. "Take her to the cells."

"Don't wait too long," she calls over her shoulder in a voice lighter than the weight crushing her chest. "I just might forget the process after playing solitaire for a few hours." The frustration snapping in his jaw gives her a moment of satisfaction before Adriel marches her into a narrow hall with little light.

"You're playing a dangerous game," he hisses the moment they're alone.

"What do you care? You're just as bad as he is." There is a flare of light in his Caribbean blue eyes, a setting of his jaw. Brushing whatever it was aside, he straightens his back and pushes her forward.

"This is insane!" Eleni stomps from one side of the room to the other. "What is she thinking?"

"If you continue to yell, Tinkerbell, I'm going to rip your heart out. I promise." Colin's threat is a low rumble, stopping Kegan mid-stride.

"We should've seen this coming and taken steps to ensure Mallory was safe." Kegan points out, shoving a hand through his hair.

"We? I think you mean *you*," Eleni snaps.

"El!"

"What? Am I wrong? Wasn't protecting Nora his *one* job?" Whirling to confront him, Eleni jabs a finger in his direction. "Maybe if you weren't sleeping with her, you'd have a level head on your shoulders."

"Enough!" The force of Colin's roar rattles the windows in their casings. "What gives you the right to condemn him? A man that suffered centuries of isolation for crimes you and others like you, hell even I, committed?"

Eleni's chin notches. "All I'm saying is-"

"No. You're scared and you're coping. But trust me when I say this Eleni, you're wrong." Colin takes a step back, arms spanning his chest."This isn't a good look on you."

"She's just worried about Nora, Colin. It's fine."

"It's *not* fine. We're all concerned. The best thing we can do now is retrieve her before fate etches the markings onto her soul." As Colin paces the space between living room and kitchen, he digs a cigarette out of a fresh pack. The dark glare Kegan aims in his direction has him stuffing it back into the pack. "Which is easier said than done. Rome commands thousands."

"Do we have a plan?" Eleni mumbles around the thumbnail her teeth are chewing to nothing.

"Get her back. In one piece." Kegan's grumble leaves no room for dispute.

"You're thinking as a man. Not as a Guardian," Colin points out. "That book is as much your responsibility as Nora is."

Kegan meets Colin's hard stare with one of his own. Waves of trepidation skitter across his spine as he imagines what Colin is trying to say. *He better hope he doesn't say what I think he's saying.* "What's your point?"

"We cannot let Rome read that spell." Colin whispers the words, but the severity isn't lost on Kegan.

Heat boils within his blood so quickly, Kegan is incapable of holding back his instinct. Hands shake at his side, his shoulders trembling with the effort it requires keeping from planting Colin on his ass.. "I will not sacrifice her for some damn book."

"Think about what you're saying." Colin plows a hand through his hair. "You're this close to being pardoned." The width between his thumb and forefinger is nearly non-existent, drawing Kegan's mute stare. "You'll throw it away?"

"Colin, in case you missed it." Kegan freezes, his words sharp and deadly. "I'm willing to let the whole damn thing burn." No way will he sentence Nora to an eternity of pain and torture because duty demands it. If Colin has any hope of forcing him to do so, he'd better be ready to kill him.

The three of them are quiet for the next few minutes, each lost in their own thoughts before Colin offers a nod. "Then we be smart about this."

"Going in there puts us at a disadvantage," Eleni muses.

"Not going condemns Nora and the rest of humanity by the time Rome is done. Who says he'll stop there?" Kegan tosses a look between Colin and Eleni hoping one of them will have an answer that satisfies him.

"I have to meet with Melchom." Colin swipes the dagger off Kegan's coffee table. "Don't do *anything* until I get back. That's an order."

As Colin flashes from the living room, Kegan and Eleni spend the next minute in quiet contemplation. This woman is important to both of them for different reasons. If they can agree on nothing else, they have that. When he meets her eyes from across the room, the hard set of her shoulders sparks a glimmer of hope inside him. "Tell me we're not waiting for him to get back."

"Fuck, no," he snarls.

Chapter 26

The moment Colin solidifies in the back alley behind the lawyer's office building, his skin prickles. After surveying the surrounding area for danger, he relaxes minutely. "You can come out."

From behind him, Colin catches Selena's elaborate sigh a second before she steps out from behind a dumpster. Shifting from foot to foot, she remains silent as Damien steps out as well. A few inches short of Colin's own height, Damien has a muscled frame that hints at raw power underneath his clothing. Eyes the same shade of blue as ice meet Colin's blatant hatred without so much as a flinch.

Colin's hands ball into fists, his knuckles whitening from the force. "What do *you* want?"

"To see this business dealt with," Damien replies in a level, yet cool voice fit for a politician. He glances over at Selena, who wraps her arms around herself and stands meekly off to the side.

"Isn't that what she's for?" Colin spits, jerking his chin towards Selena before turning back to Damien with an expectant look.

"Given the recent developments," Damien pauses significantly and nods pointedly at Selena, who visibly flinches. "I thought it wise for us to take action."

Colin narrows his eyes as he shifts his gaze between them. "Say what you need to say and get the fuck out of my life," he growls.

Damien inclines his head solemnly. "We need Kegan to retrieve the book."

Colin breaks into a snide, echoing laughter. "That's what we're supposed to be doing. It's just that you need an update every five minutes, which really hinders progress."

"No," Damien breathes a sigh. "Kegan's focus is on collecting the human, and the book isn't his top priority right now." He regards Colin with a long, piercing expression. "You have to change that."

"How am I supposed to do that without ruining my only genuine friendship?"

"Heaven doesn't care about friends," Damien says in a parental tone of admonishment.

"Well, I'm not part of heaven anymore, so why should I care what you think?"

"Because, Colin," Selena pipes up, her voice shaking. "The book is important. It's the key to everything. You know that."

Colin turns to Selena, his expression hardening slightly. "I won't betray Kegan."

Damien steps forward, his eyes blazing with anger. "This is bigger than your friendship, Colin."

"Well, you would know that better than me. You've known Kegan longer than I have and it took you what, all of five minutes to turn your back on him?"

"Kegan chose his fate when he chose loyalty to you above everything else." The flash of hurt in Damien's eyes contradicts his words.

Colin takes a step forward. "Everything else, or everyone?"

"The fate of the entire world rests on the contents of that book." Damien grinds out around a tense jaw. "And if you can't see that, then maybe you don't belong in charge."

Colin's fists clench at his sides as he takes another step towards Damien, his voice low and dangerous. "You think you can replace me? Try. Maybe you should ask yourself this first; given my obvious hatred and disdain for your kind, why has the Council left me in charge this long?"

Damien doesn't back down, meeting Colin's gaze with a steely one of his own. "The devil you know."

"Then maybe you should go back to where you came from and let me and *my* Watchers do our fucking job." Colin inhales deeply once they flash from the area. Their presence alone leaves him gnashing his teeth. "Fuckers," he mutters with a growl.

Nora paces the tight quarters of her cell, her hands rubbing her arms as she walks. The crunch of things left unnamed beneath her shoes causes her to grow increasingly tense until she notices Jess in the adjacent cell. The gentle rise and fall of his chest relieves some of the tension she carries in her shoulders.

Before arriving, she had the hope Kegan would rescue her before she could make any hasty decisions. After seeing the legions Rome commands, the odds against him would be lethal. She no sooner finishes the quick prayer when Jess's rough groan brings her to her hands and knees.

"Jess," she hisses, then throws a look over her shoulder to ensure no one is racing to their cell. When no footfalls approach, she reaches through the bars to jostle a shoulder. "Jess."

"Fuck me." The smooth flow of his voice is scraggy. As if coated in an inch of mud-caked fur.

"Are you okay? Please, tell me you're okay."

With a shift of his weight, he adjusts enough to peer through the bars. One eye swells shut under the purplish bruise that spans across a high cheekbone. The sarcasm in his reply makes her lips twitch despite their current circumstances.

"Just dandy Nora. Who needs Fiji when I have all this?"

"Good. I'd hate to find out you're just a big baby under all the tough-guy talk."

"I'm happy to play the part if it means you're going to kiss all my boo-boos away."

"Now what would that do for me, you being all tied up like that? Awfully selfish of you."

His soft chuckle ends in a wince. "Don't make me laugh."

"Why aren't you healing?"

"I suspect they crafted these cuffs from Thronen iron."

"That's bad?"

"Well, it's not good, Sweets." Shoulders bunch and shift. The exertion drains the blood from his face and racks steady breathing. "Think you can pick a lock?"

"Oh! Sure. Let me just google it."

"You must have a bobby pin or two in all that hair."

"Do you have any idea how many stupid bobby pins it would take to hold all this in place? I'd spend my life putting them in and taking them out."

"Fair enough. Look on the floor. We need anything flat, narrow, and at least a couple of inches long."

The idea of searching through things that go *crunch under your shoes* opens a pit in her stomach. Taking a breath, she crawls around on the uneven floor, hands wandering over hard debris. With so little light from the hall, Nora resorts to picking up anything that might work before dropping it to continue her search.

When her right hand skims a long, skinny object, she gives a sigh of relief until she brings it closer. Eyes squint to narrow slits as she inspects the shape. Never mind that it's too big to fit, the understanding she's holding the bone to some poor soul's finger makes her gag. Dropping it with a shudder, she forces herself to continue.

She's ready to cry uncle by the time she reaches the back corner. Each movement deepens the sharp ache in her kneecaps. Coupled with the bitter twinge in her back muscles and Nora's ready to tell Jess he's fucked. Her left hand swings up and over the floor, almost missing the cold hard sliver under the rest of the litter. There's a flutter in her stomach as she examines it under the light.

"I think this'll work."

"Awesome." He sounds tired. His voice is weary as she scurries back to the bars dividing them.

"Can you scoot closer?" As soon as the request leaves her lips, Nora pleads to call them back.

They must've banged him up pretty good. All he can manage is a dragging motion. Every so often, she catches a gasp of pain in his uneven breaths before the shuffling resumes. Her nerves are so thin, it feels like hours before she catches the brush of his arm against her fingers.

"Okay, hold still." As Nora manipulates the small titanium screw within the lock, her head spins. Fresh sweat gathers under her arms and across her forehead with the soft ticking sound of metal on lock pins. She's ready to throw her hands up when the joints in her fingers throb just before she feels one cuff fall open. One more to go. By the time the cuffs clatter to the floor, her arms are shaking.

"Do you know where they're keeping Kegan?" Nora sits back on her heels as Jess rotates one shoulder gently, then the other. Already, the wounds he sports on his face begin to mend. "Nora?"

"Huh?"

"Do you know where they put him?"

"He's not here; I came alone."

"Bullshit! No way he'd agree to something so stupid." Climbing to his feet, Jess stumbles toward the front of his cell. A few quick tugs tests the strength of the bars. Her hope that he'd forget the interrogation deflates when he passes her a questioning frown.

"He didn't know."

"What are you doing, Nora?"

"Melchom has my sister."

"And?"

"And what?"

"You can't give him the book, Nora. It'll destroy everything you love, including your sister and Kegan."

"I can't just leave her to die."

"She's going to die, anyway."

With a sigh, Nora pushes herself to her feet. Jess's words echo the ones ricocheting within her skull. Doesn't make it any easier to hear, however. "You don't know that."

"Nora, as soon as you give him that book, he's going to kill your sister and then you, if you're lucky."

Her reply dies off when the sound of footsteps rounds the corner. Armed with long spears, half a dozen demons descend on their small cluster of cells. One stands at attention while another uses a thick key to unlock her door, the other four crowd the door to Jess's.

"Nora," he hisses while taking steps backward to draw in his guards.

"I have a plan."

Her door makes a loud creak when it swings open, one guard stomping over the rubble of old bones to yank her forward. Her inhale echoes in her ears as she grabs her bag and follows along.

Kegan urges Eleni to move quietly along the twisting halls. Inside the bowels of Rome's sanctuary, the symphony's alarms are deafening. With a smirk, he retaliates by cranking up Metallica's Enter Sandman.

Slipping past him, Eleni creeps ahead only to hold up a fist as she ducks into the shadows that line the corridor. Melting into the darkness, Kegan plasters his frame against a wall just as three demons scurry past. Every instinct tells him Nora causes their excitement. "Damn woman is going to have me singing show tunes and color-coding happy pills before this is over."

"What?"

"Nothing," he mumbles as they resume their search.

Slithering from hall to hall, the two of them waste precious time trying to navigate each twist and turn. Twice now, they reach a dead-end and end up doubling back. Eleni's fist pump, when they finally stumble on an unfamiliar section, encourages his chuckle.

Less than thirty feet ahead, two scavengers stand guard over a short row of cells. Sneaking close, Kegan slows his heart, controlling every exchange of air. Every step he places is methodical as he unsheathes his dagger. Blood pumps and senses heighten as he settles the familiar weight of his blade within his hand. Once he's within striking distance, he acts.

Plunging the dagger into one's back, he leaves him to fall in a heap to better address the other. The frail body crashes into the bars behind him as Kegan slips a forearm against his neck to pin him in place.

"Where is she?"

With a frantic shake of his head, the demon searches for an escape, forcing him to apply more pressure. Any more and he fears the windpipe giving out long before he gets what he needs. "I'm not having a great day. Tell me where she is."

"Or, what," he rasps. "You'll kill me?"

"No. I'll leave you alive. I wonder how Rome rewards incompetence?"

Beady black eyes widen as fingers scramble for purchase on Kegan's arm before falling to his sides. He can see the demon considering his options, then nod as much as his arm allows. A second later, he erupts into ash.

Eleni's face mirrors his shock as he casts a shocked glare at the blonde woman wielding a crude-looking dagger. "Where'd you get that?" After a gesture to the ash pile, she passes it through the bars to him. "You're the translator?"

"Miranda."

"Who's this?" Snapping the lock off the cell, Kegan steps in, pressing a finger to the brunette's throat.

"Her name is Alysia." Miranda quickly exits the cell, her arms cradling her stomach. "When they brought us here, a bunch of demons attacked her."

"The Mercurian." Eleni stands alert from the different directions leading off from the cells.

"Would make sense," Kegan whispers. "She's alive, barely."

Eleni gives him a distracted nod before pressing for more information. "Do you know where they're keeping the other girl?"

"No." Fingers twist in front of her as Miranda throws an uneasy glance at the shadows. "They keep us separated."

"I have to keep searching." Gathering the Mercurian into his arms, Kegan carries her from the cell, stopping in front of Eleni. "She's never going to make it if you don't get her out of here."

"Tough shit." Eleni snarls, giving her head a furious toss.

Kegan sighs. *Like herding fucking cats.* "El, I need you to get these two topside."

"That's a stupid plan." Eleni hisses. "How are you going to fight them all by yourself?"

Adjusting the slight weight in his arms, Kegan mutters. "I'm not fighting them. I'm going to find Jess and Nora and get our asses the hell out of here."

"I can stay with him and help." Miranda supplies. Her face doesn't agree with the offer. "If you're spotted, I can create a distraction. Not like they're going to kill me."

Eleni's hard look doesn't soften in the slightest. "There are worse things than death."

"Just be quick," Kegan adds as he passes over the comatose angel.

"This is the dumbest idea you've ever come up with." Adjusting to the weight of the Mercurian, Eleni nearly topples sideways before she accommodates for the load. "And that's saying a lot, Bud."

"I'm immortal," Kegan grins, "give me time."

Clearly unamused and immune to his charm, Eleni rolls her eyes, then flashes the Mercurian to safety. He can't be sure why Rome wants her, since they're a relatively harmless choir, but his principles won't let him leave her behind.

"Ready for this?" Miranda appears to consider the question for longer than he'd like but manages a nod, anyway. "Stay behind me."

Taking a chance on the corridor to his right, the two of them make measured progress. Whatever Rome is doing is epic. The passageways are nearly empty of demons and they easily avoid or wait out the few they come upon.

Every piece of him searches for Nora's essence, his eyes lighting when he finally picks up the faint trail. Motioning Miranda to follow, Kegan takes a narrow staircase down one level. The sight of half a dozen demons just milling about five feet away sends a rush of urgency into his blood. Tossing a look over his shoulder, Kegan ensures Miranda is several paces behind him before he engages the demons.

His blades block their attacks with sharp rings of metal on metal, his fingers aching with each one. Catching one lunging forward, Kegan kicks him back several feet, spinning on his heel just in time to bury one blade in another's chest. The harsh scream it let out splits the thick air, no doubt alerting many others to their presence.

"That's perfect." Kegan shakes his head ruefully as he meets another advancing demon. When the song on his phone changes to *Wrong Side Of Heaven*, Kegan lets out a harsh laugh as he parries and advances with the remaining demons. Before long, piles of ash litter the uneven stone floor at his feet until only one demon remains. Bracing his legs, Kegan urges the demon to step forward with a crook of his fingers just as pain erupts within his skull.

A thick haze blankets his vision as the room spins. One hand shoots out to use the wall to brace himself as his legs tremble. Everything in him fights to stay awake when another rush of pain makes the ground rock. With a groan, he collapses sideways to the floor. His eyelids heavy, Kegan blinks twice. Just before the darkness descends, a gold statuette clatters to the floor beside him.

Chapter 27

As Colin ventures along the painted halls of the office, his smile induces a bright blush out of the receptionist before he continues to the door that reads Daniel Brittain LL.M. Flashing inside the large confines of the office, he catches the lawyer with his pants around his ankles. *Literally.*

Unaware of his presence, the lawyer drawls to the pretty blonde on her knees. A wee piece of temptation nags at him to return later. But then, patience isn't his strong suit. "Should I go back out and knock?"

With a yelp, the blonde staggers to her feet, a horrified expression twisting graceful lines. The hand she draws through mussed hair trembles as she uses the other to cover a pair of well-manufactured breasts. Lips stutter over a lame explanation when her boss dismisses her from the room, causing relief to shine in her doe-like eyes as she scurries towards the door.

"What is this sick perversion you have against me getting laid?" Melchom demands in a tight voice as he yanks on his pants. Once the belt buckle is in place, he tosses a dirty scowl in Colin's general direction. "Your timing is worse than Sunday mass."

Opting for the leather couch on one wall, Colin takes a seat. Propping his feet on the coffee table in front of him earns another withering sneer from Melchom. "You have a problem. And I don't mean those fake blonde curls."

Brushing a hand over his head transforms his lawyer like image into the one Colin's most familiar with. Complete with violet eyes and a dark smirk. "The humans like my curls. And the only problem I have is called blue-balls. Maybe you've heard of them."

"Huh? I thought that was a myth."

"What do you want?" Melchom growls, pouring a liberal amount of amber liquid in a large tumbler. "My time is precious."

"I noticed. It's amazing you function at all. Defending dirtbags and banging your secretary must really take it out of you."

With a flip of his middle finger, Melchom drains the tumbler and pours himself another. "This gig keeps the ones I defend from repenting. Claiming their souls now makes it impossible for them to give it to one of you winged assholes after they *find the light*."

"And they actually fall for this persona?"

"Hey, my numbers are up. Happy boss, makes for a happy Melchom."

"Don't refer to yourself in the third person. It's weird."

"What's this problem you think I have?"

"One of your demons has taken it upon himself to knock you off the totem pole."

Shock skitters across Melchom's ruthless appearance. "Impossible. None of them have half the power they'd need to pull that off."

"Not yet. But Rome has Nora in his possession. And the book."

"How the hell did that happen?"

Rolling a shoulder, Colin picks up a magazine and thumbs through several articles. "Trading for Mallory."

"Fuck Colin. When you guys fuck up, you don't bother with the small ones, do you?"

"We're cursed overachievers."

"Yeah right. What do you want from me?"

"Absolutely nothing. I just figured you'd like to put him down yourself and save me the hassle."

"I'll have to talk to my council first."

"Talk fast." Reaching into his boot, Colin withdraws the Thronen blade and tosses it across the table. The shadows in Melchom's eyes tell him he wasn't mistaken in its importance. "Rome's minions came at my Watchers with this. Probably has more like it."

"How certain are you?"

"Deadly.

Instead of the large marble chamber Nora's expecting, her guards lead her to a filthy room carved from stone. The few sconces offer just enough candlelight to be creepy. Since this room is smaller than the last, and sparsely furnished, the onlookers line the walls.

Near the back, a sturdy altar less than three feet long draws her attention. From the aromatic scent she catches, she figures they carved it from cedar. Draped with a bright red cloth, it boasts two fat candlesticks on either end. In its center rests an empty bookstand.

What she doesn't see are skulls, pentagrams or anything else one might associate with hell.

From a doorway on her left, Rome storms into the room like a proud peacock. Heavy footfalls are silent, though she registers the vibrations in the uneven stone floor. "Nice to see you again," he purrs, stopping in front of the altar.

"Wish I could say the same."

"How were your accommodations? Not too horrible, I hope," he continues as if she had said nothing.

Nora rests her weight on one hip. "I'd tell you I've seen better, but that might offend your cordial nature."

"Hm." Rome grins like a cat stalking its prey. "Could've been worse." After a smooth gesture of his hand, three guards haul Jess in from the darkness. When they let his body crash to the floor, Nora chokes back her moan.

They didn't bother restraining him again, but he sports fresh wounds. With his face drawn tight in pain, he rolls over to his back. The action results in various areas to bleed through his shirt.

Nora places her hands on her hips, her voice heavy with a confidence she's far from experiencing. "What have you done to him this time?"

"I sent my men to retrieve your fallen friend." Rome shrugs. "He resisted, killing three of my soldiers. The others reacted accordingly to subdue him."

"Bastards," Nora seethes, leveling a glare at the three that still hover above Jess.

"Some of them, yes." With a cock of his head, Rome rakes his gaze over her and Nora resists the temptation to physically shudder. "I've been considering your position."

Her upper lip twitches before she crosses her arms in front of her. "If you've summoned me, then you're done considering."

"I realize you make a good argument. I can't really expect you to give me something with nothing in return."

While Nora debates how best to respond, all thought ceases when she lays eyes on Mallory being dragged into the small chamber. "Holy hell."

Rushing forward, she takes the bulk of her sister's weight to guide her towards a wooden bench on their right. The blue-eyed demon sitting lazily across its frame lifts a brow in a silent challenge.

"Move."

As if amused by her command, the demon lifts his head an inch higher. Fastening a tighter grip on Mallory, Nora strikes out with her foot. Pain explodes in her toes as she kicks the underside of the bench, but she fights to keep her face impassive. Shock from her sheer audacity cascades within dull eyes. "Move."

From somewhere behind her, Adriel steps into view. His expression dares the lower demon to continue his stance without uttering a word. After calculating the odds, the demon bounces a shoulder and slinks off to a corner.

"Let me." Stepping in front of her, Adriel scoops Mallory into his arms. The gentleness in which he lays her down is hard for Nora to associate with his cold, professional demeanor.

Kneeling, she desperately looks her sister over, praying for any sign of life. A rampant fever makes her skin hot to the touch, flushing a squalid complexion. Brushing away a tangled clump of hair, Nora searches a pair of glassy eyes. Tears threaten to fall as Mallory stares back with a blank stare. Unfocused and unaware.

Nora speaks softly, hoping her voice will pierce the fog in Mallory's mind. "I'm getting you out of here, Mal." Climbing to her feet, she meets Rome's arrogant smile. "Release her."

"Why would I do that?"

"Because you need me more than you need her."

"She makes you compliant, though she holds little sway over your attitude."

"Who do you think taught me?" If Nora allows a minute to consider, she might choose her next words with more care. *Oh well.* "Until she's safe from you, you're not getting squat from me." The sight of him suddenly towering over her backs her up a step.

"That is the last time your teeth will snap at me." Words slither through clenched teeth, Rome's dark eyes bright with the aggravation she brings. "Speak the demands plainly. With great care. Any more spice from you and I'll simply remove your tongue."

"Your balls on a platter is asking too much, huh?" Light flashes in his eyes before they morph from black to a blood red. His jaw flexes. "Fine. I want my sister safe from all of your kind, and I want Jess released."

"It was neither me nor mine that fed off your sister." Grinding the words, Rome casts a frown at her sister. "By granting this, I cannot guarantee the incubus will comply."

"That's fair."

Power cascades across the room, building until the air splits with sharp cracks. Whirling backwards, she watches Mallory's form disappear. Before she can react, Rome projects an image on the cobbled stone wall. Her room offers just enough light to illuminate Mallory's now sleeping form, safe in her own bed.

"And Jess?"

Rome shakes his head. "He stays."

Chin lifts so Nora can meet his quiet stare with one of her own. "That wasn't the deal."

"I'm changing the deal." With a beckon of his finger, a short blonde steps out of from shadows to nuzzle up against his side with a sultry laugh. Her eyes on Nora, she purrs in his ear, bringing a smile to his lecherous mouth. "Have you met Miranda yet?"

Nora gives her head a jerk at the sudden turn of events, then she glimpses the medallion hanging around the girl's neck. "Bitch!" Launching herself across the short distance, Nora comes up short when Adriel clamps a hand around her waist.

"You must be Nora." Miranda hums heavily while dragging a hand along the length of Rome's chest.

"Kiss my ass," Nora spits, fighting against the steel-like grip of Adriel's hands.

Miranda levels a haughty gloat at Nora. While she never moves from Rome's side, she utters a weak proposal. "It's clear you've put little thought into this. Think of what this could mean for our families."

"You're crazy." Nora is already shaking her head in denial before the girl even finishes her paltry speech.

"It's easy for you to judge me when the angels spared your ancestors." Miranda's expression cools. "Did you know my family can only conceive one child per generation? One."

"One is more than you deserve," Nora declares, encouraging a sharp gasp in response.

"They erased us from history!

Taking a page out of Kegan's book, Nora flashes a grin full of arrogance and hostility. "Appears that they missed one."

Miranda drops her hand and changes her tone to one of desperation. "With this book, everyone will finally understand what my family gave their lives for. We'd live like queens, Nora."

"Yeah. Until your booty call turns us into cattle." Even as Nora's head spins with the craziness, she registers Adriel's hold on her loosening.

Miranda saunters across the gap, her tone coaxing. "Help us. Rome will reward you." Nora inwardly flinches when Miranda reaches out to brush a strand of hair from her face. "Why die for something you don't fully understand?"

With a force misled by her small stature, Nora puts everything she has into the swing. Agony erupts over her knuckles the moment they connect with Miranda's cheek, but the sight of her head snapping sideways is reward enough.

Adriel fights to contain her, unaware Miranda seizes the opportunity before her. Distracted by Adriel, Nora's guard is down for the slap Miranda delivers, hissing as her ring rips through layers of flesh. With a growl, Adriel shoves her backward, placing himself in front of Nora until Miranda retreats to a satisfactory distance.

Swiping at the trickling blood with the back of her hand, Nora swings her eyes to Rome. "Kill me. I won't help you."

"I have no intention of killing you." A loud commotion inside the adjacent hall draws several sets of eyes to the open archway.

When someone shoves their prisoner from behind, he stumbles forward under the meager light. "No," Nora's throat closes on the whisper as she consumes the sight of Kegan less than ten feet away.

Bile burns at the back of her throat as she notes blood on his face. When she can't locate any other wounds, the pressure in her chest lessens. Across the dank chamber, their eyes meet and his struggles resume.

Since they pulled his arms behind him, Kegan resorts to shoving his jailors off balance. After he rams his head back into one's nose, his boot prevents another from getting close enough to rein him in. Against all logic, hope blooms inside her before an overly stout demon drives an elbow into his ribs.

"Perhaps," Rome sneers, "his life is worth saving?" When he speaks, his appetite for cruelty twists his features.

"Don't even think about-" A fist slamming into his stomach cuts Kegan's protest short.

"Your kind has learned nothing. Isn't this what caused you to fall in the first place?" Rome's question booms within the chamber, vibrating off the stone around them as Miranda slinks towards Kegan. "Mortal's and their fiery blood. Worse addiction there is."

Kegan's dry laugh rings clear. "Maybe I'll check out a good rehab after I kill you."

Rome blinks. From Nora's position, she observes his smile falter just a bit. "Are you so confident in your skills to think you can?"

"If you didn't think me a threat, you wouldn't have ordered my hands bound." Kegan's grin oozes testosterone and menace to prick Rome's temper even further. Around them, Nora witnesses speculation among the legion. The mention of their leaders' fear spreads like locust.

"Enough," Rome roars, his face a particular shade of red. *Is he going to stomp his foot like a toddler next?*

"You overplayed your hand," Kegan needles. "She has no reason to sacrifice anything for me."

"No," Miranda chirps. "She loves him. Look at her face." Turning to Kegan, she drags one nail over him in her wake as she circles around behind him. "I'll admit, when Rome first approached me for an alliance, I was hesitant. Learning of my ancestor's fate was a hard pill to swallow." Nora's brain registers the dagger just as Miranda's free arm coils around Kegan's neck.

"And then he tells me you're the one who ratted them out to Michael in the first place." Miranda's pretty face twists into a maelstrom of anger as she buries the blade deep into his side.

Chapter 28

Blood spurts from the wound, painting Miranda's hands like macabre war paint. Kegan's surprise slams into Nora like a Mack truck, and when he rocks off balance, she fights against Adriel's hold to reach him. "No!"

The flow of fresh blood spills through the front of his shirt, oozing its way to the waist of his jeans. It looks blacker than it should be against his skin, pulsating with life even as it drains away. The air in her lungs grows stale by the time she remembers to exhale, but it doesn't matter. She knows this is it. This moment will define her life from here on out.

One step and another brings Kegan across the floor. His legs shake with the effort and his face drains of all color before he crumbles less than halfway. When her knees buckle, Adriel holds her upright long enough for her to find her footing, only to release her.

Running to meet him, Nora holds on for dear life as his enormous frame sags into hers. Unable to bear his weight, she lowers them to the floor with as much control as she can muster. Guiding his head to her lap, she runs a hand through his damp hair.

The sight of his blood spilling over the floor settles like lead in her stomach. Rage boils under her skin as every sense amplifies. Emotions slam into hyper-drive, consuming her from within. The desire to obliterate Miranda is so strong, it infects the empty corners of her being. The hunger is sharp; it trembles in her chest. By the time Nora can trust her voice, it sounds more calm than she would've thought. "I will kill you before this is over."

"I think you have bigger concerns than me." Miranda sneers, calling her attention to Kegan's gray color.

Wasn't he supposed to be immortal? Why isn't he healing like every other time? His movement pulls her eyes to the bound hands behind him. *Like Jess with the cuffs, maybe the cord suppresses his healing abilities?*

Fumbling with numb fingers, she works the rope free and drops it on the floor. Her mouth dry, her gaze darts from the wound to his face and back again. *He's not healing.* The next words she speaks strangle from her throat. "Save him."

Rome takes a step. "You'll unleash the spell?"

"No, Nora!" The boot snapping his head off the floor answers Jess's objection.

"He's running out of time; I need your word, Nora."

"Get your filthy hands off me." The shrill warning precedes a loud crash from outside the room.

"Now what!" Spinning on his heel, Rome directs a dark glare to the narrow doorway.

Just ahead, a few demons struggle to walk Eleni into the room. "We found her sneaking around."

"And you are?"

He can't be sure if it's relief or dismay that'll win his initial reaction as Eleni joins their little party. Her right cheek carries a red welt but otherwise she seems unharmed.

"She's one of them, Sire. The one who escaped at the college."

"Of course you are!" Rome's teeth gnash loudly. "You know, until today, I've only ever met a few of you, ever. Now you're invading my home like flies."

Eleni bumps a shoulder, her voice droll. "Well, stench attracts flies."

Rome growls. "How did you get in here?"

"I used the front door, like any other civilized being." One dark brow creeps up as if Eleni can't fathom the stupidity of his question.

"I doubt that. My men would've stopped you."

"They gave it their best effort. You should probably hand out Christmas bonuses to the ones left alive after tonight."

"We have a bigger problem, Sir. The Mercurian is gone." The same snaggletooth demon mutters before jumping back a foot.

Rome wears a look of surprise Kegan knows well. He was using her to barter with, just like Mallory. "Say that again."

Snaggletooth shares a look with his fellow demons, none of them volunteering to be the bearer of that news. "Someone helped her escape; no way she got out of here on her own."

The saucy smile Eleni gives only amplifies Rome's fury. "Was she yours?"

"Where is she?" Rome demands. His voice thins. His eyes shifting back and forth from black to red.

"Where is who?" A new voice pipes up out of Kegan's line of sight.

Rome pinches the bridge of his nose. "I'll ask again, where is she?"

"Rome! Where is who?" The same voice chimes in, this time a tad more nasaly then before.

Rome jerks a look over them. "Seems she took your Mercurian, Shax."

"Get her back!"

With a laugh, Rome blows off the other's concerns. "Be my guest; take backup."

"I made promises, Rome." The smaller demon pushes out from the crowd, grabbing onto his arm. "We had a deal, dammit."

"No longer my problem."

"We'll see about that."

The demon attempts to shift realms, but the hand Rome snakes around his throat prevents him from getting very far. Sheer terror glitters in his murky eyes as hands scrabble for freedom.

"You have threatened me for the last time." He tightens his grip until the demon's face looks ready to pop. The loud crunch of bones breaking signifies the end of his struggle. Dropping the dead weight, Rome spins toward Nora. "Now, as you can see, my patience is gone. No more games."

Kegan lays helpless, willing her to look at him.

Her arms tighten around him as if her grip alone will keep him from the ether. "Save him first."

"I need your word."

Kegan curses himself, watching her tears fall. His body burns to hold her, offer shelter from all of this. Sadly, in his current condition, protection isn't something he can promise right now. Quickly, he sends up a prayer that Nora proves to be an immense pain in Rome's ass. Let her survive the night; in any way she can.

The next words she utters are enough to break his heart, fearing what the future holds for her. "You have it."

"About fucking time!" Closing the gap, Rome jerks the knife from his side.

Nora's shrill scream matches his howl as liquid fire spills into his stomach. Letting the dagger fall with a clatter, Rome pulls her to her feet roughly. "Keep your word, and I will heal him."

The situation is unraveling too fast, drowning them all in circumstance. His chest cramps up when Nora finally meets his gaze. "In case I don't get another chance, I love you."

"I love you too." Kegan hates the croak of his voice, sounding all feeble and shit. Shaking off her guard, Eleni takes a seat next to him, and together they can do nothing but watch helplessly as events unfold.

After retrieving the bag at Adriel's feet, she picks up the dagger Rome discarded. The furious pounding of her heart ramps up with every cumbersome step. When she came up with this plan, the optimist in her saw it play out differently.

Reaching the altar, Nora pulls the book from her bag and lays it on the empty stand. Lethargic fingers fight with the twine long enough to have Rome pacing less than ten feet behind her. Resigned to the fate she carved out for herself; she peels away the thick cloth so the candlelight can twinkle at the cloudy white stone.

A quick glance over her shoulder shows Kegan holding on, but her ears catch his labored breathing.

Lifting her hand, Nora balances the tip of the blade against her palm. *Let's hope this works.* Her muscles tense when she draws the knife against her hand, slicing through layers of skin. Making a fist, she allows several drops to spill onto the altar before bringing her hand to the book.

It had taken her the better part of the day to find a stone similar to the other. As it is, this one lies just a little bigger in the anchors. With a lot of grace, Rome won't notice.

Once a few droplets of blood trickle over the stone, he stomps forward to shove her aside. Matching his enthusiasm, Miranda rushes to his side to flip through the pages.

Pain explodes in her hip and shoulder as she crashes to the floor. Air hisses from her lungs as she inches away to put some distance between them. She knew when she switched the stone this would be her fate, but she never meant for Kegan to suffer with her.

When Miranda discovers her trick, a roar of outrage breaks the silence. Whirling to confront her, the floor shudders and the walls shake from the fury Rome unleashes in full force.

Bright flashes of light burst around them. The oppressive atmosphere presses down to extinguish the candles, plunging them all into stifling darkness.

Everywhere she looks, all she can see is black. She tells herself to keep moving, scurrying over the floor until she feels Kegan behind her. When his arms encircle her, she exhales heavily. Even though it must be incredibly painful, he tucks her in tightly against his body.

Violence rents the air to create an eerie silence. When something grabs her foot in an iron grip, Nora screams.

Once the flames flicker on the candles, she prays they'll go out again. The sight Rome makes unhinged and out-of-control tightens her chest. His eyes smolder with an unquenchable rage, transforming his face into one of pure evil.

She feels Kegan's grip tighten on her, holding steadily against Rome's assault. Soon, the two of them turn her into a tug-of-war rope before Rome yanks her away. The sound of Kegan's growl slices like a knife on her heart.

While skidding painfully over the floor, her fingers claw for purchase. Stones split and chip at fingernails, her mind clamping shut on the excruciating torture.

Twisting and rolling, she kicks out. When her shoe connects with Rome's face, blood spurts from his nose. His screech pierces the quiet as he releases her foot.

Throwing himself into the fray, Jess takes Rome to the ground with a tackle that would make any pro-baller proud. "Protect Kegan."

Fumbling to her feet, she swipes up the knife again as a group of demon's circle Kegan and Eleni. Passing one weapon to Eleni, they take up a feeble position.

One tiny demon sprints forward. Snarling and snapping with sharpened fangs, she dives at Kegan. Talon-like claws wrap around his arm, peeling back shirt and layers of skin until Nora's foot connects with her face.

Grabbing a handful of pale blue hair, she drags her sideways. "Sorry, honey, he's spoken for." Stabbing her through the heart, she let the demon explode to address her next attacker.

Eleni is busy with her own attackers, so Nora stands solid. She may not fight like them, but she'll fight to the death. *Their death, right?*

No sooner does she bring another one down when Kegan's cry jerks her around to see two demons mauling him. Pulling him in separate directions, their nails score his skin. Dragging one away, Nora slams his head off the stones, stunning the demon long enough to stab him in the chest.

Staggering to her feet, something slams into her with the force of a truck. The two of them roll over the top of Kegan, falling off the other side. Each contact with the floor jars her body, knocking the wind from her lungs. When she comes out on the bottom, she swings wildly, bucking her hips to dislodge her attacker. The impact of his fist against her jaw sears light behind her eyes.

Lifting and twisting her hips, Nora shakes him loose, grinning when Kegan pins him with an arm at his throat. Unable to escape her blade, she pierces his heart with no remorse.

Clawing back to her feet, Nora searches for her second wind. Searching, she sees Eleni handling her attackers with finesse, and Jess holding his own against Rome. Every wave hits a little harder, sapping the strength from her body the longer it lasts.

Pay attention! Eyes wide as she dodges the first swing, but misses the second. White-hot pain erupts in her shoulder before the next blow snaps her head back. A sharp blade slices down into her thigh, buckling her leg.

As quickly as the demons are on her, they're gone. Liquid heat scores over her as the attackers fly backward several feet. She blinks at the hand that offers help, tipping her head back to stare into Adriel's uniquely blue eyes. "What the hell?"

A charming smile meets her confusion as Adriel passes her the lighter of two swords.

"What are you doing?" Nora blinks as her arm adjusts to the heavier sword. *Please don't let me drop this thing on my foot.*

"Following orders. I hope you have a Plan B!" Adriel calls over the racket. "Rayen, Nora. Nora, Rayen." He gives the tall demon a jerk of his chin as he takes up a defense on Kegan's left.

Nora kicks back an advancing demon before tossing a quick look over her shoulder at the quiet man. "Wish I could say it was a pleasure."

"So *do* you have a Plan B?" The moment the Hounds crash into the hall to lend their leader much needed muscle, Adriel thumbs the medallion in his pocket. As the trio screeches to a halt just on the outskirts of the skirmish, a bone-chilling roar rents the air. From where they stand, Tobias's fury scalds over the distance, the set of his jaw promising retribution.

Blocking the next attack, Nora gasps as vibrations shoot up into her arms. "Kinda flying by the seat of my pants at the moment."

Catching the lethal gait of an advancing demon, Rayen laughs. "*Great!*"

"We can't hold them forever, Nora; there's too many of them."

Eleni has a point. Focusing on the ones closest to her becomes increasingly difficult. The tremors in her arms multiply and she wills her fingers to hold on. Just a little longer. When the tip of his blade wobbles for one second, Nora drives her sword into his stomach.

Turning, she realizes she's moved too far from Kegan. Lost in the multitude of bodies, she scrambles to see anything familiar. When she finds him, it's because of his massive boots.

Pinned under a demon, he fights with everything he can muster. After he breaks the demon's nose, he adds an elbow to throw him off-kilter. Fearless, the demon readjusts long enough to pick up a dropped blade. The shrill scream he makes spurs Nora across the gap. Vibration resonates through her entire body when she collides with the demon. Her cry of outrage rings loudly in her ears while they topple head over heels.

Twisting, she rides the momentum to sprawl out on top. Fisting handfuls of hair, she drives his head into the floor over and over until he throws her off. Agony flares in her arms as she absorbs the fall. Fatigue creeps into her bones, settling in for the long haul. Stumbling upright, she takes in a deep breath. Every muscle screams with exertion, quivering uncontrollably. *Don't go down!*

Through her fog, she hears Kegan calling her name with a fear she hopes never taints his voice again. Hands swipe at the loose hair in her eyes, then she bends to pick up her sword.

The jagged sting in her scalp rips her backward before her feet leave the floor. Vile onyx eyes meet hers a second before Rome tosses her at the nearest wall.

After she bounces off the unforgiving stone, Nora crashes through the altar directly underneath her. Crawling to her hands and knees, Nora groans with the strain. Kegan's roar sounds miles away, though, in reality, he lays less than ten feet from her. As if she telegraphed her intent, a boot kicks her onto her back. Gasping for breath, she presses a hand to her side as the effort leaves her vision swimming. Her struggle to breathe around the agony distracts her from Rome's intent. When the sole of his boot presses down on her throat, her hands abandon her side to claw at the cool leather.

"Bitch!" The bellow Rome shouts over the noise, gains everyone's attention, drawing the hair on her arms to stand on end. Seeing the precarious position she's in, their allies surrender.

Eleni and Jess drop their weapons before they're pushed to their knees. Adriel and Rayen lower their swords. However, their identical glares dare anyone to try putting them on their knees.

"Do you have any idea what you've done?" Rome scream peppers her face with spit. "You screwed my ass to the wall!"

Fingers pull at the weight of his boot. Legs kick and flail for purchase as he applies more pressure. Oddly, her life doesn't flash before her eyes as everyone says; instead, it is a quick succession of images of the ones Nora loved most.

From the corner of her eye, she sees Kegan move. Desperation fills his eyes as he does his best to get to his hands and knees.

Kegan's throat closes, his mind battering at him to move his ass. Wincing, he rolls over, the most straightforward movement impeded by his body's weakened state. She fought so desperately to keep him alive, no way he's going to lie here helpless as she dies.

Grunting, Kegan pulls on every shred of willpower remaining. Agony swarms through him when he pushes himself up to his knees. Thanks to the wound in his side bleeding profusely, the blood loss alone pitches the room back and forth.

Dragging in a breath, he sees everything. The horror on Jess and Eleni's faces, the silent resignation that Adriel emanates while the scene unfolds. Rome carries a vicious smirk, victory aflame in murderous eyes. Prepared for the path destiny is casting her on, Nora's face relaxes as her body gives up the struggle.

Beads of sweat break out on his forehead. He spent a moment on his hands and knees, bracing his weight unevenly. The quiet solitude of the fog swims in front of his eyes, coaxing him to submit, yet he gets one foot underneath himself. Rage pounds inside him as Rome draws an arm back to plunge a dagger into her small body. Digging in the toe of one boot, he uses his reserves to propel forward.

With a grunt, he covers her small body roughly. Oblivious to the torment, he wraps himself around her just as Rome brings his arm down. His breath leaves on a gasp when the blade pierces his back. Rome's confusion gives Adriel the opportunity he needs to haul him away from Nora.

Chapter 29

"No!" Her wail sends pain across her side. She welcomes the feeling as she eases herself out from under Kegan's weight to cradle his head in her arms. With a sigh, he tucks his face into her chest. "Please be okay. Please!"

Around them, candles surge, burning brighter than they're meant to as Colin strides through the middle of the chaos. For the first time since they met, she sees fear in Rome's eyes. Stumbling to his feet, he searches for a quick exit.

"I don't fucking think so. It's too goddam late." Colin growls, wrapping a hand around Rome's throat. His target fights to peel away steel-like fingers, shaking when he fails. Pinned to the wall, his form blinks in and out, drawing a dark, melodic laugh from Colin. "As I said, too fucking late. It's my party now."

"You have no power over me," Rome gasps around the tight grip, his fist pummeling Colin's back.

Colin's grin is deadly. His voice is empty of any emotion. "It would seem you're wrong."

Simultaneously, every demon still alive begins blinking in and out. Their terror floating off them in suffocating waves as they realize they're just as stuck as Rome.

"I've made it so none of you can flash out." Colin explains, as if he's explaining how to pump fuel into a car. "Someone is keen to speak with all of you. It would be rude to leave early." Turning his focus back to Rome, Colin manhandles the demon with minimal effort. She thought Rome reeked of danger; Colin carries it in spades. Every muscle in his back trembles with the restraint he shows, his body spitting sparks of electricity.

The second wave of awareness makes the room spin around her as another man appears out of thin air. Dark and powerful, he exudes violence. Violet eyes blaze while muscles coil, setting sights on Rome. Only then does Colin release his hold on the demon, letting him fall to direct his attention to where she sits with Kegan.

"Help him." Tears fall free no matter how she struggles to contain them. In her arms, Kegan lay quiet, accepting his fate in a way that leaves her cold.

Colin's eyes remain on Kegan for a long while. When he lifts them to hers, Nora recognizes the heartache she sees in their amber depths. "His wounds are fatal."

Bullshit! Colin carries more power in his little pinky than Nora's ever witnessed before. "You healed Eleni with barely a grunt," she reminds him, her voice rising in pitch.

"They stripped the power I had to heal this kind of wound many years ago." Once again, Colin eyes his friend, taking his free hand in a tight grip. "I'm sorry."

"So he's going to die?" Nora rocks her head. "There's got to be something we can do." The hand Colin rests on her shoulder does nothing to calm her emotions. The sorrow filling his eyes, nothing compared to the emptiness swelling inside of her.

"I'm sorry," Colin stutters softly.

In her arms, Kegan's color drains until he's a pale imitation of what he was just hours before. Before Nora's eyes, his essence fades as if the dam sprung a leak. It's a matter of seconds before the leak blows a devastating hole in her life. "Fuck all of you!"

"Mo chridhe. Stop." The hand Kegan lifts to pull the clip from her hair visibly trembles. She listens as he takes a deep inhale when the weight of her curls cascade around them. "It's time."

Ripe emotions cause her reply to shake, her words thick and uneven. "They can't have you. It's not your time yet." Her arms tighten around him, her eyes never wavering from his. She used to scoff and roll her eyes at moments like this in the movies, knowing that dying for someone is something that only happens there. But she found it. A bittersweet ending to a bittersweet beginning. "It's not your time."

Colin heaves a heavy sigh. "I wish that were true."

"Please, baby; I can't follow you there Kegan, I need you to stay here with me." When his eyes close, Nora gives his shoulders a gentle shake until they open again.

"He chose his fate long before he met you." Colin says quietly, resting a hand over hers gently. She couldn't bring herself to look at him. The pain she'd see in his eyes will make all this final. Nora's teeth clench as she fastens a tighter hold on Kegan. "That's such utter bullshit."

"You're questioning our methods?" The baritone voice beside her pulls her eyes from Kegan for a moment. Sharp features soften a fraction as the stranger looks down on her with eyes so pale a blue, it gives Nora the image of ancient icebergs. Behind him, she catches Adriel melt into the crowd.

"No, Damien, she just doesn't-" Eleni begins, her voice trailing off with the raising of his hand.

Nora notices the reverence with which Eleni treats the newcomer. She just can't find the will to care. "I question anything that rewards something so selfless with the gift of *death*."

"Selfless?" Clean classic lines wrinkle. "It was his duty to protect the book; it should've never come this close."

"You think he did all this for the book?" Even without the shaking of his dark head, she could see his confusion. "If he wanted to protect the book, he could've stayed home. We swapped the stones days ago."

"Then, why?" Eyes skim from her to where Kegan rests in her lap and back again.

"For me. He came here at a disadvantage because I was a fool." Nora listens as Kegan draws in a shallow breath. "He shouldn't have to die because of a choice I made."

"It's because of his choices that Kegan will be taken to the ether." While Damien speaks with a measured calm that Nora finds impressive, the tiny shudders in his jaw betray the true level of his emotions.

Nora shakes her head. "What is the ether?"

Covering her hand with his, Colin speaks quietly. "The ether is nothing. It's where all those without souls go when they die."

"No!" Nora tightens her grip, wincing when Kegan releases a soft gasp of pain. "He has a soul."

"I'm sorry, Nora." Damien takes a knee beside her, his eyes lingering on Kegan. "Us Angels aren't given souls. He should've told you that."

"He did. And I'll tell you the same thing I told him." Nora clips. "You're wrong. I love him. He loves me. That means he has at least a piece of my soul."

"I wish that were true." Damien murmurs, the pain in his eyes lending weight to his words.

"I do love you, *mo chridhe*," Kegan stutters, his voice more breath than tone.

"I love you." She whispers, bending to cover Kegan's lips with hers. His gentle sigh at the contact serves as his last breath. Before she can even comprehend it, he's gone.

With a shimmer of light, his body vanishes away from her to melt into thin air. The giant puddle of blood, the only trace that remains before that too fades. It's as if he had never been there, and if it wasn't for the weight in her chest, Nora might wonder if she imagined it all.

Lifting her eyes, Nora catches the sea of faces, watching her with a variety of emotions, but it's the petite blonde in the back that wins over. Her fingers wrap on the hilt of the blade from Kegan's back before she stands.

Without a word, or a stray look, Nora advances, fingers flexing. The large hand that settles on her wrist is enough to give her a moment's reflection. "I know the pain you feel, but you need to let this go."

Nora searches a pair of violet eyes, the nagging voice in her head reminding her of their familiarity. "I can't."

"You can, in time." While his hand never releases her, his hold lightens considerably. "This won't bring Kegan back to you."

"Melchom's right, *asteri mou*."

Shaking her head, Nora fights the itch in her fingers. "She did this."

"He wouldn't want this for you." Melchom continues. "By doing this, you stain your soul, changing you from the woman Kegan fell in love with." Casting a look at the blonde, he presses. "My heart is already black. Let me handle this for you."

Jerking her arm from his grasp, she drops the knife. "You're right. He deserves better."

Face upturned, she addresses the ceiling. "Bring him back to me. Please." She has no way of knowing if the right people can hear her or not, but she'll pray every day until they do. "Take me home."

Chapter 30

Nora hesitates just outside the cabin as a thousand anxieties roar inside her chest. She takes a deep breath and pulls the door open to step into the dark interior. Tennis shoes echo in the emptiness as she walks further inside, but the hairs on her arms remain standing as she surveys the living room, unsure whether she should proceed or turn back.

"Are you sure about this?"

Nora's heart flutters and she balls her hands into fists, pressing them against the coarse denim of her jeans. The question was familiar — too familiar. She wants to yell "No!" but croaks a defeated, "No."

"Let me do this." Eleni takes a moment to latch the door behind them, plunging them into further darkness.

"No, El." She steps into the living room, her eyes immediately going to the coffee table. They had transformed the usually neat surface into a disorganized mess. Sheets of paper scatter carelessly like fallen leaves, and books from Brody's shelves are strewn amongst them. Three glasses lie on their sides, with an empty bottle of scotch in the center.

"I'm just saying it doesn't have to be you. I can manage."

Nora stares at Eleni's lips, watching them move in a fog that her mind shrouds around her. She remembers the days when this house was anything but silent; where their feet ran from room to room and their voices filled the walls with debate. The curtains were always open, filling the space with light. But now Nora finds herself in a different home - hushed and empty. A tremor runs through her body as she absentmindedly weaves her fingers through her long hair.

"Nora?"

"What?"

"I'm sure Jess will keep you company outside."

"I know," she murmurs on an exhale, giving Eleni's hand a squeeze. "I need to do this." Shoes yelp against the polished oak floors as she maneuvers the room with practiced ease. Skirting the floor lamp and rocking chair, her nerves tighten before she disappears in the narrow hallway.

Eleni drops off to the room she shared with Jess as Nora continues to the door on her right. Locating the flat switch, she raises a hand from the bright wash of LED lights that fills the bathroom, squinting until her eyes adjust. After a shallow breath, she approaches the sink on wooden legs.

The reflection she catches in the bathroom mirror stalls her heart. Blessed with a creamy complexion that matches that of her mother and grandmother, is now ashen and sickly looking. One eye swells shut, a purple-black bruise framing the lid; the other eye's iris glazed and bloodshot as she studies the effects of the night.

A dozen small wounds score her skin in various places, but the gash spanning one of her cheeks seizes all of her focus. Already, the tissue had responded by swelling to an angry red and she's certain that soon, it'll give way to blues and purples before finally fading away. A stark reminder of all that occurred.

If given a choice, she'd keep the more intimate marks Kegan left along the column of her throat. Closing her eye, she recalls the warmth of his touch, the scrape of stubble from his jaw and the scent of whiskey on his breath when he pressed lips to skin. How long before, one by one, those memories evaporate like the fog over a glacial lake, doomed by the rising sun?

"Nora?"

The unexpected sound draws her spine straight as if by a string, even as her brain labels the voice as familiar. Nails bite into the tender pads of her palms while she chokes back a cry. Sensing Eleni on her blindside, Nora struggles to keep her voice steady. "All done?"

"Mm-hmm. We didn't bring much. Or I didn't. Jess packs like a woman going on vacation." Her friends' hesitation allows the air to settle heavily around them. "You, okay?"

Who knew one measly question could drive someone to commit murder? No, her mind screams, I'll never be okay. As if the floodgate disintegrates; wild emotions churn inside her, their sharpness overwhelming. Teeth grind together as either the air thins or her lungs refuse to inflate but the sudden lack of oxygen rocks her sideways into Eleni's firm grip. The groan that slips from her as blinding pain smothers rampant emotions, draws her friend's concern.

"He broke those ribs."

"I'm aware."

"This was a bad idea. I said this was a bad idea." Gone is the light tone as Eleni takes on the role of scolding mother, her pitch rising. "Go outside. I will finish."

The sigh she releases is too big for the room as Nora rights herself. Walking away and letting her friends clean up the mess she made is a temptation too great to ignore. Eleni would have no issue rounding everything up and stowing it in the car for Nora to go through at a later date. Hell, she's insisting.

She doubts anyone would blame her for throwing her hands up with everything that's happened in the last twenty-four hours. With that, a thought slithers in a dark whisper, words meant to bolster or break. Isn't that what you've been doing your whole life? Guilt promises to consume her before it mutates into anger.

"I'm done hiding El." Her words clip in a tight voice to leave no room for argument. "I know you mean well, but we both know you can't protect me from the mistakes I've made." Almond-shaped eyes narrow, forcing Nora to raise a hand to ward off the impending discussion. As she does, every thought comes to a stop when she spots the dried blood covering her hand. "Omigod." The squeak of her shoes drowns the sob in her chest as she spins around to confront the mirror again.

Woven through strands of tangled hair, blood soaks the front of her shirt and gathers under haphazardly broken nails. Every breath is tight against the stitch in her side as she scrambles to turn on the hot water, dunking her hands under the spray. Her jaw clenches as she scrubs a bar of soap over her hands until the skin gleams a rosy pink. The signal her brain sends out, warns her she's scouring away layers of flesh, but the image of his blood claws its way to the forefront. As if understanding her dilemma, Eleni steps froward to turn off the water, covering her hands without a word. For the first time since entering the cabin, Nora meets her friend's probing eyes.

"What can I do?"

"Clean out my dresser?"

"Done."

"And I'm sure Ezio is hiding under the bed."

"I'll get him." Her chin notches as her expression changes from concern to determination. Set to purpose, Eleni moves on to leave Nora battling the urge to run. It takes almost a full minute to slow her breathing and her heart to resume a steady rhythm so she can stutter forward.

She's less than a foot away from Kegan's bedroom door, the countless emotions growing until she can think of little else. She's foolish to believe she'd experienced anger, betrayal and despair before the crash course lessons served mercilessly a few short hours ago. The packed weight of their voracity consumes everything until only an empty void remains.

"Just do it." Nora breathes, wipes a hand across her thigh and turns the door handle. Thankfully, the moonlight that filters through thin, open curtains eliminates any need for extra light.

Ahead, crisp white sheets lay in a bundle with the deep red comforter at the foot of an enormous bed. On her right, his tall dresser rests on its side, drawers knocked askew. Odds and ends that typically gather on the top now lay scattered to the four corners. When the dresser came to a stop, it shattered the full-length mirror. After spitting shards of glass across the thick carpet, it's unrecognizable. A gaping hole in the wall just above the mirror forces her head to tilt as she imagines his enormous fist striking out in anger.

"I'll never forget that sound."

"Huh?"

"I've witnessed countless moments of despair over the years, each of them unique." Eleni mumbles from the hall, as if hesitant to intrude. "All of them pale at the one Kegan made that morning. I'll go to my Maker hearing that sound."

Nora nods stiffly. She came tonight with the insane idea of closure, a balm to ease the heartache crippling her. Instead, there's only more pain. She's almost convinced herself to leave when a single item pulls her from the doorway, deeper into the room.

Under her shoes, broken glass from the mirror tinkles softly until she's close enough to hook a finger into the discarded shirt. Gathering it close, she buries her face into the material while remembering the smoothness of the buttons under her hands. The memory of him parting it over her chest jerks a moan free as every inhale carries the scent of his soap, tormenting her with its innocent cruelty.

Inside her head, a roar builds until her legs buckle, dropping her to her knees where even the bite of glass piercing denim does little to help. Wrapping her arms around herself, Nora fights the need to empty the contents of her stomach as wave after wave of nausea waters her mouth and brings fresh tears to weary eyes.

"Damn every one of you!" Bent, her words tear from a throat raw after hours of venting her rage. Tipping her head back, Nora regards the ceiling for a response. A bolt of lightning, flash of wrath; something besides the oppressive silence taking over her life. When nothing happens, an emptiness spreads through her chest to leave her cold and shaking. The hand Eleni places on her shoulder seems to ground her emotions, albeit temporarily. When she meets her gaze, Nora flinches from the anguish that skitters across her friend's face.

"This isn't helping you, asteri mou."

Unable to trust the voice hiding inside her, she nods and allows Eleni to pull her to her feet and lead the way back through the house. As they walk, rampant memories race at her heels until they reach the safety of the front door with suitcase and cat carrier in hand. Nora pauses long enough to snake the keys off the small hook near the door, then barges out into the night.

While Eleni makes quick work of loading up the car, Nora lets the cool air calm the pitch in her stomach. She'd once thought of this place as a sanctuary, where the cruelness of the world couldn't reach her. If she never sees it again, it would be entirely too soon.

At the car, Nora pries her fingers back from the set of keys, offering them to Jess, who sits stoically in the passenger seat. The nod he offers drops blonde curls over green eyes, before he lumbers to the abandoned motorcycle in a familiar long-legged lope.

Nora holds the soft fabric of Kegan's shirt to her chest, feeling the warmth of it despite her cold exterior. She can sense Eleni glance at her from the corner of her eye and offer a nod of silent understanding. All around them, the thunderous roar of his motorcycle summons a fierce energy that courses through Nora's veins like wildfire.

After as deep of a breath as she can manage, Nora pins her gaze straight ahead and pulls the car door shut with a finality she can't voice.

Epilogue

When the frigid winter breeze seeps through his t-shirt, he wraps arms around his middle. He probably should've taken the time to dress appropriately, but all he could think about when they reached a decision was getting back here.

It's late enough in the morning that the plows had already come through, making the streets more accessible than the sidewalks. Still, now and then, he finds a slick spot to slow his progress. After what feels like hours, he reaches the end of her driveway.

A study of the house on the corner lot shows a new bright red front door, though the driveway begs for the attention of a shovel. Ahead, the garage door stands open, waiting for someone to bring the trash bin up from the curb. Inside, he glimpses a motorcycle under a light tan tarp. Unlike every other house on the street, this house isn't bragging Christmas cheer. Something he'll need to rectify.

Adjusting his backpack, he waves at two teens clearing the neighbor's walkway. After a short negotiation, the boys take his money and one sets to work clearing snow. Now all that's left to do is ring the damn bell.

When it opens, he isn't expecting to see Mallory with a hesitant smile. Glancing up at him under the fringe of thick lashes, she regards him quietly.

"Can I help you?"

"I'm looking for Nora Brennan."

Eyes narrow as she tilts her head. When Damien said she'd lose all memory of those few weeks, he hadn't expected to be one of those things.

"Will your visit make her smile or cry? Because if you're here to shatter the tiny world she's built, I'll skin you alive. And I promise to enjoy every moment."

"I believe you." Lips quirk in an amiable smile. "I'm shooting for the first scenario, but there might be a little of the second."

She jerks a nod, as if unconvinced by his words. Still, she steps back into the house to holler up the stairs. "Nora, there's someone at the door for you."

While she's finally up and around after months of being saddled with grief, Nora isn't up for visitors. Now and then Jess comes by under the pretense of social calls. Once a week, Colin peeks in on her. Volunteering as her Guardian, he spent weeks on her couch before he's satisfied with the barriers and alarms he set up around her house enough to leave for any length of time. She's aware they worry over her lack of acceptance of Kegan's death. Unlike Eleni, though, the guys don't hover like a hospice nurse counting every piece of food that passes her lips.

"Who is it?" With her hand resting on the smooth banister, she pauses for some sort of reply. Mallory's lack of response snaps already fragile nerves.

Smoothing a hand over the wet tangles of her hair, Nora takes each step with care. Thick socks on wooden floors are a hazard that took some getting used to when she first bought the house.

When she reaches the first floor, the door blocks her view of said visitor. Mallory stands just inside the kitchen, sipping her tea. Quiet as a church mouse.

Fingers curl on the doorknob as she swings it open. The words she has ready to refuse the visit die in her throat just before the ground rocks. Slowly, she drags her eyes up and over the impossibly tall frame. Big, black boots shuffle on the new welcome mat. Jeans hug massive thighs, dipping low on his narrow waist. His plain gray t-shirt looks too thin for the current temperatures. When her eyes inch upward, the lazy tilt of his smile launches her toward him.

Dropping his pack, Kegan catches her with little effort, holding her tight. With a spin, he braces her against the doorjamb before claiming her mouth with a hunger Nora only finds in her dreams.

Lips explore, taste and devour. Her purr of delight is instantaneous. Hands reach up to burrow into his hair, as if to pull him closer still. When he inches back a fraction to look into her eyes, Nora's lungs stop functioning. The sight of Mrs. Willow's teen boys elbowing each other with a laugh serves as a douse of cold water.

Sinking to her feet, Nora latches onto his arm to tug him inside before she closes the door behind him.

"How are you here?"

"They let me come back."

"How? Why?"

His chuckle does little things to her stomach as the heat unfurls quickly. "I think listening to you all day, every day, wore them down."

Heat fills her face as Nora recalls some rather vicious prayers. "You heard me?"

"I wish I did," he breathes, dragging a thumb along her jaw. "Where I was, there was no sound, no light. I couldn't feel my body, but I *knew* my heart was breaking. I spent so much time convincing myself it was all a dream and that I'd wake up. Then I did. The moment they told me their decision, I wasted no time getting back here. To you."

"What took them so long? It's been months!"

"I'm pretty sure they grew tired of listening to you. They're not known for extending forgiveness to our kind."

"Colin thought maybe you'd get your appeal. Since we never put the book in danger of being used."

"Ah yes. Turns out the redemption I was looking for is right here. With you."

"What does that mean?"

"It means, *mo chridhe*, that I will live a mortal life."

"I thought you needed a soul."

"Turns out, your soul is big enough to share a small piece with me. I plan on spending the rest of your life being worthy of the gift. If you'll have me."

Nora's grin threatens to split her face in two as she buries her nose in his neck. "I'm never letting you go again."

A chuckle vibrates within his chest as his arms snuggle her tighter. "I believe you. Heaven itself couldn't stand in your way."

From inside the kitchen, Mallory witnesses the scene unfold. The gray fog her sister has been living in lifts away, her smile happier than she's ever seen before. The look the stranger equally carries for her is so intense it warms her blood.

His laugh hearty, he scoops her sister off the floor to take the stairs leading to the second floor two at a time. With a squawking meow, Ezio scrambles to follow.

The decision to let the two of them catch up in private comes quick. After she snags her thick coat from the rack, Mallory grabs her purse and slips out the back door. Absently, her hand rests on her growing stomach, as flashes of Eli run through her head briefly.

There'll be time later to tell Nora about her current condition. For now, she'll let her sister enjoy the time Heaven stole from her.

If she'd been aware of the attention her condition draws, she'd run back to the house and lock herself in.

About the author

Sarah is a Michigan native, living in Northern Iowa. A mother of four, she still copes with the idea her youngest is in college. Married seventeen years, Sarah and her husband learned quickly that communication, laughter and resisting the impluse to maime makes their marriage work. He continues to be one of her most energetic cheerleaders.

Writing had been a secret passion of hers since high school, after an English teacher knocked the dust off. While being the typical stay at home mom, she took classes and workshops to refine her skills. After a lot of anxiety, and a bout of self-doubt, she's excited to introduce the characters that live in her head to the world.

When she's not writing, she's a grandmother of four granddaughters and a soon to be grandson, as different as the seasons. Between the rambunctious nature of children and the neurotic nature of her three Great Danes, life is interesting. If asked, she'll tell you she loves every minute of it. Even if some of those minutes result in ice cream, buckets of coffee and a little solitary confinement.